NIKKI N

I've adored writing and reading since forever and have always been a sucker for love stories so I'm delighted to join the fabulous HarperImpulse team!

I write short stories and fun, touching, sexy contemporary romance and really enjoy creating intriguing characters and telling their stories. A finalist in writing competitions since 2010, including Novelicious Undiscovered 2012, I'm a member of the fantastic Romantic Novelists' Association.

I blog about three of my favourite things – Writing, Work and Wine – at www.nikkimooreauthor.wordpress.com and am passionate about supporting other writers as part of a friendly, talented and diverse community, so you'll often see other authors pop in!

You can find me at https://www.facebook.com/NikkiMooreAuthor (Author Page) or https://www.facebook.com/NikkiMooreWrites or on Twitter @NikkiMoore_Auth to chat about love, life, reading or writing … I'd love to hear from you.

Crazy, Undercover, Love

NIKKI MOORE

HarperImpulse an imprint of
HarperCollins*Publishers* Ltd
77–85 Fulham Palace Road
Hammersmith, London W6 8JB

www.harpercollins.co.uk

A Paperback Original 2014

First published in Great Britain in ebook format by HarperImpulse 2014

Cover Images © Shutterstock.com

Nikki Moore asserts the moral right to
be identified as the author of this work

A catalogue record for this book is
available from the British Library

ISBN: 978-0-00-759176-3

This novel is entirely a work of fiction.
The names, characters and incidents portrayed in it are
the work of the author's imagination. Any resemblance to
actual persons, living or dead, events or localities is
entirely coincidental.

Automatically produced by Atomik ePublisher from Easypress

This story is dedicated to;

My wonderful children for putting up with me disappearing into my writing room at odd times!

My friends and family for their unwavering support and belief that one day I would get a publishing deal.

The wonderful members of the Romantic Novelists' Association, the most friendly and professional organisation I've ever been a part of.

The fantastic HarperImpulse team – we've got the love!

And a special mention to my aunt, author Sue Moorcroft, who has been a constant source of support and inspiration to me. Without her clear constructive criticism, valuable advice and emotional cheerleading I'm sure it would have taken me much longer to achieve my dream

Chapter One

DAY ONE

– Friday –

I should have said no; it would have been the smart – aka sane – thing to do.

But there was a time limit on the offer and Amy caught me in a moment of desperation after I'd woke to yet another thick batch of overdue bills and polite job rejections. The feeling tripped a *yes* straight off my tongue, and now I've realised that maybe this isn't such a good idea, it's too late. I'm dashing across the city, yanking my purple case along behind me on squeaky wheels. So I can't back out now; I'm committed. More importantly the reason for agreeing to this crazy Plan B, on the basis that sensible Plan A isn't working, stands. It's probably my last chance to hang onto life as I know it. Sounds a bit dramatic, but there it is.

The bitter wind increases its howling across the West India Quays footbridge, tearing through my belted winter coat. 'Bugger it!' I shudder. As well as being freezing, the force of the gale is making staying upright a challenge. My favourite (yes, okay, impractical) stiletto ankle boots are battling for grip in the snowy slush.

1

I'm so bloody cold it'll be a miracle if my ears are still attached to my head, in fact they've gone completely numb, and there's also a familiar ache starting deep in my throat. Great. I don't need to get ill on top of everything else. To finish off my bad mood, the Arctic draught is trying to pick my hair out of the stylish knot I spent ages on. It's hardly going to look professional if I arrive looking like the loser in a pro-wrestling match or as if I'm stuck in the jungle on *I'm a Celebrity…*

Glancing at my watch, I speed up, heels rapping out a clank-clank-clank on the metal bridge. Being late will hardly impress, either. Unfortunately, fate is conspiring against me, because as I break into a jog the jolting combined with the wind finally frees my hair. A rain of kirby grips slide into my collar and down my back. *Seriously? Come on!* Stopping with a skid, I yank my thick red waves into a ponytail, using the emergency hair band from around my wrist.

Setting off again, I pray the anticipated snow will hold back for another few minutes. It's not looking hopeful; the air has that weird ozone smell to it and the temperature's dropped loads already, grey-white cauliflower-like clouds crowding in uncomfortably low like a suffocating blanket. Yep, I'm probably going to get snowed on and I can't help feeling it'll be fair enough; bad karma for being so sneaky. What I'm about to do makes me want to dig a giant hole in the ground and leap into it head first. But working as a temporary Personal Assistant for the CEO of my ex-employer is an opportunity too good to miss.

Of course, it may all blow up in my face. Jess certainly believes it will, saying I'm making a massive mistake. She might be right, but I think it's a risk worth taking. I've got to at least try: I owe myself that. So now I have one weekend in Barcelona to change things, whatever my best friend thinks, and if I don't, at least the lump sum I'll get will keep the rabid debtors at bay a while longer. In honesty, though, I really need the plan to work. It *has* to work.

Coming to the end of the bridge, I let out a panicked yelp as I step onto the concrete and slip on a patch of ice, regretting grabbing the handrail when my bare hand freezes to the slick metal. Peeling it off, I pick my way across a courtyard, cutting through a narrow concrete alleyway between a Japanese-themed bar and a towering hotel. The multicoloured lanterns and white fairy lights are still hanging in all the windows, even though Christmas was over a week ago. Of course leisure and retail are going to maximise the festive season and people's celebrations; there's more money in it for them. God, I've turned cynical. Sad, really, because I've always adored this time of year. But at the moment merriment and holidays are way down my list of priorities and for the first time I really didn't enjoy Christmas, even though I was home with my family and friends. I think I understand Scrooge's pre-ghosts-of-Christmas perspective now. Bah humbug.

I look for the car as I emerge onto the street, feeling sick and sweaty in spite of the chill in the air. Have I missed my ride? I'm only a couple of minutes late. Something cold kisses my cheek and I glance at the sky. Snow begins to eddy and swirl around me, getting in my eyes. No doubt I'll end up with black Alice Cooper tracks down my face. I'm wearing cheap mascara – haven't been able to afford the branded waterproof stuff in ages.

A wave of utter weariness drags me down. Perhaps this chance has slipped away. If so, standing here could make frostbite an unwelcome reality. How long to wait before I jack it in and head home? But then a swish black town car turns the corner and pulls in at the kerb with a quiet purr and I know this is it. It's on. Time to meet the CEO.

Pasting on a shaky smile, I step towards the smart uniformed driver, holding back a laugh at the luxurious vehicle he's stepped from. The formality reminds me of *The Apprentice*, when Lord Sugar emerges grumpy and grizzled from a flash car. I was a middle manager, so we were never kept in this style.

'Can I help you?' The man meets me at the back of the car, posture as rigid as his voice, whilst the wind whips grit and whirling snowflakes about us.

'Good afternoon, I'm Charley Caswell.'

He peers down at me. 'You are?'

'I am.' At least, I was last time I checked. 'Would you like to see some ID?'

'That would be helpful, thank you.'

Oh. I was joking. This is a bit weird.

Sliding a hand into my bag, I flip my passport open at the last page, placing my fingers strategically along the side to hide Wright, the second part of my double-barrelled surname.

He gives it a quick glance.

I stop breathing.

'Thank you, Miss Caswell. Wait here a moment please?'

I nod, tucking the passport away and thrusting half-dead hands into my coat pockets. I should have swiped a pair of gloves from Jess on the way out of our flat. She's used to me borrowing her stuff.

Focusing on the driver as he taps on the tinted rear car window, I watch the glass slide down but can't hear his conversation with the passenger. The tension in his shoulders as exchanges rattle back and forth between them is obvious, though.

Gritting my teeth to stop them chattering, I scrunch my eyes against the awful weather. What's taking so long? I can't be busted so soon, surely? When registering with the latest batch of agencies, I only used the first part of my surname, the one I originally dropped when moving to the city, a change made back then to escape my upbringing. But for this weekend – at least initially – I needed to be safely hidden behind the name Charley Caswell, rather than marked out as Charlotte Wright.

The ex-employee.

The troublemaker.

'I said, now!'

The order erupts from the window like something snarling with teeth and my eyes fly open. My stomach clenches in knots as the driver straightens, turning to fight his way back to me. Holding my breath, I wonder if I'm destined to go home with no prospects, no money and only numb toes and damp hair to show for my efforts.

'Shall we go?' he asks, stamping his feet for warmth.

My cover isn't blown. 'Yes!' Oops, probably a little too enthusiastic.

He doesn't seem to notice, opening the boot and gesturing to my case. 'May I?'

'No. I mean, I can manage. But thank you.' I grab it and shove it in before he can. I won't be waited on. If my independence is one of the few things I have left, I'll guard it like a precious possession.

'Fine, Miss Caswell,' a tiny glint of humour warms his eyes, 'but are you going to at least let me open the door for you?'

'It's Charley,' I flash him a grateful smile as he swings the door open, 'and if you're going to insist... Yes, thanks.'

Mr CEO is on the phone as I get in, so I take a moment to appreciate the cosy, immaculate interior of the car. Heavenly. Smooth, black leather seats, walnut finish on everything, TV screens in the back of the headrests in front of us. Nice. I sink back with a sigh of relief, then ruin it by fumbling around trying to click the metal tongue of the seatbelt into place. My fingers are burning and tingling as they start to thaw, so it makes the job that much harder.

Finally buckling myself in, I glance up. And my mouth drops open. My hands clench and lust strums my knickers.

Oh ... wow! I did *not* count on this.

I had a vague idea Alex Demetrio wasn't bad looking but I've never seen a proper picture. He's got an aversion to being photographed and any pics successfully snapped would appear in *Hello* or *Tatler* – not my type of reading material. The only photo I've seen was in a corporate brochure and he was standing scowling in the middle of a crowd. All I could tell was he had the same dark colouring as his father, the previous CEO.

So it's a complete shock he's one of the most astoundingly gorgeous men I've ever shared oxygen with, Brad Pitt-beautiful. Frozen, I admire his short, ruffled black hair, slightly olive skin and strong, sculpted face with angelically defined cheekbones. I've worked with good-looking men before but this guy is magnetic.

Thank God he's on his mobile speaking in a language I can't quite place and therefore oblivious to my unprofessional, uncharacteristic gawking. Then his gaze swings to mine and he loses the thread of his conversation, frowning. Bugger. Has he caught me staring? Embarrassing. But he shakes his head, responds to something the caller says and turns to face the window.

I wish ignoring *him* was so easy, but the deep-blue eyes I caught a flash of were captivating, framed by enviously long, black lashes that might make him pretty if he wasn't so … manly. Icing on the cake (and I love my cake) are the kissable Tom Hardy pillow lips. *And* there's The Body. Wide shoulders, broad chest and long muscular legs sprawled out in front of him. He's not just hot, he's mega hot.

This big handsome guy, a man who looks like a film star or a model in an American underwear ad, is the CEO? Unbelievable. Just my luck. My heart clunks to the pit of my stomach, feeling like it catches some vital organs on the way down. After all the gossip Tony circulated about me, and given the reason I'm here, my boss for the weekend is the last man in existence I can be attracted to.

I study him covertly, trying to swallow moisture back into my mouth. Being immune to his appeal fails in spectacular fashion, as an unfamiliar burn of heat sweeps along the back of my neck, spreading down my chest. I just manage not to wipe damp hands along my trouser legs. What's wrong with me? Although a redhead, I never blush; something I've always been thankful for.

Boy, am I in *Trouble*.

There's no time to dwell on the thought because he ends his call, throwing his phone onto the seat between us.

'So. Who the hell are you?' He demands as the car pulls out into the insane London traffic.

Chapter Two

Teeth snapping shut, my shameless appreciation of his outrageous good looks nosedives. Is he for real? Why so rude? But I must keep him on side, can't lose my cool, so I breathe in slowly, the scent of new leather making me feel slightly sick.

'Well?'

'Charley Caswell. Pleased to meet you.' Forcing a brittle smile, I thrust a hand towards him. 'The agency sent me to assist you over the next few days?'

His handshake is brisk and he withdraws as though I have a contagious disease. I ignore the tingle in my palm at his touch.

'I know why you're here,' he replies, 'I instructed the agency to hire someone. It's just that you're ah,' a pause, 'not what I was expecting.'

His gaze flickers over my chest, which I've always hated because my boobs are so big they make me feel like a low-grade porn star. Flushing, I button my suit jacket, trying to put aside the unwelcome excitement choking my oxygen supply.

Stop it. I should be offended by the quick glance, not flattered.

Be professional. I have to convince him I'm a sane human being, earn a little of his trust.

Rerunning his last remark, *not what I was expecting* I connect it with his downward glance. Is the problem I'm not a man? *Not* okay. But confrontation isn't what I came here for. 'I appreciate my first name may have caused some confusion, but I assure you I've lots of experience as a PA.' It's not exactly a lie. I was a PA for a year and a half during my climb up the corporate ladder. I'm sure the skills will come back to me.

'I haven't got any problem with your experience, after all you've been vetted by the agency.' He jerks open one of his jacket buttons and shifts his long legs restlessly. 'But I've had ... issues with female staff in the past. My executive assistant has a burst appendix and is in hospital recovering and apparently no one could step in at such short notice. Or they're still on leave.' He looks less than impressed.

'Well, we're barely into the New Year, and people do have a right to take holiday don't they?' I shouldn't say it but I feel sorry for the employees he has such high expectations of. 'And if you're limiting the number of people who can assist you to men,' I know by the flickering pulse in his jaw I'm right, 'you are narrowing your field a bit.' I won't argue outright about his blatant sexism, but I can't let it pass unnoticed.

'Maybe,' he agrees stiffly, looking at me with narrowed eyes. 'I suppose I just expected more. A sense of duty perhaps.'

Sidestepping his remark: 'So, what *issues* are you referring to about women anyway?' Carrying out my plan is going to be a teensy bit problematic if my gender means he won't even listen to me.

'Some people can separate work from their personal lives, respect professional boundaries,' he says coolly, 'but unfortunately others don't have that ability.'

'You're joking?' I laugh. Is he suggesting men do and women don't, or that he's so attractive every female who works for him will try it on? Okay, he's hot, but a large proportion of the female population demand equality and respect, and he's hardly giving off those vibes.

'No, I'm not.' He frowns. 'I was trying to be the opposite of funny.'

'Okay.' I bite the inside of my mouth. Talk about taking yourself too seriously.

'What are you smiling at?' he barks.

Blanking my face and voice, 'Nothing, sir. Absolutely nothing. I apologise, I didn't realise I was.'

'Don't be silly. You don't have to apologise for smiling.'

I ache to exclaim *I don't, Sah?* in a surprised, mock southern drawl, with a splayed hand to my chest whilst fluttering my eyelashes, but hold back.

'And don't call me sir. I hate it.'

He should try sounding less stern then. 'Yes s – I mean, Mr Demetrio.'

'Alex.'

'Yes, Alex.' I want to ask if he's sure letting me use his first name is appropriate given his need to maintain boundaries, but it'd probably be pushing it.

A horrible thought chokes me. Is the point about boundaries something he tells all female staff or is it just directed at me? Does he know who I am? A trickle of cold sweat runs down my spine, the droplet trickling into the waistband of my trousers.

'What's the matter?' he asks, broad body swaying with the movement of the car. 'You look like you've been told your grandma's been run over by a bus.'

'N–nothing.' I shake my head. Paranoia is setting in. Studying his face for any hint of a hidden agenda, I clock only bewilderment and annoyance shining in his eyes and curling his mouth. 'But let me assure you I've no problem keeping my work and personal lives separate. I'm more than capable of being professional.'

'Good.' He runs a tanned hand through his hair, leaving it ruffled in messy spikes that make fireflies circle in my stomach. 'Keep it that way.'

'No problem.' Crossing my arms and legs, I turn to stare out the window, wishing I could leap out of it. Gorgeous or not, the man needs a major attitude adjustment. Plus his behaviour has reinforced why I'm off men; my career and putting my life back together are what matter, not a pretty face and a hard set of muscles.

During the next few minutes of suffocating silence I gaze at passengers in passing cars, smiling slightly as I take in a piece of leftover mistletoe stuck up hopefully in a rear windscreen. Alex alternates between fiddling with his phone and staring out of his window.

'Miss Caswell, I should apologise,' he mutters, glancing at me from the corner of his eye.

I look over at him. If he's trying to say sorry it's a poor attempt, 'And are you?'

'Am I what?' He looks half confused, half cross.

'Apologising?'

'Yes, I am.' He lets out an exasperated laugh, a shade of tension dropping from his expression. 'I'm sorry.'

Scrutinising his face to gauge his sincerity turns out to be a dangerous move, because my breath catches in my throat, my heart beating so hard I can detect every pulsing rush of blood.

Whoosh, whoosh, whoosh.

My brain and body are definitely not on the same page. My head says *stay away!* in massive, neon, flashing letters whilst a warning klaxon sounds, but my rebellious sex drive is suggesting it's right and natural to slide along the seat towards him and–

Stop! Check yourself Charley. This isn't like you. Angling myself so the door handle digs into my left kidney, I use the discomfort to refocus, fixing on one of Alex's defined cheekbones to avoid getting lost in his deep-blue eyes. 'Apology accepted,' I reply at last. He seems genuine enough. 'However, I'd ask you not to judge me by other people's actions. You don't know me.' *Do you?*

'You're right.' He sits straighter, eyebrows folding together. 'And I know it must sound like I'm making a generalisation, but I have my reasons—'

'I'm sure you do, but you don't have to explain them to me.' I interrupt. Better to keep my distance.

'Thank you.'

I nod rather than get caught in further conversation but am aware of him studying me as I turn to the tinted car window. The dual carriageway and metal barriers slide by outside but I don't see them, too distracted by irritation and confusion. At him. At myself.

Yeah, I've got to keep my distance.

However, it doesn't take much for my attention to boomerang back to Alex. When he pulls out a computer tablet and starts flicking things across the screen with a long-tanned finger, my gaze lands on his muscular thighs, superbly shown off by expensively tailored trousers. The idea of being flung over his shoulder and carried off to his cave and ravished pops into my head. It doesn't make sense at all; I can't stand male chauvinists. Which is surely what he is if he thinks no woman can make it in the corporate world without surrendering to romance. I mean, what about men? They're just as guilty as getting involved in workplace relationships.

Added to which, growing up with three older brothers who delighted in winding me up at every opportunity means I hate chauvinist behaviour. In my teens they always taunted me about kitchen sinks and ironing boards and how real women should have dinner on the table when their husbands got home. I lost count of the number of times they provoked me into losing my temper or embarrassed me in front of my latest crush.

Now we're all adults I've forgiven them their comments. They only made them to get a reaction. Still, I learnt from the older generation in my home village that some men really do view women like that. Outdated attitudes I was keen to escape. So it's easygoing, supportive guys I date, not alpha males who have liquid testosterone running through their veins. Men like Alex.

No, it can't be genuine attraction. It's a hormonal thing, I've been sex-starved for too long. Perhaps it's time to change that. Just not with Mr Standoffish.

Stamping hard on the brakes, the driver gives a muffled curse as the car skids to a stop with a squeal of tyres. I'm wrenched out of my thoughts and, despite my seatbelt, fly sideways with a lurch, ending half-sprawled across Alex's lap, my boobs against his shoulder and my hand on his upper thigh.

It's very hard, and very hot.

Chapter Three

'Oops, sorry.' Straightening, I gaze into his eyes, cheeks scalding, heart racing again. It takes enormous willpower not to squeeze his thigh to test exactly how firm it is.

'No problem,' he replies, 'it was an accident.' He lifts my hand off his leg. 'But if you don't mind, you can have this back.'

'Thanks.' I can't help noticing how big and warm his hand is, the palm rough against my fingers, which flex automatically, fingertips brushing his wrist. His touch transmits a basic message to my ultra-aware body and my unruly hormones go into party mode again. 'Mr Demetrio,' I breathe.

'Yes?'

'I ... um.' Hot and extremely bothered, my skin tingles with waves of sexual awareness. My toes are curling, no, practically corkscrewing in my boots. Bet he's phenomenal in bed. Not that it matters. *Snap out of it.* Clearing my throat. 'Nothing.'

'Sorry, sir,' the driver calls through. 'Someone cut across me to get to the exit. I don't think he saw me.'

'No problem,' Alex replies. 'The main thing is we're all okay.' He looks down at our joined hands and frowns.

I snatch mine away, sliding across the back seat as the car starts moving again. With a small shake of his head, Alex retrieves his tablet and resumes work.

Rubbing my shoulder where the belt burnt into it, I cast around for a distraction. 'How far to the airport?' Fresh air and a change of scenery may do me good.

He glances at his expensive gold watch. 'Another twenty minutes or so.'

'Right, thank you.'

'Is there a problem?'

Shifting on the leather beneath me, I open my jacket, needing to cool down. 'No, not at all, I was just wondering.' The seatbelt tightens across my chest as the car purrs up a slip road and comes to a roundabout. I need to get a grip. Back to the task at hand. What would a new employee with little knowledge of his business ask?

'Can you brief me on the arrangements for this weekend please? And provide some background information about you and the organisation?' I know the casino chain inside out and can list the types of companies sitting alongside it under the umbrella organisation, but if I show that knowledge off he might get suspicious.

He turns to face me. 'Didn't you do any research? Or ask the agency to brief you?'

I take a deep breath, refusing to react to the implied criticism. 'There wasn't enough time. The agency gave me the broad outline, but once I accepted the assignment, it was a rush to pack and get across the city. Plus my phone died, so I couldn't look it up online.' Liar. I switched to a pay-as-you-go mobile months ago and only have enough credit to make emergency calls to Jess whilst abroad. Raising my eyebrows, I inject gratitude into my tone. 'So if you wouldn't mind?'

'Fair enough.' He stretches his arms out then drops them, the movement making me aware of how big and broad he is. 'This weekend is for the AGM,' annual general meeting I translate silently, 'of Demetrio International. The organisation has Greek roots but we trade worldwide.' The car rocks slightly as an articulated lorry roars past.

'You don't sound very Greek.' It pops out.

'What do you want? *Dios* and *agape mou* in darkly accented muttered tones?'

My stomach squelches. That actually sounds quite nice. But it appears to be a sore point. 'No, of course not. Sorry, I didn't mean anything by it.'

'No,' he sighs, 'I'm sorry for snapping. Anyway, I came to the UK as a child from Corfu, went to boarding school and then on to study at Oxford.' Which explains his unaccented English. 'I can speak some Greek. German and French too.'

'Right.'

'My grandfather built the original companies, primarily based on shipping, oil and transport.' As he speaks a crooked smile curves his mouth, making my knickers twang. 'When he met my grand-mother, who's British, she was a high-ranking army officer. After they married she left the army and had my father and younger sister within a few years but wanted to do something as well as raise children. Together they set up and managed a number of vineyards across Europe, olive farms and some restaurants and bars throughout the Greek islands. That was the start of it.'

'She was an officer,' I echo, impressed. The corporate induction information mentions the organisation's humble beginnings, but I didn't know his grandmother was in the army. She must have been a tough lady.

'Yes, but it's not well known. Pretend you didn't hear that.'

'No problem.' I mime zipping my lips. So he likes his privacy. It must be pretty difficult to achieve. After all, he's a wealthy, young and dynamic CEO and therefore someone naturally of interest to the press. The David Beckham of the business world. I could be intimidated, but he's still a person who eats, sleeps and breathes, even if it's hard to ignore the cut of the sharply tailored suit, hand-crafted leather shoes and healthy sheen of his skin. And that he could probably buy the flat I'm mortgaged to the hilt on a hundred times over.

'Thank you. So, my father came into the business in his twenties and ran the company alongside my grandfather for over thirty years, expanding the enterprise, until seven years ago when I became CEO. My grandfather retired very late, my father earlier than planned, and they convinced the Board someone in the family should run the company.' His expression turns grim.

Shifting in my seat to look at him better. 'Can I ask a question?'

His shoulders tense. 'It depends.'

'On what?'

'On what the question is.'

Wow. Talk about uptight. 'I wanted to ask how old you are,' I say easily, 'but if it's a national secret, one of those *if I tell you I'll have to kill you* pieces of information, please feel free not to answer.'

Opening his mouth, he pauses, then shocks me by throwing his head back and laughing. It's a low, rumbling sound and does funny things to my insides. As he chuckles, the tension seems to leak from him.

'No, it's not a national secret,' he murmurs, giving me a wide, genuine, ridiculously sexy smile, 'and I can tell you, but I won't have to kill you. So if you're looking for a merciful death to escape this assignment I'm afraid you'll be disappointed.'

'What a shame,' I drawl, playing along. Then freeze. God, are we flirting? I mustn't, I can't, even if it's accidental. I've been here before and look how it turned out.

Disaster.

Major bloody disaster.

No, it's fine. I shake my head internally. He's just being nice and I'm doing the same. 'So, how old are you?' I'd put him at thirty-five when he's scowling and twenty-seven when he's smiling. Funny how a change of emotion can make such a difference to someone's face.

'Thirty-one. Why?'

'You said you'd been in charge for seven years, I wondered how old you were when you took over, given the level of responsibility. Twenty-four. Pretty young.' Ouch. Most people that age are still finding themselves, dabbling around the edges of life, and there he was, running a massive organisation.

Lips compressing, any humour flees. 'I'm the oldest son and they trusted me,' he states, face going curiously blank.

I'm intrigued about the story there but it's none of my business. 'It wasn't a criticism, just an observation.'

'Yes, well, back to the facts. The business has grown more recently to include chains of hotels, casinos, media companies and a small banking arm. The organisation currently employs over ten thousand people.'

Interesting how he refers to it as 'the organisation' and doesn't take personal credit for it, like he's talking about something someone else has done. But he should be proud. He may not have clawed his way to the top through hard grind, but he's made the business more successful since taking over and he must work punishing hours for such rapid expansion. The spoilt rich playboy I was worried he might be would surely have run a company into the ground over the years, or at best let it stagnate?

'Thanks for the summary.' I cross my legs. 'So what do you need this weekend?'

'You're here to support me, set up presentations, attend meetings, take minutes and so on. Any problems with that?'

'No, none whatsoever.' I may be rusty but I'll manage.

'Great. Do you need to know anything more right now? It's just that I need to finish off some emails.' He waves the tablet at me.

'No, that's fine. Go ahead.'

'Thank you.'

As he turns back to his task, I twist my hands together. This plan has to work. If I don't get a proper job soon, a move back home is in the offing, along with asking Jess to buy me out of my half of the mortgage, which I know she'll struggle to do. To my shame I've not been able to pay my share for the last two months. She can't afford to keep propping us up, we both know it – we just haven't had the conversation yet. I guess we keep hoping something will change, that something good will happen. Maybe this assignment is it?

Blowing out a long breath, I chew my bottom lip. Imagine having to move back in with my parents after so many years of independence. They'll think they were right all along, that I should never have left the village. I can just picture having to face everyone. They'll be so smug my adventure to the big city didn't work out because they all love living in a quaint little corner of the world with traditional values. I shudder at the thought of being on the receiving end of all those pitying looks, the object of gossip. And the thought of leaving London makes me breathless. Before Tony arrived I had a job I loved, a nice flat, a fun social life, dates with creative musicians and jobbing actors, a fantastic circle of friends and great colleagues. Most of that's gone ... I can't handle losing the last of it.

I wonder what my ex-colleagues are up to. Do they still have the same nights out, the after-hours parties? Despite being manager I was still part of the group, and Kitty (best croupier in the casino, according to her) and I were friends. I worked really hard, sometimes stupidly long hours, but I played hard too. Kitty and I had lots of adventures together, occasionally joined by Jess, and got ourselves into some pretty memorable situations. Walking through the city barefoot in the rain at three in the morning because our high heels were killing us; wearing giant cardboard boxes painted and taped up to look like Rubik's cubes for a fancy-dress party; playing poker on a random rich guy's yacht moored up at Canary Wharf. If I have to move back to my parents', I'll miss the bright lights of the city, the music and gigs, bustle of people and our laughter, usually fuelled by a mixture of white wine and Cosmos.

There haven't been any fun nights out in months. I miss them. I glance over at Alex. Fun isn't a word I'd use to describe him. Okay, so he's laughed and cracked a couple of smiles and this is a business situation not a social one but still, he's wound so tight, is so snappy and defensive. Perhaps not surprising given the responsibility he's had since he was twenty-four – just three years younger than I am now. Maybe he doesn't get a lot of down time.

I don't think I'd be ready to take on a role with such massive accountability. Alex is responsible for keeping thousands of people in jobs; it's a hell of a pressure for one person. No doubt he's got a great team, but at the end of the day it all comes down to him. Could I do it? Would I want it? Building on a Business Studies NVQ from college, I got a distinction in a distance-learning professional qualification in people management and business administration a few years ago whilst working full-time and it damned near killed me. I loved learning and it helped when applying for the management job, but my social life went into sharp decline as a result. I was constantly turning down dates and cancelling plans in favour of staying in to do research or write assignments.

It made me wonder whether you can hold down a high-level job and still have time for other things, like love and family. None of the guys I dated during that time understood what I was trying to achieve. One of them labelled me a geek, nose stuck in a book when I could be out enjoying myself. He was right, I am a geek, and proud of it, so the stereotype didn't bother me. The issue was that he didn't respect my ambition and desire to better myself. Which makes my current situation even more agonising. I loved working hard and contributing to the bottom line of a company, leading and being part of a team. I have to get that back if I can.

Sitting up, I anchor myself in the now. Even if I wouldn't want to be CEO, there's clearly an upside – the job must *really* pay – because our car's stopping on the edge of a private airstrip. The smooth concrete runway is frosted with ice and surrounded by snow-covered shrubs, grass and miles of empty space. The mega-wealthy really do live in a different world. I expected a charter flight from a regional airport, not a private jet like on *Criminal Minds*. This is well out of my league, but oh, what a lovely league. Undoing my seatbelt as the car stops, I try to hide my eagerness to get on the plane and look around. There's still an excited little girl inside the corporate woman.

'Ready?' Alex asks, unbuckling his belt.

'Definitely.'

He smiles and it ignites a tripwire straight to my knickers. Thankfully the driver opens the door so I scramble out the car, handbag clutched to my side.

'Thank you.' I nod at the driver, holding my hair back from my face in the battering wind.

'No problem, Miss Caswell.'

Trailing after him, I shiver as he walks to the rear of the car.

As he pops open the boot lid I reach across him to grab my case but he's too quick for me, hauling it out onto the concrete. 'Allow me.'

Acknowledging his win with a wry smile, I watch him lift out a weekend bag, suit carrier and briefcase, before carrying everything over to the awaiting cabin crew.

Climbing from the car, Alex tucks all gadgets away in his pockets and strides over to his driver, clasping the man's shoulder. 'Thanks Evan, have a safe journey home and enjoy your long weekend off. Say hello to your wife for me.'

'I certainly will, sir, on all counts. Thank you.'

'Good. I'll see you here on Monday evening?'

'Yes, I'll be here. You have a safe journey as well.' Tipping his cap, he marches back to the car.

Interesting there's a respectful relationship between the two men. But then, it's only female employees my temporary boss has a problem with, isn't it?

Alex walks over to join me as the long black vehicle pulls away smoothly. 'Ready to go?'

Not at all. My feet are stuck to the floor. If I get on the sleek-looking plane, that's it, no going back. Plan B. Temporary PA. In Barcelona. Undercover ex-employee. Working with the hot CEO. But what would I say if I don't go? To Alex? More, to myself, for not at least trying? So I take a deep breath and reply, 'Sure.'

He points at the metal steps set against the side of the luxury plane. 'You first.'

'Thank you.' Careful to watch my footing as I clank upwards, I pray I won't slip and tumble backwards on to Alex. There's an inherent clumsiness running through me like a current and I've no wish for it to be on show this weekend. It's something I can normally keep under wraps, but my reactions this afternoon have been anything but normal so far.

I duck under the door frame as I step aboard. At five foot nine I usually feel like a towering behemoth, especially since I hit that height at thirteen and curves erupted all over the place. It doesn't help that adorably petite women seem to occupy the world. Wearing high heels makes me even taller but they give me confidence. I ignore the little voice inside my head whispering Alex is a good few inches over six foot and I don't feel like a behemoth standing beside him.

Entering the main cabin, I hold back the uncool gasp longing to break free, but my eyes feel a metre wide and my mouth drops open. When people talk about the height of luxury, they're not kidding. Plush velvety black carpet gives the cabin a cosy feel and a dozen matching executive chairs and small, expensive-looking tables are bolted to the floor in three groups, instead of the narrow, torturous seats on the planes I usually fly on. The plastic walls are white with the bottom half navy, almost the same shade as Alex's eyes. Everywhere I look there are lights and sockets.

Alex squeezes past me, oblivious to the tiny space between us. Shame I can't say the same. My nipples stand to attention at the waves of heat emanating from his body and my cheeks flush. It's become a humiliating habit in the last hour.

'Bathroom through there,' Alex nods to a narrow door across the cabin, 'why don't you sit, get comfortable?' His tone is offhand. 'Just like all the rest.' He mumbles beneath his breath, looking furious.

'Pardon?'

'Nothing.' He shakes his head. 'Just … sit down and strap up.

We're taking off soon.'

'Please don't tell me to shut up!' But I drop into one of the padded chairs anyway and glare at him.

Something in his gaze flickers and he strides over to crouch down in front of me, putting his hands to my waist. What the hell is he doing?

Chapter Four

'I said strap up, not shut up.' Staring into my eyes, he grabs both ends of the seatbelt, pushing the tongue decisively into the buckle. I clutch the armrests. 'I'd *never* speak to a staff member that way.'

If he hadn't gone on about boundaries earlier, the intense expression on his face might make me wonder if he finds me attractive. He held my hand for longer than necessary when I took my little trip into his lap too ... but no, those are crazy, unwelcome thoughts.

'Sorry,' my mouth is suddenly so dry I worry my lips will stick to my teeth, 'my mistake.'

'Yes, it is.' Grabbing the spare end of the belt with a sure hand, Alex tightens it slowly and smoothly. The practical action is so erotic it's ridiculous. Frozen to the seat, I'm ultra-aware of his broad shoulders and how close he is. I inhale his crisp, sexy aftershave; hear the even sound of his breathing; notice the tiny lines at the corner of his blue eyes, which add an extra zing of charisma. Skin fizzing, my nipples peak again and I gulp. Hard.

All the reasons for staying professional are forgotten. I want to lean forward, drive my hands into that thick, dark hair and kiss him, nibble on that biteable lower lip and get lost in the sensation of his tanned, confident hands all over me.

'No problem,' he says, with a funny twisted smile, breaking the spell, standing to take the chair opposite.

'Huh?' I blink, dazed. Why does he look so annoyed? What was all that about?

As the plane lifts off, I stare at the carpet, my body humming along with the vibration of the aircraft. My emotions feel as tangled as the Christmas lights Jess and I recently bundled up and shoved away in the hallway cupboard.

I'm attracted to a man I can't have.

It's that complicated and that simple.

As soon as the seatbelt signs ping off, Alex wordlessly moves across the cabin. Sliding a slimline laptop from his briefcase, he's soon fascinated by whatever is on it, but his focus is *so* fixed it feels like he's freezing me out deliberately. Is he angry because after what he said in the car about female employees and my reassurances he picked up my physical reaction to him? *Awkward.*

Fanning my face, I catch the eye of the pretty, blonde cabin attendant. 'Can I have some water please?'

'Of course, Madam.' She smiles politely.

Moments later she places a sparkling water in front of me, complete with perfectly squared ice cubes and a succulent slice of lemon. I hold the glass to the light, half expecting it to be encrusted with diamonds, or the water to be flecked with gold. I flush as I catch her watching me quizzically, before she edges away like I'm a mad woman.

Gulping back some water, my thoughts flow toward Alex again. It's strange, playing it cool with men has never been a challenge. Perhaps because until now they've only ever provoked lukewarm reactions, as opposed to scorching-hot ones?

Alex is still frowning at his laptop when I look over. Admiring his long muscular frame, thick dark hair and gorgeous face, lust packs me a punch and I feel like I've been knocked out by a world heavyweight. What is it about him? I've known plenty of fit guys, men who are handsome and charming. I even had a brief thing with a wealthy banker; not my usual type at all. He was really attentive, lavishing me with luxury gifts and treating me to expensive meals, but when I wouldn't sleep with him on our fourth date he backed off. To be honest, I was glad not to have to dodge his calls.

Alex is more than good looks and wealth, though. He has a confidence and complexity which make me gravitate towards him like the moon to the Earth, even though his ideas about women should repel me..

I have to put distance between us.

Shame it didn't work with my assistant, who I was definitely not interested in. Cringing, I rest my head against the padded seat, mind zipping back to the time that work went from good to ugly without stopping at bad.

Then

My manager John was supportive and lovely, with years of experience that I learnt a lot from. The last of the old-fashioned gentlemen, he and his wife doted on their four grandchildren, even with his late shifts, and I loved listening to his stories about their youngest granddaughter's quest for a full working monkey tail. He made coming to work a pleasure and everyone was sad when he retired early.

'I'll be leaving in three months' time,' he sank into the chair behind his desk, 'and I think you should apply for my job.'

'You do?' I dropped into the chair opposite. 'I've only been your PA for fifteen months.'

He smiled at me, adjusting one of the photos on his desk by a millimetre. 'I've been part of your journey from casual bar staff to temporary front-of-house receptionist to supervising the whole customer-care team. You had some of the best sales when you worked on the floor – the customers love you – and your local marketing campaigns were very innovative. You were appointed PA because I've watched you grow passionate about the casino and thought your manner and organisational skills were exceptional.'

'Thanks.' I smiled, warmed by his praise.

'I'm just calling it as I see it and in the last year you've only improved. You've got a knack for finances and the customer and are a capable young woman.' He picked up his trademark silver fountain pen, placing it in the pot on his desk. 'Which is why I campaigned so hard for the company to fund the business admin course.'

'Yes, and I've really appreciated the support, the way you've let me interview colleagues, and have extra days off, or swap shifts.'

'I know you've appreciated it.' He sat further forward. 'It's been obvious in your dedication and energy.'

'I'm glad,' I smiled, tapping my Biro against my notepad. 'And you know I value your opinion.' I hesitated. 'I am interested, but I'm worried it might be too soon.'

'Nonsense.' He waved a hand as if swatting away a hyperactive fly. 'I have complete confidence in you. You know the job better than anyone, and you've seen me doing it up close and personal for long enough.' He was right. Part of the reason for becoming his PA was to understand what it took to be a manager. 'I think you've got the skills for it,' he continued. 'You just need to believe in yourself. Nothing ventured, nothing gained and all that.'

I hid a smile. He always came out with clichés. They were part of his charm and impossible not to inadvertently copy. 'Thanks for the vote of confidence. I'll give it some serious thought and let you know what I decide.'

Discussing the idea of applying with Jess, who'd replied with a heartening, 'Go for it!' I was stunned to be offered the job after a demanding recruitment process. My team leadership experience was limited and I was certain there were better-qualified candidates but John's reference and the policy of internal progression meant I was given the chance to prove myself. For the first eighteen months I did, and it was fantastic. Mandy, the assistant I recruited directly from the reception team, was lovely. She was eager to please and efficient and we got on well. Then she went on maternity leave and decided not to return and I got handed Tony Ferrier as part of an internal transfer I never got to the bottom of.

In his mid-twenties, broad–shouldered, squat and slightly pinkish, he reminded me of an ex-public school boy, swaggering around the place from the beginning. But he was polite enough, did his work with a minimum of fuss and didn't create any drama, so I didn't think I had reason to worry. At first we got on okay and shared a few jokes.

One Monday I came into the office and frowned, studying him. 'You look a bit green Tony. Are you all right to be here?'

'Yes,' he smiled looking sickly, his normally pink cheeks pale. 'I've been on a stag weekend. The after-effects are getting to me, that's all.'

'Right. Well, take it easy, drink plenty of water,' I disappeared into my office and came back out, handing him a pack of tablets and can of energy drink, 'and make use of these.'

'Thanks.' Taking them from me gratefully: 'Do you suffer with hangovers often then?'

'No. I keep a stock of stuff hanging around for staff. It comes from most of them working into the early hours. It's hard for them to fall asleep when they finish, they're still buzzing, so there's a tendency to go for after-work drinks.'

'Right.' He sighed and rubbed his head.

I smiled sympathetically. 'Have you got some quiet work you can do?'

'Filing?' he asked hopefully.

'Okay. I'll take the phones for a few hours while you do that and then why don't you knock off early? I can handle things on my own.'

'If you're sure ... I wouldn't want you to think—'

'I don't. It was a special occasion, wasn't it? And you've been doing well the past few weeks. Everyone's allowed a night out occasionally.'

'Thanks. If you don't mind, I'd appreciate it.'

'It's fine. I know you won't make a habit of it.' A statement rather than a question, just so he knew I wouldn't put up with it on a regular basis.

'No.' He groaned, rubbing his forehead again, 'I won't.'

'So was it good?' Leaning forward I pressed a few buttons on his handset to forward his calls to my phone, then looked up at him.

'What?'

'The stag do? What did you get up to? What's the equivalent of tying someone to a lamppost nowadays?'

I glanced up, noting how bloodshot his pale-blue eyes were.

'It was my older brother's do. We made him dress as a woman and tell everyone we met that it was what he did to relax.'

I laughed, stepping back. 'Oh, dear. Very mean.'

'It was quite funny. It took some persuading but I won. He always says I get my own way, whatever I want,' he said, returning my smile before going quiet. Our gaze held for a few seconds longer than polite and his smile widened.

Uh-oh, I thought. That's not where I was going with this.

'Anyway,' I changed direction briskly, 'I'd better get on with some work. And you've got that filing to do,' I reminded him pointedly.

'Yes.'

As I backed away, he held his place, still smiling at me, still trying to maintain eye contact. As I went back into my office I had a twinge of unease but dismissed it quickly.

Everything was fine for a few weeks. Then, one Friday afternoon, I dropped a file, muttering under my breath. Tony appeared next to me, squatting down to help gather up the papers, handing them to me, fingers brushing against mine.

'Thanks,' I fumbled out breathlessly, flustered by my show of clumsiness. As I stood up I realised too late we were way too close. But to step away too obviously would be rude so I stayed put, shuffling the paperwork into order.

Staring into my eyes, he brushed something off my cheek. 'Eyelash.'

28

'Thanks.' It was a line, and an old one, but it may have been genuine, so I said nothing, just smiled and looked over my shoulder. 'I've got a report to finish so…'

'Yes, it's due in tomorrow morning.'

'I'll get to it then.' I paused awkwardly, not sure if I should say something after all.

'I'm really enjoying working with you, Charley. You're a good boss,' he said, seeming to emphasise the last word.

Phew. He got that all we had was a professional relationship. 'Good, great. Pleased to hear that. See you later.' Turning, I swept into my office and was soon immersed in the sales data I was analysing. Forgetting about Tony and any fears I had that we were being too familiar.

But two weeks later he started 'accidentally' brushing against me in the outer office where he sat, as well as making mildly suggestive comments. I said nothing initially. I'd look stupid and paranoid if I raised it with him and had misunderstood what was going on.

I'd always thought there was nothing wrong with office romances if everyone was happy and they were handled sensitively, but they've never been for me. Especially with a junior member of staff, who'd be in an unfair position if things went wrong, given the imbalance of power. So the company's anti-workplace relationship policy suited me fine. It was a moot point anyway. I didn't find Tony attractive and there was something about him I was starting to dislike. So I gave him subtle 'back off' signals, hoping he'd get bored and leave me alone but it only increased his determination. One day he cornered me in the file run.

'Fancy dinner with me tonight, Charlotte? Just the two of us.'

My back was to him as I flicked through confidential files in a cabinet, so he didn't see the face I pulled or the deep silent breath I took to control my annoyance. By then there was a niggle about the potentially patronising way he spoke to female staff, but none of them had come to me and there wasn't enough evidence to raise it with him.

Shutting the drawer slowly, I turned around. 'Thank you for the offer, Tony, but it's not a good idea. I'm your line manager and would prefer to keep this professional. Our contracts also make clear relationships between colleagues aren't allowed.' I forced away the urge to demand he call me Miss Wright. I didn't ask any other team members to and didn't want him to feel I was singling him out.

'Right. I see. Sorry.' He smiled tightly.

'That's fine.' I nodded. 'So, if you don't mind?' I waved a file in the air.

'Don't let me stop you.'

The way he looked me up and down made me edgy. Was he intending to make me squeeze past him? 'Would you mind moving please?'

'Sorry. Of course.' He stepped back to let me pass.

Striding out, I chanced a look over my shoulder. He was staring after me, grey suit rumpled and pale-pink tie askew. The whole incident was another odd one, but hopefully he'd got the message.

The next day when I came in for the evening shift, he was sitting on the edge of my desk.

'Evening, Tony. Can I help?' Claiming my chair, I gestured him to take a seat opposite.

'I've been thinking about what you said yesterday,' he acknowledged, 'and we can remove the problem.' He paused, gave a smirk. 'If you weren't my boss we wouldn't have a conflict in dating.'

My lower jaw momentarily dropped but I calmed myself, switching on my computer. 'Sorry, what are you suggesting?'

'If working together is a problem, we could change that.'

'How exactly?'

Shrugging, he stretched his arms above his head as if totally relaxed. 'Maybe if you worked at another casino?'

I stared at him in disbelief, wanting to wind his arms round his neck and throttle him with them. Anger sent tingles along my skin. I couldn't comprehend what he'd said. Inappropriate didn't begin to cover it. It was so bloody arrogant. I should give up a job earned through hard work just to have the opportunity to sleep with him? What alternate reality was he lodged in?

Going into hyper-formal mode, I straightened in my seat, squaring my shoulders. 'I'm surprised at the suggestion, Tony. I'm very happy here and have no desire to transfer. And I have no desire for us to be involved. If you're going to stay you'll need to respect that. Can you work as my assistant on those grounds?'

'Sure.' He tried to look indifferent but a muscle ticked at the corner of his mouth. 'It was just a thought. And after the way we talked, and you smiled at me—'

'I was being polite.' But guilt nagged at me. Had I encouraged him? Been too friendly?

'It was just a thought, as I said,' he reiterated stiffly.

'Good. Then I think we should regard the topic as closed.'

'Good,' he repeated. 'Everything you need is waiting in your in-tray. Goodnight.' Standing abruptly, he stalked out.

After he left, I was unnerved enough to rush through the door onto the casino floor for a walk around. I needed to be around people, try and forget I'd just been propositioned by my assistant.

After sleeping on it, I hoped for the best and that he'd have abandoned his weird ideas. I was conducting staff appraisals for front-of-house staff the following morning so didn't see him until lunchtime. There was no mention of the previous night's conversation and I didn't get an apology, but for a while it was better. The invasion of my space stopped and so did the inappropriate comments.

Then one evening I was working on a head-office project on rolling out succession planning across the London region. Tony had stayed on to pull data off the system, but was tense, motions jerky, not making direct eye contact.

'Tony, we're all right aren't we?' I asked, pouring us coffee. We were at the meeting table in my office, papers spread out around us, other staff either down on the casino floor or in the security or cash offices.

'What do you mean?' He looked over, frowning.

'Our conversation the other week—'

'Sure,' he shrugged but his expression had gone hard, the planes of his face standing out starkly. There was a gleam in his eye which made me uncomfortable.

'I just thought … you don't have to be embarrassed. We can—'

'Forget it,' he ground. Holding the milk jug up: 'White or black tonight?'

'Black, thanks.' I stared at him but he ignored me, hypnotically stirring sugar into his coffee. He was upset, so trying to pursue the conversation would obviously fall on deaf ears. I let it go, thinking he was having an off day.

'Has your brother got married yet?' I prodded, to change the subject.

'Yes. Big wedding last weekend. He's all settled with his perfect blonde princess and Mercedes and new partnership at his law firm now.'

The bitter tone and twisted expression told me more than the words did how competitive the sibling rivalry was. 'Ok–ay.' Clearing my throat, I turned a printed spreadsheet over. 'Shall we look at this one now then?'

'Yes,' he agreed, yanking it towards him.

I remember thinking: *He'll get over whatever he thought might be happening between us. He's got other things going on.*

Then odd things started happening.

Staff meetings mysteriously moved so I'd miss them, appointments were changed in the shared diary so I didn't know when corporate clients would be arriving, making me look and feel hopelessly inept. Deadlines were altered, making me prioritise work in the wrong order and have to ask for extensions or face the embarrassment of sending it in late. I started keeping a paper diary so I could track deadlines accurately, make sure I wasn't going mad. If I was out of the office, Tony would get everyone looking for me as if I'd gone AWOL, and would apologise quietly after the fact, saying he hadn't seen the external appointments in my diary. When I asked what was going on he'd express innocence, saying he'd been confused.

I was so frustrated. His behaviour was unreasonable, but I wasn't sure what to do. It all seemed so intangible and I wasn't sure I could prove the 'confusion' was anything other than genuine human error. So I looked at our policies and procedures, researched sexual harassment online, went onto forums for research. It didn't feel like he was bullying me as such and he was the junior employee. When I read all the horrifying true stories on the message boards and chat rooms of how people had ended up going off sick with work-related stress and falling into depression, even losing their jobs, houses and marriages, it made my own fears seem silly.

I settled for making notes of the date, time, location and content of any worrying conversations or events in my moleskin notebook, and called Human Resources. I didn't name myself or Tony, wanting to guard my privacy and in hindsight, my pride. The HR Manager advised me to try and resolve the issues with my staff member informally and if it didn't work to raise a formal complaint under the grievance procedure or take him through a disciplinary process, which would be taken seriously by the company. She took pains to ask if I felt physically threatened in any way but I couldn't honestly say yes at that point.

Coming off the phone feeling better, I was determined to have a clear, minuted conversation with Tony, where I'd tell him I knew he was trying to undermine me and wouldn't stand for it. That it'd be regarded as insubordination and a potential conduct issue. But before I had a chance, one awful evening cut my time at the casino short.

I never saw it coming, not what happened. Despite the storm warnings on the horizon I should have noticed.

Chapter Five

Now

'Miss?' The air hostess pops up next to me.

'Argh!' I jump, wrenched from the past, hand jerking around the glass on the tray. A wave of cold water sloshes over the rim into my lap. Yelping, I make an 'ah–ah–ah' sound as the icy liquid soaks through my trousers. It can only be this freezing because all the ice has melted. How long was I brooding for?

Alex frowns at me and I fall silent with a self-conscious grimace, standing to mop up the mess.

The stewardess shakes her head, pointing out the window. 'Sorry, you'll have to wait until we've landed. I'll bring you a towel to sit on. Can you fasten your seatbelt please?'

'Huh?' I glance out the narrow cabin window, gobsmacked to see it's night time, thousands of twinkling lights appearing as the plane banks to the right.

She brings me a thick navy towel. 'Thanks,' I murmur, tucking it under me. I watch as she takes a seat by the emergency exit, trying to ignore the flutter of panic in my stomach. I absolutely hate landing, always worrying the plane won't brake in time and will overshoot the runway or that despite being strapped in I'll get tossed around the cabin somehow. I may have watched too many disaster movies but it's the first episode of *Lost* I blame, when the plane crashes on the mysterious tropical island and the beach is awash with broken fuselage and torn bodies.

Compared to the stress of being near-destitute, landing should be easy, but rationalising doesn't stop me moulding my body into the damp seat, or my short bitten nails from digging into the slick leather armrests.

'Once we've disembarked it's a twenty-minute drive to the hotel,' Alex says curtly, powering down his laptop.

I nod, staring at the headrest of the opposite chair and smarting from his tone. I don't know what his problem is but he's going to have to get over it. And I'm going to act like the strong independent woman I was before Tony bowled into my life. I will deal with Alex head-on ... if I get off the flight alive.

The plane begins its descent. Screwing up my eyes, I start counting inside my head. The engines slow and my breathing comes in short, sharp bursts through my nose, jaw clamped tight. We hit an air pocket, dipping down, then up, and I let out a quiet squeak, ears popping. *Please don't crash, please don't crash, please do not crash.*

There's a muffled protesting squawk from the stewardess and I sense movement but dare not open my eyes. What if the crew are preparing for an emergency landing? I'll freak out completely. Better to stay in blissful ignorance.

I get a shock as long warm fingers curve round mine in silent comfort. I tilt my head and squint out of one eye and find Alex beside me, a serious expression on his face.

'We'll be fine,' he whispers close to my ear and I shiver. 'Just keep breathing.'

I didn't have him down as the compassionate sort, but the thoughtfulness and his comment make me smile. Does he think I'm so scared I'll stop breathing? That'd be a great front-page headline. *Woman hyperventilates to death on plane, too wimpy to cope!*

'Okay,' I murmur, 'I'll try.'

'Good.'

His deep-blue long-lashed eyes stare into mine. My chest squeezes my heart into my throat, or at least that's what it feels like. The connection of our hands brings us close enough that our arms are aligned, his shoulder against mine.

'You've already dropped your end of the deal,' he remarks.

'Pardon?'

'Oh good, you are still breathing. For a second there I wasn't sure.'

Smart-arse, I think and can't stop another smile from erupting. I shift away a bit. Maybe if we're not so close ... 'Landing might present a challenge but I'm pretty sure I can cope with drawing breath.' Is the shadow of stubble on his jaw getting darker? God, he's sexy.

He cocks an eyebrow, a bit Sean Connery as James Bond. 'From the shade of white you're currently sporting I wondered how much oxygen was making it to your brain.'

'Gee, thanks!' Mouth dropping open, I go to wrench my hand away.

His fingers tighten, stopping me. 'Relax! I'm kidding. You really are anxious about flying aren't you?' He nods to the towel peeking out from under my legs. 'Is that why you spilt your water?'

'Yes.' No, it's because I'm clumsy as hell when I forget to pay due care and attention. 'It's not the flying, though, it's the landing bit. I really don't like the transition from air to ground.'

'Why didn't you say something earlier?'

'I need this assignment.' I pause. 'And we couldn't exactly boat across.'

He's not quick enough to hide his smile. 'No, but I would have tried to make it easier for you if I'd known.'

An automatic response *would you really have cared?* almost breaks free but he's showing he cares now. 'It doesn't matter,' I say lightly, 'but thank you.'

'So how do you usually cope?' he asks after a moment, a deep line appearing between his dark eyebrows. 'When you go on holiday?'

'Er.' I glance around the spacious cabin, avoiding eye contact. Then peek at him. 'Don't laugh.'

'It can't be that bad. What is it?'

'I drink.'

'So? Other people drink to calm their nerves.'

'No, I mean, I *drink*. Three or four vodkas usually help achieve the right sort of numbness.'

'Three or four? Over the course of the flight?'

'Um, not exactly.' Please don't let him think I'm an alcoholic. 'First one is when the seatbelt lights blink on.' Does he know he's stroking my knuckles? It's making my insides go hot and funny. 'Second one is when the plane starts banking for approach. Third is usually as we start our descent and I might slip a fourth in during descent.'

'How do you get away with it?'

'Miniature bottles,' I admit shakily, as the stroking of my fingers gets faster and a waft of his sexy aftershave invades my nose. 'I swig them quickly and discreetly.'

'I see,' he deadpans. 'Well, it's medicinal I suppose.' He pauses. 'It, ah, must be interesting for your boyfriend trying to get you off the plane standing upright.'

'I don't go on holidays with boyfriends, only friends,' I blurt. Why did I tell him that? 'And I'm usually a little relaxed, but they know the score and help me through passport control. It takes about twenty minutes to really hit anyway. By that time we're on the coach and I nap until we get to the hotel.' Does he know our knees are touching? My leg feels like it's on fire. I edge it away discreetly.

'Sounds like you have it all figured out.' He squeezes my fingers, looking concerned. 'But why not just ask your doctor for sedatives if it's that bad?'

'Like I said, I'm okay with taking off and being in the air, it's the end part. I don't see any point in being knocked out for the whole flight.'

'Really?'

'Yes. Why would I want to waste my time asleep when I could be doing something else instead?'

He tilts his head towards mine, getting so close I start going cross-eyed. 'Like what?'

'Reading, watching a film, talking to my friends. You know, normal leisure stuff.'

'Right.'

He says it like I'm talking about a foreign concept. Doesn't he get any time off at all?

He shakes his head. 'Interesting.'

'What? You did ask.'

'Not that.' He leans over and points out the window. I can feel his warm breath on my cheek and shiver. 'We've landed.'

'Really?' I look out the Perspex. He's right. There's a vast expanse of tarmac visible in the night outside, peppered with landing lights and a control tower. 'Oh, yes.' So involved in our conversation, I hadn't noticed. It's a first – the Earth and I reacquainting ourselves without the benefit of alcohol. 'Thank you so much,' I beam.

He pauses, staring at my mouth then glancing down at our entwined fingers. A strange look crosses his face and he releases my hand quickly. 'No problem. Besides, it would hardly be good publicity if a member of staff suffered an anxiety-driven heart attack on my private plane. I also need you fully functioning tonight so we can have a proper briefing session. You can't do that drunk.'

'But I haven't had anything to drink! That's why I was getting anxious.'

He doesn't answer, busying himself with straightening his tie and undoing his seatbelt.

'Alex?'

'Time to get off,' he snaps. 'Come on.'

'Fine,' I say stiffly. Undoing my belt I bolt from the chair, feeling unexpectedly stung by his briskness. How could I have forgotten who I was talking to? Why was I deluded enough to think he was being sweet and compassionate, even friendly? Why would I even want him to be? He's not my friend, he's my temporary boss, ensuring he's upholding his duty of care. I can't make the same mistake again; get too close to someone I work with, even if last time it was accidentally. Been there, done that, got the diamanté t-shirt.

Grabbing my handbag and coat from under the seat, I stride over to the exit, where the crew have gathered.

'Have a pleasant stay in Barcelona.' The blonde attendant smiles.

'Thank you.' Doubtful. 'Bye.'

Picking my way down the metal stairs, I can't see a transport bus, so set off towards the airport buildings, assuming our luggage will follow. It's milder than London but an unkind wind still whistles along the concrete so I pull my coat tighter.

'Charlotte,' Alex calls behind me. I carry on walking. He can tell me what he wants to when he catches up.

'Charley. Charley!' he yells.

Stopping with a sigh, 'Yes?' I try not to let frost coat my voice.

He runs up. 'No. Over there.' He gestures back over his shoulder to a car I hadn't noticed parked twenty feet or so behind the plane.

My eyes widen at the gorgeous lines of the black low-slung sports model. 'Seriously?' I breathe, skirting round him to start back.

'Yes.' Falling into step, Alex raises an eyebrow. 'You like it?' Frowning, 'Or is it the status thing?'

Legs eating up the distance, I stop next to it, running my hand along the smooth bonnet. Something about the car reminds me of Alex. Powerful. Slick. Sexy. 'Status? No. It's not that. Cars aren't my thing but … well, it's kind of beautiful.' Like him. No. Stop it!

'My kind of woman,' he murmurs appreciatively before looking horrified at his comment. 'I mean, I like the way you think. I mean – never mind.'

Smiling inside, I dip my head to study the Maserati badge, amazed to see Mr CEO so uncomfortable. It doesn't fit with the smooth, self-contained persona. I like the slip, it makes him seem more normal, more approachable.

I know he's staring at me but stay silent, waiting for him to unlock the car. A pinging sound erupts from his suit jacket. Taking out his phone, he swipes a tanned finger over the screen and reads something, face tightening and draining to white. Whoever sent him the text should run and hide. Now. He looks dangerous.

'Excuse me.' Moving away, he touches the screen again and holds the phone to his ear. 'I need to speak to you,' he barks. 'I need some advice.'

He tilts his head whilst listening to the caller and the sound of something cracking in his neck carries over the space between us. Ouch, tense.

'She just texted me,' he lowers his voice, 'saying I need to agree to the latest demand or I can't see her.'

Whoever she is, I wonder what her price is. I can't imagine black-mailing a man to stay with me. Is that how the mega rich run their relationships? Fascinated by the idea, I edge closer. Unfortunately Alex notices and scowls, pointing a beeper at the car and gesturing with his chin for me to get in.

Flushing, I open the door and slide into the bucket seat. Bugger, caught out.

Respect the boundaries, Charley. Be professional at all times.

Easier if the man concerned wasn't so contradictory – and so bloody intriguing.

He joins me in the glamorous car as I'm sliding my hands over the blue and black interior, fiddling with buttons and admiring the inbuilt SatNav. Caught in the act, I tuck my hands under my legs and bite my lip.

'It's fine,' he growls.

The compact front seat means there are only a few inches between us. Too close for comfort, both for my wild hormones and if he's going to have a go at me.

'I'm sorry,' I offer, when he simply starts the engine with a low purr and says nothing. 'For overhearing, I mean. Is everything – are you okay?'

Raising an eyebrow, probably at my description of what was actually blatant nosiness, he fastens his seatbelt. 'Fine.'

Which means no, but he doesn't want to talk about it. The quiet spins into an elongated silence but thankfully there's distraction in the vibrancy and colour of Barcelona as we leave the airport. Damp greenery and concrete roads give way to high-rise towers and numerous heaving shops as we enter the city centre. The street lights are like strobes in the night as Alex accelerates through, but I see that some of the trees have twinkling lights threaded through their bare, twisting branches, possibly the remnants of Christmas. It would be nice to be able to explore the city, but I'm not anticipating much downtime.

I glance at Alex, handling the Maserati like a pro, apparently comfortable with driving on the right-hand side. The confidence is attractive. I'd be a quivering wreck at the thought of driving this car; it's probably worth about five times my old salary. Though I guess when you're a billionaire the cost of a high-spec luxury vehicle is like buying a pack of chewing gum.

For distraction I whiz down the window and stick my head out, breathing in smoke and the faint tang of cooking food. Normal city smells, not much different from London, although there is one huge difference – the temperature. Jess might disagree with what I'm doing but she still cares, texting earlier to warn me not to pack thick jumpers because, according to the internet, the average temperature in Barcelona for this time of year is twelve degrees. Practically tropical compared to the minus numbers on the thermometer in our home city.

My attention flickers back to Alex as we stop at some traffic lights. He seems less stressed, idly caressing the steering wheel as he waits to pull away. Would he do the same to me if I asked him? No. Stop it. Stay focused. *Business*. Then I completely ruin it. 'You really like this car.'

Broad shoulders loosening, he flashes me a wicked grin, kind of wolfish. 'Wrong.'

'Really?'

'Yes. I don't like this car, I *love* it.'

'I can tell.' Pausing, 'I didn't think you'd drive.'

'Why, because I have Evan?' He shrugs, long legs flexing on the pedals as he changes gear effortlessly and pulls away. 'It makes sense to have a driver back home because I can handle calls and send emails, but on shorter journeys I prefer driving. It's relaxing.'

'Even on the wrong side of the road? Do you come to Barcelona often?' I cringe as soon as it's out there. It sounds like a cheesy pick-up line.

He doesn't notice. 'A few times a year, maybe.'

'Do you travel a lot for work?' Curiosity kindles. What's life as a CEO really like?

'I'm based in London and Corfu and spend about sixty per cent of my time travelling.'

'That must be inconvenient for your wife or girlfriend.' It just slips out.

'What makes you think I have one?' Alex throws me a questioning glance.

'Well, someone like you is bound to.'

'Someone like me? Elaborate.'

Dangerous territory, back away. 'Nothing, it doesn't matter.'

'It does. I want to know what you were going to say.'

I puff out a breath, fringe ruffling up with the expelled air. *Keep it simple.* 'You know,' I shrug casually. 'Rich, powerful, professionally successful.'

Alex lets out a harsh laugh. 'Is that all you think I am?'

I'm not sure what he means. 'Isn't it enough? They're attractive … attributes to some women.'

'You sound like a politically correct adviser from a dating

agency.'

'Well, what would you have me say?' I flash. 'Top Ten Things to Look For in a Guy?'

'If it's the honest answer.'

'Fine.' I straighten, as much as I can in the tiny seat. 'For some women—'

'You included?'

'What does that matter?'

'I'm interested,' he shoots back, 'humour me.'

I sigh. 'Okay. For some women those things would be essential, but I think sharing common ground, experiences and beliefs is more important. And I'm more impressed by intelligence, ambition and a good sense of humour than power or money.'

'Isn't ambition the same as power?'

'No. Ambition is about making yourself a better person, wanting to get somewhere. That place doesn't necessarily have to be somewhere you'll hold power. What about people who study to become teachers?' I think of Jess. 'They're ambitious enough to get a degree and qualified teacher status but it's not necessarily about working up to a head teacher post, it's being passionate about educating children, getting them ready for life.'

'If you say so.' He chuckles. It's not a kind sound. 'Still, going back to the things you value, you sounded more like an employment agency looking for staff than a woman looking for a man.'

'You asked for my opinion, I gave it.' I cross my arms. 'Besides, I'm not looking, so it doesn't matter.'

'My apologies, how dare I suggest it.' He glances in the rear-view mirror, signals and changes lane. 'We'll talk theoretically instead. If you *were* looking, you're expecting me to believe those qualities would have priority over a man having a good job and fat wallet?'

Turning to him, I open my mouth to spit out an answer. His eyes are narrowed, bitterness twisting his mouth. He's obviously had a bad relationship, and it's made him cynical. I can't help wondering what happened, who she was. The woman who texted him?

Whatever. It doesn't mean he's entitled to make assumptions about me. Breathing in deeply, I do my best to stay calm. 'I'd rather be with someone who respects me and supports me pursuing my goals and who's a struggling artist, than be with someone who showers me with gifts but has a massive ego and demands complete control.'

'Is that a fact?' he drawls as we roll to a stop at a junction.

'Yes!' I sigh again. 'Maybe we should change the subject.'

'No, come on, I'm interested.' He glances both ways before signalling and pulling out with a low roar of the engine. 'Not many people are so generous with their opinions.'

Crap. Rapid back-pedalling required. 'If I've spoken out of turn Mr Demetrio—'

He cuts me off with a sideways look. 'It's Alex, remember? And you haven't. So, are you saying money doesn't matter at all? If you met two men, liked them both and the only difference was one was rich and one wasn't, you wouldn't pick the one with the money?'

There's no right answer. Given his cynicism, I will look like either a gold-digger or a liar.

'See,' he mutters, 'you can't deny it. You're as motivated by money as the next woman. The only difference is some admit it.'

'That's not fair,' I shoot, shaking my head. 'And I won't admit to something that's not true. The money would be a bonus but it wouldn't be the deciding factor. I'm not one of those women who go out with the intention of bagging a billionaire.' Attempting to lighten the mood, 'Although if I *were* looking, a man with the ability to buy me a few more pairs of shoes wouldn't be completely unwelcome.'

'So it is important then.'

'I was joking! It's not about the money.' But I'm a hypocrite. Part of the reason I'm here is cold hard cash. Though it's got no link to any attraction I feel for him.

'If you say so.' He accelerates and I'm pressed back into the seat. 'Let me put it another way. If you won the lottery, you'd take it?'

'That's not the same and you know it,' I retort. 'I'd be an idiot not to claim the money ... and FYI I'd probably share it with my family.' Crossing my arms. 'Fine, you've got me. In the grand scheme of things, money *is* important, especially when you haven't got any. Not that you'd know anything about that. But I'm talking about being able to pay the mortgage and put food on the table, not spending thousands of pounds on one item of clothing or blowing silly amounts on lavish parties.'

Alex nods as we pull up outside the hotel, yanking the handbrake on and cutting the engine. He shifts in his seat to look at me. 'Not all of us draw huge salaries or are stupid about spending,' he surprises me by saying, 'but well done, very passionately delivered.' He searches my face for something, then the shutters come down. 'I could *almost* believe you.' Climbing gracefully from the car, he leaves me frozen in my seat, mouth hanging open.

Did he just call me a liar?

Chapter Six

I'm angry and hurt but my conscience tugs at me. I *am* a liar, until I find the right moment to tell him who I am and the reason I'm here.

But he doesn't know that. So why is he assuming I'm being dishonest?

If it was anyone else who'd said it, my instinct would be to argue, but it won't help, so I take a moment to cool down. Grabbing my mobile from my bag, I check for a signal. The little tree icon and message welcoming me to Spain show I'm linked to the local network. I send Jess a quick text.

Hi, here safely :) Got off plane in one piece! Know you think I'm wrong to do this but I need to. Speak later. C x

Dropping my phone into my bag, I hope I'll still have a best friend by the end of the weekend.

I wiggle from the car, aided by a red-uniformed concierge who rushes over to hold the door open for me. If I'd expected Alex to wait I'd be disappointed. He's already gone into the hotel. Charming.

Studying the grand white frontage of the building, I thank the man, receiving a nod and smile in reply, before I click up the broad stone stairs and through the gold-gilded door into the lobby. Spotting my infuriating but dishy boss at the front desk, I stride across the vast, high-ceilinged, black-marbled room. The differences between the traditional façade and the modern interior of the hotel work surprisingly well together.

Hoping Alex will acknowledge me and perhaps apologise turns out to be pointless; he's deep in laughing conversation with the pretty brunette receptionist who's tapping quick fingers over a computer keyboard, their gazes tangling. Not that I'm bothered.

'Here you are, sir,' she says with a flirtatious smile and some exotically rolled r's, 'the Mediterranean. I have two key passes. There are two guests staying, *si*?'

My eyes widen. He's not expecting us to share a room? No way. Not appropriate, a bit sleazy, and how would it look if anyone found out, given the rumours Tony's spread about me? It's absolutely nothing to do with how my rebellious hormones might cope with the challenge of sleeping a few feet away from Alex.

He looks round at me. 'Oh, there you are. Sorry I didn't wait for you but I wanted to get started on check-in. I thought you might be wrung out after the plane journey.'

Meaning my nerves on landing. Drats. He has his faults, but he's actually pretty thoughtful.

His gaze flickers over me, making my skin fizz, and he frowns. 'Are there any other rooms available?' he quizzes the receptionist.

She checks her screen. 'No, sorry sir. We are fully booked.'

'What about other hotels in the area?'

'I can make some calls but it is unlikely given the time of year. It's very busy.'

'Right.' He runs a hand through his dark hair. 'Of course.'

I start to feel self-conscious. 'What's the situation?'

'We were expecting Stuart to accompany me,' he throws over a broad shoulder. 'For a woman, different arrangements would have been made.'

He usually shares rooms with male colleagues? But he's mega

wealthy, could probably buy the whole hotel with his pocket change. He doesn't *seem* gay ... and he warned me off earlier. Was it all a cover?

Embarrassingly, he catches me studying him. His eyebrows fold down together, then his mouth quirks up on one side. 'It's a suite with two separate bedrooms.' He shakes his head. 'It's for convenience. Your room would be accessible from the outside corridor as well as the lounge of the suite.'

I release a breath. Separate rooms and he's not into men. Not that I care, about the latter, I'm just pleased he isn't suggesting we share a room, as Tony probably would have done.

'Charley?'

'In that case, no problem. Take it.' It'll be a pain to try and find somewhere nearby and I doubt we'll be in the suite much anyway.

'If you're sure? That's helpful, thank you.' After a moment Alex hands me a key card and I take it, careful not to let our fingers touch. I so need dinner and then bed. I'm exhausted, and annoyed with him. Some time to get my head together would be heavenly.

'I will call someone to take your bags up,' the receptionist says in her lovely lilt as the concierge rolls up with our luggage in a gold trolley.

'We can manage,' Alex replies, 'but thank you.'

I raise an eyebrow. For a billionaire he's oddly humble. From the bewildered expression on the receptionist's face she thinks the same but simply nods, handing Alex a slip to sign and asking if he knows where he's going.

'Yes, thank you.' Walking round me, he starts unloading our luggage, looping the strap of his bag diagonally across his broad chest, retrieving his briefcase and folding the suit carrier over the same arm. When he bends over to grab the handle of my case with his free hand, I step forward.

'That's okay, I can get it,' I say hastily.

'It's not a problem, honestly,' he looks up at me.

His dark lashes are so ridiculously long. I edge away. 'Honestly,'

I echo, 'I'm fine.'

'I'm trying to be a gentleman. Are you always this stubborn?'

'I'm not being stubborn,' I defend. 'I just like taking care of myself.'

Picking my case up, he gives me a small smile that curls my toes. 'Being independent is admirable but it's okay to accept help sometimes. Now let's get upstairs and get rid of our bags so we can eat. We have a table booked for eight thirty.'

'We do?' I squeak. Being with this guy in a professional setting is one thing, but at a cosy table for two?

'It's what usually happens when people go on business trips together.' He gives me a pointed look. He's right, damn it. Leading the way to the lift, he stabs a small round button set in a gold panel. 'Besides, we need to discuss the schedule and how we'll work best together.'

With me blindfolded so I can't see your gorgeousness? The knee-jerk thought flashes across my brain.

'Or do you suggest we sit separately and shout across the restaurant at each other?' he asks drolly.

'No, of course not,' I mutter. Couldn't he have filled me in on the plane? Although I guess he had other work to do then, and it's not for me to challenge. But won't dinner be a bit uncomfortable? My cheeks go hot with irritation as I mentally rehash his snotty remark in the car about almost believing me.

His blue eyes focus on my face like a satellite tracking device. 'You're a funny colour again. Are you all right?'

'Uh-huh. Just a bit warm.'

He stares down at me, eyes narrowed, but thankfully the lift arrives with a discreet ping. He gestures for me to go first and once we're both in stabs the **P** button. Excitement leaps up. I've never stayed in a penthouse before. Have I fallen asleep and woken up in the middle of *Pretty Woman*? But of course, I'm not a prostitute and sex is definitely *not* going to form part of the arrangement for the next few days.

We sink back against opposite walls of the lift. I fan myself, trying to cool down. The memory of his words reverberates through my head and a pressure builds behind my jaw.

'Did you mean it?' I blurt.

He raises an eyebrow, 'Mean what?'

'What you said in the car? About not believing me? What I said about men and money?'

'I didn't say I didn't believe you. I said I almost could.'

'Same difference,' I shoot back. 'And not very nice.' Then I snap my teeth shut so I don't say anything I might regret.

He looks at my hands where they're clenched at my sides and then back at my face. 'As far as I'm concerned that discussion was simply an interesting debate.' Shrugging broad shoulders, 'But if I upset you I'm sorry.'

It's hardly the apology of the century but sometimes you have to work with what you've got. 'Thanks.' I pause, 'An interesting debate?' Hmm. 'Have many of those?'

'No,' he looks thoughtful, 'not really.'

The lift doors open and we walk to the end of a long black-carpeted corridor decorated with white and cream flocked wall-paper and elegant crystal chandeliers.

'You can access your room here.' Alex indicates a door set into the wall adjacent to the main suite entrance. 'But come in through the suite and take a look around. You'll be free to use the lounge and bar. You've got to see the view, it's spectacular.' He swipes his key card over the reader on the door frame and takes our stuff in without waiting for an answer.

The door clicks shut quietly as I wander through the hall with its luxurious gold-toned carpet. Alex deposits our luggage against a wall as I enter the lounge, but I'm barely aware of him.

The suite's gorgeous, more like a posh flat on the Thames than hotel accommodation. The room is done out in calming beige tones, with plush gold-hue carpet. Two white oversized leather sofas form an L-shape, strategically placed in front of panoramic windows overlooking the brightly lit city below us and the wide blue Mediterranean beyond it. At the end of each sofa is a glass vase filled with white roses on a black table and there's a small bar with optics in the closest corner of the room.

The only hotel room I've ever stayed in with its own bar was bright yellow with orange and blue swirly covers on narrow twin beds. The bar consisted of a tiny fridge full of miniature bottles costing a bomb and a wonky wooden shelf above it holding a selection of neon plastic tumblers. I may have been a manager but the money wasn't fantastic and London is so expensive unless you live on the outskirts and commute. Our flat is pretty much in the heart of the city so holiday budgets never stretch to much.

Inhaling the scent of polish and subtle fragrance of the roses, I try to look unimpressed but epically fail by zipping over to the window and pressing warm fingers against the cool glass to take in the view. Amazing. It feels like I could fly. I'm lost in the moment, swept away in the heady sense of freedom and feeling of weightlessness from being so high up. 'It's beautiful,' I murmur at last, turning round to find Alex right behind me, only a foot away, 'absolutely breathtaking.'

He steps forward. 'I couldn't agree more.' But he's not looking over my shoulder out of the glass, he's staring at me, eyes intense.

Breathless and crowded and incredibly excited, I step back but hit the window. There's nowhere to go. A wall of heat builds in the space between us, a magnetic force field pulling us together.

But Alex obviously doesn't feel the same. Shaking his head as if rousing from a dream, he swings away. 'Dining room through here.' His tone is abrupt. Without waiting, he marches into the next room.

Stumbling in my high heels to catch up, my brain is so muddled that when Alex halts in his tracks I slam into him, my boobs crushing up against the warmth and hardness of his back through his suit jacket. 'Sorry.' My face and certain areas below my waist heat instantly.

Going rigid, he throws an accusatory glance over his shoulder as he puts space between us. He looks so stern I want to giggle, but hold back. Stepping away, he stuffs his hands in his pockets, glaring out the window. I frown. It was his fault for stopping like that, so one apology is enough. Leaving him to brood, I run a cursory glance over the long glass table and red velvet chairs, which could comfortably seat a football team, before hurrying back into the lounge. I gasp as I notice the baby grand piano tucked away in the other corner and go over to it. Sweeping my hand over the curved lid, I recall the weekly piano lessons Mum insisted on. She was right to make me take them. Being able to play an instrument is a joy and music has always been there for me, giving me the escape I longed for as a teenager.

Alex marches in, an unreadable expression crossing his face.

I snatch my hand away. 'Sorry, it's probably just for show isn't it?'

'I don't know. I've never really thought about it.'

'Never? But if you've stayed here before … ?'

He smiles wryly. 'I hardly even noticed it's in here. I might have the first time, but that was a long time ago.'

He looks suddenly exhausted, the lines bracketing his luscious mouth, making it more noticeable. An overwhelming need to order him to sit down, fix him a drink and tell him to lay his head in my lap sweeps through me. *Hang on a sec. What?*

As he shakes his head, it drags me from my thoughts. 'Can you play?' He looks genuinely curious.

I nod, latching onto the question gladly. 'I'm reasonable, had lessons when I was younger. Occasionally I teach myself songs. I'm lucky enough to have a good ear. Still, if I'd kept tuition up I'd be much better now.'

'Do you get much of a chance to play?'

'Only when I visit my family and use the one in the village pub.'

'The pub has a piano?'

'Yes. It's a bit of a mishmash really, traditional versus quirky. Chess matches on Mondays and Rock Karaoke on Wednesdays and Saturdays, live music on a Friday, but it works, you know?'

'Not really.' For an instant he looks wistful, but the expression passes. 'But I can imagine.' Nodding at the piano: 'Use it whenever you want.'

'Thanks.' I don't like that I'm touched by his suggestion. 'I uh, think I'll go and unpack.'

'I'll show you to your room.' He strolls over to an unmarked door tucked away in the corner.

Grabbing my case, I follow him. When the door clicks shut behind me the room suddenly feels tiny even though it's huge. Alex in my bedroom. Unsettling. Tempting.

'Here you go.' Oblivious to my feelings, he throws the curtains open to reveal a sensational view of the teeming port. I swing my case onto the queen-sized bed, unzip it and hover. I can't unpack in front of him, it's too personal.

Alex checks his watch. 'I'm going to take a quick shower and change for dinner.' He starts tugging at his tie.

'Right. I guess I'll do the same. How long before I need to be ready?'

The tie comes off and is tucked away inside a pocket. 'Half an hour?' He undoes his top button as he saunters past me to the door.

I catch a glimpse of olive skin over broad collarbone with a hint of chest hair in the open neck of his white shirt. Hormones take over. He's mouth-watering. *Stop undressing.* I beg silently. *No, keep going.* Oh, heck. His lips are moving but I'm deaf to any words. 'Pardon?' I ask.

'I asked whether you'll be ready for dinner on time.'

'Yes, no problem.'

'No problem?' A smile plays around his mouth. 'If you are, you'll be the first woman of my acquaintance capable of it.'

'Maybe I'm not like the other women you're acquainted with then,' I lift my chin, holding direct eye contact. 'I'll be ready,' I glance at the slim silver watch on my wrist, 'by eight fifteen.' Twenty seven minutes. It's not long but I'll do it, just to show him.

'I look forward to it.' His smirk says he fully expects me to fail.

It feels like I'm at the Olympics, on the starting line. I fling open my suitcase, ready for the gun to fire to begin the race.

'I'll see you soon.' His hand is on the door handle, straight-faced but a glint of humour in his eyes.

'Fine.' Picking up my wash bag, I fight back a smile.

'I'll be waiting in the suite.' He pulls the door open.

'Perfect.' My fingers inch towards my black stilettos.

'Actually, I'll knock for you.'

He's determined to not give me an extra second isn't he? 'Suits me,' I say lightly. I put a hand on one hip, striving for casual, turn and manoeuvre myself so the other hand can grope around in the case behind me.

He watches every move. 'I'll leave you to it then.'

'Okay.'

Shaking his head, he slides from the room and I spin round to my case. Just as the door swings shut, his voice echoes through the tiny gap, 'I'll be waiting.'

It makes me laugh and I shake my head.

Right. Focus. Twenty-five minutes left. I lay out minuscule black lace underwear and a favourite evening dress I packed with two others, just in case. Tight, deep-purple, strapless and with small jewel-encrusted pockets, the hem is just above the knee. It's one of those dresses that makes you feel good, boosts your confidence. And the hotel is so posh I have to dress up.

I pelt into the bathroom but am still able to appreciate the modern black and white tiles, the corner bath with jets and the gloriously huge walk-in shower. It's divine. Imagine waking up to this every day. Bliss. Pulling on a shower cap, I push a button and step into the hot blast of water. I'd love to wash my hair – it's gone wild from snow and wind and dry cabin air – but I don't have time. Scrubbing with branded complementary shower gel and realising Alex is probably showering only a handful of feet away, my eyes slide shut. Imagine what he'd look like without his formal suit, stripped bare. Broad chest, long muscular arms and legs plus other interesting parts. He's bound to be a dream naked. The man looks built. I bet he has a six-pack.

I inhale sharply, nipples tightening, an answering throb between my legs. No, stop it. To shake loose the dirty thoughts, I turn the temperature down, gasping as the icy needles chill my skin. It does the trick, reining my hormones in. Turning the shower off, I step from the cubicle, whip off the shower cap and dry briskly with the fluffy bath sheets, finishing up with lashings of moisturiser. Applying light make-up, I unpin and brush out my hair, tying it in a messy topknot and spraying it with gloss-effect hairspray.

Darting into the bedroom, I tug on underwear, ignoring the horrible slide of fabric on cream-dampened skin. Scrambling into the dress, I adjust it to sit right on my waist and hips and hold my boobs in. Threading on dangly jet black earrings and a matching chunky necklace, I spray on perfume before bucketing around the room for a quick tidy. I check my watch as I strap it back on. 8.13 p.m. Last thing is to slide my size-eight elephant feet into black suede-effect stiletto heels.

Although expected, the loud rap at the door still makes me jump.

'It's Alex,' his voice is muffled, 'ready?'

'Yes,' I holler, 'come in.'

Alex enters as I'm reaching across the bed to grab my clutch bag.

'That,' his voice sounds strangled, 'is impressive.'

Standing, I note the new form-fitting black suit and pale-blue shirt that sets off his eyes spectacularly. No tie tonight, top button undone. I prefer the slightly more casual look on him and gulp. 'Thanks. I said I'd be ready in time.' I can't help gloating.

He smiles, acknowledging my victory. 'Yes, you did, though I was talking about– Ah, never mind, you look very smart.'

'Thanks.' *Smart?* I can't remember the last time I've been so deflated by a compliment. It's not as if we're on a date, it's a work dinner and we're just colleagues, but would it have killed him to dream up something better than *you look smart*? It's what Mum said on the first day of school or what Gran might remark about one of my more modest dresses. Huh. 'Shall we go then?' Moving past Alex, I grab the door handle.

'Charley.'

'Yes?' I'm startled to find my nose practically pressed against his shirt front when I spin around. Too close. Way too close. He smells gorgeous and my knees go liquid.

He puts some room between us. 'I was just going to say that ...' he trails off, rubbing the back of his neck.

'Yes?' A long uncomfortable pause follows. 'What is it?'

'Nothing.'

A silence drags out. I'm ultra aware of my bare legs and tiny underwear, the raw urge to bridge the distance to him, push my hands into that thick, dark hair and kiss him. I tighten my grip around the door handle, using it to anchor me to reality. It's difficult. His eyes are so blue staring into them all day would be no hardship at all.

'I mean, I just remembered,' he says in a deep rock-star husky voice, 'that I need to make a quick call.'

I blink. Now, just as we're going to dinner? After how keen he was for me to be ready on time? It must be important. It's after office hours, so perhaps it's his girlfriend he needs to phone. In the car he said he didn't have one, but his definition of girlfriend and mine might be different. I don't like the twitch in my stomach at the thought.

'I'll go downstairs then.' I murmur. 'Meet you in the bar?'

'Yes. I'll be down shortly.'

'Okay.'

'Okay.'

I'm pinned to the door by the intense expression on his face. It's like he wants to say something but can't quite get it out. *What? Please don't tell me about your girlfriend. I don't want to know.*

'I'll bring a copy of the schedule down with me,' he states.

His reminder that this is work is the perfect push to break away.

'Great.' Whirling around, I leave as fast as possible on my high heels. I need time. I need space. And for the sake of my sanity I need to see him as my boss … not a man.

Chapter Seven

'Bugger!' While talking on my mobile to Jess, I hunt for a quiet corner in the hotel bar. The call will cost money I don't have, but this is an emergency. 'Bugger, bugger, bugger!'

'What's wrong?'

'The CEO. Alex. He's gorgeous! Tall, dark-haired, ruggedly handsome and heavenly-bodied. Every time I'm with him I practically swoon, like a girl from those regency novels you devour. Or I basically drool. It's so embarrassing. What am I going to do?'

'Well, if you'd listened to me you wouldn't be in this situation in the first place. I told you, it's not right—'

'What's not right is what Tony bloody Ferrier did to me. Jess, please,' I beg, 'less teacher mode and more best friend. You still love me, right?'

'Yes,' she sighs. 'Of course. Okay, so you're finally going gaga over a man.' She chuckles, lightening up. 'I must admit I was wondering if it'd ever happen.'

'That is *not* helpful.' Spotting a free table, I stride across the room and sit down, ordering a glass of white wine from a passing waiter with a series of elaborate hand gestures. 'And I'd hardly say going gaga. I'm just struggling a little to stay professional, that's all.'

'Sorry, but a little? You just said you nearly swooned.' She laughs.

'I'm glad you think this is funny. Remember that when you're having to pull me out of a giant tub of ice cream and prise the empty wine bottle from my cold fingers because it's all gone wrong.' Then I interject quickly, '*Don't* say it.'

'Fine. And you're there now, so we have to deal with it, I guess. Hmm. He's gorgeous. Well, I agree it would be better if he was fat, old, smelly and bald.'

'If only. And what's really annoying is he's totally not my usual type.' I nod a thanks to the waiter as he places a glass of wine in front of me.

'Why? Because he's not a sensitive soul like the ones you usually go for who look like James Blunt on a bad day? Have you ever wondered if the guys you date aren't really your type, and that's why you never commit to them?'

'Hey, watch it.' I take a large mouthful of the wine. 'You're not so hot on the commitment front yourself, are you?' I wince. 'Sorry,' I rush. She's been in love with my oldest brother Tom for years, since a heated kiss on her fifteenth birthday caused mayhem and havoc in both our families. It almost ended our friendship when he rejected her. We don't talk about it but I've always known he's part of the reason she's never had a serious relationship. Maybe one day it'll work out between them. If anyone deserves a happy ending it's Jess. 'Besides,' I switch subjects, 'you're forgetting Nick. He wasn't my usual type and that didn't work out.'

'Yeah, he was a banker rather than an artist or musician, and a real man's man. But he was also an ass who only wanted a trophy girlfriend. That was never going to be you. You're too intelligent for a start.'

'Doesn't feel like it at the moment. Anyway, stop trying to get on my good side just because you're losing the argument.'

'I'm not! We've been friends for over twenty years, and you can be pretty annoying, I'll give you that—'

'Hey.'

'But you do have *some* good qualities.'

'Gee, thanks.'

Jess sniggers. 'Pleasure. So, what's he like apart from not your usual type but gorgeous?'

Maybe if I just focus on the negatives. 'Arrogant, cynical, defensive and sexist. Oh, and stubborn. Entrenched in his views.'

'Wow, that's quite a list. And er, I hate to point it out Cee, but you're not unfamiliar with the concept of stubbornness yourself.'

I cut across Jess, on a roll. 'He fluctuates from distant one minute to laughing the next. You never know where you are with him. He's also kind of old-fashioned. You know,' another gulp of wine slides down my throat as if by magic, 'complete sentence construction, wanting to carry my bags, not believing in employing female staff.'

'Speaking the Queen's English? Offering to help you? How dare he?' she mocks. 'Complete and utter bastard.'

I smile, knowing I'm caught out. 'All right, perhaps I'm being a bit harsh but you can't quibble the last one.'

'That I get and it's not acceptable.' She pauses, mulling it over. 'How old is he?'

'Early thirties.'

'Miss Caswell.' The deep voice is unmistakable.

Flicking a quick look over my shoulder, I freeze. Of course Alex is standing right behind me. The pit of my stomach drops down to my toes. God knows how long he's been there for. Oh, crap.

'Still, he doesn't sound that bad,' Jess is still chatting away, 'from the way you described how hot he is, I think I could overlook some of the rougher edges. Or possibly train him,' she muses. 'Maybe I should pop across Europe and check him out?'

'Um, I'll get back to you on that. Gotta go.'

'Something wrong?'

'You could say that. Speak later.' Flipping my phone closed, I stand reluctantly. How much has he heard? Everything including my comment about Tony? Talk about incriminating. Talk about blowing my cover. It would be just my luck if he kicks me out of this classy hotel with no belongings and no money and I'm left stranded in Barcelona.

Taking a deep breath, I swivel around. 'Alex. I didn't realise you'd be down so soon.'

'Obviously. So would I have overheard the entire character assassination if I'd arrived earlier?'

Phew, he probably didn't hear me mention Tony. Then mortification singes my face as I realise what he *has* overheard. 'I'm sorry.' Screwing my face up, 'Er, what exactly—?'

'Arrogant and sexist were mentioned. Old-fashioned and cynical also featured.'

'I'm so sorry. Is there any point in saying some people might take some of those as compliments, in particular the old-fashioned part? You know,' I squeak, wishing I could vanish in a puff of black smoke, 'as in traditional values? Moral fortitude?'

'I might have done, because I don't think there's anything wrong in being polite or articulate, or being worried about something other than the latest fashions or music, but they didn't sound like compliments the way you said them.'

'No, I get that,' I confess, squirming now, 'but it was because...'

'Because?'

Because I was convincing myself not to like you. I can't say so or the conversation will leap from humiliating to downright excruciating. 'It doesn't matter. I apologise unreservedly. There's no excuse for it. I don't suppose there's any way we can move past this?'

'It's too late to get another temp,' he confirms, and I hate his voice being so cool and rigid after the rapport we built in the suite, 'so I'll try to forget it, even though every word is indelibly engraved on my brain.'

'I'm so sorry. Again,' I offer quietly, feeling awful. I can't believe I was so indiscreet. My head was just so all over the place I didn't stop to think. Not my usual style at all.

'Yes, well.' He stares over my shoulder, jaw tensing. 'Just forget it.'

There's nothing else I can say and the silence quickly becomes unbearable, so I look around the room. What might be Catalan art hangs on the cream walls and lots of small square mahogany tables with clean lines are dotted around trendy brown leather and purple velvet sofas. The long, wide black bar is backlit by purple and red UV lighting, with metal high-backed stools grouped together, elegant square chandeliers hanging overhead. Full-length windows overlook the marina, the boats bobbing up and down gently on the calm sea.

Alex lets out a heavy sigh. 'Shall we go through for dinner?'

'Please.' As I grab my almost-empty glass and clutch bag from the table, I stumble and Alex's large hand shoots out to grab my elbow. I wrench it away, feeling like I've been branded, the heat of his fingers transmitting a tingling message through my skin straight to my tiny underwear. 'Th–thanks.'

Turning around, I struggle to walk in a straight line, my knees are trembling so hard. Alex wordlessly follows and a young brunette waitress greets us at the entrance of the restaurant. Why do they all have to have such glossy dark hair? Not everyone has celebrity-shiny tresses, some of us mere mortals are challenged with hair that curls and waves and demands complete freedom, no matter what we might do to control it.

'¡Hola! Table for two? Penthouse suite, si, Mr Demetrio?'

Alex nods and we trail after her as she sweeps through the packed room. The clink and tinkle of cutlery and the glow of lit candles mix with muted conversations to create a warm, welcoming atmosphere. Alex's jacket brushes my bare arm as he walks beside me. I ignore the shiver it causes.

'By the way,' he says in a low voice, 'I know I said we'd forget about it, but I do want to clarify one thing.'

'Yes?'

'I employ women.' His sideways look says he's disappointed with my assumptions. 'I'm not stupid. I've seen the benefits of gender balance. Some of my best senior managers are female, which is why six of them sit on the Board.'

'Out of how many directors?'

'Ten.'

'Oh.'

'It's only my executive assistant I insist is male. Not that I have to justify anything to you.'

'Of course not.' He's defensive, but I can hardly blame him after what he overheard.

We come to a beautifully laid table by the window overlooking the grand vista of Port Olimpic. It's pretty, lights from passing boats shining and twinkling off the dark water, the rhythmic lap of waves against the jetties barely discernible.

I gulp as we sit down. It's exactly the kind of set up I've been dreading – intimate and romantic. I flick a wary glance at Alex. His total concentration is on the menu. I frown as I finish off my wine. The last thing I need is to get drunk and sloppy and let my identity slip too soon. No more alcohol tonight. Reaching for a glass of water, my hand twitches and knocks it over, and I watch in horror as it sends a cascade of good old H20 directly towards Alex. But he's quick, pushing back from the table like his chair is on wheels.

I jump from my seat, grabbing a napkin. 'I'm so sorry. I didn't get you, did I?'

He stands, waving a hand to someone behind me for assistance. 'Luckily for me, no.'

My gaze drops to his trousers to check and I move towards him, hand extended reflexively to mop up.

He grabs my wrist before I reach my target, 'I said you missed, Charley.'

'Yes, of course. S–sorry,' I stutter as he releases my arm. Was I really just about to rub his crotch? Dear God. Sloping back to my chair, I wish I could slide under the table and hide, especially when not one, but two members of staff arrive to sort out the mess I've made. My face starts to burn. I've always been clumsy but today I've hit a new record; the water in the plane, almost falling over in the bar, and now attempting to give Alex a shower and rub him down. I should come with an Official Government

Warning: *Spending time with this girl may be bad for your health/ clothes/sanity.*

The staff leave, taking away everything bundled in the fine linen tablecloth. People are staring, but Alex is consulting his phone, so I bury my nose in the menu. The waitress returns, laying out a new tablecloth and placing cutlery, napkins and crystal glasses out precisely. She gives me a small reassuring smile when I peek over the top of the leather-bound booklet. 'Thank you. Sorry.'

'No problem, madam. It has happened before.' She moves away, distracted by the next diner needing attention.

'Now the drama's over,' Alex tucks his phone away, face taut, 'shall we order?'

'I apologised. It was an accident.'

'I know. So have you decided?'

'No. I need a minute.'

'If you must.'

My teeth snap shut. He hasn't forgiven me for my comments. Fingers gripping the menu, I focus on reading. Despite my turmoil I'm impressed by the delicious selection of Mediterranean dishes with international influences. 'It all looks fantastic,' I murmur finally. 'I think I'll have the *carré de cabrito glaseado a la miel con setas.*'

'Rack of honey-glazed meat with mushrooms?' Alex translates fluidly. 'I love a woman who's not afraid to eat properly.' He shakes his head. 'Sorry, I shouldn't have said that.'

'It's fine.' Waving his apology away. I can hardly criticise his behaviour when I'm so confused – and horrified – by my own.

Taking a breath, he neatly changes direction. 'Have you been to Spain before? Your accent isn't bad.'

'Thanks. I took Spanish at school.' I also handled occasional calls from international clients when at the casino, so I'm not as rusty as I might be.

'Not French?'

'Most of my friends took that.'

'And you didn't want to take the obvious choice.'

'Guess not.' I notice again the clarity of his blue eyes and the laughter lines that bracket his mouth.

'It doesn't surprise me.'

'What do you mean?'

'At the risk of backlash, you're quite strong-minded. You don't seem like the kind of person to shy away from going your own way. You were probably about eleven if it was the first year of secondary school,' he pauses and I nod, 'and there would've been peer pressure to take the same language as friends, but you didn't.'

Alex's stare is unnerving. Is there something stuck to my face? Before there's a chance to check, or ask him what his remark means, a waiter appears at my elbow. 'You order first,' Alex nods.

'Thank you.' I reel off my order and focus on picking up my iced water without incident, as Alex orders in Spanish just as well as I did. While drinking, I clock a glamorous blonde at the next table checking Alex out. She's dining alone and has no shame about who the target of her interest is. I get the feeling that if I wasn't sat here she'd be in my chair right now starting a conversation with him. She catches me looking and I glare at her, then wonder why. It's nothing to do with me.

'So.' The waiter retreats. I set my water down, hiding a smile when Alex eyes my glass warily. 'How come you know how to speak Spanish? And where did you go to school?'

'Let's talk about work, shall we?' Alex bites. 'It's why we're here, after all.'

'All right.' I rummage through my bag for pen and paper, annoyed at his tone. He really has got a ten-ton chip on his shoulder. Anything personal about him is clearly off the table. Rearranging my plate and cutlery to make room for my mini-notepad, I lift my head to find Alex frowning. 'Is there a problem with me taking notes?'

'No. As long as you're careful with them. Sensitive information leaking onto the market could be disastrous.'

'I didn't know we'd be discussing trade secrets,' I joke, then fall silent when his face doesn't change. 'Don't worry. I know how to protect data.' I lick my lips. Now for the killer question. 'You do trust me don't you?'

'I don't know you. But perhaps I'm being overcautious. I keep forgetting the agency vetted you.'

'Uh-huh.' I clear my throat uncomfortably. They didn't vet me well enough, otherwise they'd know where I used to work. And the way I left. 'Well, if it helps, I'll write in shorthand. It's a bit of a dying art so not many people can read it nowadays. I learnt it—'

'I don't need your life history,' he says shortly. 'Let's just get on with it. I'll start with the running order of the AGM.'

I clench my fingers around the pen. God, what on earth is eating him?

Chapter Eight

While I work my way through a sumptuous main course and a satisfyingly chocolatey dessert, Alex goes through the schedule for the next few days, picking at his own meal. Unwinding incrementally as he talks, his voice softens, broad shoulders becoming less rigid. I take notes, but mostly listen as he describes key events and gives background on employees we'll be seeing for one-to-one meetings.

'Is this one of your hotels?' I ask when he finally trails off.

'No.' He leans back in his chair. 'I tried that once, but it didn't work. I couldn't focus on the AGM, kept being pulled into issues or noticing things that needed correcting. Here I'm part of a visiting organisation. I can let other people do the worrying.'

'Cool.' Oops, not the most professional language.

But he surprises me by grinning. 'Yes, indeed. Cool.'

Is he laughing at himself, recalling my comment to Jess earlier about complete sentence construction? Why can't he show his sense of humour more consistently? It would make it so much easier to read him, understand how I can earn his trust.

He leans forward, resting crossed arms on the table. 'Aren't you going to finish that?' He points at the half-eaten chocolate cake in front of me.

'I can't,' I answer regretfully, pushing it aside, my taste buds still delighting over the smooth richness of the icing.

'What a waste,' he shakes his head sorrowfully.

'I know, sorry. I'll pay for it if necessary.' It's an empty gesture. I'm broke.

'I wasn't serious.'

Thank God. I bet the meal would cost a fortune. 'Oh.' The light-hearted moment gives me an opportunity to ask what I've been wondering about. 'So?'

'So?' he echoes.

'We've done the business bit. Now will you tell me where you learnt Spanish?'

'No point.' Shrugging, he picks my dessert fork up and toys with it, his large hands on the tiny utensil looking like something out of *Gulliver's Travels*. 'It's boring. And I told you enough about my background earlier.'

Blimey. Talk about guarded. I was hardly asking for his inside-leg measurements. Did he train at spy school or something? The thought is ironic, but then I realise I could totally imagine him as a secret agent, one of the hot guys from *This Means War*.

'Fine, you can keep your secrets,' I smile, 'but you've got to give me something. Nothing too personal, I promise.'

He raises an eyebrow, but plays along. 'You'll just keep badgering until I do, won't you?' He shakes his head when I simply smile. 'Fine. Go on then.' he grumbles.

'Okay,' I tap my finger on my chin. 'You're the CEO of a world-wide organisation, so … what's the funniest thing someone's ever done to impress you? Or the weirdest interview you've ever conducted?'

'You wouldn't believe me.'

'Try me.'

Relaxing back in the chair: 'All right,' he smiles, 'but you asked, just remember that.' Does he curve his lips slowly and sexily on purpose or does it just come naturally?

'I will. I'll remember if I wake tomorrow scarred by your stories that you're responsible for the trauma.'

One corner of his mouth curls up further. 'I can live with that if you can.'

'Oh, I definitely can,' I spark, before sitting back in shock. I'm flirting. Inappropriate and Not a Good Idea. Then another thought. Dread seeps through me. What if I did do the same with Tony? That despite saying I wasn't interested I actually led him on? Hot nausea rolls in my stomach, so I take a deep breath to deal with it, tucking the notion away. The horrible feeling is soon forgotten as Alex shares some of his funniest and strangest experiences, ending with one particularly close to my heart, given my co-dependent relationship with sweet food.

'Then there was the woman who wanted to work in our PR department and sent in handmade baked goods every day for two months.' He takes a swig of water and I'm hypnotised by the movement of his strong throat muscles as he swallows, the dark stubble just under the skin.

'No! Two whole months?'

'Yes. Pies, cakes, fresh bread, cookies. The staff in business support were ecstatic.'

'I bet they were, but how did sending all of those things in relate to her application?'

'She wrapped everything in copies of her CV.'

'You're kidding!'

'I'm not. I think she wanted to prove how successful a targeted PR campaign could be.'

'Well it's an interesting approach.'

'And a tasty one.' He pauses, straightens his face. 'Unfortunately she hadn't read the job details properly.'

'Oh no, what?' Propping my elbows on the table, I lean in.

He shifts closer and shares in a conspiratorial whisper, 'The post was based halfway across the world and she wasn't looking to relocate.'

'No,' I groan, laughing, 'after all that?'

'I know. But if she couldn't even read the ad properly there wasn't much hope was there?'

'Everyone makes mistakes.' My comment somehow changes the tone of our conversation because his eyes fix on the darkness outside the window, face paling.

'That's right. People do,' he rattles out, like unrelenting hail striking glass.

'I didn't mean anything by it. I wasn't talking about you. Are you all right?' My hand creeps across the tablecloth, wanting to comfort.

Swinging his attention inside, he looks down at my fingers, blinks, tucks both hands away under the table and forces a smile. 'I'm fine.' Meaning he isn't. 'Apologies. Right, I've shared my war stories. Your turn now.'

The most recent battle can't be mentioned yet. I need more time before mentioning Tony. 'No war stories. Ask again.'

'Tell me where you grew up then. What was it like?'

This is easy. 'I was born in a pretty little village, Holmes Brook, which I always think sounds like a nursing home. It's on the Dorset-Hampshire border. It has the one pub, a village hall and a few shops. It's surrounded by fields and has a river looping around it. In theory I had a good amount of freedom.' Describing it takes me back to sunny summer days filled with the smell of hay and a wide expanse of blue sky, the taste of sweet crunchy apples and evenings that took forever to dim.

'Sounds idyllic,' he murmurs, echoing my thoughts. 'So why freedom in theory?'

'I've got three older brothers and one of them was always following me around keeping watch.' I smile fondly. 'It drove me nuts. I know they were just looking out for me, though.'

'I can understand that. What else?'

'Our family home is massive and on the outskirts of the village, with a duck pond next to it. My favourite part is the apple tree at the bottom of the garden. I used to love climbing it and throwing apples at my brothers' heads.' I laugh, then halt. *Too much information, Charley, his eyes will start glazing over soon, wrap it up.*

But he sighs and shares, 'Sounds great to me. We had olive trees, but we weren't allowed to climb them.'

'We?'

'I have a younger brother.'

'Oh. Well I'm sorry if I've given you tree envy,' I joke.

'So you should be,' he smiles.

There's a silence and I realise we're staring into each other's eyes. 'So er, anyway,' I bluster, 'I ah, met my best friend Jess when I started primary school and we ended up buying a flat together in the city.'

'And what do your parents do?'

For someone so fiercely private he's very interested in my life, but the more open I am, maybe the more he might trust me. 'Dad was something in Defence for years, used to commute, got retired young, so chairs lots of committees on a voluntary basis. Mum devoted herself to us but took on charity work as we got older, running the WI, organising local events. I guess part of it is there's family money and those are some of the expectations.'

'Are your family well known in the village?'

'You could say that!' Laughing, I attempt to push the bitterness away. 'They've always been the centre of everything. The spotlight was always on them. And on us.' I didn't mean to mention it, but he's a good listener.

'That was a problem?'

'It taught me to be cautious,' I admit, picking up my napkin and smoothing it out, 'what people think of you matters in a small village. They don't let you forget your mistakes in a hurry, that's for sure.' Absently, I fold the napkin at the corner, then back in on itself. 'So you don't take many risks.'

'What does that mean?'

'Are you sure you want to hear this?' I look up at him, fingers still working the napkin, folding and refolding.

'Yes. Indulge me.'

'Okay. Well, I tried to make Mum and Dad proud, but disappointed them when I moved to London. It was the only real risk I've ever taken, but I had to do it. As beautiful as the countryside is, staying in a rural community wasn't for me. I wasn't happy,' I sigh, realising I've folded my napkin into a swan shape. Setting it aside, I laugh self-consciously. 'I worked as a silver-service waitress in the next town over when I was seventeen. Anyway, me wanting to move away caused ructions and my parents spent months trying to talk me out of it. They'd rather I lived locally and got engaged to a nice village boy.'

'So how did you manage to leave?' Alex shrugs out of his suit jacket, hanging it on the back of his chair.

I won't let my eyes wander down to check out his broad shoulders in the crisp blue shirt. Staring at his face, I admit, 'In hindsight I could have been more mature, persuaded them it was my risk to take.'

'And in reality?' There's a twinkle in his eye. He knows what's coming.

'I was eighteen. Let's just say there was some bad behaviour.' I roll my eyes, recalling my teenage flouncing and yelling. 'They finally backed off when I declared I wasn't going to live my life according to what other people wanted and was moving to the city whether they were happy about it or not, even if I had to live on the streets. I started packing a rucksack to make my point. Mature, hey?'

'You were young,' he excuses.

'Yes, well ... they didn't exactly give me their blessing, but we stopped arguing at least,' I smile wryly.

Too personal to share is that it's still there between us. Going home is always tense. My parents love me but still don't agree with my decision. The distance hurts but I'm not sure how to bridge it. It's the reason they don't know how broke I am or how close to failing. The plan is to tell them only if I absolutely have to. I don't want them to think they were justified in the opinion that staying home would have been best for me. Whatever has happened, I'll never regret making my own way in the world.

'I know what you mean,' Alex confides, a shadow crossing his face.

'You ran away from home too?' I try and lighten things, scrub the glint of unhappiness from his eyes.

'No. Not quite.' He goes still. 'I never talk about it.'

But he needs to. 'Well, I've trusted you with my teenage angst. Why not tell me about yours?'

'It's nothing controversial. Neither is it something exclusive to my teens. And it's hardly angst. It was just what you said about the spotlight being on you.' He picks the napkin swan up, turning it over between his long fingers. 'I understand. Being part of a family-run organisation as successful and wealthy as ours doesn't exactly give much opportunity for privacy. It's always bothered me. That's why I do the press conferences for the business when I have to, but don't give interviews about anything else.'

I've got something in common with a billionaire. Who'd have thought it. Gazing into his gorgeous eyes, a shared moment of understanding flows between us and I gulp. I can't do this.

'That was pathetic,' I tease to break the connection. 'Tell me one of your actual secrets.'

'It wouldn't be secret if I told you. And besides,' he says po-faced, 'you'd have to sign a gagging order if I did.'

I'm not entirely sure he's kidding.

'You went to a state secondary school, right?' Alex moves the subject on swiftly before I can comment on his surreal remark. 'Why didn't you go private?'

'Mum said it would be good for us, give a better grounding in reality. I wouldn't have wanted to go to a boarding school anyway.'

'And why London rather than anywhere else?'

'I left school with respectable grades, and took a Business Studies NVQ and a few A levels at the college in the nearest town. In the first year, I went on a theatre trip and fell in love with the city. After that it was just a question of time.

'It's great, so full of hustle and noise and people and shops and different places and experiences. It's such a change after my child-hood, was exactly what I wanted, no ... needed. I wouldn't want to raise children there but I'm a long way off that yet, so it's not an issue.' Woah, where did *that* come from? Why would he care about my plans to start a family one day? He doesn't comment, but his expression goes shuttered and distant. TMI?

'Did you go to uni?' he simply asks. 'Or have a gap year?'

'No, straight to London. I did plan to go to Africa as a volunteer, help build schools and see a bit of the world.'

'But?'

'But I missed the application window.'

'Why's that?'

I glance away and mutter something.

'Sorry, what was that?' he asks.

I sigh. 'I got glandular fever.'

Alex throws his head back and laughs, 'The kissing disease?'

'Yes, okay, I've heard that one before.'

'Sorry. So was it? Down to kissing?'

It's like he's completely forgotten himself. That this is just work. Worryingly, I like it.

'No comment,' I reply cheerfully.

'Fair enough.' He drops the swan and traces a finger on the tablecloth. I wish for a flashing moment it's my skin. 'Did you know we send our managers out to Africa for charity projects?'

'Yes, I—' *almost applied*. I manage to stop in time. Too close. 'I saw it on the internet.'

He frowns. 'You said earlier you hadn't managed to research the company.'

Damn, caught out. 'That's right,' I think fast, 'but I'm talking about when I was looking into it at college, surfing the net. I remember seeing something about Demetrio doing it as part of a corporate programme.'

'Really? I can't remember when we started it.'

'Well I'm twenty-seven, so this was about nine years ago. '

'That makes sense. I went out there for the pilot scheme around that time, whilst my father was still in charge.' Suspicion slides from his face and I let out a breath.

How funny. Would we have met under different circumstances if I hadn't become ill? Mind you, Africa is a huge country and what would be the chances of us volunteering in the same village? I don't know why I'm even thinking it. We occupy different worlds. And there's the giant issue of the reason I'm here, along with his glaring mistrust of women.

He isn't for me.

Alex clears his throat. 'Charley?'

'Yes, Alex?'

'You went somewhere else.'

'Sorry.' Time for bed. Standing, I grab my bag from under the table and shove my pad and pen inside it. 'It's late. We should call it a night. Everyone else has.'

Alex blinks and unfolds himself from the chair, glancing around the restaurant. 'I hadn't noticed.' Looking puzzled, he pushes his shirtsleeve back to check his watch. 'It's almost eleven!'

'Still an hour away from turning into a pumpkin, though?' I tease.

'Something like that.' He shrugs back into his suit jacket, rubs a hand over his emerging stubble. The rasping sound makes my pulse kick and my hands tighten around my handbag.

We meander back to reception and the silence is companionable enough as we wait for the lift, but there's a tension about him; in the line between his eyebrows, the way his hands are shoved in his pockets. I wonder what he's thinking.

Once in the plush interior of the lift, I lean against the wall. 'Thanks Alex, it's been a nice evening. I know I upset you earlier, but I'm looking forward to working with you this weekend.'

Shifting away, 'Yes,' he says in a clipped voice, staring at the lift doors, 'I think we covered all we needed to.'

Huh. What did I say? I don't understand the super-formal censorious tone after we've got on so well. I wish he'd stop running hot and cold. It's unnerving. He's like two different people: one the stern CEO and one the normal, down-to-earth guy. Trouble is, I never know which he's going to be.

I dart out into the corridor as we arrive at our floor, pawing through my bag for the key card. 'What time do you want me?' I ask over my shoulder.

'*Pardon?*'

My cheeks burn. Did he think I was making him an offer? 'In the morning, what time do you want to make a start?'

'Seven please. Let's meet at main reception.'

'No problem.' Running the card over the reader, I shove the door open. Stepping into my bedroom, I turn and look at him as I clutch the door handle. 'Night.'

'Yes, goodnight.' His reply is muted by the door as I swing it shut, but his magnetic blue gaze is the last thing I see.

Chucking my stuff onto the dresser beside the wide bed, I start stripping off with a suspicion it's going to be a long night.

Chapter Nine

I'm not wrong. After texting Jess to explain why I cut short our call earlier and say I'm off to bed, she responds with a simple message.

Oh dear! Okay Cee, talk in the morning x

Trying to settle, I flick through the channels before turning off the TV, pick up a fashion magazine but hurl it on the floor within minutes, grab my e-reader and shut it down after a few pages. Deciding to attempt sleep because I need to be at least semi-human tomorrow, I'm frustrated by twisting restlessly into the early hours, sheets wrapping themselves around my sweaty body. I switch on the air-con, but get too cold, so I switch it back off. Nothing feels right. At one point I'm so irritated I shout a string of swear words into the dark.

It's no good. My physical state's not the problem. Working with Alex is bringing up all sorts of conflicting feelings. I find him so compelling but who's the only one left who can help me, meaning he's off limits.

Like oil bubbling from an underground well, the memory of my last horrible night at the casino, the reason for my current situation, rises to the surface.

Slotting confidential papers into the cabinet, I tilt my head from side to side to get rid of the kinks in my neck. Time for home and a hot bath. Tony should be filing this stuff away, but I don't trust him. The thought's no sooner there than he swaggers into the room, shutting the door behind him decisively.

'Not gone yet? You're free to call it a day, Tony.' *Go away.*

He doesn't answer, but is suddenly right behind me, trapping me against the drawer. Not particularly tall, he is nonetheless stocky, built like a real British rugby player, and it makes me feel crowded. Feeling the heat of his body against my back, a needle of fear pierces me. We're alone in here with the door shut. I rapidly calculate how many members of staff are out on the casino floor. Not many, it's a Tuesday, one of our quieter nights. It's unlikely anyone would come up here at gone eight.

'You're working late,' he says in my ear. 'Why can't I?'

'I'm expected to cover some of the late shifts. You aren't,' I answer stiffly. 'I'll see you in the morning.' Orders aren't my usual management style, but my patience is razor-thin. When he doesn't move I grind my teeth. 'Is there something in particular you want?' Slamming the drawer shut with a metallic bang, I turn to elbow past him.

Before I know what's happening, he grabs my ponytail and throws me roughly against the cabinet. 'Hey!' I squawk. He's too close for me to plant a knee between his legs.

'You know there's something I want,' he breathes, making horror jump in my chest, 'but you're so stubborn! Little Miss Boss in her tight suits and high heels, taunting me with her sexy body every day.'

A hot hand runs over my left hip and squeezes hard. I wince and try to back away as the hand continues a path upwards. In that moment, outraged and scared after weeks of uncertainty, I come alive. This can't be happening. No way. I won't let it. Scorching anger rockets. Bringing both arms up in the few inches between our bodies I thrust them apart and break free. 'Get *off* me! Now!'

Grappling with me, Tony steps back, accidentally tearing my silk t-shirt in the process. There's a loud rip, but I don't care. Luckily he gives me just enough room for escape. As I turn to run out, I catch sight of the industrial-sized stapler on top of one of the cabinets. So when his fingers brush the bottom of my ponytail, I pivot around and feign a swing at the side of his head. Wrenching himself out of the way, he stumbles backwards.

'What the hell are you doing?' he roars. 'Are you crazy? That would have been assault.'

'So is what you just did to me!' I shout back, equally angry, but with a tremor beneath my volume. Watching him, keeping hold of my makeshift weapon, I back out into my office, deliberately opening the door to the main staircase so I can call for someone if I have to. Stuffing my things into my bag, I pick up the phone as Tony strolls in, calmly smoothing his tousled hair.

'Hi. Can you call a taxi for Tony please?' I ask the duty security guard. 'He's ready to go home. Thank you.' Replacing the handset with a click, I look at my assistant coolly, trying to hide how shaken I am.

'It was just a bit of fun,' he says sulkily. 'Talk about overreacting.'

I put a hand up. 'You're having a laugh! That was no one's idea of fun and I've told you repeatedly I'm not interested. There's something seriously wrong with you. Now get out.'

He takes a step towards me but stops as I brandish the stapler. 'This will seem mild in comparison to what I'll do if you take another step, Tony. And I'm more than happy to call the police.' It's all bravado, because underneath I'm shaking to the core, wondering if he'll flip and I'm going to be an unsolved murder on *Crimewatch*.

His eyes narrow and he looks like he's seeing me for the first time. He slouches his shoulders, puts on a kicked puppy dog expression. 'There's no need for that,' he says meekly. 'I'll go now.' A pause 'I–I'm sorry. It was crossed signals, that's all—'

'That,' I gesture to the filing room and then my ripped top to emphasise my point, 'was nothing to do with any confusion on your behalf. You knew exactly what you were doing.'

'B–but,' he gawps at my tone, 'I—'

'We'll deal with this tomorrow.' When I've had a chance to calm down, have called HR and arranged to have him suspended, sought their advice on whether to involve the police or not. 'Now go home,' I insist. My hand hovers over the radio at my hip and the panic button I can press to summon security. Why the hell I didn't think of using it in the file run I don't know. Shock probably.

He flushes. 'Fine. I'm gone.'

A slammed door and rapid footsteps follow. I wait a minute before calling the security office again. 'Did Tony get his taxi okay?'

'Yes, he just left.'

'Thank you.'

Sinking my head into my hands, I sit there for a long time, waiting for the shaking to stop. After a while I drag myself out of the the chair and walk with heavy feet down to the front desk. 'I'm not feeling well,' I tell Lynda. 'Can you track Evelyn down and ask her to cover for me please? She's on silver duty tonight.'

She looks up with a quick smile. 'Sure. She's around somewhere. Hope you feel better soon.'

'Thank you. Night.' Stepping onto the street, soggy after a summer shower, I stumble numbly to the tube station, feeling like I'm caught in a nightmare I can't wake from.

The next morning, having shared my horrid experience with Jess over a few glasses of wine and having had a good night's sleep, I feel steadier. Steeling myself for the day, I put my most modest suit on. I could feel bad about what I'm about to do but I've given Tony enough chances to understand what's acceptable and he went too far. The blue smudge of a handprint on my hip and yesterday's ruined top agree. The only regret I have is not calling the police last night. Too late to worry about it now, though, and I can decide what to do after speaking to HR.

I sweep into work at half eight. Tony's not due in until eleven because of a dental appointment, so I've a few hours to make the necessary calls and see if an HR rep can attend to help me suspend him.

Roberta, the new receptionist, in to catch up with some paperwork – probably trying to show willing – hails me with a wave. 'Morning. You need to go straight to the conference room,' she tugs her hair behind her ears, 'you've got visitors.'

'Really?' I frown, 'There's nothing in my diary for this morning.'

'They arrived twenty minutes ago and said when you came in you were to see them. I think one of them was from HR.'

Huh. Weird. Perhaps someone overheard or saw something last night so they're here in anticipation of my complaint. 'Fine. I'll see them now. Can you pick up calls please?'

'No problem.'

Skirting around the black marble desk, I push open the gold-plated *Staff Only* door and run up the stairs, swinging around the door of the conference room with a polite smile on my face. 'Good morning, how can I help...?' Trailing off, I take in my regional manager sitting at the head of the meeting table with a grim look on his face. A woman I don't recognise is sitting beside him in a formal grey suit, jotting something in a notebook, a copy of the disciplinary procedure in front of her. 'Nigel, what are you doing here?' I frown.

'Sit down, Charley,' he orders.

Sinking into the nearest chair, I fold my hands on the table. 'Did you hear about what happened last night?' I ask, perplexed.

'Unfortunately, yes,' he replies. I open my mouth to tell him the situation, but he carries on talking. 'That's why I'm here. It gives me no pleasure to do this ... but I have to suspend you. We've had serious sexual harassment and bullying complaints lodged against you and you need to be off work while we investigate the allegations.'

'*What?*' The absolute bastard. My seat sticks against the carpet as I spring out of it and my feet get tangled in the legs. Steadying myself on the table, I stare at my boss. 'What are you talking about?'

'Luckily the complainant won't be involving the police, which is helpful. Otherwise we'd have to use the prosecutions policy as well, which as you know would make things more protracted.'

'Again, *what*?' The room goes blurry around the edges.

Nigel grinds his teeth and utters a sentence that clearly makes him uncomfortable. 'Your assistant has alleged you've been putting pressure on him to enter into a...' distaste colours his voice, 'personal relationship and last night you tried to force physical contact on him—'

'But it was him! He—'

'It's best you don't say any more,' the woman sitting with Nigel intervenes, expression bland. 'Have a careful think about the allegations and wait for the investigatory interview to give your account. Sorry,' she shakes her head, 'I should have introduced myself. I'm Sally, one of the HR Managers. I'm here to explain the process. My role is—'

'I know exactly what the process is,' I say, speaking carefully. 'I'm a manager. Just take my stuff and go, right?' I long to get down on the floor and have a tantrum at the utter unfairness of all this but need to stay calm. Being anything other than professional will go against me. 'Just send me the paperwork in the post. I'll see you in the investigation meeting.' I nod tightly. Stalking out, I take the stairs at a near-run, intending to leave immediately, face burning and chest itchy with humiliation. How can this be happening? How did he get to them so quickly?

On the verge of bursting into reception, I realise I left my personal diary and other bits in my office last night. Turning around, I slam into Big Baz's chest. Reminding me of a very big, very dog-eared version of Danny Blue from *Hustle*, he's the longest-serving, sweetest security guard. He's not usually here at this time of day, unless we're cashing up. Which we're not. I wince. He's here for me. Another wave of humiliation hits.

'Sorry Charley. Can't let you back up.' His eyes are sympathetic and it's some consolation he looks genuinely pained.

'There are things I need.'

'Make a list, luv, and call with it later. I'll arrange for one of the boys to drop it round to ya.'

'But—' He crosses his arms and shakes his head. 'Okay,' I surrender. This is bad enough without attracting extra attention.

Following me into reception, he has the grace not to lay a hand on me, but it's still a thousand times more awful because a few people I manage are drifting in, faces bewildered as they watch me heading out with Baz in my tracks.

The heat of mortification deepens, but I force a reassuring smile, 'Just a bit of a mix-up. I'll be back soon. Everyone keep on working hard.' I feel like a criminal. Usually Baz's services are for throwing out drunks or poor losers who've been parted from their cash because they don't know when to stop gambling. But I'm neither of those. Still, as I step out the front doors, tears of frustration and anxiety scorching my eyes, I wonder if the second label is apt. Have I lost? Tony has already cost me so much. Respect, confidence in my abilities, and now, perhaps, my job. Am I like a gambling addict who doesn't know when to quit?

More than anyone, I should know that in the end, the house always wins.

Now

There's so much worse to come, my mind skitters away from it. Checking my mobile, I'm shocked to find it's two in the morning. Throwing myself face down on the bed, I hold a pillow over my head and scream '*argh*' into the mattress, long and loud. That finally seems to do the trick and I fall into oblivion.

Chapter Ten

DAY TWO

– Saturday –

By half five I've already woken three times and I decide to give up on sleep. Needing time to shake off a foul mood and bleary daze of exhaustion, I grab a black coffee from the machine in the corner of my room.

Pulling back the navy double-lined curtains, I gaze out of the window at the awakening city. Mopeds are zooming along the narrow roads in the dusk, and in the growing light I can make out the skyscrapers looming over other smaller but more architecturally compelling buildings. I know from the tourism magazine on the dresser that along the coast people from the mainly Catalan population are already making their way to the numerous textile factories, to the production lines that form the foundation for hopes that Barcelona will one day be a major fashion capital.

Padding to the other window, I squint down at the marina. The sea looks so peaceful with the first few rays of sunlight glimmering over it, so inviting, that with eyes gritty through lack of sleep I long for a refreshing swim. Setting the cup down, I flick through the hotel brochure. Fantastic – the heated indoor pool opens at six, no doubt for guests wanting an early-morning workout. I have more than enough time for a few laps before meeting Alex for breakfast. While I search for the swimwear I stuffed in my case at the last minute, I realise it's only been twelve hours since I left London in the bitter cold. Feels more like twelve years.

I pull out the black bikini from my trip to Turkey with Jess a couple of years ago. It was such a great holiday – sunbathing, sightseeing, water sports, laughter, drinks by the bar. I was too busy to take a break in the six months of last year when I had a job, and I now regret it. All the experiences missed in favour of long hours and dedication ... and look where I am now. No proper job, no money, no prospects. Shaking the maudlin thought off, I wash quickly and brush my teeth, tying my hair in a low ponytail. Yanking the bikini on, I turn to the mirror, frowning at how little it covers. There's an obscene amount of rounded cleavage on display aided by the push-up top and the bottoms are cut ultra high on the hip. It's one thing wearing it on a beach and another at the facilities of a posh hotel, but unfortunately I'm stuck with it. It's not like I've got the money to buy an alternative from the discreet boutique tucked away in hotel reception.

Pulling on the white, luxury towelling robe from the back of the bathroom door, I push my feet into matching slippers and leave the room, key card safely in my pocket, yawning widely as I follow signs to the gym, spa and pool. Alex and I are in the penthouse suite on one side of the top floor, but the other side of it houses the leisure facilities in an atrium. Traipsing along a short corridor and through a series of white doors, I wave my key card over the inbuilt sensors and gasp at the white-marbled women's changing rooms.

After a moment I wander out to the pool. The room is gorgeous; the domed glass ceiling overhead letting in the early-morning sun; lush palms and vivid purple flowering plants surrounding me and filling the air with a heady floral fragrance. It looks like I'm the first one here to enjoy it this morning. Kicking off my slippers and shrugging out of my robe, the heated air feels glorious on my skin. After a quick rinse under one of the poolside showers, I dive into the pool, looping through the blue in a U-shape before rising to the surface. It's sheer bliss. The water is soft and warm and I feel brighter and happier already, the sharp tang of chlorine in my nose, my ponytail sticking wetly to my back.

Swimming to the edge, I curl my legs against the side, grab the rim of the pool and push away hard, doing laps on my back before flipping over into an efficient front crawl. Fifteen minutes later I start tiring, so finish off with a few leisurely laps before climbing out and reclining on the nearest lounger. The padded navy cushion is cosy and the rising sun warm through the glass above me. I'll just dry off for a few minutes before going back to my room.

I jerk upright with a gasp when there's a splash and drops of water splatter me. Looking around for the culprit, I see a dark shape moving effortlessly through the pool, but I can't make out whether it's a man or a woman. Well, as long as they don't splash me again we'll both be happy. Lying back down, my eyes drift shut. I'm aware of the moisture on my skin evaporating in the humid air. One more minute, just one and I'll get going...

'Charley. Charley!'

The voice intrudes and I fight to open my eyes, focusing slowly on the delicious face from my x-rated dream. Lifting a hand, I run my fingers over his cheekbone, trace a thumb over the rough stubble on his jaw and slide my palm slowly round the back of his neck. I smile drowsily, pulling him down toward me, lips parting. 'Alex,' I croak.

'Bloody hell!' Wrenching his head away, he grabs my hand and yanks me into a sitting position, hauling me out of my fuzzy dreamscape. 'Charley, it's time to wake up.'

Blinking the world into focus, I foggily realise what I've just done – touched Alex in a way that's definitely not within working boundaries. Bright anger battles with dawning humiliation. Shit and double shit.

'All right, I'm awake!' I shake myself free, trying to ignore the flash of broad tanned chest with a sprinkling of hair, and the abs so defined they're countable.

His comment resounds in my head. He's right. It's time to wake up, to the real world, where women who come onto colleagues uninvited ruin their professional reputations. Especially if they might have track records of that type of behaviour *and* the recipient is firmly against workplace relationships. Not that he knows about my track record yet but, when he finds out, me having grabbed him is hardly going to prove my innocence.

Irritation at myself and him ignites and sparks. Why was he so close to me when I was sleeping? And did he really have to yank me up like that?

'Charley?' he asks roughly.

Twisting on the lounger, unable to meet his eyes, I scramble over to my robe, hauling my arms through the sleeves and tying the belt with quick jerky movements. 'I'm awake,' I reiterate, 'don't worry.' I bite the words out without turning, panic squeezing my windpipe. 'See you in reception in a while.'

Bolting from the pool, I push through umpteen doors and jog down the corridor, not stopping until back in my bedroom. The next half an hour is hell. Shampooing my hair in a blistering shower, I scrub my body with exfoliator, trying to erase the embarrassing encounter with Alex along with the chlorine from my skin. All the while the mantra running through my head is *don't think, don't think, do not dare to think.*

Sprinting into the bedroom whilst drying with a fluffy towel, I brush my hair and pull it into a loose bun, yank on black underwear and perch on the bed to pull on dark-patterned tights. Then I climb into a grey sleeveless tailored dress with a short tulip skirt, grab the matching jacket and slip on a pair of black patent stiletto heels. Hanging the towel in the bathroom, I catch sight of my pale cheeks, bloodless lips and puffy eyes. Not a good look. I hurriedly apply the basics – pressed powder, eyeliner, clear lip gloss – and comb my fringe down with shaking hands. How will I face Alex?

I was going to kiss him.

And he knew it.

Oh, God.

I'll just have to make the best of it. Apologise then maintain the biggest physical distance from him.

Arriving in reception, the polite professional smile I've pasted on falters when Alex steps forward from the front desk clad in a sharp black suit and narrow black tie, looking like he's about to attend a funeral. Dark but devastating. Great. I address a spot above his left shoulder. 'Shall we go in for breakfast?'

He drags his gaze over my outfit and frowns, carefully fixing his attention somewhere around my right earlobe. 'Something's come up,' he says curtly. 'I've got to sort out a problem with a new acquisition. Go ahead and eat without me.'

'B–but,' my throat goes achy and weird, 'if it's a business issue I should help you with it. Don't you need me?'

He pauses, eyes raking over my face, expression guarded. 'No,' he replies tightly. 'I don't. I'll see you later. Don't look for me, I'll find you.'

I don't get a chance to say anything before he stalks off. Obviously he's annoyed because of what happened by the pool, but that was just rude. And what can I do when he's not given me the chance to say sorry? And what will I do if the almost-kiss has blasted away any professional respect he has for me, undermining my credibility? My plan will be totally shot.

The anxious thoughts whirl around in my jumbled head twenty minutes later as I push aside food I've only toyed with. Finishing my fresh orange juice, I stare down at the tablecloth, something inside hurting. I've got the horrid feeling it's not just Alex's opinion of me as an employee that matters. It's his view of me as a woman too.

Despite everything, I want him to like me. We had such a good time at dinner last night. He was so funny once he relaxed, and I opened up to him more than I'd planned to. I enjoyed his company.

And he is respectful of women after all, and—

No. Oh no. Don't do it, Charley.

I'm being sloppy and sentimental. It's the exhaustion of lost sleep talking, the stress of the last few months. Alex doesn't – *can't* – matter to me in that way.

I text Jess, not expecting an answer because of the time difference.

Morning sleepyhead, need to talk later. Made a complete fool of myself with Alex this morning. Could do with some advice. C x

As I order another juice and decide whether to wait for Alex as requested or go look for him, my phone vibrates.

Morning, no probs, but now I'm intrigued! Shall have to wait until 2nite to find out what the big mystery is. Until then, advice = whatever it is, keep your cool! J X

Easy for her to say – she isn't stuck with The Most Gorgeous Man Ever for the entire weekend. Tucking my phone away, I jump as Alex appears beside me, one hand in the pocket of his exquisitely cut trousers, his buttoned-up suit jacket showing off his broad shoulders and flat stomach. Pure lust erupts inside me, along with a vision of the mouth-watering body I caught a glimpse of by the pool. Then Jess's advice ping-pongs around my head. *Keep your cool.* It might not be easy to follow, but it is sensible. Winter ice cool, that's what I'll go for.

'Hello,' I clip politely. 'Ready?' I grab my bag and stand up.

'Yes, thank you.' His voice is equally bland. 'Ready to go and run over the PowerPoint presentation?'

'Yes, thank you. Lead the way.'

After striding across the lobby, we climb a small flight of carpeted stairs leading to a short corridor filled with gold-handled doors. He holds one open for me wordlessly.

'Thanks.' I slip into a large conference room, more like a hall. Stepping over to a box-filled table, I tuck my bag away as Alex stalks to the front of the room. 'I'll just get set up,' I call over. 'Give me five minutes.'

'No problem,' he responds distractedly, fiddling with his laptop.

A few minutes later I'm satisfied the name badges, delegate list, notepads and pen pots are laid out properly and walk along the blue-carpeted aisle created by the two sections of chairs set out in lines. Stepping onto the slightly raised stage, Alex is standing at the podium, adjusting the microphone with a deep line cutting between his dark eyebrows.

He gestures to the wireless laptop set on a glass table over to the side and I nod, hustling over to it. Sitting down, I tap a finger on the Enter key and a sign-in screen appears.

'Password?' I prompt.

'Sorry, I didn't expect it to have gone into sleep mode already.' I jerk as the words flow directly into my ear, his warm breath sweeping over my cheekbone. A shiver runs up my back. I can't sigh out loud, so I hold my breath instead. 'Here.' Reaching across me, he types his password in whilst I try not to flinch, holding my position as I will myself not to stare at his long lashes and the faint stubble along his jaw. He's close enough I can smell his trendy male scent. It's gorgeous; clean, masculine and sexy. Just like him. As I start to unwittingly lean closer, he straightens.

'Okay?' he asks.

'Yes.' I breathe out.

'Well?'

'Yes?' I swing my head to look at him.

'It's ready for you to use.'

I must look blank because he gestures to the laptop, mouth curving in a slight smile. 'Care to rejoin me on planet Earth so we can get started?' He pauses. 'I interrupted your nap earlier, perhaps you're still tired?'

The mild sarcasm makes me flush. 'That was an accident. I

didn't mean to fall asleep. I just didn't sleep properly last night.'

'Hmm,' slipping me a sideways glance, 'I know the feeling.'

Not sure what he means, I ignore his comment. 'Look Alex, I owe you an apology. I shouldn't have—'

'Now's not the time. Let's get on with this.' Not waiting for an answer to his comment, he strolls back to the microphone.

I bite my lip. 'Fine. But we'll talk later,' I mutter crossly under my breath. 'That's a promise.'

The next few hours are ridiculously busy. It's exhilarating, even if not the work I'm used to any more. After syncing the laptop to the massive SMART board above the stage, we run through Alex's presentation three times before he's happy with it. He has a clicker to control the slides, but insists I know the timings in case of technical faults, in which case I'll use the laptop to change the slides.

I greet the few dozen employees and some of the shareholders as they flood in, Alex explaining to me in a low voice that anyone not present can vote by proxy or electronically. Giving out badges, ticking off lists and making small talk, I enjoy the buzz in the air. There are probably about two hundred attendees and they all look pleased to be here.

Whilst coffee is served ahead of the meeting, it strikes me as bitterly ironic to be representing the global umbrella organisation of the company in the capacity of a temporary PA when my ultimate ambition was to fast-track into a promoted position elsewhere in the group. If it weren't for Tony, one day I might have been attending an AGM as a senior manager. It's not fair.

Face burning with troubled thoughts, I'm glad when Alex nods at me across the room to get started. I close the doors and dim the lights, hotfooting it onto the stage to join him at the glass table, adjusting the laptop so it's right in front of me. As Alex rises from his seat, I notice a faint sheen of sweat across his forehead. If it was anyone else I'd wonder if it was nerves, but he's so self-assured I scrub the idea. Maybe he's not feeling well.

'Ready?' He buttons his jacket and licks his lips. I nod, puzzled. Is he okay? Without another word, he walks over to centre stage.

'Good morning everyone,' he says, adjusting the microphone slightly. 'Are we ready to begin?' Conversation dies down and people turn their heads to give their full attention. 'Good,' he replies, 'then I'll start. I'm Alex Demetrio, CEO of Demetrio International.' I can see his hands where they're resting on the podium. His fingers are clenched and white, but no trace of doubt shadows his clear, firm voice. 'Welcome to our AGM.'

The presentation should be boring because I've heard it so many times, but it is fascinating because Alex warms after the first few minutes, confidently running through annual reports for the previous year and year to date, explaining the financial forecasts for the forthcoming two. He looks more comfortable and I'm pleasantly surprised when he is wryly humorous about the privileges and pitfalls of running the company. It's honest and brave and interesting.

'I also want to thank the senior team and all support staff for their hard work and dedication, which make all the difference to the success of the organisation. The Board of Directors and I truly appreciate the passion and energy of our employees.' Alex gazes across the audience, taking the time to meet people's eyes, smiling so widely his cheeks must hurt.

His voice drops slightly and several people lean forward to hear better. 'I've gone through the finances, the strategies and the ambitions, how we're going to expand, but I want to talk about something else I feel we should focus on over the next three to five years. Something important. Something worth doing. I hope you'll agree with me and understand why.' His face becomes serious and I'm mesmerised, like everyone else. 'What I want to say is this. Every one of us has a responsibility to the companies we run, to each other and to other colleagues, to local economies and markets. But we also have a responsibility to the wider world. That's why we'll continue to fund hundreds of charities with a diverse range of good causes, as well as maintain a drive for carbon-neutral working and energy efficiency across the whole organisation. It's also why there's an Economic Social Responsibility programme for managers, which includes spending a month abroad in Africa helping to rebuild villages. I'd like to show you a short film of that now before I continue.'

I can't help but be inspired by his passion, especially when he plays footage of the organisation's best and brightest management trainees covered in sweat, caked in mud and heaving cement and bricks in the scorching sun. They interact with smiling villagers, children getting underfoot and kicking footballs to the cameraman against upbeat background music. It's more usual to see TV celebs or pop stars, or a British prince or two undertaking this kind of work, but even without the glitterati, the short film is moving and captivating and the result at the end is a new school for the community. It's truly heart-warming. Imagine being able to make that type of difference to people's lives. Imagine how it must change you as a person, to be something that is so much bigger than yourself. I sigh. I might have gone on the programme if things had turned out differently. The metallic taste of rage floods my mouth. Tony Ferrier has robbed me of so much. I feel sick.

The film ends and Alex reclaims the microphone. 'What you just saw is the reason we're proposing to extend the programme from one month to three, open it to other employees and double the number of people we send over there.' Alex pauses to let everyone adjust to the idea. 'It's also why there's a plan to increase the yearly donations by an extra...' My mind boggles as he announces a number with an inordinate number of zeroes. A few men in the front row blanch. One wearing a loud purple tie looks as if he might fall off his chair. I hold back a laugh, wondering how many shares he owns.

'The other thing I want to suggest is in the information pack you were sent.' Alex booms. 'There's a saying that charity begins at home, but I think we've been missing it. My family are from

Corfu and the company was started three generations ago by my grandfather, but we're also British and the UK feels like home.' His voice wavers for a split second and I wonder if anyone notices. 'We need to launch more projects in the UK. Community projects in deprived areas, housing where there are shortages, a national apprenticeship scheme so that we can drive down the number of NEETs across the country, that is young people not in education, employment or training. We have an ageing population and no default retirement age, so we need to respect the experience of the older generation while also helping the next into work and out of poverty. We need to take action *now* and lead from the front and hope that other businesses follow. We'll improve our corporate image and increase the motivation of our staff, but more importantly we will feel proud.' He pauses. 'We will *be* proud. Who,' he demands, looking around the room, 'is with me?'

The room is silent, then clapping begins. I feel like I'm at some political pep rally. I fully expect to see Barack Obama appear with Michelle, but there's just Alex, who can be both so distant and in the next moment so charming, standing at the front of the stage, charged with compassion and energy. For a moment I lose my breath. He is such a complicated guy, but everything he's just said fills me with warm positivity.

The rest of the meeting is quick, shareholders approving the previous year's accounts and dividends per share and voting overwhelmingly in favour of Alex's plans, ending with the composition of the Board. Everyone is re-elected and Alex seems satisfied as he wraps up, summarising the last slide.

'Thank you all for your time,' he says finally, smiling. 'Now I'm going to go and lie down in a dark room with a glass of Retsina.' A small laugh erupts from the audience. 'You're all welcome to stay for light refreshments next door before leaving, unlike the members of staff staying for breakout sessions and a working lunch, followed by a long afternoon of individual meetings. You know who you are!' He waits a beat. 'If there are no questions?'

he addresses the room. 'Good. Enjoy the food and I wish you all a safe journey home. Thank you. Oh, and a belated Happy New Year to you and your families.'

As Alex steps from the podium, people stand, stretching and chatting and making for the door. I exit the PowerPoint and start shutting down the laptop. I'm really confused. Who is the real Alex? The formal, sharp closed-off guy, or the witty, compassionate one?

I shouldn't care. It doesn't matter to me who he is – as long as he believes my story when I need him to.

Chapter Eleven

'What do you want me to do next?' I ask Alex as I zip his laptop into its bag.

'Can you take notes during the group sessions?' he asks absently, checking his smartphone. 'They're rotating coffee breaks with team meetings and group thought showers,' he continues, swiping a finger across the screen. 'We need some ideas for a new rewards programme for customers and employees. It'd be helpful if you could capture the ideas.'

'Sure,' I say easily, looking over at the small group of managers chatting in the corner. It's gratifying to see it's an almost even mixture of men and women. 'See you later then?' I sling the laptop bag over my shoulder against my handbag.

'Hmm?' He taps something else on the phone. 'Yes.'

The phone seems permanently attached to either his ear or hand. Would it kill him to look at me when he's talking to me? With a quiet harrumph, I turn to scoot over to the awaiting group.

'Charley?'

'Yes?' I glance back.

'Thank you.' Alex gives me a grateful smile with a flash of white teeth, dark-blue eyes crinkling at the corners.

Almost staggering under the force of it, I return the smile weakly. 'Uh-huh.' The man is too bloody gorgeous for his own good.

Hotfooting over to the corner: 'Hi, I'm Charley, Mr. Demetrio's assistant for the weekend.' A round of greetings and a few waves meet my words, with one familiar blonde woman nodding more rigidly. 'I'm going to take notes of your session,' I explain. 'Shall we get started? I think we're in the room across the hall.'

An hour later I've made four pages of notes filled with their ideas and have even contributed a few suggestions, all met with approving nods, though the blonde – Sara Eden – was less enthusiastic. She might have been the woman eyeing Alex up at dinner last night, though I can't be sure.

Taking notes at three more meetings, it's soon time for lunch in the main conference hall, which has been arranged with round tables and matching chairs dotted around the room. Sitting with a few managers from the first session, I breathe in the scents of savoury and sweet food, listen to the group gossip about work and partners and kids, and slowly relax, though not enough that my appetite returns.

Staring blankly at the tablecloth, I recall Alex's remark about having a happy new year. I love the end of one year and the beginning of another. It's an emotional milestone, not just a fresh page because the month has changed, but a shiny new calendar on the wall. No matter how rubbish the past twelve months have been, you can hope the next twelve will be better. God, the next twelve *have* to be better for me. It doesn't feel likely at the moment.

It takes me a minute to realise it's gone quiet. The man next to me clears his throat and coughs.

'Are you all right? Do you need some water?' I query but his attention is fixed above my head. I swing around and notice Alex beside me. 'Oh.' Pushing my plate away, 'Hi.'

'Hi.' His gaze flickers over me then round the table. Do I imagine it slides over Sara more quickly than the others, as she flicks her hair and looks at him from under her lashes? 'Sorry to interrupt.' He touches my shoulder. 'I need to talk to you about a few things please?'

'Of course.' Standing, I stack my practically full plate in the middle of the table. 'See you later everyone.'

'Don't go without on my account.' Alex frowns at my food.

'I'm done thank you. I'm not very hungry.'

His eyes flicker over my body and darken, making me flash burning hot, but he says nothing, gesturing to an empty table across the room.

Following, I smile when he edges a glass of water out of my reach as we sit down. He hasn't forgotten my clumsiness last night.

'How are you finding it?' He leans forward. 'Everything all right? Any questions?'

Nodding to show it's all under control. 'Fine, yes and no. Are you pleased with how it's going?'

'Reasonably, yes.'

'Oh. Only reasonably?'

Searching my face, 'It's not a criticism of you. Just other things I need to sort out.'

I give him a relieved smile. 'Right. But you'd say, if there was anything I needed to improve?'

'There isn't.'

'All right,' I lower my voice. 'It's just that … this morning, by the pool. I owe you an apology—'

'Oh, that.' He straightens his tie. 'Let's not dwell on it. It's already forgotten.'

'Is it? I don't want to dwell on it, believe me, but you made the comment about me napping and … I don't want you to think I make a habit of—'

'I'm sure you don't,' he interrupts. 'And I'm sorry. About my comment.'

'No, *I'm* sorry. It was unprofessional,' my nails curl into my hands and I drop my voice to a whisper, 'to touch you like that. I didn't sleep well last night, was a bit fuzzy when you woke me. That's the only reason it happened.'

'It was?' I must imagine the glint of disappointment in his

rapidly shuttered gaze. 'Of course it was.' Shaking his head: 'Look, I was a bit hard on you. Let's just forget it. We've other more important things to focus on.'

'Okay.' Forget it? I still remember the sensation of his warm stubbly skin under my fingertips, his thick, dark hair soft against my palm. 'There were things you wanted to brief me about?'

'Just a reminder you'll be with me this afternoon taking notes at management meetings.'

'I remember. It's probably quicker to type them straight into your laptop. Is that okay?'

'Whatever you want.'

You naked in my bed? Thank God I don't say it out loud. And that my dress is thick enough he can't see the effect the thought has on my nipples, which immediately go hard and bead.

'If that's it then?' I squeak. Clearing my throat, I rise from my chair.

His voice stops me. 'What did you think of the presentation? It went well, didn't it.' His smile is a touch arrogant.

I won't feed his ego by telling him how inspirational he was or how much he impressed but I'll give credit where it's due. 'I liked your plans for the UK projects.'

'Thanks.' His fingers tap on the table. Quick, slow, quick, quick, slow. 'I believe they're worthwhile, especially if it means other people get involved.'

'I'm sure they will.' Pushing back from the table, 'Catch you—'

'What's the worst thing about your job?' he asks quietly, leaning forward.

Being sexually harassed by your creepy assistant? No, not the place for *that* conversation. Crap. What do I say? Think about it from a PA angle. 'You're not about to go off and do some *Undercover Boss* thing are you?' I ask, to give myself time to think.

'What?' He looks blank.

'The TV programme? Where CEOs go undercover on the front line to find out what's really happening within their companies?

Then deliver the findings back to the Board?'

'I don't watch much TV. And I'm sure most of it's garbage anyway. And no, I'm not doing undercover whatever it was, I'm just ... interested.'

'Right.' I place my chin on my hand in a deliberate thinking pose and make a mmmm sound. He stifles a smile. 'Well, I guess it would be rapidly shifting priorities.'

'Really? I didn't think you'd be bothered by that. You can't handle the pressure?'

'Of course I can! I'm just answering your question.' I take a breath. 'And just because I don't like it, doesn't mean I can't do it. Does that make sense?'

He nods jerkily. 'Strangely, it does.'

What's going on with Mr CEO? 'So what are the worst things about *your* job?' I follow a hunch.

'Nothing. I love it,' he answers robotically, dragging a hand through his hair. 'Why?' he shoots defensively.

I sit back in surprise. 'I was just asking the question you asked me.'

He sits back too, frowns. 'Ye–es,' the word slides out. He's thinking. Considering. 'But that's different.'

'Because I'm a junior member of staff and you can tell me what to do?'

He waves off the remark. 'It's not about hierarchy in that way,' he replies, 'but I suppose it is.'

'Meaning?'

'You can share things. But I'm the one in charge.'

'So you can't share? Or won't?'

'I can't let any doubts or weaknesses show.'

'Rubbish! You're as human as the rest of us. Aren't you?' Yanking my notepad and pen from my bag: 'But just to keep you happy.' I scrawl on my pad as I talk. '*I, Charley Caswell,*' I declare, '*promise not to blog/post/tweet/socially broadcast/sell to the papers/tell anyone anything Alex Demetrio discloses to me, or which happens, during the course of this assignment. Forthwith—'*

His white teeth click shut and he rolls his eyes. 'Very good. You've made your point. Now put it away.'

'Yes, sir!' Putting the pad aside: 'So, the worst thing about your job?'

He starts fiddling with the arrangement in the middle of the table, a finger playing with a row of red beads entwined with the flower stems. I gulp and squirm in my seat. 'The travel,' he murmurs.

From the way he's acting I was expecting something a bit juicier. 'Oh. That's it?' I raise one eyebrow.

'Isn't it enough?'

'I'd love to travel more, see the world.'

'Yes but you don't see the world, only an endless series of hotel bedrooms and conference facilities. If I'm lucky I eat in the restaurant, but I usually order room service so I can work at the same time.'

It sounds lonely. Joyless. 'I hadn't thought of it like that. When you see it in movies it seems glamorous.'

'It's not.' His expression is grim, lips pale. He's wound so tight. I feel a ridiculous urge to offer him comfort, but that's not allowed. 'It's tiring and relentless.' He sighs. 'Especially when there are people you'd rather be spending your time with.'

A girlfriend? My mind magics up an image of him kissing a skinny blonde. Ick. A friend? The look on his face doesn't invite further questions so I settle with a soft, 'I'm sorry.'

'Don't be,' he grinds out. 'I wasn't looking for your sympathy.'

But he does need someone to talk to, and if it's me, perhaps he'll listen in return when I tell him about Tony? 'I'd never dare offer you sympathy,' I answer, tongue in cheek, 'but what else?'

'What else?'

'What else do you not like about the job?'

'I really shouldn't—'

'Just say it, Alex. No judgement, I promise.'

He checks if there's anyone around to overhear but most people are picking over the fresh fruit and light desserts laid out on a long table on the other side of the room. My nose twitches at the rich aroma of coffee but I don't want to leave the conversation, not when he's showing trust in me.

'Chairing disciplinary panels or grievance hearings,' he shares. It's quiet and torn from him.

It's also a perfect opening. 'You get involved in those?'

'Yes, if they get to a certain stage in the group, not for the smaller companies. It's rare, because they go through management, and directors hear appeals, but a few times I've been hearing officer where it's involved very senior people.'

Maybe he wants me to interrupt, stop the flow of words but I won't. I shift further forward in my chair so he can keep his voice down.

'It's difficult sometimes,' he confesses, 'because you never really know what's happened, especially in a grievance where it's two people at odds. There's that saying about two sides to every story, isn't there? Well, I've found each person has their own views and the truth generally falls somewhere in the middle.'

I wonder what he'd say about my situation. Will he believe I provoked Tony? Or deserved what happened to me?

He runs a hand through his hair again, leaving it spiked up and ruffled. I prefer the messy look. He looks younger, sexier. I shake my head and focus on listening. It's the safest option. 'And?' I nudge. He hesitates. 'It's fine as long as you don't talk about particular cases, isn't it?' I ask. 'You won't be breaching any confidentialities.'

'No. Still, if an employee overheard me talking about it, even in general terms—'

'I'm an employee.'

'Not a direct one. And not after this weekend. Besides—'

'Besides?'

'Nothing.' His cheekbones darken.

He's not– *Is he blushing?* No. It must be a trick of the light.

'Maybe your employees would appreciate you not taking this stuff lightly. Maybe they'd be gratified to hear how much care you take, that if they were ever to go through a formal process you'd be serious about the responsibility.'

'I hadn't thought of it like that,' he concedes, drumming his fingers on the tablecloth.

'It's part of how we learn, isn't it? Exchanging views with others, sorting through the different opinions for the ones which make the most sense to us.'

'Not many people share their views with me. They'll tell me what they think if I ask but don't offer their thoughts freely. And I'm not sure how honest those opinions are.'

'Ah.' They probably don't dare. One wrong opinion might get them fired. Yet from what Alex just said, and from the impression he gives of being fair, I don't think it's likely.

'It's the bullying allegations I find hardest,' he circles back. 'Is it a manager being a bully or them trying to proactively manage someone, bring them to account, and the employee not liking it?' Blowing out an exasperated breath: 'In the end it comes down to someone's perceptions, and those are coloured by their personal attitudes, experiences and emotions. Unfortunately, by the time those cases get to me, sometimes too much has happened. The working relationship is at breaking point. It's sad. We've lost good people that way.'

Would he class me as one of them? 'I can see what you're saying.' I stretch across the table, grab a glass and pour some water into it, carefully. Letting delight at his emotional intelligence show would be premature. But it gives me hope.

As though a cork has popped from a bottle of suppressed feeling, he keeps going. 'The biggest thing for me is that I'm fair. Disciplinaries and grievances involve real people. You're making decisions about their employment that can really affect their lives. What if I get it wrong?'

'You have doubts?' I take a sip of water, the liquid cool on my tongue.

'Of course I do. Even when it's a robust process. There have been cases where I've had to make judgements based on the balance of probabilities.'

'What does that mean?' I probe. Throwing my head back, I gulp down the rest of my water. When I put the glass down Alex's eyes flicker back to my face. Where was he looking?

'Taking all the evidence into account and deciding what's most likely to have happened.'

'Sounds heavy.' I kick myself. What an insensitive way to describe something which obviously causes him anxiety. Even worse because I know more than anyone the depth of distress caused by those situations.

He raises both eyebrows. 'That's one way of describing it.' He gives a one-shouldered shrug, his beautifully cut black suit gleaming in the overhead lights. 'I suppose even the justice system isn't infallible, they get it wrong sometimes, and innocent people get sent to prison.'

'But you're not condemning people to be locked away.' Shaking my head, 'You're too hard on yourself, Alex. And anyway, if you get it wrong, there must be someone to scrutinise your decision?'

'No. I deal with cases at appeal stage, so the next step is tribunal.'

I shiver. It's the perfect 'in', the perfect moment to move forward with the crucial part of the plan I came here to see through. I should tell him now, whilst he's in this mindset, never mind where we are. With a deep breath, I go for it. 'Actually Alex, on that subject there is something I wanted to—'

'I hate going to tribunal,' he announces, 'though I guess no employer likes it. But I've seen so many vexatious claims made by people to get money, usually through a pre-hearing settlement.' Temper smoulders in his eyes. 'They drag everyone through the mud, uncaring of how much stress they cause.'

His condemnation immediately gets my back up. 'Don't you think that's a sweeping generalisation? Some of them must be genuine cases. What about their stress? And don't forget they've paid out money to have the case heard and someone has thought it credible enough to make it to tribunal court.'

He stares at me, blue eyes rapidly cooling and capable of causing the Arctic to chill by a few more degrees. 'If they're genuine I can't understand how it couldn't have been resolved earlier. It's the sexual harassment cases that bother me, where it's so hard to tell whether there's been any actual harassment or not, and who, if anyone, is responsible. You never know exactly what's happened between a man and a woman in the workplace, especially without witnesses. That's why it's easier to remove any possibility of those kinds of claims.'

His comments hit the biggest raw nerve possible. 'Perhaps some aren't resolved earlier because people feel unable to come forward?' I retort. 'They might be embarrassed or ashamed, or think they can handle it alone. Or not see it coming until it's too late.'

'These are grown adults we're talking about, not playground schoolchildren.'

'It's not immature to be scared, or to worry about the ramifications of your actions. And how can you cast judgement if it hasn't happened to you?' I stop, take a breath, dizzy with anger. '*Has* it happened to you?'

'No.'

'So you don't know what it feels like, what choice you would make.' I spring out of my chair, hold myself steady with my hands flat on the table, shaking. 'And how are you going to remove the possibility of those claims? Unless you're going to try and segregate men and women, you've got a problem. And it's not necessarily about men and women, is it? There could be a same-sex claim.'

'Segregation?' He looks shocked, rising from his chair. 'Don't be silly. I meant having a no-workplace relationships policy. For everyone, whatever their sexual orientation.'

Feeling stupid for my hasty remarks, I turn sunset red. 'You can't get people to control their emotions like that, Alex. They're not robots. Haven't you ever heard the heart wants what the heart wants?'

His face closes down. 'Sometimes what the heart wants isn't what the person attached to it needs. And in my experience, a lot of the time it's hormones doing the wanting, not the heart.'

Is he saying he sleeps around? 'Do you think it's realistic to expect people to adhere to that kind of policy? Plus it wouldn't necessarily stop sexual harassment claims.'

'It can minimise them, and yes, if the clause is written into the employment contract.' He rubs his temples. 'It's not about feelings, Charley. It's about trying to keep the organisation alive and productive. It can't be either of those if it's imploding because people are falling out when it all goes wrong. Which it inevitably does.'

'Wow. That's cynical.'

Tucking his chair under the table, he nods, 'What can I say? Sometimes, sadly, it's the safest way to be.'

I shove my chair under the table, making the glasses rattle. 'You're right,' I state, staring him directly in the eye. 'That *is* sad.' His mouth falls open. 'Now if you'll excuse me,' I seethe, unable to see clearly, think clearly, 'I'm going to get some fresh air.'

'Take as long as you like,' he barks.

Stomping from the room, I wonder if I've blown it and if he means I shouldn't bother coming back at all.

Chapter Twelve

Luckily for me he doesn't. When I return from a brisk walk around the block, I find him waiting in one of the meeting rooms with a group of managers. Pointing to the laptop he's set up in my absence – which I must have left in the hall in my haste to escape, oh, pants – he nods, 'Charley. Are you ready?'

There's no chance to tell him I'm sorry. He had a right to express his views, and maybe they didn't gel with mine, but I made it personal. Out of order. Unprofessional. I was overly sensitive because of my situation. I should have stayed calm and under control. Why can't I keep my emotions in check around him? I never had these problems at the casino. Is it the pressure of the last few months or is it about Alex himself? *No. Focus on work.*

I take notes and after everyone leaves I write up a sales strategy and answer email correspondence while Alex dictates to me. I become absorbed, fingers flying over the keyboard with his rapid-fire thoughts. I'm envious of his energy. How he does it, has presumably held the same pace for the last few years, is incredible. I feel like an amateur in comparison, tired after one day.

Rotating my head to ease the kinks from my neck, I feel a crunch and a tension headache starts. Alex has stopped talking, so I look up. He's standing at the window, shoulders wide and set, hands deep in his trouser pockets.

'Alex?' No response. Standing, I step closer. 'Alex?' A sharp pain stabs in my forehead, aching discomfort digging in deeper. I need to get to my room and take some painkillers otherwise I'm liable to be laid out with a migraine for the next few hours. Still no response. Muttering in exasperation, I move closer, waving a hand in front of his face. 'Woo–hoo, *Alex?*'

He jerks, grabbing my hand and holding it down between us. 'Yes?' he frowns.

'Is there anything else you need me to do?' I wiggle my fingers, hand tingling against the slide of his skin.

'The last email's sent?'

'Yes, just now.' A pulse blooms in my right eye socket.

Releasing my hand, 'Sorry.' Glancing down at his watch. 'Good. Yes, that's all for now. I'll see you in the lobby at seven thirty for drinks.'

'Pardon?'

'Drinks,' he exclaims, 'the liquid things before dinner?'

'Thanks for the explanation,' I say dryly. 'I just thought we were done for the day.'

'No, sorry. You're expected to come to the party tonight.'

What? I'm knackered, especially after only a few hours' sleep. Plus this headache is expanding to epic proportions. I also need space from the bright exciting tension sitting in my lower belly and coating my nerve endings when I'm near him.

It's not good.

This is not romance.

This is business.

'Party? No one at the agency said anything. When you mentioned one earlier I figured it was for the AGM attendees.'

'It's for the employees here and any others who can make it. Stuart usually attends so I'll expect you to be there. Is there a reason you can't be?' He glowers. It's framed as a question but is an order. But then, he is the boss and I need to be reasonable, especially since I still owe him an apology for earlier.

'No, there isn't.' I put my hands on my hips. 'But would it kill you to say please?'

'What? I—' For a moment I think he's about to start shouting, but he throws his hands in the air and starts laughing. 'Unbelievable,' he mutters under his breath, stepping closer to me. I back up as a wide chest fills my vision. 'Please Charley,' he says theatrically, a mock pleading expression on his face, and fun, relaxed Alex is back again. 'Please, please, please … come to the party.'

I shake my head and grin, then scowl as the motion pulls sharp claws through my head. 'All right, all right,' I say, pretending reluctance. 'But do I get a break?'

'You're about to get one, and you proved yourself so efficient at getting ready last night,' he cocks an eyebrow, 'that you should have an hour or so to yourself before meeting me.'

I chew the inside of my mouth but say nothing. He doesn't know I need extra time to let the migraine tablets take effect. 'Fine. But before I go, I need to talk to you about something and I owe you—'

'An apology?' He massages the back of his neck, as if feeling my pain, like conjoined twins. 'We seem to be having this conversation regularly, don't we?'

I flush. 'I'm not usually so argumentative. I shouldn't have called you cynical. I'm sorry.'

'Yes, well, I'm sorry if I lost my cool. You're right. I *am* cynical – whereas you're an optimist. We both have strong opinions and we're not likely to agree on this particular point so I think we should agree to disagree.' A strange look passes over his face, as if he's made a decision. 'Let's just see the assignment through as quickly as possible.'

The headache intensifies. 'Sounds good to me.' It doesn't. I should be wishing for the weekend to be over with as much as him but the thought he wants rid of me is appalling. Then I'm appalled that I'm appalled.

His phone vibrates inside his trouser pocket and he plucks it out, going pasty white at whatever is on screen.

'Alex, are you okay?'

'Pardon?' He gazes at me blankly, black eyebrows pulling together.

'You look awful. Maybe you should sit down for a minute.'

'I'm fine,' he says swiftly, but sways like a tall tree in a high-force gale. I think of Alex as solid and strong, but right now he's vulnerable.

'You're plainly not.' Ignoring my headache, I grab his elbow and jerk him towards a chair about seven feet away.

'What do you think you're doing?' He tries to pull his arm free but I hold tight, hooking my fingers into his silky, expensive shirt.

'Helping. You look like you're about to fall over.'

'I don't need anyone's help.' But his deep voice is hoarse. 'Leave me alone.'

'Sit down,' I insist. Spinning around to swap our positions, I shove at his chest lightly, slowly backing him towards the chair. Five feet to go.

'I said I'm fine!'

'Did you get bad news?' I say softy, pushing his chest again, trying not to accidentally grope what feel like glorious pecs. He steps back. Four feet. 'Is there anything I can do?'

He looks at me oddly. 'What would you be able to do?'

'I don't know.' But the energy he directs at the question allows me to push him another foot or so backward. Getting there. I shiver. He's *so* gorgeous, even more so when he's off-balance. It's not fair how attractive he is in his formal shirt and tie, his body so close I swear I feel its core temperature. 'But I'd try,' I say desperately to distract myself. 'I'm just offering—'

He huffs. 'Well, I don't need you. Stop offering and go away. Go and get ready or something.'

'No.' I press my other hand against his chest and press again. Two feet. Nearly there. 'Look, I'm not trying to be difficult—'

'Seriously?' He rocks out a laugh that does funny things to

my knees. 'You've done nothing but present me with difficulties!'

'Thanks a lot!' I give him a final shove borne of frustration and, of course, he chooses that minute to cooperate. He lands squarely in the chair and the momentum carries me forward. I stumble and end up sprawled on top of him, bum on his hard lap, hands clinging onto his shoulders for balance.

'Oh,' I squeak.

'Oh,' he echoes.

We lock eyes, his pupils dilating. His gaze drops down to my mouth. 'You're really quite beautiful you know,' he says huskily.

The rumble of his voice, reverberating through his broad chest and against my breasts, strikes a chord in my misbehaving body. He thinks I'm beautiful!

It's a mere sparkle of thought, because I squirm on his thighs and his hands clench on my hips ... and he jams his mouth down on mine.

The kiss is demanding and rough and he curves an arm around my back to yank me closer. I know he's taking his frustrations out on me but I'm not scared in the way I would be if it were Tony. The fear goes deeper as warmth spins inside me. It's not fear about my physical safety; it's about guarding my heart.

I pull away but really don't have anywhere to go, lying across his lap with his arms wrapped round me. 'What are you doing?' I choke into his mouth.

He lifts his head just enough to hear the words and confusion clouds his face. 'I'm not sure,' he admits. I expect him to let me go but he kisses me again and it's not rough any more. It's how every girl longs to be kissed for the first time; slow and sweet and sexy. It's much worse than his misplaced anger. More dangerous. I try to fight it but it's useless. I hold out for all of two seconds then breathe in his fresh scent and become aware of the smooth texture of his shirt where my hands have moved to his taut upper back. I can feel the hot muscles shift under my palms. The heat of his solid body presses into mine, chest to knee, and the sound of our heavy breathing and the way his thumb rubs along my jaw slays me. I give in. I melt. I can't think, only feel, gripping onto him to stop from slipping off his lap and flowing into a puddle at his feet. Raging warmth spreads through me. Embarrassingly I let out a kind of half moan, half squeak, and the pressure of his mouth increases. He groans in response and the kiss gets slower and steamier.

Taking out my hair band, he runs gentle fingers through my waves and all traces of a headache fade. Tingles zing along my spine as one of his hands drops to cup my bum. He stands, lifting and putting me on the edge of the meeting table. The glass is cool beneath my thighs through my tights as my skirt hitches up. He crowds closer, flexes his fingers on my bum, prompting an answering tug between my legs. Woah! I gasp and grab fistfuls of his thick dark hair as the kiss goes on and on, gaining energy and spark. His hips press between my thighs and it's obvious he's enjoying this as much as I am.

Take me now, I think foggily as he lifts his head. Maybe I say it out loud, I'm not sure. Either that or he's a mind reader.

'Here. Now,' he mutters gruffly into my neck.

In that instant I almost say *Oh, yes please*. I don't care as long as this feeling carries on. I don't give a monkey's if someone sees us.

Huh? Hang on a second.

I freeze as the extent of my desperation hits, like a bucket of ice cubes has been tipped down my back. This is so wrong. How would it look if I was caught on the table with the boss? More importantly, what will Alex think? If I do this with him, he might believe I did the same with Tony.

What on earth am I thinking? What happened to asking Alex to help me out of a hole? Getting my life back? That's the problem. I wasn't thinking.

I wrench my mouth from his, tug my hands from his hair. 'No,' I croak and my body, the traitor, is screaming to stop being so stupid, to get back in there, to strip his shirt off and unzip his trousers and enjoy this one mad moment. 'I said *no*.' I'm talking as much to myself as him.

'*No?*' Alex stares at me, luscious mouth damp and red from our kisses, hair standing up in spikes from my passionate tugging.

'No.' Pressing his chest, I slide off the table and smooth my skirt down. I swear it's one of the hardest things I've ever done. But necessary. 'You're my boss.' Grabbing the band from his hand, I twist my curls into a bun.

The dazed look in his blue eyes lifts, replaced by something else. Backing away, he stalks across the room and slides his suit jacket on. 'The fact I'm your boss,' he coolly does the buttons up, 'didn't seem to present a problem when you were hanging on to me and whimpering.'

I gape at him. Arrogant sod. 'I was not whimpering.' Was I? 'You took me by surprise, that's all.'

'Did I also take you by surprise this morning by the pool? Is that why you tried to kiss me then?'

Anger ignites from a spark to a raging fire. 'I told you the reason that happened. Is this what you're like when you don't get your own way. You go on the attack?'

He laughs, 'Attack? You're giving me too much credit. I'm just pointing out the truth.'

When he moves to his laptop and carelessly starts shutting it down, the dismissal drives me over the edge. Humiliation mixes with fury in a whoosh of adrenaline along with a healthy dose of bitterness and regret. If it wasn't for one of *his* employees, I wouldn't be in the position I'm in now.

'I can take the truth! So you should be able to as well. The truth is it was inappropriate for you to kiss me. You made,' *a move on me first*, is the intended sentence but his head jerks back.

'That's enough.' His eyes are dark, flat like a shark's, generous lips compressed.

I don't like the way he's looking at me. The anger and disappointment, the raw contempt making me shudder. *Shit.*

113

He picks up the laptop. 'I suggest you think carefully before you finish your accusation, if you're building up to a sexual harassment claim. I shouldn't have kissed you, you're right. I wish I hadn't. But let's not lie. The heat was mutual. And I won't let anyone say I'd make any woman do anything she wouldn't want to. Especially a member of staff.'

Dismay hits. It's the worst thing he could think. Cringing, 'I don't mean that, I'd never—'

'Save it,' he interrupts, 'I'm not interested.'

God, what a mess. He actually thinks I'm trying to build a case when I'm trying to do the opposite. As he sails to the door, I rush after him. 'No. No way. You're not just going to walk out. I did not accuse you of sexual harassment and I wasn't about to. Okay?' I grab his arm. 'Alex. Alex! Look at me!'

He glances over his shoulder, hand on the door handle.

'I want to be completely clear. It *was* mutual. But I was going to say you made a move on me first. Not that you made me do something I didn't want to. I just can't get involved, all right? I can't.' I lower my voice, 'It's not about you.'

'It's not you, it's me?' he says sarcastically. 'How original.'

'I know it's a cliché, but yes. Believe it. You said yourself I'm honest with you, tell you what I think, so why I would I lie about this?'

He stares at my face, eyes softening. Blows out a hard, fast breath. 'Okay, I'm sorry I jumped on you about it. And you're right, I shouldn't have ignored my own policy. Truce. Let's forget it ever happened. I will.' He yanks open the door, gives me a shadow of a smile. 'I'll see you at the party.'

After he leaves, I stand in the middle of the room, recalling his knowing touch, his incredible kissing, his hot, hard body. But it's his words that keep boomeranging back on me the most. *I wish I hadn't kissed you.*

I should be relieved.

Instead I feel lost, when I have absolutely no right to.

Chapter Thirteen

'You kissed him?' Jess shrieks down the phone. 'And it was amazing?'

Sometimes a girl needs her best friend, even if the bill is going to be astronomical and you might have to sell possessions to pay for it. Oh, God. This is going to give her so much ammunition. 'He kissed me first, but yes, amazing, like you wouldn't believe.' I can't stop thinking about *that* kiss. Ironic, given Alex wants to forget all about it. But I've never felt that intense rolling need and heat in the pit of my stomach before, which even now won't go away. A need that's making me twitchy and restless. 'But I had to stop,' I sigh. 'It's just too complicated. I mean, what is it with me and this guy? It wasn't bad enough he overheard me on the phone to you yesterday? That I'm deceiving him? I'm a disaster zone. What's wrong with me?'

Sitting down on the edge of the bed, I grab hold of the floor-length hem of my electric-blue dress to make sure it doesn't get caught in my strappy black stilettos.

'There's nothing wrong with you,' she chuckles. 'This is an area you're understandably sensitive about. Before you say it, I know he doesn't know that yet, but he will, and he'll get it, I'm sure. And the other thing, well, it's obvious isn't it? Like I said last night, you fancy him. But not just that.'

'Oh?'

'You *like* him,' she says in a sing-song voice. 'It's the fireworks they talk about in films and books. Chemistry.' The last remark holds the shadow of regret, but neither of us says anything. We both know she's thinking about Tom. 'Think about your reaction,' she picks up the thread. 'How often do you get so mega clumsy and mess up so much around a guy? How often do you go against your sensible side and kiss someone you hardly know? Never.'

I can't argue. She's right.

'Uh-huh,' I answer miserably. 'So what do I do? And why aren't you using the opportunity to lecture me about it after you told me not to do this?'

'It's a bit late for that now, and as you pointed out yesterday, I love you.' Her tone becomes brisk. 'Now, get some perspective. Take a step back and think it through. You can either ignore the chemistry, or do something about it.'

'I guess so.'

'You just have to be prepared to accept the consequences of whichever one you go with,' she finishes.

'All right, I get it! I'm not one of your key-stage-three kids. Honestly, why I put up with you.' We both know my grumbling is good-natured. Her directness always comes from a kind place and I value it. It's funny Alex thinks I'm opinionated. If he met Jess, he'd think me practically mute in comparison. Argh, why does it always go back to him? I shake my head, smooth my hand over the bed covers, spreading out the wrinkles.

'Well?' she demands.

'Don't worry, oh wise one. I will humbly follow in your enlight-ened footsteps.'

'Very funny. So now I've shared my wisdom what are you going to do?'

'I'm going to do what he wants – forget about it. Then try and lay my hands on a padlocked chastity belt.'

'Well, good luck with that,' Jess laughs. 'Whilst you wrestle with

116

your libido I'll be on another date with Jake, and I'm thinking it's going to be a *late* night.'

I smile. Jess has always been able to pull me from the blackest of moods, even when we were teenagers and mood swings were a daily battle. 'Okay, I'll let you go then. See you Monday evening?'

'Maybe, maybe not. It depends. I might see Jake on Monday night. If he manages to keep me entertained sufficiently for the next thirty-six hours.'

I shake my head. 'Just do me a favour, text me on Monday so I know what your plans are, that you're safe?'

'Yes, Mum.'

I huff. 'Just promise you'll take care of yourself.'

'I will.'

Ten minutes later I stride into the lobby, searching for Alex. I'm running a little behind, on the phone with Jess longer than planned. I can't see him, and wait around for a while before going to the reception desk and asking if he's left a message for me.

'There was a gentleman here a while ago, Señorita,' the mous-tached man says in a heavy Spanish accent, straightening a pile of papers on the desk, 'but he left. Maybe he has gone to the function room in the basement?'

'Thank you. If he comes looking for me can you tell him where I've gone please?' The basement? Sounds interesting.

'Of course.' He nods.

'Thanks.'

Clicking straight from the lift into a massive nightclub, I pause. What a place. I'm impressed by the modern art-deco mirrors and spinning lights, red and black paintings and sofas contrasting with the white moulded walls, red cushioned stools at the long bar. Nice. There's a table heaving with food in the far corner and pink cock-tails are being held aloft by waiters and given out indiscriminately. Moving closer, I smile at a brunette waitress and scoop one up. Taking a sip, 'Mmm, Cosmo,' I murmur, savouring the sweetness of fruit rounded off by the citrus tang. Perfect.

117

It's two hours before I spot Alex in the heaving mass and by then the food's been tidied away, I've had three cocktails and have shouted-talked at loads of people I don't know. The party is pounding. It's in the drunken dancing (mostly out of time with the throbbing beat), the squash of people at the bar, the yelled conversations above the music and the stuffiness of the room caused by shared body heat.

'Ooh, there's Alex,' I blurt to the woman I'm talking to, a pretty girl with a beauty spot on her cheekbone, wearing a short black dress. I don't know who she is, nor does it matter. We've spent the last twenty minutes admiring each other's shoes and dresses.

'That gorgeous creature?' she yells in my ear. 'Go get him.'

Grimacing, 'It's not really like that.' But sweat prickles along my upper lip as I take in how tall, dark and knicker-meltingly handsome he is in his tux. What is it about men in tuxes? The James Bond effect?

She stares at me, arching a well-plucked eyebrow. 'No. Of course it isn't,' she mouths into my ear in an amused tone.

I laugh. 'Have a good night. Nice to meet you.'

'You too.' The woman is forgotten as I hotfoot it across the room, staring at Alex. Dodging damp, bouncing bodies, I pray no one will step on the hem of my dress.

'Alex, there you are,' I shout above the music, reeling when he turns and a wave of alcohol fumes hits full force, nearly taking me out. I move closer to hear him.

'Charley. Where've you been? You're late,' he growls, the sugary sweet smell of drink wafting off him. How much has he had? I thought he'd stay sober for company social events. He's mentioned his reputation and what people think often enough.

'I don't care, I'd wait for her,' a short, round guy to Alex's right laughs, leering at me.

'Yeah, me too,' another colleague, a tall sharp-faced, red-haired man agrees. 'What's your name, love?'

Alex glares at both of them. 'This is Charley, my temporary PA.'

'I was only a bit late. I went to the lobby but you'd already come down here. I've been socialising for the last couple of hours,' I explain, ignoring the way the men with him are openly checking me out.

The shorter man elbows the other and turns to me. 'We all know Alex usually has male assistants. You must be special.' Leaning forward, he waggles his eyebrows, holding out his hand for me to shake, almost falling into the cleavage displayed by my halter neck.

'I'm up here,' I say sweetly, pointing to my face. 'And that's right, I am special.' Grabbing his hand, I shake it firmly and apply pressure to a particularly sensitive spot Jess once showed me and am gratified to see his eyes widen. Releasing his hand, I step back. 'I wonder if you might excuse us for a few minutes? I need to talk to Mr Demetrio about an urgent business matter.'

'Sure, sweetheart, whatever you say.' Backing away, flexing his hand with a slight nod to convey he got my point, he winks at Alex, 'I like this one, she's got balls.'

'Enough,' Alex barks at them and they both mumble a sorry before sloping off.

I roll my eyes and turn to find Alex staring down at me, 'What?' I ask self-consciously. 'Nothing.' Nodding, respect shines in his gaze. 'Sorry. They're senior employees but can be a bit silly with a drink inside them.' Frowning, I w–would have inter– interven– stepped in if necessary y'know.'

I look up at him. How far gone is he? His blood alcohol content appears to be climbing by the minute. 'I know that, thanks. They're okay.' I wave after them. 'But I don't need anyone fighting my battles for me.' I pause as a cheer goes up for the cheesy seventies pop song that comes on. 'Before anyone collars you, can we talk?'

He moves closer. 'What do you want?'

'Huh?' I shiver. His warm breath on my neck is like heaven, barely-there stubble grazing my cheek.

'What do you want t'talk about?'

'Let's go somewhere,' I suggest.

119

'Where?'

'Hotel bar?'

He casts an *I don't think so* look at the mass of people between us and the lift. 'Too far. Need to be here. 'Vailable for people. And I don't think I sh–should go anywhere with you.' He sways. 'Need to protect myself.'

'What?' I frown. 'Why?'

He shrugs, gazing over my shoulder.

'For God's sake,' I exclaim, 'what do you think I'm going to do to you?' Grabbing his sleeve, I jerk him over to the quietest corner of the room, away from the bar and dance floor. I'm sure if he was less under the influence of whatever alcohol he's necked he'd resist more. Instead, he settles for a mutinous expression, marred by the fact that he can't focus his eyes properly. I prop him up against the wall with a hand on one shoulder, worried he'll slide to the floor if I don't.

A slow song comes on and the calmer melody means I don't need to shout to be heard. 'I just need to make sure,' I say, 'that you really understood me earlier. About what you thought I said. About—'

'The kiss?'

'Yeah.' I bite my lip. 'It was—'

'Incredible,' he sighs, looking dreamy.

'What?'

'What?' he repeats sharply, drawing himself up a few inches. 'Nothing.'

I frown up at him. 'Alex, are you okay?'

'Uh-huh.' He nods but it's skew-eyed, like his head isn't on straight.

Still, pinning him to the wall after seeing him in a tux is giving my fizzing hormones all sorts of naughty ideas. What I'd like to do to him...

We're jostled by the crowd as they dance past us in a conga. My boobs brush up against his jacket and I hear him breathe deeply.

'You have to leave,' he orders, glancing around the room furtively as if afraid someone's watching us.

I follow his eyes but see only a bunch of people having a good time. 'I'll go up to my room shortly.' *As soon as I've made sure there's someone to look after you.*

'No.' He shakes his head. 'I mean you have to leave Barcelona. I can't work with you.'

No! I need this. Dismayed, I start firing out words. 'Alex I'm sorry, I am. The bits I'm responsible for anyway. You kissed me, I kissed you, but I realised it was a bad idea and I lost my temper because of your reaction. I wasn't thinking when I said what I did, but you misunderstood. I thought you got that. I thought – I want to stay,' I argue. 'Let me stay. You need me. For work, I mean.' Alex stares over the top of my head, not replying to my comments. 'God, can't you even look at me? And are you drunk?'

He drops his gaze to where my chest meets his, to my clenched hands gripping his upper arms. His jaw is working, eyes hazy and unfocused.

'Are you even listening to me?'

'Listening seems to be a bit of a challenge at the moment,' he mutters, 'and yes, I am sh–slightly intoxicated.' His eyes cross. 'Happy?'

'Not really. And why can't you listen? Have you gone deaf from the noise?'

'My ears are perfectly fine, along with other parts of me,' he laughs ironically.

What's he on about? Maybe drinking isn't a regular thing, perhaps he can't handle his alcohol. As CEO running a massive organisation, and with his work ethic, he probably doesn't get much time to kick back and relax. 'Sorry, I'm still not getting it. Why are you having problems listening?'

'For the same reason Bob's eyes almost fell out of his head.' Putting space between us, he looks me up and down. '*That* dress.' He points at it like it's a living thing that's done wrong.

'What about it?' It's ankle length with no high splits and it's not that low-cut, so I don't see what the issue is.

'It's clingy,' his voice rolls out in a slur. 'It shows off every gorgeous curve.' He bangs his forehead with a fist. 'No. Inappropriate Alex.'

Wow, Mr Stern CEO really has left the building. 'And now you're talking to yourself,' I sigh. 'Look, I'll forgive you if you forgive me. So can I stay until Monday?'

'Nope. Going home t'mrrow. Mind made up. Sh–sorry.'

'But why?' I cry.

'Just too difficult.'

'That's not fair, I've worked hard for you today! And I flew, even though I was afraid to.' I'm horrified by his comment. I've been so difficult he'd rather do without me, even though he has one-to-one meetings tomorrow he needs support for. He thinks I'm unprofessional. Tears scorch my eyes. It's what I was accused of at the awful disciplinary hearing. Unprofessionalism. Inappropriate conduct. Even though it wasn't true, it still stings. I won't let myself give in to those dark thoughts, though. I have to fight. 'You can't do this, Alex!'

He shrugs, eyes going opaque. 'Can. I'm in charge.'

The blood boils in my veins and I'm sure the colour's reflected in my face, a knot of tension tangling behind my ribs. 'I don't understand you,' I choke. 'One minute you're genuine and funny and the next minute you're closed down and arrogant.'

'As I said, I'm in charge.' His face is set, though his eyes are still a little crossed.

'Fine,' I huff. 'I'll go home. But don't expect me to be happy about it.' I can always try and change his mind tomorrow, once he's sober. Whirling around, I hike my skirt up and stalk towards the exit. Seeing the taller man from earlier, I stop him, sloshing his drink over my dress accidentally. 'Bugger. Sorry.' I breathe in. Rein it back, Charley. 'Your boss has had enough to drink,' I tell him. 'I suggest you get him some water and painkillers.' I spin away then back again to hold his arm. 'Oh, and about a gallon of black coffee. Otherwise he's going to suffer in the morning.'

I am so furious with Alex as I get into the lift that, despite my advice to his staff, I wish on him the biggest, worst, most clanging hangover possible.

Chapter Fourteen

A glass of red wine in the hotel bar doesn't help calm my temper, nor does going to my room and flinging clothes into my case, in the event I can't convince him to let me stay. Swearing loudly doesn't make a jot of difference and even throwing my shoes against the wall doesn't curb the frustration thundering through me. 'Argh. Bloody, bloody man!'

I'm too wired to sleep: angry, hurt and charged full of sexual energy I can't do anything with. I can't believe it's going to end like this. Sent home early like a disgraced teenager, no reference, no hope and back to square one. I hold back tears of impotent fury. Suddenly desperate to be free of my dress, I start wrestling with the ties behind my neck. A knock rattles the door. Whoever it is has the worst timing ever. Another knock.

'Charley, open up.' Alex. His is the last face I want to see. 'I'll stand here for as long as it takes,' he says flatly, banging on the door again.

I square my shoulders. *Just get it over with.*

Wrenching the door open, I come close to taking it off its hinges. Hanging onto the ties of my dress where it's tangled with the fingers of my left hand, I stand tall. 'What do you want?'

'To talk.'

Starting to push the door closed, 'Not now.'

He shocks me by shouldering open the door, stepping over the threshold. 'Yes, now.'

There's a leap of excitement in my belly at his action. Down girl. 'If you think I'm letting you in here whilst you're drunk—'

'I'm not any more.' He kicks the door closed behind him. 'I've had three espressos and lots of fresh air.'

I take him in. The tux jacket is open, bow tie undone, ends hanging loosely around his neck. The top few buttons of his shirt are open too. His hair is standing up in tufts and his eyes are bloodshot, but sharper than they were. 'You're not swaying or slurring,' I observe, backing up to put space between us.

'Like I said. I've sobered up. I'm sorry. I don't drink very often, or very much.'

I can't help it, he looks so ropey – adorable – but ropey, my mouth lifts in a smile. 'I could kind of tell,' I say. Then stiffen my shoulders. 'That doesn't mean you have the right to barge in here, though. Who do you think you are?'

'A man who's sorry for upsetting you downstairs?'

'Really?'

'Really,' he repeats solemnly. 'Sit down.'

'I'm fine standing thanks.'

'Do you ever do as you're asked? Thialo! You can be so stubborn sometimes.'

I flounder, mouth opening and closing like a goldfish. But he's got me. Of all the things he could call me on, this is the one he's right about. 'I am stubborn,' I admit tiredly, sinking down on the edge of the bed, even though everything in me says to stay standing on principle. 'Thialo,' I test the feel of it on my tongue. 'I thought you didn't usually speak Greek?' Remembering his remark about it in the car to the airport. Was that only yesterday? Hard to believe.

'I don't, not really. Only when I visit my family,' Alex starts pacing up and down the room, measuring the dimensions with his steps, 'but I learnt as a child and sometimes it comes out, especially when...'

'When what?' My arm's starting to ache from its position behind my head, but I'm worried if I try to untangle my hand I'll flash him.

'When I'm stressed.'

'I'm sorry if I stress you out.' I rub my face with my free hand, exhaustion beginning to take hold. 'I don't mean to. It's not my intention to be … *difficult*.'

Wincing, 'I know you don't,' he says rapidly. 'That's not—' He abandons the sentence with an exasperated huff. 'There are just other things going on in my life right now that are making it hard for me to keep perspective.'

'Hence the mission to get falling-down drunk?' I raise an eyebrow.

'I wasn't aiming to go that far.' I let out an unladylike snort, picturing the way I had to steady him against the wall earlier. 'I needed a release valve.' He grimaces, 'But picked the wrong one.' Rubbing the back of his neck: 'To be honest, I'm embarrassed. I don't usually behave like this. You've hardly seen me at my best this weekend.'

'Meaning?'

'Telling you far too much, getting drunk, ordering you home. I'm not myself at the moment. I pride myself on being professional and I don't think I have been.'

I'm hardly one to talk, after trying to kiss him this morning and falling into his lap this afternoon. 'Or perhaps you're being yourself,' I suggest.

'What are you saying?' he scowls.

'Perhaps you're being the person you're meant to be? The only time I've seen you looking anything approaching happy is when you let your guard down, when you've relaxed enough in conversations to forget yourself and the formal CEO persona.'

'Some of us don't have the luxury of doing what we want. Some of us can't just run away to the big city.'

'Hang on. I told you how much grief my parents gave me for that. You think it was easy? It wasn't. Mum still resents me for not staying close and Dad hates that it upsets her. I'm glad I did it but it's there under my skin every day, the hurt I caused them.' I sigh. 'I guess nothing comes without a price.'

'Now you're the one being cynical. I thought you were the optimist. Look, I didn't come here to argue. And I certainly don't need any complications.' Yanking his hand through his messy hair: 'But I've been unfair to you. You were right downstairs, you have worked hard. It's not your fault if I can't handle things.'

'Handle what things?'

He neatly sidesteps the question. 'I'm sorry for upsetting you.' His attention is caught by the pile of clothes heaped in the case, blue eyes zeroing in on a lacy red push-up bra. He inhales sharply, looking away. 'Of course, if you want to stay for the rest of the assignment you can.'

'Right.' I slide off the bed and absolutely nothing more comes out my mouth.

'You don't seem very happy,' he frowns. 'I thought you wanted to stay.'

I can understand his confusion. I should be biting his hand off. I should be overjoyed. It means I can stick to the plan. 'Do you *want* me to?' Where did that come from? A warning klaxon sounds in my head, telling me I'm too close to the edge.

'What does that matter?' he asks, pacing forward.

'Do you want–me–to–stay?' I demand, unable to hold the words safely inside. We're almost nose to nose. I'm still hanging onto the ties of my dress and my arm is aching something chronic.

'Of course I don't!' His admission stuns me into silence.

Ouch. 'Why?'

'Because.'

'Because I'm difficult?' I whisper, disappointment slashing through me.

He lets out a kind of growl and then, 'Not you! Keeping my hands off you. *This!*' Scooping me up, he kisses the breath out of me, hands moving to grip my face, tongue seeking mine.

Oh, *that.*

The clash of our mouths and bodies is fast and furious and my defences dissolve. I find the strength to yank my fingers from my dress ties and drive both hands into his hair, tunnelling into the soft spikiness, lost in darkness, holding onto him. My dress slides down to my waist and he breaks away to look down at my boobs swelling out of the strapless black bra.

'Beautiful,' he breathes.

I can't help it, I love the look in his eyes. Then he kisses me again, asking for even more, to go further. God, it feels so good. His body is so hot, like my own personal radiator. Sweat breaks out across my skin and I push his jacket off blindly, tearing his shirt from his trousers and wrenching it open. Groaning, he presses open-mouthed kisses down my neck, panting as I run my hands over his bare, slightly hairy chest, tracing jagged patterns.

My palms run over his toned pecs and abs, feeling the bumps and ridges.

He is so world-alteringly gorgeous. And so incredibly built.

Thinking doesn't feature. Lust tugs between my legs, tingles spreading outwards. Edging nearer, I push against his hard, glorious body, wanting to get closer, the ache of need throbbing at the back of my throat.

With a muffled groan, he reaches around and unzips my dress, shifting so it slithers to the floor. He grabs my thighs with big, hot hands and I wrap them around his waist. And then I'm pinned against the wall and he's kissing me again, igniting trails of fire in my blood.

My head goes back against the patterned wallpaper. I can't believe he wants me so much. My back arches, nipples springing to life. It feels like I'm unravelling and tightening at the same time. Alex pushes me higher, hips rocking urgently against me. I can feel how turned on he is and can't wait until he's inside me. Deep. Ruthless. Ready to thrill. His mouth travels down to suck at a sensitive spot under my ear, to nibble at my collarbone, moves to lick and then suck on a perky nipple through my bra. The pleasure and need is unbearable, torture.

'Ohhh ... yes, yes,' I call hoarsely, body temperature rocketing, sense of reason sliding away. I've never been so turned on in my life.

'Yes?' His voice is rough and he unhooks my bra, a shiver of delight speeding down my spine in immediate response. He tugs the material out the way. My body is shaking with excitement as Alex's tongue circles my nipple, then his hand is in my lacy black knickers, which are damp with wanting him and his clever fingers are strumming a rhythm that sends me into a shuddering mass of jelly in his arms, demanding release. He slips a long finger inside me and presses forwards and I yelp, then moan blissfully and bite his shoulder, skin slightly salty on my tongue. I want him to stop what he's doing with his hand so I can return the favour, but if he stops I might kill him. I think I'm going to ... 'Yes. Just there ... Ooohhhh. Alex.' Everything clenches, muscles spasm, shivers shoot up my spine, hot waves of orgasm hit and I fall apart, biting down harder on his shoulder.

'Wow,' I moan afterwards, dropping my head back against the wallpaper.

Taking a shaky breath, he slides his hand from my knickers and hoists me up and I lean in and kiss him, running my tongue along the edge of his bottom lip before biting gently. He jerks. At the same time, I run my hands down his unbelievable abs and unzip his trousers, slipping my hand inside his jockey shorts. He's up for it in every way that matters and I moan at the rock-solid feel of him pulsing beneath my fingers.

Trembling, his hands tighten round my hips. 'Charley Caswell, you are one sexy woman,' he says huskily.

The use of my fake name tweaks my conscience. He doesn't know who I am or why I'm here. I should stop. It's not fair on him. Then he pulses in my hand and my fingers close in response. Who am I kidding? 'Your turn now,' I say throatily, staring into his intense, blue eyes, and he suddenly flinches, body going bow-straight and still. I can feel the tension in his shoulders and arms.

'Stop,' he orders, voice barely there. 'No,' he says louder, pulling his hips away and releasing my legs so they slide down his. I'm left standing against the wall wearing only my knickers. 'Shit.' He runs a hand through his hair, nose flaring as the scent of sex rises between us. 'I'm sorry. I can't do this.'

'Alex,' I choke. 'You're going to stop now?' Pointing at the bulge in his trousers.

He flushes, picking up his shirt and shoving his arms into it. 'We shouldn't do this. We work together.'

I go cold, common sense flooding back. It sounds like a cop-out, but he's right. It doesn't make sense. I'm risking everything. He also has some obvious baggage. His reasons might be different to mine, but having sex would be a really bad idea. Still, the abrupt rejection kills, and doesn't prevent me wanting to launch myself at him and finish stripping him off for hot, dirty sex on the bedroom floor. I bite my tongue to hold back a moan, then inadequately cover my boobs with my hands. 'Can you...?'

'Sure,' he says crisply, passing my dress to me and deliberately staying as far away as possible. If he's not careful a girl could get a complex.

'Thanks.' Pulling it over my head and smoothing it down my body until the hem hits the floor, I cross my arms around my waist to hide my braless boobs. 'Can we talk?'

'No.' His face is shuttered and I hate it. 'I've got to go. Now,' he says grimly, fastening shirt buttons and bending over to put his shoes on. I don't even know when he took them off. My mouth falls open at the sight of his sexy bum bent over right in front of me. My hands clench in my dress. I will not touch him.

'It shouldn't have happened,' he plucks his bow tie off the bed. 'It was a mistake, a big one. I'm leaving. We've got an early start in the morning.'

'We have.' A queasy feeling settles in the pit of my stomach. This is embarrassing. A mistake? A big one? Even if I agree, he's making me feel like a heap of crap. 'And you're right,' I shoot out as he turns towards the door, 'it would be better if it hadn't happened. It was … crazy. But Alex, we're both adults. You don't have to run off as if I'm expecting you to propose marriage.'

He emits a sharp laugh, swinging round. 'If only you knew.'

'So, tell me.'

He hesitates, frowns. 'Can't, sorry.' Setting off towards the door again.

Hot colour floods my face, 'So I'm good enough to mess around with, but not to talk to?'

'Charley,' he recoils. 'It's complicated. I'm not in the market for a relationship. For anything. You wouldn't—'

'Understand? Nope. No way. You can't do better than that? Do you know what?' I shake my head, seething anger and sexual frustration driving me. 'Don't do me any favours.' Bucketing forward I grab his jacket and shove it at him, 'And don't let me keep you.'

He seems shocked, holding the jacket against him. 'Charley—'

'No. Off you go.' I can't remember the last time I felt so humiliated. I pretty much push him across the room, needing him out right this minute.

He opens the door and a growl escapes me when he pauses in the doorway. 'Wait.'

'What?'

'Before I leave…'

'Yes?'

Lowering his voice, 'I need to know that you won't tell anyone about this.'

I frown. 'What?'

He smooths down his dark hair, erasing the spikes caused by my frantic clutching when we were kissing. His sharp cheekbones are bright red, eyes darting over everything but me. He looks how I feel. 'You're making this harder than it has to be.'

'I apologise,' I say coldly, stepping back. 'Why don't you try explaining to me in words of one syllable what you mean. Maybe then I'll be able to follow.'

Rocking back on his heels, he shoves his hands in his pockets. 'Don't be like that. It's just – I have to exercise a certain amount of discretion because of my role, my reputation. I fight hard to keep my private life private. So, can I trust that this will stay between us?'

Understanding dawns, and with it, gut-turning disappointment. He doesn't trust me. It's upsetting on a number of levels, not only the one related to The Plan. 'Oh. Oh, wow. You're actually *asking* me not to tell anyone. Gee, thanks. What's the next step, get your lawyers involved and serve me with a gagging order?' The remark hits home because his cheekbones darken further. 'Alex, I feel sorry for you,' I say quietly, sweeping together some of my tattered dignity. 'That this is the world you live in. I don't think anyone could pay me enough to. Don't worry,' looking him up and down I raise an eyebrow, 'I'm not one of those kiss-and-tell girls. I definitely won't be telling anybody what just happened.'

'Do you mean that?' he grinds out.

'I told you earlier today, anything that happens this weekend I'll keep a secret.' I make sure to hold his gaze, let him read the sincerity in my eyes. I hope they're glowing at him. I hope they're scary glowy. I'm so bloody angry.

Letting out a whoosh of breath, he gives me a brief grateful smile. 'Thank you.'

For a bright guy, he's being *so* dumb. How can he not realise how badly he's just offended me?

'Don't thank me Alex,' using the most freezing tone I can manage, 'I'm only thinking of myself.'

He frowns. 'What do you mean?'

'Simple really. I wouldn't want anyone to know how incredibly stupid I've just been.'

An emotion I can't interpret flares in his eyes. 'Charley, hold on—'

'Good night.' It gives me overwhelming satisfaction to slam

the door in his face.

Stumbling across the room, I throw myself on the bed. 'You bloody idiot,' I mutter at myself. 'What the hell were you thinking? Remember why you're here!' Crawling under the covers, I can't stop the memories flooding in.

Chapter Fifteen

As I lurch into the flat after being suspended, dazed and dizzy, I feel like part of me has died. The fear sets in alongside the shameful humiliation. I slouch on the sofa and give in to it for endless hours while Jess is at work, staring dry-eyed at the wall, unable to compute what's happened.

When I realise I'm shaking with cold, shock and hunger I make myself move. Showering and pulling on a pair of jeans and a vest top, I force some soup down and call our Human Resources department, getting a copy of every relevant policy I can think of emailed to me. Pouring over them, I highlight paragraphs and make notes. Drinking strong, black coffee and pinning my hair back, I drag my disordered thoughts together and am interrupted only by one of the security guards arriving with my stuff.

'Thanks,' I say brightly, looking him straight in the eye. I won't be pitied, or act like someone who's already lost. 'I appreciate it.'

'No problem,' the man – one of Baz's new recruits, Ian – gives me a quizzical smile and I wonder if I look a little manic. 'Baz said it was important to get this to you,' he prompts nosily.

'It is. Thank you. Bye.' I slide my diary, files and notepads from his grasp and wait until he's trotted down the stairs before bumping the door closed with my hip. As I do, a piece of paper flutters to the floor and I sweep it up. The tears threatening all day finally spill over as I read the note.

Whatever it is, we're all rooting for you.

I let go for a few minutes then wipe the tears away and march into the kitchen, where I've set up camp at the table. If they're rooting for me I'd better get on with it.

Some time later, Jess slams in. 'What the hell is going on?' She throws her bag into the corner, stripping her coat off.

'Huh?' I look up from my diary, where I've been backtracking to all the times Tony has said or done anything inappropriate over the last few months, to write up a chronological sequence of events for the disciplinary investigation. It feels good to be doing something meaningful, taking control.

'I called the casino on my way home to see how you got on with sorting out Tony and they said you left this morning.' She sets her hands on her hips, temper written across her face. 'Then Kitty took me aside. Is it true?'

'What?' Sitting back in my chair.

'You've been suspended?'

'She shouldn't have told you that.'

'She's your friend as well as your colleague, and as if you wouldn't have told me.'

'Of course I would, but I wanted to tell you myself! Sorry.' Sucking in a breath: 'I didn't see any point in ruining your day too, so I was waiting for you to get home. That b—'

'Bastard Tony,' she finishes. 'Yes. What did he do?'

'He's accused me of sexual harassment—'

'He wishes! The little—'

'And bullying.' I rise to get fresh coffee started. 'They're taking it seriously. So I'm suspended until they've investigated and decided on an outcome.'

'Which will be that he's talking a load of crap.' She drops her hands from her hips and shakes her head. 'I don't know how you can be so calm.'

'I wasn't.' Handing her a chocolate biscuit from our heart-shaped tin: 'When I got home I was a total mess. Had a bit of a meltdown, then got it together.' Spooning sugar into her favourite mug, I pour hot water in and stir. 'I'm calmer now because I'm doing something about it. And I know it will be okay. Because they know me. And because I didn't do anything and he has no proof that I did.'

Thrusting the mug at her, as I say it I truly believe it.

'What?' I cry.

A young mum with a baby in a pushchair swerves sharply to avoid me, the crazed-looking redhead. 'What?' I repeat, moving off the path to sit down on the crisp green grass. 'And people believe him?'

I've escaped to the leafy surroundings of Hyde Park. After two days in the flat getting my paperwork in order and waiting for an invite to a disciplinary interview, the walls have started closing in on me. I'm worried about running into someone from work, in case they ask me questions, or worse, avoid me out of awkwardness, but I can't take it any more. Besides, if I'm as innocent as I keep telling myself, hiding away will only make people think I have a reason to be ashamed. I can't let anyone doubt me.

'People who know you don't,' Kitty answers gruffly in my ear.

'He has no right to say anything to anyone. This is all confidential. And what about people who don't know me?'

'Look, people always kind of think stuff goes on between bosses and their PAs. Just because it's the other way around doesn't mean they won't buy into it. How many films and books have you read about office romances? And you and Tony work closely together, you're stunning, and some people, *not* me, think he's not bad looking, in a blond chinless kind of way. It wouldn't be impossible you'd be involved.'

I close my eyes, chest tightening. 'Yes, but that I'd try and force him? That I'd bully him? This isn't *Indecent Exposure!*' I grab a handful of grass and hold onto it. 'I'm demanding as a boss, ask for loyalty and dedication, but I'm not like that.'

Kitty clears her throat. 'I know. Look, I have to go in a minute. I'm calling from work and the place is crawling, two guys I've never seen before and some woman from HR.' She hesitates. 'I'm saying the next bit as a friend and as someone who believes you. You have to realise it doesn't look good. You're gone and he's still here, so he can say what he wants.'

'Well I'll be putting a stop to that,' I say bitterly, clenching and unclenching my fingers in the grass 'HR are going to get it in the neck for letting him talk about any of this.'

'I don't blame you. But it might already be too late.'

I'm sure my heart stutters. 'What do you mean?'

'Shit, Charley,' she says feelingly. 'It's not just here they're talking about it. I had a call from Suzie at the Manchester site about an hour ago, and then Josh got a call from Aaron in Brighton. They've all heard about it. And then I got a text from my cousin Mel, who works at that investment bank in Canary Wharf. There's a bit of a buzz going round. She recognised your name.'

'Oh, God. Oh no.' I slump forward, forehead pressed against knees, tears leaking from the corner of my eyes. Years of my life, of tough grind, and my professional reputation, any hope of furthering a career in the City, all down the drain. Even if at some point it's proved I'm telling the truth, my name will be tainted. People will always think O*h yeah, isn't that the girl who...?* And even if they believe I didn't harass or bully him, there'll be those who wonder if an affair gone wrong was the root of the accusations.

'This is so unfair,' I explode, 'It'll be across the whole city in nanoseconds. I kept saying no. I told him to back off.'

'I'm so sorry,' Kitty murmurs, voice quickening. 'You know we all respect you.'

'Yeah.' I smile weakly as I think of the note from Baz. *We're all rooting for you.* 'I know.'

'I'll be a witness if you want,' she offers, 'I can tell them—'

'That you never saw anything? That no one did? He was careful, Kitty. He never did anything when anyone was around.' Letting go of the grass, I pull at the hem of my Asian-patterned maxi-dress. It's sunny today and my skin is warm, yet I've never felt colder inside. 'Thank you for the offer, really. For the show of solidarity, but there's no point in anyone else getting dragged through the process. And we shouldn't even be talking about this. It could get me in trouble.'

'I could give a character reference. Say what an amazing manager you are—'

'And he'll just say we're friends as well as co-workers. Please. I'll be fine,' I say briskly. 'You all need to get on with things, pretend I'm still there and ordering you around.'

'Okay, I get it. But rest assured, that pig won't get an easy ride from us.'

'That'll just give him extra ammunition that "bullying" towards him is widespread, and land you in it too. Don't give him that. Just be polite and professional, all right? I'm still your boss, so that's an order!'

'Yes, boss. I hear you.'

'Good,' I say softly. 'Thanks for the call. Now, get back to work.'

'Take care of yourself. Hope to see you soon.'

'You too.' You have no idea how much. Ending the call, I lie down on the grass, seething.

The disciplinary interview three days later initially goes well. The appointed investigator, Mitchell, an American senior manager from one of the southern casinos, listens as I tell him my view, staying calm but getting my point across. I detail the events that unfolded, my responses, and utterly deny all allegations of either sexual harassment or bullying. I answer all his questions honestly and pray the sincerity shines from my eyes.

But one thing becomes abundantly clear during the interview.

As much as I wrote down what was happening and how I handled the matter, I can't prove that it's what happened. My phone conversation with HR for advice was anonymous – and I curse myself for my pride, because at least I'd be able to show I was having problems with him if I'd given my name – and my only notes are in my diary, which, as Mitchell points out, I could have written at any time.

'How do you explain them being in different-coloured pens?' I say, losing my cool.

'I take your point,' he remarks, 'but you could still do that retrospectively.' Pushing a sheet of paper towards me, 'Now can you comment on this please?'

Casting my eyes over the list of times and dates: 'What is this?'

'A call log from HR. A record of durations of phone calls between Mr Ferrier and HR Advisers.'

I flinch. 'What do you mean?'

'This,' he slides a bundle of paper-clipped pages over, 'is a rough transcript of file notes of those conversations. Taken in real time, with dates on them. Mr Ferrier has agreed that these can be shared with you for the purposes of the investigation.'

'I bet he has,' I hiss, flipping through them. The bastard. Every time we had a run-in, any time I gave him advice to leave it alone, he called HR. Five conversations in which he names himself and states his manager's behaviour is stressing him out, that she's making him uncomfortable, that she's making unreasonable requests and advances. That he doesn't know what to do because he doesn't want to lose his job.

Shoulders slumping, I look at Mitchell. 'What do you expect me to say? It's all lies.'

But it's tangible evidence, I know that.

'Is that your formal response?' Mitchell scrawls something in his notepad.

'I suppose so,' I whisper, pole-axed. Tony planned this. He made sure he had a back-up plan. Right down to looking so concerned after the evening he put his hands on me in the file room. Bruised me. He apologised so I'd calm down, not call someone right away. So he could get to them first. He played me. I just don't know why. Because I rejected him?

'It looks like we're done for today,' Mitchell says. 'Unless you have any questions or anything further to add. Do you want me to run through what happens next?'

'No,' I say numbly, lips tingling. 'I know what the options are.' Action or no action. Back to work or disciplinary hearing. And after this I have a horrible feeling which one it'll be.

The investigator sees me out. If it's any consolation, he looks sympathetic. Not that sympathy will make any difference to the outcome. He will have to make a recommendation based on what the facts appear to tell him.

And nine days later I have my answer, darting out of a three-hour disciplinary hearing holding my hand over my mouth as I barrel into the back of the first taxi I can hail. Holding it together in the meeting room cost me, jaw clenched to stop from crying out, only able to nod my understanding of the outcome.

On the balance of probabilities it is reasonable for the panel to form a view that something untoward occurred and the allegations are therefore proven. Given your position in the company and the breach of trust and confidence in the contractual relationship, our decision is to summarily dismiss you without notice. A letter detailing the outcome and your right of appeal will be sent to you within five working days.

It was awful. The death of hope. But worse was Tony's smirk at me when no one was looking. What the hell have I done to him to make him go this far?

My P45 arrives a week later but I ignore it, too busy lodging an appeal against the decision. I can't say the process was unfair, but I put a letter together stating I've done nothing untoward, and although I can see that Tony has more evidence than I do, I have a previously clear disciplinary record and a reputation for being a fair manager within the company. Plus no one actually saw or heard me do anything to him, so how can they prove I did? Sending my appeal grounds off, I wait for the invitation to the appeal hearing.

It's worse than the first hearing. There's no new evidence and the appeal panel simply review the original panel's decision based on the information to hand … and then Tony gets teary, exclaiming how much this has affected him, how mortifying it's been to reveal he's been harassed by a woman senior to him, how he's had to seek counselling for depression.

'What?' I spring out of my chair. 'This is ridiculous!'

Tony flinches away, gripping the edge of the table and keeping his eyes downcast as if too scared to look at me.

Everyone on the panel – two men and a woman, strangers – and others in the room glare in disgust at my outburst and its apparent impact on their quaking employee.

I can feel what's coming. Tears scorch my eyes and my neck goes hot and itchy. I won't give him the satisfaction of crying in front of everyone.

'Apologies,' I announce. 'But I think I'm done. Obviously nothing I say will matter when I'm contending with this,' pointing at Tony's theatrics. 'And I won't sink that far.' I stare at the panel members in turn and none of them looks away, they're so sure I've done wrong. 'I understand the facts appear to say one thing, but if you knew me, how passionate I am about the company and what I've given over the years, and if you could see through him,' I gesture at Tony with my chin, 'you'd know the truth would speak another. Thank you all for your time.'

Spinning on my black stilettos, I tug my suit jacket down, eyes burning as I fling the door open. Launching myself down the corridor, only a firm hand on my arm stops me breaking into a run.

'Wait.'

'What?'

Mitchell, the investigator, at the hearing to answer the panel's questions, looks down at me. 'I'm sorry.'

'What for?'

'You were credible. I never said you were lying when I presented the case. Just that the evidence against you was stronger.'

'What good is that? It doesn't change anything.' My face screws up. 'Doesn't change what I've lost.'

'I wanted you to know.' He checks the door behind him. 'I have to investigate the facts, and present them as I find them.' He looks torn, brown hair neatly combed down, tie perfectly straight, but fingers of both hands rubbing anxiously together.

I soften minutely. He's making sense. 'I know. But as I said, it means nothing now.' My nose tingles. Tears aren't far off. 'Goodbye.'

'I work for the company. I'm in a tight spot,' his voice follows me as I exit into the stairwell.

Not as tight as the spot I'm in, I think, erupting into sobs as I clatter down the stairs, barely able to believe how my career with Ionian Casinos is ending.

Securing proper work after that's impossible. Raising a tribunal claim doesn't help, because word gets back to Tony and he and his friends call all the reputable agencies and main employers in central London, telling them I was fired for gross misconduct and the reasons why. It's clear he wants me gone and forgotten, but I can't let it go without one last try, if for nothing more than the reason that he could do this again and wreck someone else's life. So I lodge the claim, pay my fee and wait for my day in court, if it gets that far.

But in the meantime the job search is lousy. The most recent reference I can provide has *dismissed for GM* under Reason for Leaving and it's not one employers look for in prospective employees. So I stop using it, and my failure to provide a current satisfactory reference is the killer. It's competitive enough in the recession, with the labour market so buoyant with redundant people, that without a reference my chances are slim, if not downright skinny.

After a month I start leaving the years at the casino off applications, writing that I was unemployed, but then I don't have the experience required to show I'm suitable for the jobs I want. Desperate, I take cash-in-hand gigs, dropping off leaflets, delivering food for shabby takeaways, pulling the night shift and trudging into the flat at 3.00 a.m. It's soul-destroying, and salary-wise nowhere near what I've been on. Some days I can barely scrape myself off the mattress I feel so down. I fall behind with bills, which isn't an issue at first, juggling things around, making minimum payments to credit cards, slicing out luxuries like the gym, turning down invitations to night outs. Still, it only takes two months before things get sticky financially. And during that time, when it's clear conciliation isn't a possibility, the tribunal service writes to me, telling me my case will be heard but that the other side have requested a postponement to prepare their case, which has been granted. While it gives me more time to prepare, too, it also means more waiting. There's only so long I can hang on for, and one day in a fit of despair I hit on the idea of registering with agencies under a different name, using the internal reference John wrote for me when I applied for his job. Removing the reference from the company letterhead and putting it on a blank sheet of paper with his personal address on, I know there's little risk of them contacting him, because he and his wife spend their time abroad on cruises. The deception feels wrong but it's necessary.

Life continues in a cycle of desperation and near-misses, of eating beans and recycling clothes and scraping together pennies from the back of the sofa. The day I face what an absolute mess I'm in comes too soon.

'I have to tell you something,' I turn to Jess, pulling on an oversized navy hoody ready for my pizza-delivery job. Looking unattractive is a must when you're a woman rolling up at people's doors unaccompanied. You never know who you're going to face.

'Uh-oh, sounds serious,' she answers, head stuck in the fridge hunting for dinner ingredients.

'It is. I don't know how to say it, though.' I tie the laces on the ratty trainers I bought from a charity shop after selling my expensive ones.

'Just say it.' She backs out and drops some cheese and ham on the side, pulling a carton of eggs from the overhead cupboard.

'I can't pay my half of the mortgage this month,' I rush. 'I'm so sorry. I've tried everything; extending my overdraft, getting a loan, selling stuff. But I'll give you everything I've got.'

'Charley—' She steps towards me, holding up her hands.

'I gave you cash for the bills last week and thought I'd make enough this week,' I rabbit, 'but the pizza place dropped two of my shifts. They can do that because I'm only a casual worker. And—'

'Charley, stop. Stop!' Hugging me tight, she whispers into my ear, 'Take it easy. Don't do this to yourself. I can cover it for a while, I have some savings. I have faith you'll get a decent job soon.'

'Thanks. But you're my friend,' I sniff into her neck, holding her desperately, feeling so, so sad, heart aching. 'Not my bank.'

Pulling away, she mock punches me. 'Too right. I won't charge you two thousand four hundred and thirty-seven per cent interest for a start.'

'I'll pay you back,' I promise fiercely.

'You will,' she smiles, 'because I'd hate to have to come after you and break those beautiful long legs of yours.'

Sticking my tongue at her, I grab my keys off the side. 'Thank you, Jess. I really mean it. It's more than—'

'Hey, enough. Chin up, shoulders back. You have pizzas to deliver, remember. Which reminds me,' she rifles through her rucksack, stacking her pupils' books on the side for marking later. 'I picked these up for you today,' chucking a personal alarm and a torch across the kitchen. Of course, I miss them and she sighs as they clatter to the floor. 'One day your clumsiness is really going to be a problem.'

'Yeah. But at least I've always manage to control it at work.' My face drops. 'Not a problem at the moment, obviously.'

'Go,' she shoves me out the door, 'and I want a pizza with anchovies brought home for breakfast.'

'Yuck!' But her request has the desired effect and I tuck my sadness away.

Over the next few weeks the balance in our relationship shifts and doesn't feel right. Apart from when I go home for Christmas, I spend a lot of my time in the fragrant pizza delivery van contemplating my future. Jess can only keep us both afloat for another month at best and I can't ask my parents for money, can't admit the depth of my problems. If I move home it's better they think I chose to, rather than knowing I had to. It might be time for me to call them. Tomorrow, I decide, Friday night after their habitual fish-and-chip supper. Heartbreaking, but necessary.

The next afternoon my friend Amy calls, saying she can get me alongside someone useful for a weekend. It's someone who might be able to help me, who has the power to rectify the wrongs done, if I can convince them to listen and to believe that Tony is a liar and a fake. Someone who might make the tribunal claim against Ionian Casinos unnecessary.

Alex Demetrio, CEO.

Chapter Sixteen

DAY THREE

– Sunday –

Now

I drop my towel, tugging on underwear, followed by a white top with a formal grey trouser suit, pairing it with my favourite red stilettos. I'm still seething about Alex's behaviour last night but, yanking a brush through my hair, I can't decide if I'm angrier with him or myself. Him for being so insensitive, me for losing all brain power and fooling around with him in the first place. I hardly know him and I let him put his hand down my knickers. That's not my thing at all. My hand stills. No, it's not. So Alex is different.

Damn it.

Jess is right. I *do* like him; the guy he is when he forgets to be Mr Uptight CEO. And since that first moment on Friday, the physical attraction has been a current so strong, swimming against it has been exhausting. Last night it was go with it or risk drowning. It was well worth the pay-off physically, but look how it ended.

God. How could I have been so stupid, given how much I have

to lose? I might have compromised everything with my lack of willpower.

He said I could stay. All I had to do was say thank you gracefully and keep my hands to myself. But I couldn't manage it. When he kissed me I lost all sense of myself, my priorities, the reality of my life, Plan B. All for a guy I've barely known for thirty-six hours.

Shit.

Can I really go to Alex now and tell him about Tony? Ask him for his help, ask him to believe that Tony is the bad guy, ask him to settle out of court so we don't have to go to a tribunal? He's so cynical and mistrustful of women, surely he'll either think I was willing to sleep with him to get him on side or that I *was* having a thing with my ex-assistant. Because if I would have slept with him, why wouldn't I have slept with Tony?

I'm not going to know until I see him again, until I gauge what he thinks of me. But I've got to face it; I've potentially blown the plan, gained nothing that will help secure my future, only a sum of money that will help repay some of my debts. The whole weekend may have been for nothing.

There's only one way to find out if that's the case or not.

Grabbing my bag, I stick my head out my bedroom door to see if Alex is in the lounge. No sign of him. Putting my game face on, I close the door behind me and sail across the room, knocking at his bedroom door. 'Alex? Al–ex?' No answer. I glance at the clock above the mini-bar. We're almost late for the first meeting. I knock again, and then a third time. 'Alex?' Nothing.

What if something's happened to him? What if he's had a heart attack from the stress and long hours? It can happen to the young as well as the old. My chest squeezes with panic, even though I absolutely should not care. Bugger it. I bang on the door with the flat of my hand then thrust it open, all but falling into the room.

I jump back, shocked, as Alex spins around from a spot by the window across the massive bedroom. He's dressed in nothing but a pair of tight jockey shorts, talking rapidly into his phone, frowning darkly.

God, what a body. Perfection.

I go straight into reverse, backing into the lounge, but he gestures me to stay put. Huffing, I lean against the door frame, making a huge effort to focus on the view outside the window, instead of the one inside. If ever a man was built for the screen or ad campaigns it's him. I can't help peeping at the phenomenal body I had glimpses of last night. Super-defined, hair-roughened upper body, long muscular thighs, gorgeous toned bum in the clingy underwear ... My palms are itching to touch it all. *No, enough. Don't go there.* Pretend *it* didn't happen.

'Tell her no,' Alex hisses down the phone, 'I won't do that.' He pads across the room towards me. 'I'm really late,' he tells the caller. 'I have to go.'

He's too close. Inhaling his fresh clean scent is unavoidable and something goes ping in my pelvis. He sucked my nipples and gave me an orgasm less than eight hours ago. Oh boy. I try to edge out of the room again, but am stopped by Alex's ferocious glare. Does he really have to keep me here, in sight of *that* body? Is this some sort of torture for slamming the door in his face? Because it's working. I'm biting my lip to stop from drooling. Focusing on the ceiling helps, along with singing a little ditty in my head *dum de dum dee dee.*

'Then call her bluff,' Alex bites, his tone dragging my gaze to his face, which has grown pale, dark stubble visible in contrast. He expels a harsh breath. 'Well, we'll see won't we? Speak later. Bye.' Throwing the phone onto the bedside table, he rushes over to the mirrored wardrobe. 'Sorry,' he mutters, 'I don't usually run late.' He grabs a suit and shirt off hangers.

'It's fine. Is, ah, everything okay?' I shouldn't care, but he looks so stressed I feel sorry for him.

'Huh?' He gives me a black, glowering look – Heathcliff, eat your heart out – and shakes his head. 'No!' He takes a deep breath. 'I mean, thanks, but don't worry about it. It's personal. Therefore not your problem.'

Ouch, if that isn't a knock-back I don't know what is. Me slamming the door in his face hasn't caused him any regret. If it had, he'd be willing to confide in me. Then I remind myself of the cold facts. He's not my friend, he's my boss. *Grow up, Charley, he doesn't owe you anything. He doesn't have to tell you anything. And you shouldn't want to know. Not if you're still sticking with the plan.*

'In that case,' I say stiffly, 'can I wait in the lounge please?'

'No, stay. Run through the schedule, remind me who we're seeing when.'

'I'd rather not, when you're—' pointing at his bare chest.

He glances over at me. 'Please, we haven't got time for this.' He looks pained. Hauling on his trousers, he zips and buttons them. 'Just tell me.'

'Fine.' Taking a deep breath, I turn my back and recite the meeting times from my notepad over one shoulder.

'Thank you.'

'Are you done now?' I ask, stuffing the pad back into my bag.

'Almost.'

Craning my neck, I peer over my shoulder. His shoes are on and his shirt is three-quarters done up. 'Thank god for that,' I mumble.

'Pardon?' He looks up, fingers on the last button.

'Nothing.' I clear my throat, eyes fixed on the bed he slept in last night, after he did naughty things to me and – *stop it.*

'Are you okay?' he asks.

'Yes, thanks,' I croak. Nothing a full memory wipe wouldn't cure.

'Charley?' Alex straightens his tie knot, pulls the suit jacket on. 'About last night—'

'We need to go. We're already late for the first meeting,' I rattle, looking over his shoulder, scared he'll read too much in my face.

'I know,' he mutters, shoving his phone in his pocket, 'and with a blinding hangover I'm hardly looking forward to work, but this will only take thirty seconds.'

'Thirty seconds we don't have. Let's go.' He doesn't look

hung-over. Tired yes, with the bags under his eyes, but otherwise he looks as polished as usual. Marching into the lounge, I hear him follow.

'I didn't mean to insult you. I just had to check.' He slaps a hand against the door above my head, whispers in my ear, making my heart pound.

Anger rockets. I give the door an almighty tug and he releases it. 'I don't want to talk about this now, Alex.'

'There are reasons I have to be careful.'

I step into the hallway and turn to him, the insensitive way he acted spinning back on me. 'You're right. You said. You have a rep to protect, right? Who knows who might get the wrong idea, leak it to the press? *The CEO and the Temporary PA*,' I add ironic quote marks with crooked double fingers, 'imagine that on the front page of the tabloids.'

'Stop it.' He jerks me back into the suite by my wrist before dropping it as if burned.

Ignoring the scald of his touch sparking all the way down to my toes, 'Silly me, I apologise. Talking in the corridor is probably too public for you.' I regret it as soon as it's out.

'You're angry, I understand that. In hindsight I could have handled it better. That doesn't mean we can't—'

'No thanks, no repeats, I'm not going there again.'

His eyes narrow. 'Actually I wasn't offering. I was going to say it doesn't mean we can't work together for the time left.'

He's offering the perfect opportunity to move on, so it's not disappointment filling me, it's relief. It is. 'Great. Good. Let's get on with it then.'

'Good.' He slams the door behind him then winces, putting his hands to his head.

I can't help it. As cross as I am, a tiny smile steals across my face.

'It's not nice to take pleasure in other people's pain,' he rasps, then ruins it by giving me a self-deprecating, crooked smile in return.

'I know,' I reply. 'But I'm guessing you've not had many hang-overs in your life.'

He shakes his head carefully, 'No'

'And maybe I'm *not* nice,' I add.

His blue eyes heat up. 'Oh, I think you are.'

'Shows how much the alcohol has addled your brain then,' I say lightly, hurrying down the corridor to call the lift. I cannot fall any further under his irritating but oh-so-exhilarating spell.

An indeterminate amount of time later, I'm ready for escape. And if this is how I feel, God knows what state Alex is in. We've done five back-to-back meetings and there are four more excruciating, energy-sapping ones left to go.

The effort expended on ignoring him is costing me. No matter how much I focus on typing notes into his laptop, every time I glance at him, hear the confidence in his voice, every shift of his mega-hot body, even the smell of his aftershave, triggers the memory of what we did against my bedroom wall. The fact he's sitting in the chair we shared the kiss on yesterday doesn't help. Neither does the fact that when he sat down in it earlier I could see the same burning awareness in his eyes.

'Did you get that last bit, Miss Caswell?' Alex's voice reels me back to the present.

'Of course, Mr Demetrio.' I read the last sentence back to him. Is he trying to catch me out?

'Excellent. Thanks.' He turns to the last of the morning's managers. 'I think we're done, Mr Reilly.' He shakes the man's hand. 'Time for lunch.'

'Yes, sir,' the man replies in an attractive Irish lilt, smiling over at me with even white teeth when I glance up. Jess has a thing for accents; she'd love this guy.

Alex glowers at me across the table, so I focus on saving the document and shutting the laptop down. I don't know what his problem is. Maybe it's his hangover. Closing the laptop lid, I pelt out of the room, intending to search for food and respite from his disturbing presence. The plan fails on both counts because when confronted by an array of delicious Mediterranean dishes, the desire to eat curls up and dies, and I turn away with only a small bowl of green salad to find Alex heading straight towards me holding a heaped plate of food, expression intent.

'We need to finish our conversation.' He follows me to a table, sitting down uninvited. He digs into a steaming pasta dish, appetite seemingly unaffected by his hangover or any emotional turmoil.

'Sorry, I'm on a break.'

He finishes a mouthful, giving me a searching look. 'Yes, but this isn't about work.'

'I'm not...' I lower my voice as we attract attention from nearby tables, including a number of employees from this morning's meetings, 'I won't talk about this here.'

'I agree, which is why we're going to the suite when we've finished lunch.' He forks up more fragrant pasta, the ripe smell of sun-dried tomato sauce wafting across the table.

I lean back, 'I don't know how you can eat that with a hangover.'

'I just feel really,' his attention drops to my chest, 'really, hungry.' I push aside the lurch of lust in my stomach. 'And don't avoid the topic,' Alex growls. 'Upstairs. Ten minutes.'

'Don't order me around!' I flare. 'And besides, some things are better left unsaid. We're out of here tomorrow. We won't have to see each other again.' It's not a question, so it's weird my voice rises at the end.

Alex sets his cutlery down, 'You're right. We won't have to.'

He's agreeing with me, so I should be pleased. Instead it cuts. 'Then there's nothing to talk about.'

A member of his staff sits down at the next table, so he lowers his voice. 'I still want you to hear me out.'

'I'll think about it.'

'I wouldn't expect anything less,' he replies po-faced.

'Are you laughing at me?' I ask suspiciously.

'Wouldn't dare, I'd be too scared,' he drawls, then gives me a small amused smile and devours the last few mouthfuls of food, peering at me through long, dark lashes.

Bugger, he's more gorgeous than ever. Is it because he's even further out of reach, or because I know how clever his hands and mouth are? 'I can't imagine you being scared of anything,' I say, to distract myself from his physical appeal.

'You'd be surprised,' he frowns. 'Aren't you going to have that?' Gesturing at my untouched salad with his fork.

'Not hungry. I'll grab a snack during tea break.'

'Make sure you do. I wouldn't want you fainting on me, we've got lots to do today. Speaking of which, I've agreed to fit in an extra meeting, so we may finish later than planned. Sorry.'

More time in his company, fantastic. 'Whatever you need. You're the boss. As long as you're not going to spring another party on me.' I shut up as I remember how last night's party ended. With stuff fantasies are made of.

Alex seems lost in thought too, then clears his throat and shifts in his seat. 'You're still doing a good job.'

'Thanks. I wondered if you thought so after the way you asked where I was up to.'

'That was only because we were going so fast. I was worried your hands would cramp. Stuart's do.'

I'm touched. It's nice.

'You didn't think I was trying to catch you out because you slammed the door in my face last night?' he demands.

'No!' I squirm.

He leans forward, tanned hands sliding across the tablecloth towards me. I look down at them. Thinking of what they did to me. 'Business is business, Charley. Anything else is separate. I don't let personal feelings colour my working relationships. I'm better than that.'

'You're a robot then, or a saint, if you can switch off your emotions that way. It must be lovely to compartmentalise so easily,'

I say sweetly, pissed off at him but not sure why. 'Tell me,' I goad, forgetting where we are, forgetting I should be trying to get back in his good books, 'does your halo ever slip?'

A nerve pulses in his jaw, 'You know it does.'

'I do?'

'You were there last night when it did.'

'Oh?'

'In your bedroom. Against the wall.' His voice goes that rock-star husky again.

I squeeze my thighs together. 'So I was,' my voice climbs, 'but are you referring to before, during or after?'

'You're still annoyed.' His fingers wrap around mine, stroking them, drawing me in. 'Whatever you say about forgetting it, we have to talk. In private.'

Why is he touching me like this in public? He's just making it harder. My chair scrapes along the marble floor as I reclaim my hands and push away from the table. I can't give in to this. 'Far as I'm concerned there's nothing to discuss. So if it's about your privacy again, what I said stands,' I whisper. 'I don't intend to tell anyone, ever.'

'Charley.' Alex springs from his chair and sways, going pale green.

'I'll see you in the meeting room later. I need to go and clear my head.' I catch sight of an open-mouthed employee sitting at the table next to us, shamelessly eavesdropping. 'And as for your privacy, guess that was an epic fail, huh?'

Alex follows my eye line and glares at the man, who immediately finds something riveting to study on the opposite side of the room. It would be comical if I wasn't so desperate to get away.

My luck is out. Recovering, Alex skirts the table and wraps a hand around my elbow, towing me over to the window, our backs to the audience. 'See what I mean?' he says roughly. 'I have no privacy. And everything seems to make my life more complicated.'

'Am I supposed to feel sorry for you? To empathise with a

billionaire with properties around the world, no worries about job security or money, no commitments tying you down?'

'No commitments?' Pinching the bridge of his nose, Alex blinks. 'What do you know? What would you call running a high-profile company? It's constant, twenty-four seven. There's always someone or something calling on my time, somewhere I have to go, some place I have to be. Added to which I have a—' He stops, the sentence hanging in the air between us.

'What?' I'm intrigued, my temper slinking away. This is the real man, the honest one behind the corporate image. We all wear masks. Some people just wear them better than others.

'Nothing. It's nothing you need to know about.' Yanking his mobile from his jacket pocket as it makes a beeping sound, he reads a text. Swears. Curls his fingers around the gadget like he'd crush it. Rubbing his neck, he stares broodingly out the window.

It makes me feel bad for him. 'I'm sorry if I've made assumptions about your life,' I offer, 'but it's only because I don't really know about it.'

'Why would you?' He turns his attention back to the phone to re-read the screen and mutters absently under his breath, 'You're only a temporary employee.'

Ouch. I suck in a sharp breath, his comment unexpectedly painful.

'Of course I am,' I reply in a carefully modulated tone. The Queen would be so proud. 'Well, I have an important call to make,' I fib easily. But then I'm used to lying. To Alex, to myself. 'I'll see you at the next meeting.'

'Hmmm?' He barely knows I'm here while he taps out a text.

'That is so rude,' I mumble under my breath. Talking louder: 'See you in a bit.'

'Yes. Fine.'

I leave him by the window, dark head bent over his phone. It makes him look lonely and I wonder how many genuine emotional connections he has in his life; ones that aren't business-related.

It doesn't matter. I can't be part of his world. So I don't know why his comment about me being a temporary employee hurts, like I've lost a treasure that was almost within reach.

No. I'm being an idiot. A romantic fool.

Once I'm back in the suite I lock the interconnecting door to the lounge and lie on my bed with an icy cold flannel over my face, hoping the shock will bring sensible Charlotte back. Hoping the plan can still be salvaged.

Chapter Seventeen

There's a knock on the door a few minutes later. Bolting up, I fling the flannel into the bathroom and go to the door.

'Charley, I know you're in there. Come out please, we need to talk.'

'Can we do it later please?' I put a hand against the grain of the wood.

'I'm sorry I was rude earlier, burying my nose in the phone,' he says softly, and my face burns. He heard my mumbled comment. 'But I expect you in the lounge in two minutes,' he insists, voice hardening.

The way he speaks makes me think if I don't come out he'll come in, forcibly if necessary.

'Fine.' Wrenching the door open, I charge smack into Alex's broad chest. We untangle ourselves in a flurry of arms and muttered apologies.

'Sit down,' he orders.

I stand, arms crossed.

Rolling his eyes. 'Oh. Right. You don't like orders. *Please*?'

'Do we have time for this?' I perch on the edge of the sofa cushion.

He checks his watch. 'Twenty minutes. I don't think our conversation about last night can wait until later.'

'Go on then.'

Studying my blank face, he heaves a short sigh. 'Firstly, I'm sorry if I upset you. You know I've got stuff going on but I should have paid more attention to what I was saying. I didn't mean to be disrespectful.' He rubs his face.

'Thank you,' I reply, somewhat mollified. 'But does being a temporary employee mean I'm a second-class citizen or what?'

In the act of taking off his suit jacket and throwing it on a chair, he freezes, eyes zeroing in on me. 'Don't be silly.' A disbelieving smile kinks the corner of his mouth, 'Why would you say that?'

I shrug, feeling oddly caught out, 'I don't know,' my gaze skitters away, 'it was the way you said it. Only a temp.' Am I making a big deal out of nothing? He was just stating a fact. 'It doesn't matter.'

Unfreezing, Alex prowls over and sits on the other sofa, at right angles to me. 'It does matter, you saying it makes it matter. Tell me, Charley.' He scoots forward until he can peer into my face. 'You know I care a great deal about my privacy. But it's not that. I don't think it's appropriate to offload my personal problems onto my staff, even agency ones. It would be unfair. They need to see me confident, not confused. Otherwise what would...' His white teeth click together.

'What?' I lean forward despite myself.

'It doesn't matter,' he repeats, shifting back on the sofa.

'It does matter, you saying it makes it matter,' I echo his comment.

He exhales, eyes twinkling. 'Very good, you got me.'

'So?' Crossing my legs, I think about taking my shoes off but mustn't get too comfortable. 'Tell me. They need to see you confident, not confused, otherwise what would what?' Prodding, 'What would people think, what would they do? Have you ever wondered if you worry too much about what people think? Image isn't everything.' Remembering his hasty exit last night, 'Or is that it? Why you left like that, what the request to not tell anybody was about? You're worried about people knowing you got hot and heavy with a lowly staff member?'

'Yes!' Alex admits.

Stunned, I fall silent, mouth open.

'But not like that,' he explains. 'It's nothing to do with you being junior. I don't think of any staff as lowly. I respect them, I'm glad of the hours and effort they put in, their passion and energy. Wow, I must really be off my game if you think—'

'I don't. Not really,' I confess. Though he can be arrogant, I can't pretend he's some high-handed bastard, even if it would make it easier not to like him.

Nodding to accept my admission he goes on, 'It's about me flouting the "no workplace relationship" policy, Charley. It wouldn't do my credibility much good, would it? I had my work cut out when I introduced the clause into the contracts a few years ago. In fact it got quite divisive. So if it was publicised that I wasn't sticking to it, there would be one hell of a backlash.'

'If it's been that troublesome, why have the clause?'

'As I said yesterday, I think it offers the best level of protection for people.'

Except it didn't protect me from Tony, I think bitterly, rage bubbling up as I think of what he did.

'You've gone pale.' Alex looks concerned. 'Are you okay?'

'Yes. I probably should have eaten properly, like you said. Please don't say I told you so,' I add.

He smiles crookedly, eyes crinkling, and my hormones sizzle. 'I won't.' He goes to the bar and returns with a sealed packet. 'Ginger biscuits. It's not much but it might help.'

'Thanks.' I'm touched, more than I should be. I take the packet with care to avoid making physical contact with him.

There's a silence between us as I nibble on a biscuit. 'Maybe you could retrain as an air steward,' I muse after a moment, forgetting myself.

'Pardon? Why would I need to?'

Pointing at him with the edge of a biscuit, 'You might enjoy

159

doing something else. You don't seem happy being CEO.'

He rockets off the sofa and marches to the window, shoving unsteady hands into his pockets, staring outside. 'You're wrong. It's something else bothering me.'

'Maybe, but I don't think I am wrong.' Rising from the sofa, I slope over to him, afraid he might bolt. 'I'm sorry. I shouldn't have said that. But I did. And sometimes it's better to face things head-on. You don't like what you do, don't enjoy running the company.'

'I told you, I won't confide in employees.' The angle of his head changes, arms going angular and stiff.

'You already did last night. About me running away to the city. *Some of us don't have the luxury to do what we want*. And down-stairs, *it's constant, twenty-four seven*.' I want to stroke the back of his neck, offer him comfort. I can't. 'And I won't be an employee after this weekend.' What the hell am I saying? Am I nuts?

'But what if I offer you an ongoing assignment?' he challenges. 'What if I'm so impressed I tell the agency you should stay on somewhere? Are you going to give that up just in case something *might* happen between us, when I've already told you I can't get involved?'

Rather than my mouth watering at his gorgeousness, this time it's at the prospect of continuing work. I could stay in the city, with Jess. Get my old life back.

He must see the greed in my eyes. 'See? You'd want it. And I can't get involved, especially with someone I work with. It just messes everything up. I won't perpetuate one mistake with another.'

'Oh. I'm a mistake.' A mess to be cleaned away. Like I was for Tony. 'I get it.'

'You don't.' Spinning around he glowers at me. 'You don't understand anything.' His voice breaks. 'Why would you? We lead completely different lives.'

Frustration bursts to life hot and fast. 'So help me understand.'

'You don't know the consequences—'

'Of what? What do you think I'm going to do? Are we back

160

to privacy again, is this where you whip out the gagging order?'
I shake my head, 'You hide behind your clause and your professional reputation as an excuse. But I think it's about sharing part of yourself with someone else. You don't like people getting too close.'

'You're wrong.'

'Am I?'

'It's not a fear of intimacy.' He flashes back. 'I'm not some commitment-shy teenager. Give me more credit than that.'

'For God's sake, what is it then?'

'I just don't want to let anyone down!'

'Why would you? How could you possibly let anyone down by trying to have a normal life?'

'Because then that's all I might want!'

His anguish shuts us both up.

After a moment he admits. 'You're right, okay? I hate my job, I'm not happy. Being good at something doesn't mean you love it.' He looks pained, and then as if ripped from him: 'I do it because I have to. It's my responsibility. But there are so many things I miss out on. I don't have any hobbies, I do nothing for fun. The closest I get is running on the treadmill and lifting weights whilst listening to business reports on my earphones. I feel completely out of touch with the real world. I've got no idea what programmes are popular and I can't remember the last time I read a book.' He stops, looking horrified. 'This is bullshit. I've got nothing to complain about. A lot of people would kill to be in my position. Listen to me,' he mocks, 'the ungrateful rich guy who wants to escape his money-padded cell.'

Even if I didn't feel the wild magnetism to him, he's a person in torment. 'You feel guilty because you don't want it,' I attempt to console him with words, 'but that's okay. Everyone should be able to choose their own lives. It's normal to feel hemmed in if that's not the case.'

'Maybe.'

'Freedom is one of the most important rights a person has,

Alex, you only get one chance at this funny old world. The question is whether you can do something to change your situation.'

'Could you walk away from everything you are? Could you let your family down, abandon your responsibilities?'

'I feel like I already did. I didn't fit into my parents' plan for me when I came to London. I've always felt like a disappointment for being career-minded and doing my own thing.' Traipsing to the sofa, I sit down.

Alex follows, standing above me, hands on lean hips. I make sure I look at his face rather than the dangerous area in my direct eye line.

'There's nothing wrong with being ambitious,' he replies. 'And why wouldn't somebody as bright as you want to use their brain? Despite your occasional clumsiness, you're the type of person who could set their mind to anything and be successful. You're attractive, confident, quick. I know I'm impressed.' He sits down on the sofa.

His unexpected comments warm me, soothing the sore spot ripped open by Tony's recent actions. It's the rawness most of us have, the little voice whispering insidiously that we're not good enough and never will be. 'Thank you,' clearing my throat, 'and did what I said help?'

'Maybe. I'll think about what you said. If only you could help solve some of my other problems.' He chuckles darkly.

'Like the woman who texted you yesterday, who you were talking about this morning?' As soon as it's out there I regret it. None of my business.

'What do you know about it?'

'I was standing next to you. You said *she*. Just forget it,' I say stiffly, rising. 'I'll get my bag. We should go.'

'I'm sorry.' His voice stops me. He sighs, shudders. 'Have you ever loved someone so much the thought of them being taken away makes you feel like shutting down?'

I gulp. He sounds tortured. Oh, God. Did I nearly help him cheat on someone last night? He doesn't seem the type, is too principled, but you never can tell. I have to know. Sinking back down on the sofa beside him: 'No,' I answer. 'I've never felt that way about anyone, not romantically.' Hint, hint. Have you? I keep going when he stays silent. 'I'd be gutted to lose a family member, obviously, and I've felt like that about other things.' With a certain degree of irony, I think about my job, flat, friends…life.

'What do you do?' he asks.

'Do?'

'When it happens. How do you stop from shutting down?'

'I don't know.' I shift, caught off guard. 'Honestly? Sometimes you don't. Sometimes you let it happen, shut down, and then you,' I grope for the right words, 'reboot. And you decide whether to fight, or walk away.'

'I bet you didn't.'

'Didn't what?'

He smiles, traces a finger along the back of the sofa near my shoulder. 'Walk away.'

But perhaps I should have. I feel like the worst kind of deceiver sitting with him, sharing thoughts and feelings, while he's oblivious to my motives. 'What makes you say that?' I ask.

'You're far too stubborn. No offence.'

I smile. 'None taken, you're right.' I gather my thoughts. 'But wrong too, because I've gone through something really tough and walked away for a while.' In the weeks after the appeal when all I could do was rail against the unfairness of it all, before I decided to stop being a moaning Myrtle. 'Then I decided to fight,' lodging the ET, 'which I thought was the right thing to do. And in some ways it still is, the principle is important. But, lately I've been wondering if sometimes hanging in there is worth it, if it isn't more damaging to keep going when you know the cost is stacking up.' I look at him, a guy who is hurting, clicking that he'll see my fibs as a betrayal no matter what my justification. 'When you end up doing things you don't like.' An idea crystallises. 'Sometimes maybe walking away is the best thing to do all round.' Is that what I should do?

'I can't walk away,' he grinds, 'no matter what the cost.'

'Why? And no doubt you have unlimited funds, but I was talking about emotional costs.'

'I know,' he interjects. 'But there's no choice, not when it comes to this.'

I feel sick thinking he's part of a couple. Or was he pining after an ex last night and I was some substitute? 'So, who is she?' I grimace. 'This woman you love so much.'

'Who is she?' He jolts like I've stuck a cattle prod somewhere unmentionable and electrocuted him.

'The reason you've been so stressed?'

'Yes. Her. Louise.' He lopes over to the bar and cracks open two bottles of cola. 'Here.'

'Thanks.' I accept it gratefully. 'So. Louise? Who is she?' Taking a thirsty gulp.

'My wife.'

'*What?*' I splutter and cough, leaning over to cup a hand over my nose, scared drink will shoot out of it. *Please no. Not a married man.* There's never been a whiff of it in the papers. This cynical guy actually loved someone enough to walk them down the aisle? Wow. I can't pinpoint the odd feeling in my chest at the thought.

'Are you okay?' He pats my back a few times and I block out the warmth of his palm through my suit jacket.

'Uh-huh,' I wheeze. Scooting forward, I put the bottle down rather than break it with tightened fingers. 'I didn't know you were married.' Please tell me this isn't one of those stories where his wife doesn't understand him and that's why he almost strayed.

'Not many people do.' He touches my shoulder as I sit up, gazing deep in my eyes. As if unable to stop himself, he tucks my hair behind my ear, making my skin go goose-bumpy. 'Very soon we won't be married. Our divorce is almost final. We've been separated for two years.'

'Right,' I mutter. Alex has integrity, and as far as I know has never lied to me, despite concealing his wife's existence, though by the sound of it that's been from the world in general. Reaching forward and grabbing my drink again, I take a big gulp, feeling confused. Am I relieved because if he's being honest I haven't helped him semi-commit adultery, or because it means he's available?

'Aren't you going to ask me any more questions?'

'Nope. I'm whipped. I had a late night last night.'

I definitely don't want all the gory details about his ex, about how glamorous and high-society she is.

'I know.' He stares at me meaningfully. 'I remember some fierce red-haired she-monster slamming the door in my face.'

'That was nothing,' I say lightly. 'You should see me when I get my hulk on.'

'Yes. I'd hate to see you when you're really ferocious.'

'Positively scary.' I wiggle my eyebrow and manage to put the half-full bottle on the table without spilling it. He smiles and I smile and then we're smiling together and I feel that unbelievable spark between us. The tingle along the back of my neck warns me not get in any deeper.

My smile fades and I stand up, but Alex grabs my hand.

'Where are you going?'

Gesturing to the wall clock: 'We need to go.'

'We have a few minutes. I got sidetracked, haven't said every-thing I need to.' He tugs on my fingers and I try to ignore the zing it creates between my thighs. 'I feel bad about last night—'

Mortification burns and along with it, pride surfaces. I'm not some naive little school girl and I won't have him feeling sorry for me. 'I'm sorry I slammed the door in your face but don't worry about it, I understand. You have baggage. We all do. Don't lose sleep over it, I won't.' Liar, liar your pants are positively roasting.

He pulls on my hand. 'Well, I might. I don't usually do that sort of thing.'

'What?' I ask, sitting back down. 'Fooling around with women you hardly know?'

'Um.' He rubs the back of his neck, avoiding eye contact. 'Not exactly.'

'Wow.' That makes a girl feel special. Picking up the bottle, I start to peel the label off.

My thoughts must be reflected in my expression because he closes his intense blue eyes then reopens them, 'I don't usually kiss women I work with,' he growls. 'Or immediately ask them not to disclose it. I acted like an insensitive idiot and insulted you. I'm sorry.'

'It's fine,' I respond neutrally. 'You've already told me you got spooked because we're working together and you can't appear a hypocrite. We're going round in circles. The only thing I'm not sure of is whether you live like a monk or not.' Why did I say that? He'll think I'm fishing.

Hesitating, he runs a hand through his hair. 'You need to understand, the world I live in has its own rules.'

'And?'

'You go out socially as a couple for business or PR reasons and it makes sense to extend it to other areas. It's convenient. But any arrangement I have, both parties are clear what the rules are.'

I laugh in disbelief. 'Yeurgh! It sounds so … cold.' I look at him, puzzled. It's so at odds with the hot-blooded guy I've started to know. The one who kissed me, the one who pinned me against the wall. I blush. 'And if you want the correct definition, I think you mean friends with benefits, which isn't exclusive to your world. More disturbing is the way you're talking about casual relationships like they're contracts. I'm sorry Alex, but people's emotions don't behave according to a set of logically laid out terms and conditions.'

'I wasn't inviting a commentary on my private life.'

'What were you doing then?' Anger sends a sparkle of pain across my temples.

'Explaining my actions last night.' A pause. 'The truth is, I panicked.'

'Panicked? Because I might tell people?'

'Yes. But mainly because I can't make the same mistakes again. Too many people get hurt.' He stomps all over my attempt to ask him what he's on about. 'It shouldn't have happened. I should have had more control.'

Slamming the bottle down on the table, I rear up. 'Don't be so ridiculous, or patronising! We were two consenting adults. You hardly ravished me against my will. We're not in some regency novel where you're the lord of the manor. We live in the modern world.'

'But those kinds of books are about honour, aren't they?' He comes out of his seat to tower over me. 'About keeping it and losing it? And this situation is about honour. It's something instilled in me since childhood. Honour is a big thing in the Greek half of my culture, modern world or not.'

'Seriously?'

'Seriously.'

'So what compromised your control?' I demand. 'What made you lose it?' *Say I'm not like the others.* Even as I think it, I know I shouldn't.

He shoves his hands in his pockets. 'I'm not thinking straight with everything that's going on. And you're absolutely gorgeous … and you wanted me.'

'So anyone half-presentable, up for it, and within reach would have done.' As much as I don't want it to, my voice trembles. 'Thanks very much.' I spin away. 'I'm just going to grab something from my room. I'll see you down there.' I march across the room, movements stiff and jerky.

'Charley, come back.'

'I don't think so.' Slamming the door, I lock it tight, needing a few moments to myself.

Men!

Chapter Eighteen

The sound of my fingers pounding away at the laptop seems disproportionately loud, as Alex and his Chief Finance Officer Greg agree on a list of actions with corresponding timescales. There's a different feel to this meeting and I wonder if they're friends as well as colleagues.

'Quarter three,' I correct them.

'Pardon?' Alex's head lifts.

'I think you mean quarter three, not two.'

Frowning, he checks the paperwork. 'You're right, thank you.'

'Of course.'

With a final comment of, 'We need to watch those costs and we'll be on track for quarter four,' Alex stands, and I do as well. 'That's it, we're done.' He shakes his CFO's hand, 'Thanks for your time, Greg. Have a good flight home in the morning.'

'Same goes, but perhaps we can have a drink in the bar later?'

'That would be good.' Alex grins then after seeing him out turns to face me, unbuttoning his jacket. 'Charley, I think you took my comment the wrong way earlier. I know it came out wrong.' He raises his eyebrows, looking at me hopefully. 'Really, really wrong,' he tacks on gravely.

I shrug and stare out the window, trying not to let the comment mean anything, determined not to get further involved for the sake of my sanity.

'I care even if you don't,' Alex says roughly.

A tap on the door cuts off whatever else he was about to say and his face goes blank. 'Good afternoon, you must be Tony. How are you?'

My blood freezes in my veins, time slowing.

It can't be.

But it is. Alex's broad shoulders block the doorway, shielding the person from view, but as the visitor answers in a deferential tone I recognise the voice.

'Yes. Fine, thank you sir, and you?'

I struggle to draw in quiet, even breaths, instead of short, panicky ones. What the hell? What's he doing here?

'I can't complain,' Alex says formally. 'Take a seat.'

And with that, in swaggers the man who turned everything in my life upside down, who ruined my career, my credibility and my prospects. I drop into my chair, head down to hide my face, giving myself a moment to think before he sees me.

Oh, God. I can't be here.

The room falls away, Alex and Tony's voices going muffled like I'm underwater. My ears pop and light spots in front of my eyes join together so that my whole vision goes bright white, warm clamminess spreading over my body. It's scary and disorienting. Sweat beads my forehead and I tuck my chin closer to my chest as I fight to breathe, to think. In, out. In, out. What am I going to do? I can't let them see me this way – weak. It'll pass. It *has* to pass. Thankfully the oxygen starts filtering back into my body and my sight starts clearing. It must be a stress reaction. Sitting still while it lifts completely, I wonder if Alex or Tony noticed.

There's the shifting of furniture and bastard-face sits down to my right. I catch a waft of the aftershave I disliked so intensely, and raw emotions hit, coagulating in my stomach. Fear, anger, seething frustration, sadness ... jamming into a ball of concrete in my throat. I shiver, blood whooshing through my veins, heart

169

thudding. Ba–doom, ba–doom, ba–doom. I can't look at Tony, there is so much turmoil inside, but at last my pride kicks in, and I sit up straighter.

Of all the ways I'd imagined seeing my ex-assistant again this wasn't one of them. I had daydreams of dramatic scenes where I'd tell the world what he'd done, giving an impassioned speech for justice that'd bring tears to people's eyes and a spontaneous round of applause. Then he'd get his comeuppance somehow, before crawling into a deep, dark hole, never to be seen or heard from again. And I'd magically get my old life back. Yes, all a bit *Dynasty* I know, but the mind works in funny ways.

I definitely didn't think I'd be stuck in a small room with him and another person oblivious to the undercurrents. Plus I'm at a massive disadvantage. If Tony greets me by name it'll blow my cover, and Alex will find out the truth in the worst way possible. I quake, but anger and resentment step in. *Don't let him win again. Don't let him see you rattled. Take control.* I stare at the thick black carpet, then study the polished glass table, the shiny metal of its legs, the huge square windows and white blinds, until I'm calmer, steady.

Then, lifting my chin, I look directly at Tony, gaze raking over his straw-yellow hair and pinkish complexion, which drains of colour with the shock I read in his flinty eyes. His attention switches to Alex and back to me and his lips shape something before he recovers, suspicion narrowing his glare.

'Is there a problem, Mr Ferrier?' Alex asks, eyebrows pulling together.

'No.' He studies my face but I stare back at him blankly. Let him wonder. 'I thought your assistant was a man? Did he leave?'

Alex glances at me. 'No. He's ill. Miss Caswell came via an agency.' He doesn't notice Tony raising his eyebrows at my assumed name, too busy shuffling the papers next to his elbow.

'Let's begin. We've held a number of these meetings today and this is the last of them.' Smiling at me: 'Sorry, Charley, I should have said. This is Tony Ferrier. He's a new management trainee, due to go off to Africa with the expanded programme soon. He's acting manager of our flagship branch in London. Do you know it?'

He can't know that every word is like a stiletto grinding splintered glass into my bruised heart. 'Yes, I know it,' I respond politely, though inside I'm seething.

I don't believe it. Tony has taken my job twice over. First in ejecting me from it and second in stealing it from me. It must be recent or Kitty would have called. God, they must hate working under him. I freeze. What if he starts coming on to them too? As manager he's in a stronger position than he ever was. I have to find a way to block him. Wait. Was this what it was all about from the beginning? Getting my job?

'Thank you, Alex.' I conjure a smile to aim at my temporary boss, then turn it on Tony, baring my teeth. 'Nice to meet you, Mr Ferrier.' Not.

Tony's gaze flickers between Alex and I, probably trying to work out how much Alex knows.

'Pleased to meet you, Charley. I used to know a Charlotte,' he muses, 'she was an interesting woman.'

'I'm sure you've lots of stories to tell, Tony,' Alex interjects smoothly, 'but if you don't mind, now isn't the time for them.'

Tony shifts his attention. 'Yes, of course,' he agrees, 'sorry. Sometimes I just get carried away with memories of happier times, like—'

'Ouch!' I cry, jerking my hand away from a piece of paper.

Alex reaches over to touch my arm, 'Are you okay?'

A spot of warmth grows in me at his concern.

'Charley?' His big hand wraps around my wrist and the zing of it, even in these circumstances, amazes me.

Tony's eyes zero in on the physical contact, his expression first assessing then worried. He runs a finger along the inside of his shirt collar.

'Yes, Sorry. Paper cut.' I slip my arm from Alex's grip, hold up my bleeding finger, glad my distraction worked. I wonder why, given his obsession with privacy, Alex would be so hands-on in front of another employee.

'If you're sure.' He swivels back to Tony. Strange he doesn't notice bastard-face's pallor when he notices everything about me. 'So, quarter one, the beginning of the financial year.'

Tapping out the notes of their conversation, I find the sound of Alex's deep voice oddly soothing. Weird. I do my best to ignore Tony, getting lost in the Q1 report, facts and figures I know back to front and sideways, as I was at the casino until late summer, half-way into quarter two. They're stats I input into spreadsheets and analysed myself. My rage grows exponentially and I stab the keyboard keys, wishing they were Tony's face.

After five minutes, during which Tony takes credit for the successful results and high profit margins, never mind all the hard work of the entire staff, my jaw is aching from clenching my teeth so hard. It's an incredible effort not to spring out of my chair and start ranting at both of them; Tony for being such a devious bastard and Alex for trusting one.

'Thanks. I think we're done. Good results, nice to meet you.' Alex shakes Tony's hand twenty minutes later and I want to warn him to go and scrub them with high-end detergent. Saving the document, I log off the laptop, needing to get away and re-gather my thoughts. But it's backed up and takes forever to co-operate. I fight the urge to fling it across the room at Tony as he stares at me with a creepy smirk.

Alex's mobile rings. 'Excuse me, I have to take this,' he says, exiting swiftly, shutting the door behind him.

Dismay wallops me. *Don't leave me alone with him!* I want to yell.

No. You can handle this. And if he lays a hand on you, just scream the bloody place down.

Crossing his arms, Tony squares his rounded rugby shoulders and raises a menacing eyebrow. 'Hello again, boss. Going somewhere?' he sneers.

I can't help it, I snigger. He's ridiculous, trying to be some tough East End gangster or something. The stance and comment are probably designed to intimidate, but have the opposite effect.

'Are you being serious?' I snort. 'Is that all you've got?'

Flushing, he drops his arms. 'I wouldn't be so confident. My best has already floored you, hasn't it?'

He's not as broad as Alex. In fact he's a lot smaller than I remember. I step closer and realise I tower above him. 'I think floored is a bit of an overstatement. After all, I'm here aren't I?'

For months I've been shadowed by him and his actions, but he isn't a monster, I see it now. He's just a man. A spoilt, immature, playground bully who likes to dominate, who finds sneaky ways to take what doesn't belong to him because he's not good enough to earn them like everyone else. Adrenalin hits with a surge of primitive anger, my heartbeat accelerating, blood pressure rising. Really, what else can he do to me?

I haven't been a victim so far – because I kept on fighting, kept getting back up, so I definitely won't be a victim now.

How do you beat a bully? I think back to black-haired Sally Benson in primary school who tripped me over in class and called me names every day for weeks, and how that was resolved.

You show bullies no fear.

I chuckle. 'If that's it...' Snapping the laptop shut, I place it on Alex's pile of stuff, pick up my bag and circle the table, 'I'll be off.'

He steps into my path. 'You don't get off that easily,' he spits. 'Are you going to tell me?'

I stare him down. 'Tell you what?'

'What the hell you're doing here!'

'What does it look like? I'm working, no thanks to you.'

'Oh dear,' he moves nearer, 'been having trouble finding gainful employment?'

The statement is so inadequate to describe all the pain he's caused it chokes the words in my throat. Fury flashes and I step right up into his face, teeth gritted... and he flinches.

He's scared of me.

I know the moment will be etched in my brain forever, a glowing memory I can hold onto when things are tough. I'd never hurt anyone physically but this man deserves to hear what I think of him.

'Not as much as you'd like,' I snarl, my hands curling into tight fists. 'You're pathetic. I said no to you and you didn't like it, so you had to make me pay, and you couldn't get a management job like a normal person so you had to slither your way into mine. Sad.' I shake my head pityingly. 'And now you're asking stupid, obvious questions.'

'Not stupid. You seem awfully close to the CEO, I was just wondering if you were trying out a different line of work.'

His comment is intended as an insult but I'm more interested in the anxiety shining in his eyes. *I knew it.* He's worried I have a personal relationship with Alex which might give me the advantage. He doesn't need to know he's wrong, not if it's an illusion that'll help me.

'Wouldn't you like to know,' I reply, smiling very slowly and very suggestively, hoping I'm convincing.

'You're talking crap,' he says flatly.

'Am I?' I raise an eyebrow. 'Or do I know the way he likes to be kissed because I sat in his lap and did it yesterday afternoon?'

He must see that truth in my eyes. 'You conniving bitch.' His tone is almost admiring. 'You've certainly changed over the last few months. After all, you said no to me because of the contractual clause, yet here you are shagging the guy who wrote it.'

I want to tell him not to talk about Alex like that but the drama needs to play out if I want to get rid of him. Plus it feels good. 'I hate to burst your silly little ego,' I say sweetly, 'but it wasn't the clause, Tony. It was you.' I stab a finger at his chest. 'I didn't want *you.*'

He steps towards me. 'I don't believe you.'

I jerk out of reach. 'Believe it.' My voice is concrete. 'I'd rather lop off my right arm than sleep with you.'

'You bitch!' he raises his hand. 'You'd better be ready for a fight at tribunal. I'm going to tear you apart.'

'Bring it!' Maintaining eye contact, I refuse to back down. 'But lay a finger on me and I'll scream, and you'll regret it.'

'I completely agree,' Alex says from the doorway.

Tony whirls around to face him and panic claws at me. Oh God, not like this. I know what conclusion Alex has come to and need to say something, but disbelief and shock whisk my voice away.

'Get out,' Alex orders.

No, no, no. 'R–right,' I whisper.

'Mr Ferrier.' Alex points at the door, shoulders tight and vibrating with tension. 'Leave now please. I'll find you later.'

'Sir—'

'Out.' The broad back he turns on Tony is an immovable barrier, a clear dismissal. With a look of impotent fury, Tony slams out of the door.

'What the hell was all that about?' Alex demands, staring at me with narrowed blue eyes.

'You didn't hear the whole conversation?'

'No, just your last comment.' He grabs my elbows, pulls me against his chest. 'Are you okay? What did he do to you? You're bright white.'

Letting out a jittery laugh, I look down, feeling guilty, body shaking as the adrenalin of confronting Tony drains away. Do I tell Alex everything now so Tony can't get in first? Slipping from his arms with no lack of regret, I go over to the window, looking out to sea and wishing I was far, far away.

'There's no way I'm having one of my managers, any member of staff, intimidate or make another feel uncomfortable,' he speaks into my silence. 'It's completely unacceptable.'

'Yes,' I murmur, summoning the bravery I need to tell him the truth.

Then he moves and puts his arm around my shoulders, catching me off guard and skittering my breath. I can feel the warmth of him down my entire body. I tremble harder, back shuddering, teeth chattering. Then I let myself go for a moment, closing my eyes and resting against him, drawing on his strength. It feels so sinfully good. And so heartbreakingly right.

His arms tighten. 'God, you're really shaken, aren't you?' He puts his mouth to my ear, voice croaky. 'You're all right now. Tell me what happened.'

I feel so safe, so secure for the first time in ages. I want him to keep holding me.

'Charley?' he prompts.

'H–he just got a little close and—' My shoulders slouch. I want to tell him the truth but when I do, I really think I'll lose him. All he'll see is the betrayal. I bite my lip. It's okay to be a little selfish sometimes, isn't it? To want to hold onto a good thing for as long as possible.

His phone beeps. 'For God's sake! This is getting ridiculous.' He drags it from his pocket with a telling sigh. 'I'm so sorry. Can we meet in the suite at half eight? Will you tell me then? We need to go over a few things for tomorrow anyway. And you'll be safe up there. I'll make sure he stays away, I promise. Have a few hours off. I have to sort this out.'

'Okay.' I smile, my cheeks feeling tense and unnatural. 'Do what you have to do.'

He brushes a finger down my cheekbone. 'You're sweet.' Walking across the room, he pauses, giving me one of his heart-stopping crooked smiles. 'What I said earlier. Last night wasn't just because you were there. Or that you're gorgeous. It was you. You talk to me like I'm a normal person. You make me feel … normal.'

Without waiting for my reply, he leaves. I slouch back against the window, mouth gaping.

What am I supposed to do with that?

Chapter Nineteen

Muttering as my watch ticks past eighty forty-five, I pace the golden carpet, coral-painted toes sinking into the thick pile. Where's Alex? He said he'd be here. Ten more minutes and I'll go look for him.

Over the past couple of hours I've tried to relax after the jolt of encountering Tony and the ton of confusion brought down by Alex's admission. A quick dinner and long, hot bath helped, but I can't stop wondering where Tony is and what he's doing. Has he tracked Alex down, or has Alex gone to find him? Are they talking about me right now? Is that why Alex is late? Maybe I should start packing my case again. Every muscle in my body clenches at the idea.

Sitting at the piano, half afraid to touch it because of how expensive it looks, I plunk a few keys tentatively to de-stress, and launch into 'Chopsticks', playing faster and faster, fingers pressing the keys harder and harder as my frustrations flow onto the ivories, the force making my wrists ache.

When Tony said those things about my closeness to Alex and me changing, he was right *and* wrong. He touched a nerve. I've changed. But maybe not for the better. My hands stumble and I crash out some discordant notes, pulling a disgusted face. I switch to a Coldplay number from my teens, from a time when I sat at the piano for hours learning songs from the charts.

Tony is wrong about me. Isn't he? Fuelled by sheer desperation, my principles have flexed enough to take this assignment under false pretences, but they *haven't* bent so much I'll use my body to get ahead. But the fact Tony believed me straight away leaves a bad taste in my mouth. I've compromised my own moral code to get alongside a stranger, to try and gain his trust. The last few months have been so awful I'm now lying to a guy who doesn't deserve it. It's easy to think you can do something to someone when you see their face in a corporate brochure, but once you meet them in real life it's different. Especially when you discover they have pretty major trust issues and don't leave themselves vulnerable to people very often.

And they start to trust you.

And you like them.

And they tell you that you make them feel normal.

And you know with every fibre in your body that's a good thing.

My hands still, the last notes echoing in the sumptuous room, my head slumping down onto my hands with a plink-thud sound.

What am I *doing*?

Jess was right. I should never have come here, should never have pursued this crazy plan. I might have lost some of my trust in the world but I don't want to be someone who is comfortable betraying people. And I definitely don't want to be someone Tony Ferrier approves of.

I can't do this.

Lifting my head, I realise something else. I don't want Alex to think of me that way, as someone who lies and deceives and uses. Fingers flitting over the keys again, I look out the window at the Barcelona skyline, at the buildings and lights, before turning my attention to the sprinkling of stars I can make out in the distance far above the sea. The darkness they occupy is simple and absolute. The sight gives me perspective and everything in me goes quiet.

It's clear now. I have to abandon my plan and come clean with Alex. I'll tell him the truth about what I came here to do, but am no longer going to pursue it. I'll live with the consequences. It might not help my career or financial situation, but I'll know that in the end I did the right thing.

I lift aching fingers from the piano, curl my hands into loose fists, study the clock. Time's running out. Where on earth is he?

Knocking on Alex's bedroom door to make sure he hasn't fallen asleep or lost track of time, I tut when there's no answer. I run into my room and slip some flats on. Checking the restaurant, with no joy, I rocket into the bar as the next logical choice. I'm completely underdressed in my blue skinny jeans and clingy grey long-sleeved top but don't care, scanning the room.

Spying Alex at the bar, drink in hand, talking to Greg, his CFO, I can see from the way he's slouching it's not his first drink. Strolling over to them, I tuck my hands in my pockets and dredge up an easy smile. I need to play it strategically, not take issue with Alex for being late. 'Hair of the dog?' I check. 'Or a re-run of last night?'

Glancing over his shoulder, Greg gives me an easy nod. 'Hello again.'

'Hi.'

Alex swivels around, suit jacket on the back of the stool, tie ends dangling loose around his collar. Damn, how does he always look so good?

'Charley.' He grimaces, 'Am I late? What time is it?'

'Almost nine.'

'You didn't stand her up did you Alex?' Greg nudges him with a light elbow.

I open my mouth to reply but Alex gets in first, straightening in his seat. 'Of course not. It's not a date. We arranged to go over some work-related matters.'

'That's right,' I agree smoothly. Does he think I'll blurt out what we did last night? Or that earlier he as good as told me he likes me? 'We agreed to have a post-meetings brief,' I explain. 'Are you ready Alex?'

In answer, he slides off his chair, 'Can I have a word?' He walks to a spot by the window.

Trailing a few feet behind, trying not to stare at his gorgeous bum, I bash into him. He turns, catches and steadies me, stepping away as though he's not allowed to breach the space between us. What was that scene in *Dirty Dancing*? Something about frames and Jennifer Grey muttering about spaghetti arms as Patrick Swayze tried to cop a feel. 'Thanks.'

'I was wondering,' he broaches, 'if we could meet in the morning instead of tonight. Say half seven?'

'I really need to talk to you.' I need to tell him the truth, and, as part of that, need to know whether he's spoken to Tony.

'I need time to myself tonight. I need to ... think some things through. Do you mind? It can wait until morning, surely.'

There's no point in starting an argument, it won't achieve anything. If he agrees to listen I'll know he's knackered and impatient and not in the best frame of mind. 'I guess so,' I say reluctantly.

'Thank you,' his long-lashed blue eyes warm up, reminding me of a young, dreamy Jared Leto. Sigh. 'I appreciate it,' he adds, looking so grateful I wonder how often he gets an evening off. He needs to agree some serious parameters with his staff. Lack of work-life balance can lead to burn-out. I've seen it happen and am seriously worried he's on his way to it.

'I'll see you in the morning then,' I mutter, feeling like there are masses of things unsaid between us, making me tense and restless.

'Yes. Good night, Charley. ' He reaches a hand towards me but thinks better of it, dropping it to his side.

'Night, Alex.'

Our feet must be stuck to the floor because neither of us moves.

'Are you two going to stare at each other all night or are you going to go and have your meeting?' Greg calls across the room.

Alex rolls his eyes, 'Neither,' he responds. 'Come on.' His fingers glance off my arm as he motions me to follow, their heat burning through my top.

'We've put our meeting off until morning,' he tells Greg as he reclaims his seat.

'In that case, would you like to join us for a drink?' Greg asks me, pulling out the stool next to him.

Alex freezes while reaching for his beer. Obviously he wants to talk to Greg alone.

'Better not,' I reply, 'I've got some reading to do. But thanks for the offer.' Alex picks his drink up at that, shoulders relaxing. 'Have a good evening.'

'Charley,' Alex says.

I spin round, hoping he'll ask me to stay. 'Yeah?'

He raises his beer, 'hair of the dog,' and smiles.

'Right.' I smile back and leave them to it.

Their heads are together deep in conversation before I'm at the door. I sense a bit of bromance in the air.

Good for him, I think. He needs to talk to someone.

So why, as I mulch across reception to the lift, do I feel decidedly deflated that this time it isn't me?

An hour later I'm working on a large glass of white wine whilst sprawled on one of the leather sofas in the suite. Chocolate wrappers decorate an end table and I'm surfing the net for shoe porn on the TV. I'm relaxed, but for the small quiver of nerves in the pit of my stomach in anticipation of the morning's conversation with Alex. Another crappy night ahead, then.

There's a shuffling sound, the door bursts open and Alex rolls in. 'Get a good night's sleep and remember what I said,' Greg calls from the corridor.

'Yes, all right. Night,' Alex replies and clicks the door shut. Chuckling, he wanders in and throws his jacket and tie down across a sofa.

'Sorry,' I bolt up, scrambling to clear away my mess. 'I didn't realise you were coming back so soon.'

'It's fine,' he waves a hand, 'stay. In fact, as long as we promise not to talk about work, let's have a drink.'

'I thought you didn't want to talk tonight?' I say, surprised. Wow, Greg must be the world's best listener.

'I didn't. I don't,' he reiterates. 'I'm trying something different. Let's just … relax.'

'Right.' Except I have never felt less relaxed in my life, not when I'm in the vicinity of Mr Hot CEO and there's a secret burning on the back of my tongue.

Flicking switches to turn the main lights off, Alex switches a couple of table lamps on, casting pools of light around the room. 'Much better,' he exclaims. Strolling over to the bar, he undoes a button on his shirt. *Pop.* 'Top up?'

'Please.'

He comes over with the wine bottle, pouring generously. 'Here. You deserve a break as much as I do with all your hard work over the last two days.' He hits his forehead with his palm as he walks back to the bar, 'Idiot, that was work-related. Sorry, I can't seem to help it.'

I pick up my glass. 'Thanks. Well, I'm sure it's a hard habit to break.'

'You're very generous, given what a workaholic I am.' He opens the fridge and pulls out a beer, unscrewing the top.

'I wouldn't say you're a worka—' At his raised eyebrows, I change my intended sentence, 'Okay, you are in actual fact, a workaholic.' I curl my legs around to make room as he comes over and sits down on the end of the sofa.

He throws his head back and laughs, long and loud.

You make me feel…normal. His admission echoes in my head. He can be intense and driven and a little arrogant, but this is the real man; a witty, caring, passionate guy who finds the constraints of duty stifling and who forces himself to act in a way he thinks the world expects. He can be quick-tempered, but wouldn't anyone be if they were working so hard to keep it up? It must be exhausting. Like Peter Parker and Spiderman. With great power comes great responsibility. But not always that much fun.

'What were you doing?' He gestures at the TV.

'Surfing for shoe porn,' I say promptly, then cover my mouth. 'Oops, I mean—'

'Drooling over shoes or people doing questionable things to them?' he asks, straight–faced.

'What? You can't be serious – oh, very funny,' I drawl when I catch him chuckling, laughing with him.

Then we go quiet.

Chugging down some beer, he rests his head on the back of the couch, undoing another shirt button. *Pop.* My eyes stray to the length of his sprawled muscular legs. I go warm and prickly as I remember the sounds and scents of last night's crazy encounter against the wall. My body immediately aches and I squeeze my thighs together in response.

Looking up, I find him watching me watching him. Oh boy. He undoes another button. *Pop.* How many more?

He takes another long gulp of beer, eyes fixed on me challeng-ingly as he does it. It's strangely sexy, the knowledge in his eyes. The hint of cockiness. He's so smoking hot.

He sets his bottle down. 'Charley.'

'Yes?' I inhale sharply.

'I shouldn't say this.' His gaze flips from my cleavage to my mouth. 'But I really like you.'

'You do? '

'Yes.'

He swivels to face me, crossing his legs so our knees touch. I fight the urge to slip my hand inside his unbuttoned shirt, redis-cover the firmness of his broad chest.

'Right.' His statement doesn't change anything. We don't belong together, him and I. And in some ways, him saying this now makes it worse because I'll be throwing it back in his face in the morning when I admit the truth.

But ... God. I feel like a teenager with an intense crush. Like in school when you worship the cool, good-looking, popular boy from afar and one day he comes over to talk to you. *He knows I exist*, you think, feeling as though you're going to float away into the clouds you're so giddy. That's childhood, though. Castles and daydreams. I have no room for those. There are no happy ever-afters.

Alex slides closer at my silence. 'I was talking to Greg and it dawned on me. Until now, he and my brother were the only people who make me check reality, ask myself the hard questions. But now there's you, too.'

Oh, help. Please stop. I'm already in like with you. I go breathless when his hand lifts, when his confident fingers start stroking my jaw. My heart is racing in an outright gallop. It might beat right out of my chest. 'Are you and Greg close?' I quiz. *Ground yourself. Feet flat on the floor, no floating away.*

'Yes, we met at uni.'

'That's nice,' I gulp, lost in deep-blue eyes getting darker by the second.

'Hmm.' His thumb moves to trace my bottom lip, stops in the middle, presses it in as if fascinated. 'Charley, I've got a problem.'

'What's that?'

'I stopped being able to think the moment I sat down next to you.'

Huge turn-on. 'You did?' I won't touch him. I can't, not after the way he ditched me last night. My fingers curl in defiance.

'Yes. It happens a lot.'

'Oh.'

A big hot hand curves around the back of my neck to pull me in and bring us face to face, mouth to mouth, so that we share the same air. He buries his face in my collarbone, brushing it with a gentle kiss before tracking his nose up my throat, like a wolf searching for the scent of blood. He inhales, licks my skin delicately and I shudder. It's basic and possessive and I love it. 'The way you smell, the way you feel … I love it,' he mumbles, teeth grazing the skin beneath my ear. 'I know I messed up last night, and we'll probably regret this.'

'What?' I gasp, eyes closing, neck arching further to give him easier access. I can't resist. His other hand slides up my thigh, index finger tracing the inside seam of my tight jeans.

'I heard the way you spoke to Ferrier, how you didn't want him. It tells me you don't make a habit of getting involved with people at work. So perhaps I'm the exception.'

I squirm, both at the movement of his hand and his words. This is turning into the biggest mess imaginable. 'Where is Tony?' I ask, praying my high-pitched voice isn't a giveaway.

'I sent him home, back to the UK.' He bites my earlobe. 'He was done here anyway.'

'D–did you talk to him, ask him anything?'

'No. I just got his plane ticket swapped and off he went. I didn't like the man, to be honest. Taking all the credit for those fantastic results when they're down to the staff and the manager before him.'

Safe, I think. I'm safe. It's over, for now. But I have to tell Alex the truth, before we go any further. My words are stolen as he tips me back on the sofa and plants a deep, mouth-watering kiss on me. Ooohhh ... Lifting trembling hands to his back, I tug his shirt from his trousers, my legs falling open to let him settle against me.

He moves away a mere millimetre, whispers into my mouth, 'I'll finish it this time.'

I stop being able to think. The only thing I can utter is, 'You'd better.' His skin is blistering satin, a texture I need more of, to be complete. Another kiss and he drops down to scrape his stubble along my neck. The contents of my underwear zing and my hips roll in response.

Yanking up my top, he pulls my bra down and puts his mouth on me, sucking a nipple, tweaking the other with shaking urgent fingers. I writhe, I pant, I lose all self-control. I don't care. He changes to a licking motion so he can talk. I'm glad someone in the room can. God. If he doesn't take our clothes off soon I'll kill him.

'I just need to forget,' he mutters. 'Help me forget.' Rearing up, he kneels over me, thighs taut, grabbing my top and wrenching it over my head. Jerking open the zip of my skinnies to reveal my lacy underwear, he frowns, 'Are you on the pill? I have condoms—'

'We'll use protection.' I twist under him and his warmth wraps around me and his clever fingers delve inside my knickers. 'Hurry,' I moan.

He stands and scoops me up, walking us both into my bedroom, kissing me along the way. As I slide down his body to stand, I wrench open the rest of his shirt buttons, yank it down his arms and throw it across the room. Alex lays me down on the wide bed and I reach around to sweep a book, clothing and jewellery to the floor. My mouth goes desert dry as he stands, peeling off his trousers, staring down at me with undeniable hunger. His skin is bronze, pectorals ridged and coated with a light dusting of dark hair continuing down into a sexy line between defined abs I will definitely count later.

He is universe-tiltingly gorgeous, shoulders wide, biceps hard, waist lean above his clingy jockey shorts. The only sound in this private place, a bubble where no one and nothing else exists apart from us, is the panting of our breaths, the rustle of clothing.

Alex's eyes burn into mine as he slides his shorts off. I gulp and suck in a breath on a little squeak. Wow. He is gifted in *all* the right areas. I just hope he knows how to use those gifts.

 Grabbing a condom from his wallet, he climbs onto the bed and helps me undress. I expect it to be hot, dirty and quick. But he shocks me by brushing my hair from my face, running his fingers over my cheekbones.

'Beautiful, vibrant,' he smiles gently, 'perfect.' Then he slides down my body, fixes my hips to the bed with heavy hands, trails blazing heat down the inside of my thigh with his tongue, looks up at me knowingly and gets to work with his pillow lips. They feel as heavenly as they look.

I'm soon gasping and writhing around, clutching his hair, 'Please just get inside me,' I beg and scramble out from beneath him when

186

he doesn't play fair, pinning his big, broad body to the bed. I grab the condom, open it and roll it on, licking a flat male nipple and dragging my nails down the front of his muscular thighs, kissing each mega-sexy ab in turn, laughing as his hands clench in my long red hair.

'Thialo,' he groans, 'yes.'

'Yes?' I narrow my eyes at him, and take hold of his rigid, glorious length, moving my hand back and forth, 'Are you sure you're ready?'

'Yes!' His hips jerk and he lunges up and pushes me back on the mattress, and we tangle our limbs together as he plunges into me, my wet heat welcoming him in. He moans as I raise my hips and dig my heels into his delectable bum. 'Yesss…' I echo. He's big and hard and deep, thrusting in and out, scooting me up the bed until my head hits the headboard. I feel like I've waited for him forever, even though I've only known him for two days. Back arching, I wrap my arms around him, clinging on to his shoulders. 'Harder,' I urge, breathless, desperate. 'Now.'

'Now?' His bulging biceps are either side of my head and his sexy, hairy chest grazes my nipples, causing delicious friction. He obeys my order, nudging my G-spot with every flex of his hips.

'Don't stop,' I say huskily.

'I won't,' he promises, thrusting in and out, on and on.

And I honestly couldn't tell you how long it lasts because I'm in oblivion, caught up in an alternate universe. All I know is I see stars, I fly to the Moon, I orbit the Earth and I'm sure on my journey I discover the glorious moment of the Big Bang.

Afterwards, once the foggy cloud of jaw-dropping sex has lifted, I tense. I shouldn't have done that. I *really* shouldn't have done it. I should tell him to leave now, before any more damage is done. I expect he'll bolt anyway, giving me that speech about discretion again. So when he rolls onto his back with a satisfied groan, arranges me so I'm splayed across his muscular, naked chest, and tangles our legs together, I'm astonished. And I can't summon the energy or motivation to make him go.

He strokes a finger along my clammy thigh and the simple action reignites sparks along my skin. I gasp and squirm.

'You like that?' he grins.

'Don't get cocky,' I smile up into his face. 'Two can play at that.' I wriggle against his hip and he groans.

'You win,' his arms tighten around me.

Lust pings my nipples back into hard peaks. Talk about incredible chemistry. I can't resist any longer, walking my fingers over his abs and counting them. 'Eight?' I say. 'That is just ridiculous. Are you He-Man or something?'

He laughs huskily. 'I start most mornings with a couple of hundred crunches. And don't forget I work out at the gym.'

I raise an eyebrow. 'Next you'll be telling me you're like that guy out of *Crazy, Stupid, Love* and can do that *Dirty Dancing* lift.'

'Crazy, stupid *what*? Are you trying to tell me something?' he asks playfully. 'No,' I retort immediately. 'I told you, don't be cocky.'

He kisses my hand and lowers it to rest over his heart and I can feel it beating underneath my palm. Tenderness washes over me. I wish we could stay like this forever.

What? Uh-oh. *No.*

He didn't leave or give me *the talk*, he's doing worse. He's being unbelievably sweet and sexy, and I'm a sucker for both. I shouldn't read anything into it. He could be like this with every woman he sleeps with. I clamp down on the twist of pain and jealousy robbing me of oxygen. We've made no promises to each other, and he doesn't know what I've done yet, what I came looking for. He'll think I was trying to use him, have tricked and betrayed him. The morning's going to come too soon. It's not fair to him, but I'm not ready for this night to end yet. I just want to stay in his arms, be with him a little bit longer, know him better. Surely a few more hours can't hurt. I snuggle in, squeezing his waist.

'Alex,' I blurt, 'what happened?'

He chuckles. 'I must have done something really wrong if you don't know. Do you want me to show you again?'

'No, yes, maybe later, I mean – what happened with Louise?' I rush out. I've picked about the worst moment I could, but I suddenly need to know.

'You want to talk about this *now*?'

I push away from him, pull a face, 'Kind of.'

Dragging me down to his chest, 'It's my least favourite topic of conversation given she's the most deceitful, dishonest woman I've ever met, but,' he pauses, 'all right.' A massive sigh lifts me up and down with his chest. 'We met at work. She was my PA.'

Chapter Twenty

'Oh.' *Shit.* I shiver, dismay shooting right down to my toes as everything becomes clear. His cynicism, his trust issues, his 'no workplace relationship' policy. I literally could not be in a worse position.

I'm his PA now.

I'm lying to him.

He'll think history is repeating itself.

I can't move, I'm so horrified. So I stay melded to his glorious body.

'Yes,' he repeats and adds quietly, 'I didn't think it was a good idea for us to get involved. But she was beautiful and has her own particular brand of charm when she feels like it. It only took a few weeks and we were dating, a few months before we were pretty serious.' His deep voice rumbles in his chest, the vibration reverberating through his naked skin to mine. 'I proposed. We were happy. It wasn't until I got her to sign a gagging order and pre-nup things went wrong. My family's company, the money and our reputation was too much to risk, though. I know that she always resented me for it. But it was necessary. I'm glad of it now, after everything that happened.'

'But maybe the lack of trust caused the marriage to fail?' I say, unthinking, and his face goes tight, jaw flexing. Wincing, 'Sorry.

That was too honest, and not necessarily the case.' I kiss the side of his luscious mouth. 'Sorry,' I breathe.

His expression softens. 'Although it didn't help, I don't think that's the reason it didn't work out.'

'Really? Was it because of your long work hours, did she feel neglected?'

'I – no. I never really thought about it.' He goes silent for a moment. 'I suppose at the beginning we saw each other at the office and I must have made more time for her, but ... She was ecstatic when she gave up work and seemed happy to go and spend my money so...' he trails off, staring at the ceiling.

'Still a lonely life, though. You have to spend time together as a couple to make it work; have fun together. Otherwise you can lose sight of each other.'

'Quite the relationship expert, aren't you?'

'Actually no. I've never had a serious relationship.'

He shifts under me, tips my chin so he can examine my face. 'What? How old are you? Twenty-seven? Don't you believe in them then?'

'I do. It's not that.' I free my chin, rest my cheek back on his chest. 'I just – my career's always been important to me and I've never met someone I felt strongly enough about to compromise it for.' I rush on, 'And mum started trying to marry me off from about the age of twelve. It kind of put me off, especially surrounded by all the die-hards in the village who believe women should stay home as housewives and raise children. Which is fine if that's what you want, but there should be a choice and a partnership in which both parties are happy.' I squint up at him. 'I'm not abnormal though, or anti-men. I've dated. A lot. I could be in a functional relationship if I wanted to. Anyway,' I clear my throat, hearing the defensiveness in my voice, 'you were saying, about Louise?'

'Dated, a lot? Right. Uh, Louise, yes. Well, there was something missing, something kind of crucial for a lifetime commitment.'

'What was that?'

'She didn't love me. Not for a minute.'

I lift my head, frowning. 'Are you sure? Maybe you're being too hard on yourself. Relationships go wrong for all sorts of reasons.'

'For God's sake don't feel sorry for me.' He sits up and I roll onto the mattress with a yelp, before propping myself on one elbow. I really know how to kill a mood.

He rearranges the pillows behind him and half-sits against the headboard. I feel bereft. 'She loved the lifestyle, what I could give her, who or what she thought I was, but that was it.' A deep sigh expands his chest. 'When I said it was over she wasn't happy. She's been difficult ever since. No,' he corrects, 'impossible. If only we weren't connected.'

'You won't be much longer, though.' I drag the covers over me. 'Once the divorce is final, you don't have to see her again. Unless you run into her socially?'

'It's not that.' He reaches over to the dresser and grabs a glass bottle of mineral water, strong tanned hands unscrewing the top with ease. My gaze flits down his toned body.

'What then?' I prompt, sweeping my hair around one shoulder.

He pours a couple of glasses of water and passes me one, avoiding eye contact.

What's he hiding? 'You don't want to talk about it,' I guess.

He eases the covers down to my waist. 'No. Enough talk about my ex. Let's have some fun.'

'Fun?' I feign confusion. 'You know what that is?' Before reality intervenes tomorrow, I'm going to enjoy this night and the experience; mind-blowing sex with a complex, charismatic, smoking-hot guy who makes me feel amazing.

Growling, he pounces, tipping his water down over my boobs and stomach, making me gasp. 'How unfortunate, I seem to have spilt my drink,' he drawls, 'I must be learning some of your bad habits. I guess I'll just have to mop it up.'

He proceeds to do so, using nothing but his tongue. At some point, various other body parts get involved and I pour the rest of the bottle into his lap, 'Oops, clumsy me.' I take great delight in returning the favour with my mouth until his hands are in my hair and his body is shaking and quaking. 'I've got to get inside you,' he says huskily and puts on protection and then he is and oh God, oh God, 'Alex!' I yell.

'Are you hungry?' he whispers later, raising his head from my hip, breath warming my skin.

I look down at him. Maybe I'm not as fantastic in bed as I think he is, if he can even contemplate other needs. I don't know if I'm hungry, I'm struggling to remember how to inhale. 'Uh,' I grunt.

He chuckles, grinning. 'I am.'

'Really? Hungry for...?'

He gets my drift and squeezes my waist in a tickle, making me writhe around on the soft bed.

'Not that.' He sits up, rolling his eyes. 'All you think about is sex, sex, sex, woman. I'm starving. Shall we call for room service?'

'I thought men were supposed to fall asleep straight afterwards?' I watch his eyes darken. He looks mean and dangerous and it's pretty sexy. 'It was just an observation,' I defend, edging away, my breasts jiggling.

His hot gaze zooms in on them and a firm hand clamps around the back of my neck, hauling me in for a swift kiss. 'Maybe I'm not most men. And maybe I'll fall asleep on you later,' he adds meaningfully.

'What, we order food and then I'm dessert?'

He winks. 'Maybe. Now go and find some menus.'

'Bossy!' I climb off the bed hoping the size of my naked backside won't put him off a repeat session, although it's too late to do anything about it now. He's already seen everything.

'Absolutely,' he mocks, 'but then, I am the boss.'

I pause in the act of pulling on his shirt.

'Sorry. That was stupid. What an idiot.'

'Technically we're off the clock,' I say lightly. 'You're not my boss after hours.' Tugging his shirt down to cover the tops of my thighs, I stick my tongue out at him. 'But I will go and get the menus, because I might be tempted to eat.'

Wandering into the lounge, I grab the room service cards off the side and pause, cheeks burning. Will this get charged to the room? Suppose Alex expects me to buy the meal. I'm not sure there's enough in my bank account. On the other hand I don't want to assume he'll pay because he's rich. I don't want him to think I'd make that assumption. People must use him for money all the time and I don't want him to lump me in the same category as them or his grasping wife. But if I make the offer to go halves can I find a credit card with enough available funds to cover the cost?

I'm overthinking this. It'll be fine, I'm sure.

Walking back into the bedroom, I find Alex engrossed on his phone, frowning and tapping the screen rapidly. 'Everything okay?' I ask.

He gives me a slow, sexy smile, 'It is now,' he says huskily, before carelessly throwing the phone on the floor. Something in my chest catches at the action. He's willing to put it down for me. Flinging the covers back, he tugs me closer by the hem of the shirt, 'I got bored, so I decided to check the markets. You took ages.'

'A few minutes,' I counter.

'It felt like forever.'

'It did?'

'Never mind,' he says, gaze fixed on where my boobs are pressed against the fabric of the top, before dropping to my bare thighs. 'Come here.' He pulls on the hem of the shirt again and once I'm on the bed switches his hold to the collar to bring me in for a sweet, unhurried kiss. 'Better,' he says, sitting back. 'Now hand me those menus. I've worked up an appetite.'

We lie curled up in bed together later, surrounded by plates scraped clean of aromatic Spanish dishes, both of us full to bursting. The room smells of spices and tender meats and fiery vegetables. I guess when you stay in a suite costing about a grand a night the kitchen never closes. Rain lashes against the windows, running down the glass in random patterns. It's cosy. I feel content, way more than in a very long time. I can worry about tomorrow, tomorrow. There was an uncomfortable moment when Alex insisted on accepting delivery of the meal alone in the lounge, but he was so thoughtful in passing me cutlery and napkins and condiments when we camped out on the bed (a suggestion he pulled a face at until I accused him of being uptight) that I forgave him wanting to be discreet.

Groaning and shifting, I press a hand to my overfed belly. 'I feel so fat.'

'Yes, you look it,' he agrees gravely, getting up and clearing the plates into the lounge.

As he climbs back into bed, I punch his arm playfully, 'Hey!'

'Oh, come on,' he lifts the covers and pretends to leer, 'you know you've got a gorgeous body.'

I'm incredibly, proudly flattered. 'Right answer,' I joke. 'You can have a brownie point.'

His shoulders rise and the movement rubs his wide chest against my side. 'It's only the truth. Anyway, you women are too obsessed with how you look.'

My mouth swings open. 'Maybe that's because any woman over a size six is considered obese and catwalk models are still skinny. Maybe it's because according to the media we're supposed to have impossibly glossy hair and long eyelashes and smooth, dewy skin that defies the ageing process. And anyway, isn't that a bit hypocritical? I bet the women you normally socialise with are all slim.' Why on earth did I say that?

'I'd love to say you're wrong.'

'But you can't.'

'No, I don't think the majority of them started out tiny, though, I think they battle with each other to be the slimmest. They put that pressure on each other. What they don't realise is men are simple animals. We're not that bothered about your weight or dress size as long as we get to touch it all, and play with it.'

I smother a laugh as his hand creeps under the covers to squeeze my thigh. 'You're right,' I concede, grinning. He seems thrilled at my surrender, until I add, 'Men *are* animals.'

'Well, in that case—'

And just like that I'm flat on my back, pinned down.

'No, no, I'll pop, I swear,' I giggle. 'I can't.'

'Okay.' He frees me.

I roll onto my side and within seconds he's settled in behind me, lean hips spooning my bum, a large hand resting across my ribs and holding me close. My back is against his toned chest and he presses a kiss to my hair.

'Night,' he murmurs.

'Night.'

This feels so easy. So right. I feel cared for, happy.

Alex gives a deep mutter of satisfaction and is asleep within minutes, but wrapped up in his warm hard body, my hormones and emotions are out of control, bouncing up and down. I lie wide awake for a long time, staring into the darkness. What have I done?

Chapter Twenty One

DAY FOUR

– Monday –

I wake on my stomach to murky dawn creeping around the edges of the curtains and a warm mouth surrounded by raspy, delightful stubble running a set of open kisses down my spine. I murmur drowsily, the muscles between my thighs clenching as a whiskered jaw moves to rub over my shoulder. My hair is gathered up and tucked into my neck. A hot muscular body slides against my back, pressing me into the mattress.

It wasn't a dream, Alex is in my bed.

And he stayed all night.

My head is foggy from lack of sleep and I'm barely able to lift my eyelids. I don't want to wake yet. Today is doomsday. Except I'll only be telling him to be honest with him, not to ask him for help. I'm walking away from the claim too. I can't pursue it. Not after spending this time with Alex. It's clear to me now. Some things you have to let go. Some things are just not worth it.

'Morning,' he says throatily, nibbling on my earlobe. Squirming, all I can offer is a moaned greeting in return, a flush running over my entire body. I feel feverish. Big hands slide my hands above my head onto the pillow. I'm at his mercy and open my legs, feeling wildly excited and wired, breathless.

'I thought we had to go over some work stuff this morning,' I gasp.

'It's still early,' he whispers, 'and I definitely have time for this.'

It's dangerous being dominated by him. I like it too much. A thrill of lust shoots through me and I twist beneath him, breasts swelling and nipples hardening as my hips lift off the mattress. He takes his time, covering my back with more kisses, sucking the pulse at the side of my neck. I wriggle, panting, shaking, wanting him to do it, take me on another orgasmic trip deep into outer space.

A scorching hand sweeps under my hip and a knowing finger finds the waiting heat and wetness and I grind myself against his hand shamelessly.

'Charley,' he groans, kneeling and tilting my hips upwards. I hear a rustle of foil and thank God that he carries condoms.

My inner muscles clench with anticipation, the sense of it so strong I can't breathe as I rest on my elbows. I expect a hard, demanding thrust and tense, but instead he fills me slowly, holding me steady so I can get used to the pulsing rigidity, feel every throbbing movement as he pushes in deeper. I close my eyes, arching my back, and only then does he start to move in and out, back and forth, leaning over me, his toned stomach and chest causing delicious friction across my damp back.

A purposeful hand plays with one of my nipples, sweeps down over my stomach, holds me as he pumps in and out faster and faster, groaning hotly in my ear. 'You're so sexy, it feels so amazing being inside you.'

Then we're both coming and I'm lost in sensation, my hands bunching up the bed covers, and I'm sobbing at a rush of pleasure so intense I think I might fly apart under his hands.

Sanity takes a long time to return. Will I be able to walk today? I wonder. Will he? Wow. I can't believe his stamina. There's something powerful and pleasing about someone being so desperate to have you they can go three times in twelve hours. But now it's the morning after. Bright light is spilling through the curtains. I break into a prickly sweat. It's time.

I stare at Alex as he stretches and leans over me. Short dark hair standing in spikes and peaks from where I've grabbed onto it so many times, the stubble that grazed my body earlier is evident in the dark, sexy shadow along his jaw. I breathe in the male scent of his skin. He's out-of-this-world gorgeous, out-of-this-world spectacular in bed. And so different to what I imagined when first meeting him on Friday.

'You're what my brother Kristian would call *isse omorfi*,' he tells me, splaying a hand over my tummy, translating at my puzzled look, 'a beautiful woman.'

'You should speak Greek more often. It'd be a shame to lose that heritage, though I guess it'd be unlikely, given your colouring.'

He pulls a face. 'Don't you like the way I look?'

'No,' I tease, blanking my face, 'it really sucks to be in bed with someone tall, dark and handsome, being bedded by a six-foot-something hunk. But every girl makes sacrifices, I suppose.'

'Right,' he answers dryly, squeezing my hip just where I'm ticklish.

'Stop, stop!' I laugh breathlessly, trying to get away.

He goes serious. 'Am I your usual type?' He studies my face closely.

'Why do you ask?'

He shrugs a broad, bare shoulder. 'The stuff you said to your friend on Friday on the phone.'

I roll over on top of him. 'Forget that,' I stroke his cheekbone, 'I was having a bad day and you'd annoyed me.'

'Uh-oh. No brownie points?'

'Nope.' I shake my head, 'In all seriousness, you're not my usual type. I usually go for creative guys. Tortured artists and struggling songwriters. Unconventional, free spirits.'

199

'Well I'm sorry if my suits and conventionalism disappoint,' he mutters stiffly, extracting himself and flinging the covers off, 'still, you seemed to enjoy it.' Picking his trousers off the floor and pulling them on: 'We should get up.'

A ball of steel hits me in the stomach, panic erupting. I'm not ready yet. Not ready to stop feeling wanted, and good.

'You didn't disappoint. And I've got news for you, Alex Demetrio,' scrambling out of bed, I throw a pillow at his head as he turns around, 'I don't think you're that conventional.' The pillow hits him right in the face and he scowls. 'Wanna play hooky?' I ask, holding my breath for his answer.

Glancing down at the phone in his hand, then at me, his scowl turns into a frown.

'Come on,' I pretend to pout, hands on my hips, 'we've no meetings 'til after lunch, and the company won't fall apart if you have a few hours away. When did you last take time off?'

'I'm not sure,' he admits. Eyes landing on my jiggling chest, he throws his phone down on the bed. 'Okay.' He gives me a massive grin I wish I could take a picture of and carry inside me forever. 'Race you to the shower.'

Half an hour later we're sitting at a plastic table in a run-down café just off Las Ramblas, the main series of streets running through the centre of the city down to the marina. We sip Café con leche y leche – a luscious coffee with a condensed milk and cream topping – and listen to the Spanish music playing from a tiny speaker in the corner, with a tangle of wires running from it. The paint is peeling and the cushions are tattered, but I like it. It's homely and charming in its own way.

I laugh as Alex struggles to shove a rolled-up napkin under one of the table legs to stop it wobbling.

'Bet this isn't your usual type of place is it?' I snort, popping a piece of fresh, warm pastry into my mouth and immediately wiping flakes from the front of my loose black jumper and tight grey jeans.

'Not any more,' Alex reappears from under the table. Picking up a teaspoon, he looks at its smudged, stained handle dubiously.

'What do you mean?'

'When I went to Oxford, places like this were my favourite. The scabbier the better. I could be anonymous in them. It was probably the best time of my life.' The corners of his mouth turn down and he looks sad.

'Scabbier?' I joke, trying to distract him, 'I didn't realise you knew such language, Mr Demetrio.'

He smiles reluctantly, 'Just because I speak formally in work situations, it doesn't mean I always do.'

'So why was Oxford the best time?' I lean forward, interested in his response.

'I could be who I wanted to be back then. If I wanted to pretend I was someone else I could leave the university and hang out in town, where no one knew I had money or wanted to be with me because of the family business. It's the youngest and freest I've ever felt.'

'And?' I prod.

'And, when I think about it, I feel like I wasn't young for long enough. Sometimes I feel life's passed me by a little. I…' A frown cuts a small line between his brows and he looks unsure, before confessing, 'I suppose I'd like to be out in the world doing something different; experiencing new things and meeting new people. Do you know what I mean?'

'I do know.' I run a finger over the back of his hand, feeling the connection between us. 'Moving to London was absolutely what I wanted, but doing it at eighteen forced me to grow up fast, because Jess and I had to take care of each other. In a way, we became adults too quickly.'

'Would you change it if you could do it again?' Alex asks, turning his hand over to capture mine, toying with my fingers.

My skin sparkles, body tingling. Like magic, if I thought such things existed.

I mull over his question, biting my lip. 'No,' I shake my head at last, 'because, well … I still have time to change things.' Saying it helps me realise it's true. 'I have plenty of time left, and apart from a joint mortgage, very little responsibility. How about you?'

'Unfortunately I have lots of responsibilities,' he evades and pulls his hand away, looking grim, as an elderly couple walk into the café. 'Charley, I don't know how to say this…'

'Say what?' Is he telling me it's over now? That's it?

'I can't – that is – we have to be discreet.'

'No PDAs you mean?'

'Pardon?'

'Public displays of affection. And I wasn't asking you to hold my hand, Alex,' I say, stung and irritated. 'Or kiss me in the middle of the street.'

'I know you're not expecting anything from me, which is good.' That stings too. 'But I mean what I said on Saturday night. I want my private life kept private, so when we're out in public—'

'Okay, I get it. We have to be careful. Noted.' I force myself to smile. He may have annoyed the heck out of me but I don't want our last few hours together ruined. I can also see proper anxiety in his expression. 'Come on,' I lick flakes of pastry off my fingers before gulping the aromatic sweet coffee down. Pushing the other pastry towards him: 'We went to so much trouble sneaking out of the hotel, you've got to soak up some of the local culture. Eat and we'll go for a wander, do a bit of window shopping, see if any of the street entertainers are out now they have to pay for licenses.'

'How do you know that? Have you been here before?'

'No. I watch a lot of travel programmes.'

'That's right. You said at dinner on Friday you want to travel.'

'At some point, yes.' It's a dream that seems a long way off at the moment, but I'll make it happen somehow, someday. Everyone needs goals. I raise an eyebrow as he starts devouring his croissant. 'Hungry are we?'

Cocking his head, he runs smouldering eyes over my body. 'I burnt off a lot of energy last night.'

I blush and joke. 'Well, whoever she was, she's a lucky girl.'

'Very lucky,' he says, staring at my mouth.

Shifting in my seat, I cast around for a way to change the subject so I don't launch myself across the table and break his no PDA rule. 'We should do something about your wardrobe.'

He pauses, mouth full of food, then swallows. 'What's wrong with it? These are expensive clothes, you know.'

'I know,' I nod solemnly, 'they're stylish,' I placate. 'But they're so ... bleurgh, formal. You haven't worn one casual thing, even yesterday.'

He looks blank.

'Sunday?' I prompt. 'The seventh day of the week, that people usually have a rest on.'

'Oh, yes. I knew that.' Taking another bite of croissant with white, even teeth, chewing and swallowing: 'I've got casual stuff at home.'

'Which consists of what?'

'Chinos, white shirts.'

'Whilst the suave Jude Law look is pretty sexy, a pair of jeans might be nice, especially if they show off your lovely rear end.'

'Thanks,' he smiles, looking ridiculously pleased at my comment, 'but I don't do *that* casual.'

'Why?'

'It's an image thing. I have to think about the family reputation.'

'What, are you royalty or something?' I tease. Despite him being CEO, and his social status, it's surprisingly easy to feel comfortable with him.

'No. I told you, we have old-fashioned values.'

'Come on, even princes go casual on occasion. Look at Harry and Wills. Is the world going to explode if you do? Will either of your parents keel over from a heart attack?'

He holds his hand out in a see-sawing motion. 'Fifty-fifty,' he jokes. 'The last time my brother Kristian turned up in jeans, Mum asked him to change and Dad locked himself in his study.' He stares into space before shaking his head. 'Fine, I'll take the chance, but if it all goes wrong I'm blaming you.'

'Not a problem, I've got lots of places to hide.'

'I wish I did.'

His candid comment makes me stop and think. It must be awful to feel like you have nowhere to run to if necessary. Still, if there's one thing I've learnt this weekend, he doesn't appreciate being pitied. 'You'll find somewhere,' I wave a hand, 'and if you don't, you're rich enough to buy your own private island, Richard Branson-style.'

He throws a napkin at me and I duck out of the way. 'Don't be cheeky,' he says and I open my mouth to apologise but he dead-pans, 'I can afford far more than one.'

'Good for you. That'd be nice.' I sigh dreamily, chin on my fist. 'White sands, vast azure skies, swaying palm trees.'

He flicks the tip of my nose to bring me back. 'Are we going shopping or not?' He leaps from his chair and pops the rest of the second pastry into his mouth.

'Yeah. Come on then.'

He throws a pile of money on the table without checking the bill. Although he doesn't hold my hand as we leave, a warm hand trails a fiery path down my back, making me shiver in response. Though no one can see it, I know it's there.

Talking about our favourite places in London, comparing notes, we mooch along Las Ramblas. There are a few street artists around to take advantage of the tourists, and I jump and let out an embarrassing girlie scream as a lifelike statue moves – a vampire spinning me into his arms and pretending to bite my neck with red-tipped fangs. I pull away muttering as Alex tries not to laugh, and fails, hugging me to his side when I stick my lower lip out in a mock sulk. As he lowers his head towards me, I push against his chest. 'Hey, no PDAs,' I say in a light tone, 'remember?'

'Yes,' an expression I can't read crosses his face, 'you're right.'

We stop in one of the shops at the northern end of the long, wide, paved street, tucked behind a discreet black door. Sitting in a plush, green-velvet chair filled with silk cushions, I soak up the atmosphere as I wait for Alex, trendy music pulsing from invisible speakers in the burgundy walls, a horde of young, cool staff floating around making drinks and tending to the exclusive clientele.

Alex comes out of the changing room wearing a pair of black jeans and a pale-blue open-necked top. Oh my. My knickers go into meltdown at the sight of his muscular thighs in the tight denim, the cotton of the top clinging to his wide shoulders and chest, the light shade managing to highlight how big and manly he is.

'What do you think?' he demands.

'Uh-huh,' I wheeze, nodding. I shoot a look at the nearest female assistant. She's stopped what she's doing to stand and gape at him.

'Do you like it?'

I suck my cheeks in, and gulp with great difficulty. 'Do you?'

'It's comfortable,' he shrugs. 'Think I'll go and try something else on.'

As he goes into the changing room it gives me a view of his delectable bum. I may just slide down into a puddle on the floor right now. The assistant and I look at each other. She recovers first, probably because she has no idea the contents live up to the packaging. I squirm on the chair, thinking about the things we did to each other, how warm and confident his hands are. Would it be very naughty to sidle into the cubicle and help him out of his clothes?

'You have a very handsome boyfriend, si?' The young assistant saunters over, tucking a few dark curls behind her ear.

It's too complicated to explain. My chest puffs up. 'Si,' I reply, wishing he did belong to me. Silly girl. Just imagine that on tap twenty-four seven, though. Wow.

Alex materialises again in dark-blue jeans and a black top, open at the collar. *Take me now*.

The shop assistant looks at him and turns to me with a raised eyebrow. *Why are you here shopping* her expression seems to say, *when you could be alone with him*? I completely agree, wanting to go back to the hotel room and push him up against the wall and do wicked things to him.

'Charley?' Alex crouches down in front of me, tanned skin and black hair looking sinfully gorgeous against the dark top.

'What? Yes. Fine,' I croak.

'I didn't ask you anything.' He chuckles, 'I was just trying to get your attention.'

'Oh.' Leaning forward I tuck my hands into his collar, feel the smooth skin of his shoulders, run my fingers into the hair at his nape. Our eyes connect and something around the area of my heart lurches. 'You know I like you, right?'

He smiles and the corners of his blue eyes crinkle. 'Yes. I like you too.'

I want to rest my forehead against his, close my eyes and make the world go away, but it's not an option.

'Good.' I sit back and clear my throat. 'Now go get changed and then buy some of that stuff. You look great in it.'

'Yes, madam,' he salutes, pretending to click his heels.

I sit back in the chair, head falling onto the headrest as he strolls into the changing room.

I'm going to hell.

Chapter Twenty Two

But I'm in heaven a few minutes later when we've exited the boutique carrying several posh bags and I spy a shoe shop. I drag Alex over to the large window, my eyes racing over the display. I'm a girl who loves her chocolate but shoes ... they're on another level. The ones that make me go still are open-toed and neck-breakingly high, covered with blue and purple swirls against a white background, reminiscent of renaissance artwork. Better still, one of them is lying on its side and I can see that the soles are red.

'Wow,' my breath fogs the glass.

'Nice?' Alex presses a hand into the small of my back and, after peering down into my face, grins.

'Magical.'

'So buy them.'

I check out the price tag. If I had a steady job and three months of clothing budget set aside I'd consider it. 'Can't.' It's a humiliating confession.

'I guess it is a lot to spend. Let me.' He reaches into his back pocket and pulls out his wallet.

'That's sweet, Alex, but I wasn't hinting. I don't want you to pay because you're the man, or the boss, or rich.'

'I appreciate that, but you love them.' One corner of his mouth curls up, 'In fact, from the light shining in your eyes I'm not sure which you're most excited by; me or the shoes.'

I chew my lower lip like I'm putting serious thought into it. 'It's a close contest, but they just have the edge.'

He smirks. 'Very funny. I'm not sure if they'd be very good company, but if that's how you feel, you should definitely buy them.'

I stiffen my shoulders. 'I told you, I can't.'

'Why?'

I may as well tell him. 'Because I'm broke.'

'Broke?'

'Yes.' This is so cringeworthy, especially with him being so rich. Super-yacht, luxury mansion, sports-car rich.

'Completely broke, as in you can't afford to eat?'

If only a crevice would open up in the chewing-gum-laden pavement and swallow me whole. 'Yes,' I reply tightly, 'pretty much.' I fight the urge to lay my head against his broad shoulder and cry.

'Ah,' he says, nodding.

'What?'

'The comments you made about money in the car on Friday make sense now. So, how have you managed this weekend?'

'Everything's paid for.' I shove my hands in my jeans pockets. 'Room, food and drinks.'

'What happened?'

I trail my eyes across the other shoes in the window, not really seeing them. 'I don't feel comfortable talking about it.' Now, out in public, is not the time to tell him about my chequered employment history.

'You can tell me.' He squeezes my waist and looks into my eyes. 'What is it?' he asks, trying to make light of it. 'Online bingo? An addiction to male dancers?'

'Close, but not quite.'

He sighs. 'You don't want to discuss it, I can live with that, but why are you struggling so much? Wouldn't your parents help if you asked them?'

'Yes.' I want so badly to lean on him, let him carry some of the weight.

'But you don't want to ask,' he guesses, 'because then they might think they were right, you shouldn't have moved to the city.'

I've never met a guy who understands me so well. 'Yes.'

He tugs on a piece of my wavy hair. 'And will they be right?'

'No,' I say fiercely, instinctively, 'they won't.'

'Because?'

'Because I was happy until recently, and the experience of pursuing my dreams has made me who I am. No one can take that away from me.' It spills out of my mouth and I stop. Regret and relief rise in my throat.

'So does it matter if they think they're right, as long as *you* know they aren't?'

I let out a shaky laugh. 'I guess not.'

'Everyone goes through setbacks, you shouldn't be ashamed. It doesn't matter to me whether you've got money or not and it won't to anyone who matters.'

'Easy for you to say,' I sniff, 'you're loaded!' Immediately backtracking, 'Sorry, that was rude.'

'Don't worry.' He pauses. 'My family has pots of money, the company does. Between you and me, though, I don't draw as big a salary as I could.'

'You mentioned that on the way to the hotel on Friday. So how come? And what about the designer suits, the Maserati? You're not going to tell me you live in a box under a bridge are you?' I look at him suspiciously, 'Because that I would *not* believe.'

'No.' His eyes gleam with mirth, 'I don't. I have a flat in London, one in Paris, and my own wing of the family home in Corfu. I'm not saying I don't enjoy having money, but the rest of the stuff is part of the image. There are far more important things in my life.'

'Like?' I'm confused. I thought all he did was work.

'Right at this moment, bedding a lovely redhead.'

I roll my eyes, grateful to him for trying to cheer me up. He makes life seem right. Or at least like it's okay, or might be.

No. I can't think that way. Stepping back from him deliberately to put some distance between us, I stare at the display again. It's not real, whatever's happening between us today. He's nothing to do with real life. The inflexible, solid glass of the window separating me from the gorgeous shoes is like the barrier separating Alex and me. We can see each other but we can't occupy the same space.

'Come on.' Spinning away from him, I wander down the street, looking up at the graceful Gothic architecture of the buildings surrounding us. 'What do you think is in there?' I point at nondescript double doors tucked under an archway in the side of a building, a flow of people entering and exiting.

'I don't know. Do you want to check it out?' Alex asks.

'Have we got time?'

He frowns down at his watch. 'Let's make time.'

I smile over my shoulder at him as he follows me, and watch as the smile dies from his eyes, face becoming sombre. What's he thinking? I wonder, but forget about it in the awe of the room I step into. It's like arriving in Narnia. Completely unexpected. An indoor food market is arranged in lines of stalls, the vibrant colours almost too bright for my eyes. I spin around. Red, orange, yellow, green, purple. Smoothies, fruit, cakes. Like a light glass-topped warehouse, the space is warm and filled with people. I can smell something deliciously spicy cooking and hear shoppers chattering as they buy stuff or meander down the aisles. 'Woah. Where do we start?' I ask, mouth slightly open in wonder.

Alex turns away from a stall owner with a blue bandana in her dark hair, handing me a clear plastic cup with a domed lid and a neon-pink straw sticking out the top of it. 'Strawberry and Kiwi smoothie,' he answers, gesturing down the alley of stalls I'm standing next to. 'Shall we go down there?'

'Thanks. Sounds good.' Taking a sip of smoothie, I make an *mmming* sound at the back of my throat. 'That's gorgeous. You have to try it,' holding out my straw to him.

Ignoring it, he hauls me in close and plants a kiss on me, tongue slipping between my lips. 'Tasty,' he whispers, stepping away.

'What happened to no PDAs?' I breathe.

Taking in the crowd of people sweeping past us: 'There's no one I know here. To everyone else we're just a couple enjoying a lazy day together.'

'Uh-huh,' I agree, fiddling with my hair, arranging it over one shoulder. We're not a couple, and when he finds out what I came on the assignment for we're not likely to be.

'Let's get cracking,' he says, tugging me forward.

An hour later we've walked up and down every aisle and have tried more samples than I thought possible. Tender meats and fresh seafood and sweet bread and dark fruity wine. 'Well, I'm not going to need any lunch that's for sure,' I tell Alex. 'Talking of which, shouldn't we be getting back to the hotel?' I'm surprised I'm the one to mention it.

'I suppose so,' he says reluctantly, looking around the market one last time before we push out the door back onto the grey street. 'I liked it in there. It reminded me of you.'

'Loud and full of food?'

'No. Colourful and fun.' He runs a hand through the lengths of my hair.

'Thanks. I'll take that as a compliment.'

'It's meant to be.'

He's being too nice. It's going to make telling him the truth so incredibly hard. Biting my lip, I dash off ahead of him, turning around to walk backwards. 'Last one to the hotel...' I trail off, searching for a suitable insult.

'Has to flash the other?' he suggests, eyes twinkling and intent.

'*Again?*' I exclaim, instantly understanding that his thoughts are centred around me and him naked on a bed.

'Is that okay?'

'Uh, yes!' Whirling around, I start jogging back down to the marina. To the hotel and the nearest bed.

One more time. I just need to be with him one more time

before I say goodbye.

As we approach the hotel, he takes my hand, yanking me down behind a large palm tree in a Mediterranean-style pot.

'What are you doing?' I demand.

'Shhh,' he turns to me. 'Hiding.'

'Um, why?'

'I don't want them,' he points out a couple of shady-looking men hanging around outside the hotel with cameras, 'to see us.'

'Oh, right.' The privacy thing again.

'Before you know it, we'll be all over the tabloids. I can't let that happen.'

'What about the women you get pictured with who appear in the celeb mags?'

'That's different.' He wipes his forehead with the back of one hand. He's actually sweating. 'They're my dates for public events. She knows that.'

'Who knows that?' I ask dangerously.

'Louise.'

'And that matters because?'

'Our divorce is being finalised and she's not happy about it. If she thinks I'm involved with someone, she'll drag it out even more.'

'Are you lying to me about the divorce, Alex? Is it really happening?' Kettle and pot and black for accusing *him* of being the one who's dishonest.

His intense blue eyes clash with mine. 'No.' He emphasises the word, 'Absolutely not.' Squeezing my arm to underline the point: 'It's happening. I'm telling the truth.'

I can tell he's being sincere. 'Then, for God's sake!' I snap, starting to rise.

'What?' He grabs my knees to pull me back to the floor.

'If that's what the whole not telling anyone and being discreet and no PDA thing was all about why didn't you just tell me? I would have understood.'

'I wasn't sure of you, didn't know you, and those other reasons still count. The clause thing and the wanting privacy.'

'Right.' Hmm. I want to tell him that's unfair and unreasonable, but he's got a point. I was a stranger. And in a lot of ways I still am.

I watch as the men start chatting, and one of them lights a cigarette. 'Alex?'

'Hmm?'

'Those women you get pictured with. You're not with any of them? None are friends with benefits?'

'Not all of them,' he answers absently, craning his neck to watch the men.

'What?' I ask darkly.

'Only a few,' he says quickly, catching sight of my outraged expression. 'No one special,' he adds. 'And not for a few months.'

'Oh,' I answer, mollified.

'Charley, will you do me a favour?' His warm breath puffs across my hair.

'What?'

'Can you go in first? I'll follow in a few minutes.'

'If it's that important to you.'

He gazes down into my eyes and I feel the powerful connection that keeps tugging me in. 'It is,' he whispers, tucking a piece of hair behind my ear.

'See you up in your room then. Don't take too long.'

'I won't.'

A delicious forty minutes later I'm standing in the massive shower conditioning my hair. As much as staying in Alex's bed is very tempting, I've insisted on returning to my own room. I need space and time to brace myself for what I'm doing straight after lunch.

Telling him. Everything.

When he joined me in the suite it felt as though something had changed between us, maybe because we spent the morning together. Neither of us said anything; we didn't need to. He just took my hand and led me to his bedroom and we undressed each

213

other, the rustling of our clothes and the humming of the air-con the only sounds.

He touched me like I was a rare shell discovered on a faraway beach, fragile, worn away by the sea over time, and ready to break. The incredible passion was still there, but it took second place to something else. Our bodies fit together perfectly and he held my face and kissed me with sexy tenderness. I skimmed my fingers down his spine and held him close when he was inside me. When I came, I felt more at peace than I have in a long time, tingles running through me, tears clogging my throat. And when he held me afterwards we sighed at the same time and laughed about it and I thought, *I want to stay here forever*.

That was when I knew I had to get away. Disengaging, I slid out of bed and mumbled an excuse about needing to get ready, unable to look him in the eye.

I feel sad and horrible. What's he going to say? He's so smart and confident and has such a mega-amount of pride. He'll hate me. I take a deep breath, and release it slowly. I'm a big girl. I will deal with whatever happens.

Looking down, I realise I've written *I'm sorry* in four-inch-high letters on the steamy cubicle door. Losing the plot. Still, I might as well carry on as I started.

Stepping from the shower, I wrap a fluffy towel around my body and traipse into the bedroom, door open so I can see into the lounge. There's no sign of Alex so he's probably on his way down to bag us a table for lunch in the restaurant.

An impatient knock sounds on the main suite door. Perfect. A towel is hardly the best outfit for receiving guests, but what if Alex has forgotten his key card? Another knock. Or could it be room service? Has Alex changed his mind? A third round of thumping. Better to answer before whoever it is decides I'm dead or incapacitated and feels duty-bound to kick the door down. Which could be pretty humiliating in my current outfit.

'Coming,' I call. Hurrying through the rooms, I swing the door open, a polite greeting freezing on my lips. 'Tony,' I grind out. 'Alex said he'd sent you home.'

'You wish.'

'What do you want?' I fold my arms across my body, hating the way he's looking at me. I'm in a towel, alone in a hotel room with him. It reminds me of the scene in *Pretty Woman* when Julia Roberts' character gets a visit from Richard Gere's slimy friend and ends up getting clocked. But this is real life, not a film.

'Just a quick chat with the big boss,' he answers, looking round me.

'He's not here,' I bite.

'But he is usually, right?' He shoves his way into the room and I jump back. 'Interesting that you share a suite,' he muses, 'but with separate bedrooms. Maybe you're not as a close to him as you might have led me to believe yesterday.'

I should set him right. Not that I can deny I've slept with Alex, but I could tell Tony my motivation has nothing to do with the claim. But the worried glint is still in his eye and right now I'm more worried about my personal safety than anything else. If him thinking I have Alex on side protects me, I'll keep the pretence going for now.

Pulling my spine straight, I ignore the towel rising up my thighs. 'Tony, this is getting tired.' I force a bored tone, 'Just leave.'

'You're sleeping with him.'

'You're right,' I admit with a genuine smile, thinking how earth-shattering the sex is. 'I am.'

He deflates, obviously expecting a different response. 'You are?'

'Yes.' I watch with glee as his normally pink skin goes white. A wild, reckless feeling uncurls inside me. After what he did, I want to see him squirm. 'And let me tell you, it's certainly not a big ask when it's with someone as gorgeous as Alex.'

Tony takes a threatening step towards me and although I flinch internally, on the outside I project bravado, imagining I'm the star of a TV soap. 'He's very easily persuaded with the right currency,'

215

I cross my arms under my boobs and hike them up to make my point. 'What can I say? I've got him hooked.' I stare him down, hoping he won't lose his temper and punch me. 'I don't think we'll be going to tribunal now. They'll give me a vast settlement and, in return, I'll forget all about what you did.'

'I don't believe you,' he spits.

'Well here's the proof you need.' Crossing the room, I thrust Alex's bedroom door open to reveal the messy bed and the heaps of clothes on the floor I'm now grateful neither of us tidied away. It's a crude demonstration and inside I'm cringing, but a girl has to do what's necessary.

'Oh.' Tony staggers back, heading for the main door.

'Oh.' The echo comes from the open doorway, where Alex stands glowering, all trace of our time together wiped off his face, looking like the cynical, stern CEO from Friday.

Oh, fuck.

Oh double, triple fuck.

Chapter Twenty Three

'A–Alex. Did you hear—?'

'All the important things,' he grinds out, looking murderous. 'How shall I summarise? How about sex, tribunal and a pay-off?'

I can't breathe, feeling like I'm going to be sick on my own feet. In the middle of taking a shaky step away from Tony towards Alex, I stop, feeling like a Jurassic insect frozen in amber. Spots twirl and spin in front of my eyes. I screw them shut, wishing it would make the scene disappear.

Alex shakes his head so hard when I open my mouth, a vein starts pounding in his forehead. 'Don't.' The word is so full of contempt I flinch. He whirls to Tony. 'You know each other already? Before yesterday?'

'Yes, sir,' bastard-face confirms, stepping away from me, a smug smile curling his mouth.

The fury rolls off Alex in waves, his eyes narrow, jaw tight. 'What's her name? And how do you know her?'

'Charlotte Wright.' Tony's eyes gleam with triumph. 'She was my manager at the casino. She was proven to have sexually harassed and bullied me in a disciplinary hearing. She lost her job.'

'I bloody did not! That's a lie. It was the other way around! He was after my jo—'

'Shut up!' Alex rounds on me, breathing hard.

217

I'm so stunned I obey, clamping my teeth shut. It's not an argument I want to have in front of Tony anyway.

'Mr Ferrier.' Alex stares at him, hard and cold. 'You can leave now. But you don't tell anyone about any of this. Do you understand me?'

'Yes, sir.' Tony swaggers to the door and gives me a self-satisfied smirk over Alex's shoulder.

As soon as he shuts the door behind him, I rush over to Alex, grabbing his arm. 'He's talking rubbish. I didn't—'

'Is it true?' Alex asks in an icy voice, shaking me off. 'Is your name Charlotte Wright?'

'Yes,' I cry anxiously, 'but—'

He looks like he wants to kill someone, probably me. 'And were you dismissed at a disciplinary?'

'Yes! But I didn't do it. Tony—'

'And do you have an ongoing tribunal claim against Ionian Casinos?'

I want to latch onto him physically, beg him to listen, but when I move forward, his disgusted expression scrubs the idea. 'Yes, but I'm dropping it.'

'If I called the court office now they'd confirm that, would they?'

'No. I haven't done it yet, but I'd decided to.' As I say it, I really feel it. I can't let it consume my life any more. Tony's done enough damage. It's time to move on.

'That's convenient,' he says sarcastically, face going hard, sliding forward to get in my space.

Lifting my chin, I stare him right in the eye. I may be in the wrong but I won't be intimidated. 'Firstly,' I state in a clear voice, holding a hand between us, gripping the towel with the other, 'back off. Secondly, just hold on. Don't jump to any conclusions.'

He breathes in and out, circling away to put a sofa between us. 'I respect the first. As for the second, don't give me orders. I'll do what the hell I want.'

'I'm not trying to order you around, I'm just asking you to

listen. You don't have the right—'

'The right? Cheats and liars and fraudsters don't have any rights in my eyes.' His laugh is bitter and makes me want to cry. I've hurt him, just like Louise did. I've made him think I don't want him for who he is, only what he can do for me. He is so, so wrong. He needs to understand that. He needs to hear me.

'You cold bitch—'

'Alex—'

'You're nothing but a—'

Striding forward, I don't try and hide how bloody incandescent he's making me, slapping my palm on the sofa. 'Stop it!' I shout. 'Now! It's not how it sounds. I was going to tell you! Will you just listen?'

'No,' he yells back. 'You lied to me, deliberately hid that you were an ex-employee, told me in the car on Friday you knew nothing about the company.' His mouth curls. 'I should have followed my instincts. Women aren't to be trusted. And it all makes sense now. You said yourself you're broke – win a claim of sexual harassment and wrongful dismissal at tribunal and get, what, fifty, sixty thousand – but blackmail the CEO and get even more. What a conniving bitch. You're even worse than Louise.'

Nothing else he could say would hurt as much because after last night I know how much he detests his ex. His voice is so full of venom that for the first time I feel tangible fear, a dip in my stomach. 'Alex, that's not what I was after. I just wanted a fair hearing. Tony made it up and I knew I didn't have much of a chance of winning at tribunal, so I came along to just...' I flounder.

'Just?' Alex asks softly, and somehow it's worse than any shouting.

'Get to know you, explain who I was, tell you my side of the story, and see if you might help. Or something. I didn't have a proper plan. It was short notice, I had a friend at the agency, we thought it might help and – it was crazy, stupid. But I had to do something! You don't know what I've been through because of

219

him.'

He sweeps a hand through the air. 'I'm not interested in your little sob story,' he snarls. 'And even if I believed any of what you just said, you slept with me.' His voice is deep and precise, like sharp steel cutting into my bruised flesh. 'You're just like those WAGs,' he condemns, 'willing to prostitute yourself in return for cash and possessions.'

'I am *not* the same as Louise,' I bellow, throwing both hands up in the air like they can actually stop the toxic words erupting from his mouth. I rub my temples. I need a moment to clear my head, start again, help him understand. 'Let's take a break,' I whisper, 'I'll go and put some clothes on and make a hot drink and we can talk this through.'

He laughs harshly. 'You're delusional. You really think I'm going to stick around and have a cosy pot of tea with you? There's nothing more to say, other than I won't be settling your claim and I'll make sure we fight you with everything we have.'

'I told you, there'll be no tribunal.'

'Why not?' He holds onto the back of the sofa with both hands, knuckles white. 'You're in the perfect place to blackmail me now we've slept together.'

I look down, feeling ashamed. 'Alex, I know you're angry and hurt but—'

'Don't be cocky,' he throws my teasing words back at me in a rigid voice. 'I'm angry because you've abused my trust. I'm not hurt. I have no reason to be. If I was hurt, it would mean that I cared.' His gaze is violent as he comes round the sofa to tower over me, 'And don't fool yourself.' His breath brushes my cheekbone as he enunciates the next few words, staring straight at me so that I get the message. '*I. Don't. Care.*'

The sentence sends shredding pain running through me, strands of darkness twisting around it.

'Wait!' My clenched hands are shaking with adrenalin and prickly anger. Edgy frustration makes me shudder as he storms towards the door. The gorgeous guy who takes his responsibilities so seriously, who is compassionate and good, the one who has a secretly playful side, who I'm attracted to, and who is such an angel in bed, is gone.

I have to try and get him back.

Stumbling across the room, I block his exit, squeezing myself between his body and the door, leaning back against it.

'I didn't plan to sleep with you. It just happened. I tried to tell you the truth last night, but we ended up in bed.' Reaching out my hands, I lay them on his chest, hoping he'll feel my sincerity, praying he'll look past the lies and see the real person, and the truth.

But his livid look screams *don't touch me* and he grabs my upper arms and moves me out of the way.

He yanks open the door with a loud click, 'You had the time to tell me whenever we were alone together. Including this morning.' Something tries to settle on his face but he blanks his features.

'It was never the right time. And then when it was … I didn't want it to end. I enjoyed spending time with you. You get me,' I keep babbling as he opens his mouth with no doubt another less-than-flattering comment. 'I lied about my name, and my last job and the tribunal, yes. But that's all I lied about. Everything else I said was the truth. I swear it,' I bang my fist on my chest, 'I swear I'm real, and being honest now. And I promise I never assumed because we slept together you would—'

'I've heard enough. It's good you never assumed anything,' he says coolly over his shoulder as he steps into the corridor, 'so you won't be disappointed you won't be getting paid.'

'For the assignment?'

'If that's how you want to take it.'

I crumple against the door frame, unable to believe his words. He means the sex.

He refuses to look at me. 'Get your stuff and get out, *Miss Wright*. The car will take you to the jet.' His head angles oddly. For a second I wonder if he might relent, 'To be absolutely clear,' his knuckles tighten around the handle, 'I never want to see you again. We're done.'

A vicious slam punctuates the remark. I gawk, wondering if the door will come off its hinges. I hurl myself down onto the smooth leather sofa, place my hands palms down to anchor myself. 'Shit. *Shit*. No,' I moan. A louder voice is galloping through my head. *Yes*. I bury my face in a cushion, tears leaking out, hoping that if I ignore the world, it will ignore me for a while.

I shower again, needing to feel clean. Unfortunately no combination of water and soap is strong enough. The phone rings as I stand dripping and dazed in the bedroom. 'Alex?' I snatch it up.

'It is Maria from reception,' her warm accented voice murmurs. 'Your car will be outside for you in twenty minutes, madam.'

'Thanks.' I fumble the phone back into its cradle with a hollow clunk.

Then I shake myself. I don't have long. Flinging my stuff into the suitcase, I yank on underwear, tights and a figure-hugging blue woollen dress with vertiginous black high heels, twist my hair up and dab make-up on, hoping it's enough to conceal the state of my face.

I stagger through the suite to knock on Alex's bedroom door, my movements uncoordinated and jerky. No reply. Shame, anger and defiance thread through me.

I can't leave like this. I've got to try again.

Bending over the dressing table in my room, I scrawl a series of jumbled notes, screwing them up and tossing them in the bin. The minutes are ticking by and my breathless panic increases as the moments pass. *Calm down*. Biting my lip, I take a moment to study the wide Mediterranean outside the window, the bright January sunlight glinting off white caps, sky blue and brilliant. I wonder if the sea would swallow me whole if I asked it to. It's calming, though, the view reminding me I'm a tiny part of a much bigger world, giving me perspective.

With a new sense of resolve, I go to the desk and bend over the pad.

Alex,

I'm sorry. But only for lying, not for the things you want me to be guilty of because trusting someone would be too hard. I get why, but you can't go through life never trusting anyone, even if, like me, they give you good reason to doubt them.

The money for the assignment would have helped me survive a little longer, but that was the only sum I was interested in receiving after getting to know you. This weekend started out about justice and vindication and yes, compensation for what Tony did to me, but I can see I went about it the wrong way.

I was wrong.

I didn't sleep with you to gain your trust or for a pay-off. You and I just happened. It wasn't planned. In fact it was the very last thing I was looking for. Maybe at some point you'll talk to Tony and look in his eyes for the truth and you won't find it there, because all he's ever done is lied. I know I have too, but only about what happened to me before we met and the reasons I came here, not about who I truly am – someone who likes you for the person you are behind the CEO persona.

Alex, I hope you do what you want with your life, whatever makes you happy.

Charley x

A sob lodges in my throat. Grabbing my case, handbag and coat, I leave my bedroom and shove the note under Alex's door before rushing to the lift. I smile blindly during check-out, focusing on the exit. Then there's a blank spot and I'm staring at the clouds outside the small round window of the plane. During the flight the staff do their best to look after me but I stare vacantly out of the window. I don't even get nervous on landing, I'm too numb, and by the time the wheels touch down on tarmac my eyeballs are dry and scratchy with the effort of not crying in front of *his* crew.

Stumbling from the plane into the back of the car, there is one thing I know for sure.

I'm not the same person I was four days ago. The weekend, and knowing Alex, has shifted something inside me. I'll need to figure out how to deal with it. But not now.

An hour passes and I'm delivered straight to my flat, knocking the front door shut with my hip and throwing my keys into the purple ceramic bowl on the hallway table, a sweet but gaudy gift from one of Jess's pupils. I throw my coat at the square functional rack constructed by Jess and I over the course of a long, fraught Saturday afternoon when we ended up cursing everything about self-assembly furniture, modern and Scandinavian.

I tuck my case against the wall. The flat looks strange, both new and familiar.

'Jess?' I texted her in the car but haven't received a reply. She's probably in class.

Kicking off my heels, I flex my cramped toes back and forth against the floor whilst sifting through the post. Mostly bills. I expected more envelopes but then realise the postman's only delivered once since I left on Friday afternoon. I traipse into the lounge. Painted in crisp whites and creams with wide bay windows, it looks out over a colourful bustling London street and is my favourite room. It offers little peace now. I deflate onto one of the large black sofas heaped with colourful Middle Eastern-style cushions.

Gazing at the cracked ceiling, I can't believe I was in one of the most amazing and cosmopolitan cities in Europe a few hours ago and am now back in London in the bitter cold. Now I'm home safe I can blub and shout and throw things if I want to. I wait for it to hit, but nothing happens.

So I force myself to act, stomping into the hallway and dragging my case into my room, upending everything onto my bed. Racing around unpacking, I stop only when my phone beeps. I rifle through my bag, hope soaring for a short moment. Alex?

Hi. What happened? Staff meeting, home about fiveish. See you then. J x

I should spend the next few hours looking for a job but I've got to face facts. After this weekend, my career is over. Once Alex tells the agency what I did I'll be even more unemployable. I can't summon any upset at the thought. What's wrong with me? Have I turned into an emotionless robot?

Stripping off my clothes, I stuff them in the laundry basket and change into my favourite loose boyfriend jeans and a baggy white top. I scrub my make-up off, until my skin is blotchy, and brush my hair into a ponytail. Wandering back to the lounge, I sprawl out on the sofa beneath the window and throw an arm over my face, fatigue overpowering me. I close my eyes, hoping to erase the entire weekend. Instead, all I can see is Alex's face grinning down at me, all I can hear is his deep husky rock-star voice when he's turned on, all I can feel is the imprint of his warm hands on my body.

He's just a guy. Forget him. I squeeze my arm tighter over my face and after a few long minutes I fall into darkness.

A gentle hand on my shoulder drags me from an ignorant bliss I'm reluctant to leave behind. 'Charley, wakey wakey.'

'Hmm?'

'I'm home hon, wake up.' The hand rocks me again.

'Okay, okay.' Forcing heavy eyelids open, I squint at Jess. 'Urgh. What time is it?'

'Just after half five. I ran a little late, sorry.'

There's concern in her sharp features, anxiety reflected in her grey eyes. I cast off the last dregs of sleep, sit up and yawn widely. And freeze, remembering where I am and why. Home, cast out. My face burns. 'Oh, Jess,' I groan, rubbing my forehead.

'What happened?' Shrugging out of her cropped leather jacket, she tosses it on the other sofa, her white-blonde bob darker than usual. When I glance past her, I see the night and heavy rain pressing in against the window.

Sitting and stretching, I meet her eyes. She is here now, and cares. Just like that, it rushes at me. My bottom lip quivers and though I bite down hard I can't stop the emotional devastation, the scorching humiliated tears. 'You're going to say I told you so.'

Jess sucks in a breath through her teeth and spins on her heel. 'I'll get the wine.'

When she returns with two giant glasses and a bottle of Pinot, I tell her everything, and finally cry.

Chapter Twenty Four

Back to Life, Back to Reality

– February –

As I wrap newspaper around my favourite silver-framed mirror, the black print smudges and rubs off on my hands. 'Bloody hell! Perfect.'

Kneeling on my bedroom floor, I rub my fists in my eyes and try not to let the tears escape. I hate this. Absolutely hate it. *No. Focus.* Leaning forward, I grab a fragile jewellery box Jess gave me for my fifteenth birthday and start to roll it up in more cheap newspaper.

To my utter shock, I got paid for the weekend in Barcelona, though the letter accompanying the payslip made it clear the agency would be taking my name off their books immediately. I longed to call them and say I was transferring the money straight back – there's a part of me that really didn't want to take Alex's money, however indirectly it might come to me – but I couldn't afford to be proud. So I gave most of it to Jess to make up for some of the back pay on the mortgage, and reminded myself firmly it was for the work I did, not sleeping with the CEO, whatever he might believe.

But now the money's all gone and so has the month I gave myself to find a job after I got back. It's no good. Once I found the letter from the mortgage company Jess hid in her room, stating the last two payments were overdue and threatening repossession of the flat if payments don't become more regular, I knew what I had to do. I can't ruin the wholeness of Jess's life by trying to hang onto the tatters of mine.

It's just a shame I didn't ask my parents to lend me money when I went home for Christmas, because it turns out they've invested it all in the IT security firm Tom is setting up. Now that he's back from Afghanistan and has bought himself out of the army he's trying out civvy street. I'm really pleased for him, but it just doesn't help me. Which is why I'm taking up Dad's offer to move back home and into the summer house for a while. Only until I get my life back on track. Until something good happens. I've always believed hard work and passion are the things that get you where you want to be in life, but the events of the last few months have made me think luck plays a part too. And at the moment I'm on a streak of the bad stuff.

Rising, I massage my aching back and stretch out my shoulders. I've been packing for three hours. Time for a break. Going into the kitchen, I grab a mug, throw in a teabag and sugar and flick on the kettle. How many more times will I get to stand in this room and do this?

God. This is my home, where I belong. I don't want to leave.

Waiting for the water to boil, I wonder if Alex makes his own tea. I wonder what his homes are like or if he's ever had to leave somewhere he loves. I growl in self-disgust. He keeps creeping into my head, though I do my best to drive him out. I'm sure Alex is getting on with his life and has forgotten all about me, so I need to stop giving him headspace.

I start scrubbing the oven top where Jess made us carbonara last night. The girl can really cook, but she leaves behind a mess reminiscent of a world war. Does Alex prepare his own meals or have a private chef? The second is entirely possible, even though he intimated he only put up with the trappings because it came as part of the deal.

'No, Charley,' I mutter, 'you have to stop this. No more thinking about him, wondering about him. You will never,' I scrape at a stubborn piece of dried cream on the hob with a butter knife, knowing Jess would murder me if she knew, 'see him again.' Giving the hob another wipe and throwing the cloth down, I wash my hands and pour the kettle. 'And now I'm talking to myself,' I puff out a breath, ruffling my fringe, 'great.' I stir the teabag around the mug, a suitable reflection of my spinning thoughts.

This is stupid. Surely in a few more weeks any feelings for and about Alex will be gone. Like a teenage infatuation, the emotions will fade with distance and time. I stir the teaspoon faster. I'll forget the way he looked at me, smiled, the common ground we discovered even with the difference in our circumstances, the way I could be opinionated with him and he liked it and didn't feel threatened, that he respected my career. I won't think of the laughter and banter and that when he relaxed, this warm, sweet guy came out. I will turn away from the memory of how it felt to be within reach of his gorgeous face and sexy, built body. I'll try my best to block out the warmth and excitement of the brilliant sexual chemistry between us. I won't remember my surprise that he's so much more than the spoilt rich CEO playboy I was expecting, how vulnerable he is about the family duty he takes so seriously.

Yes. I *will* forget. Definitely.

And I've dropped the ET claim, even though it sickens me to think of Tony sitting in my office at the casino. I'm getting on with my life. I have to.

The spoon, guided by my agitated hand, whirls round in ever increasing circles, clank, clank, clanking against the side of the mug until it flies free, flicking me with scalding tea.

'Ow! Bugger it!' I jump back, brushing hot drops from my arms and running my smarting skin under cold water. At least the pain stops me moping. Fishing the teabag from the mug, I add milk, jerking as the doorbell rings.

I'm not expecting anyone.

Tugging at my casual green sweatshirt, I shrug at my faded, well-worn Levi's. It's Sunday afternoon and I'm dressed for comfort, not company. Jess is out and I thought I'd be alone. The bell rings again as I walk down the hallway. *Okay, okay.* When I unhook the chain and swing the door open, I draw in a sharp breath.

'Alex!' I step back, astonished, sharp lust pinging my silky knickers. Despite humongous bags under his eyes and stubble darkening his jaw, he's still ridiculously hot. 'W–what are you doing here?' Mouth as dry as the Egyptian desert, I lick my lips. Alex on my doorstep is completely surreal. He belongs in Barcelona, at the hotel, not here. What the hell does he want?

Anxiety, hurt, confusion, anger. The conflicting emotions race through me like the colours and numbers on a spinning roulette wheel. I wait for it to slow and stop, for the ball to settle into a slot, for one emotion to win out. I grimace. Perplexity, with a massive dash of hope, seems to be the winner.

'Can I come in?' His face is unreadable, I've no idea what he's thinking.

I run my eyes over his tight black jeans and clingy grey v-neck jumper under a winter coat. They look like things from our shopping trip on that last day.

'They suit you,' I blurt. *What am I doing?* Balls. Looks like I've no control of my emotions. I need to woman-up. But he's so big and dark and gorgeous. I'm startled my memory has faded enough in the last month that I've forgotten how olive his skin is, how black his hair, the depth of his clear-blue eyes, which are now deadly serious as my gaze meets his.

'Thank you,' he replies, something flickering across his face, 'any chance you can answer my question now, though?'

'Question?' I'm so blown away by him being here I can't think properly.

'May I come in?'

There's a brief ache in my chest at his deep familiar voice and my breath snags somewhere in my throat. For a second, recalling the shouting and horrid things he said in the hotel suite, I consider slamming the door in his face. Then I remind myself I'd lied to him and hurt him, and burning curiosity to know *why* he's here overrules any anger. But I need to take control.

'It depends what you want.' I lean against the edge of the door. 'Are you here to yell and make accusations again?'

'I hope not.'

'You hope not? I was kind of hoping for a no to that one.'

'I'm here to talk.' A sliver of ice coats his voice, 'I'm hoping it won't end in any drama.'

'Well, let's do our best then,' I say irritably, waving him to go along the hall. Slamming the door, I follow. A flash of heat prickles along my skin as I catch the smell of his fresh male aftershave, so I scoop in a deep breath as I walk into the lounge.

He turns from where he's standing by the window and shoves his hands into his pockets. It underlines his height and taut strength of his body and an image of him standing by the hotel bedroom window in his jockey shorts flashes through my mind.

'Shall I take your coat?'

He sort of *prowls* towards me, like in vampire books, and I keep still, craning my head further and further back so I can stand my ground as well as maintain direct eye contact. My eyes widen as he stops a foot away and the air between us thrums with unspoken tension. At least it does for me. And I suddenly want to tell him I wish things were different, that we'd met in other circumstances.

Shrugging his coat off, he hands it to me. 'Thanks. I came here to ask you to tell me what happened with Tony Ferrier.'

'Right.' My fingers curl into the expensive wool of his coat and I can feel his body heat on it. Putting it down hastily, I point at the nearest sofa and sit on the other. 'So why now?' I ask as he perches opposite me. 'How come you want to talk like adults a month after you sent me home with such indecent haste? And why, after the unforgivable things you said, should I even have this conversation with you?' I can't help it, the anger and humiliation rolls back over me. I'm in the suite that awful Monday, on the end of his guilt-making comments and edgy pain, feeling ashamed and defiant in equal measures. Shaking my head, 'Don't you think it's a bit late, Alex?'

His jaw clenches but he consciously relaxes it, breathing in deeply through his nose, a muscle flexing in one tanned, whiskery cheek.

He smiles grimly. 'I hope not. And you're right, I made some totally unacceptable comments. I regret some of them,' his voice is deep and ragged, 'very much. In my defence, I was furious.'

I expected him to fight hard, say he had every right to say what he did. His response takes the wind out of sails that were billowing with turmoil and misery. 'Yes, I get that.' I edge forward on my seat. 'And I understood why, after what you told me about Louise and how important it is for you to have honesty and trust.' I pause, 'I'm really sorry I made you feel so– so—' I'm not sure how to describe it. He said in clear terms that day how little he was upset by what I'd done … because he didn't care. That I was no better than Louise. That he never wanted to see me again. 'Well,' I shrug, staring at the small, chipped, wooden coffee table.

He clears his throat. 'I read your note once I'd calmed down and also spoke with the agency. They said you hadn't made a complaint or anything.'

'Why would I? And thanks for arranging for me to be paid. It helped.'

He waves a hand in the air. 'You earned it.' He drags a hand through his hair as my face falls. 'I meant for the PA work, nothing else.' He swears under his breath. 'Anyway, I spoke to HR last week and they confirmed the tribunal has been withdrawn.'

'Uh-huh.' It feels like there's a question behind his comment but I don't know what he wants. Feeling exposed and vulnerable, I get up and pace over to look out the window, hiding my face.

The room's quiet except for our breathing. Thankfully, all I can smell is the sweet vanilla candle on the windowsill. If I had to handle the sexiness of his scent again, I don't think I could get through this conversation. I gaze at the regimentally positioned lamp posts and dark-brown leafless trees along the street, not really seeing them, then look to the sky. The clouds are grey, torrid rain is coming. Shivering, I wrap my arms tightly around my waist.

'Charley?' Alex prompts.

As the sky outside darkens, I realise my face is reflected faintly in the window, so I concentrate on keeping my expression neutral, in case he can see it.

'I know in Barcelona I didn't let you explain the full extent of what happened but you were pretty adamant that you'd done nothing wrong, that it was all Tony. So why drop the claim if you think you're the one in the right?'

I spin around, smiling sadly. 'I know I'm in the right, Alex, I don't need a judge to tell me that. I realise that now. And I didn't think I'd win, what with all the hotshot lawyers and things you said. Besides, I'd already decided to drop it over the course of the weekend. I'd had enough of it all. Remember what I said? Sometimes it's knowing when to walk away.'

He stares at me. 'I hate to see you so … defeated, after how feisty you were that weekend.'

I hitch my chin up, dropping my hands onto my hips as pride kicks in. 'Don't worry, Alex. I'm still that girl, and I'm not defeated. I'll be okay.' Saying it makes me feel it, and helps me believe it. 'I'm just moving forward.' I frown. 'And honestly, I'm really confused at your reaction because now your company won't have to go to tribunal. So you should be happy, right?'

'Yes. But—' He runs a hand over his stubbly jaw, making a delicious rasping sound. 'I went to the casino yesterday.'

'You did?' Fear spikes. What else did Tony say about me? How much lower can Alex's opinion get?

'Tony wasn't there, he was at a training course, but I spoke with a few members of staff in his absence.' He pauses. 'A croupier named Kitty was one of them.'

'Really?' Hope springs up. Kitty's on my side. Not that Alex will automatically believe her, but still. 'And what did she tell you?'

'She's in a difficult position, seeing as she now reports to him directly.'

'Yes.' Disappointment pulls my shoulders down. 'She is.'

There are footsteps, and warm fingers bring my chin up to look into his intense long-lashed eyes. 'But she still stuck up for you. And once she knew who I was and I'd asked her to be absolutely honest … She really doesn't like him, does she?'

'No.' I wrench my head away from his touch. It's too tempting to want to get nearer. I want him too much.

He frowns. 'I got the impression hers is a widely held view.'

'What do you want me to say, Alex? That I hate the guy? I do. I also hate that he's there, when I'm not. And I can't stand the thought of him drooling all over the female staff.' I shudder. 'But why are you going to believe anything I say? After all, I lied to you about my name, my job, my background.' I throw the challenge down but he ignores it.

'I looked over the results and accounts from the period you were manager. They were solid. Better than that. I read all the staff appraisals too. You got the best out of people, were well respected and everyone I spoke to yesterday liked you. They talked about your enthusiasm and the hours you put in.' Looking thoughtful, 'Your record was clean.'

'Yes,' I nod, a warm spot growing inside me. But somehow it makes what I've lost even worse. 'Not that it made any difference at disciplinary.'

He overlooks my tone. 'It got me thinking. So this morning I reviewed all the documents that were considered at the hearing and the appeal.'

'You did?'

'I did,' he says solemnly. 'Then I called the investigator and had a chat with him, followed by phoning the senior HR Manager and getting her to go into the office and pull some information together for me.'

'On a Sunday?'

'Yes.'

'You are *such* a slave driver.'

'Guilty.' A hint of a smile turns up a corner of his mouth. 'Though I did apologise for disturbing her roast lunch.' He studies my face, 'The thing is, I needed to know.'

I want to ask why, but instead say, 'And?' biting my lip while I wait for his answer.

'We found a file note of a call from a female casino manager having problems with a male assistant back in the summer. She wanted to discuss it anonymously and was given some advice.'

I nod, 'Me. My call.'

'I gathered. Then it got more interesting. The HR Manager went through the confidential file notes of queries from female staff who've worked at the same places as Tony over the last couple of years.'

'And?'

'There's an interesting trend.'

Gulping, I step nearer to him. 'Like what?' I whisper.

'I can't tell you the details, but it's enough that I think that Tony isn't as innocent as he painted ... and that the disciplinary panel might have got it wrong.'

'You believe I'm telling the truth?' I throw my hands out, hitting his flat stomach accidentally. He lets out a small *oof*. I didn't realise I was so close. 'Sorry. Why are you telling me this, Alex? Aren't you afraid I'll reinstate the tribunal, using this against you?'

He catches my fluttering hands, holds them firmly between our bodies, then runs his finger along the inside of my wrist. I shiver. 'And will you?' he asks roughly, eyes raking my face. 'Use it against me?'

I look him head-on, doing my best to ignore the tingles zipping up my arms into other parts of my anatomy. 'No. You'll do the right thing if you find out it's Tony who was lying.' I take a deep breath, regret making my voice hoarse. 'I was telling you the truth in Barcelona. I wasn't on assignment looking for extra ammunition, I was just desperate for someone to listen. I also needed the money, and a current reference that doesn't leave employers running for the hills.' What a titanic fail that was. A bitter smile twists my mouth. 'After I raised the claim, Tony spread rumours about me around the city, meaning I haven't been able to get a decent job since the casino. And I still can't. Which is why I'm leaving London.'

'What?' He drops my wrists, confusion racing over his face. 'Why? You love the city.'

It hurts he knows me so well. 'I've got no choice. I've no job, and Jess and I can't meet our mortgage payments on one income. My parents don't have the money to help me. So I'm moving back home, going south for a while.'

'But you can't go.' He looks upset, sagging onto the sofa.

'Why not?'

He runs a hand through his hair. 'Because I need to know all the facts. So I can decide what to do.'

'About what?' *Me? Us?* Hope reignites and I hold my breath. He was horrid the day he found out about me, but it wasn't unforgivable behaviour, not in context. It came from him being Mr Uber-cynical because of his past and the world he lives in, and from being livid. I wouldn't fall into his arms if he asked me to. Not straight away. But I might give him, and us, a chance if he said he was sorry, and meant it.

He goes still, expression distant. 'About your case. About Tony. If you're telling the truth I have to do something about him.'

'And what if you end up thinking I'm the liar after all?'

'Then I can walk away with a clear conscience, knowing

everyone's been treated fairly.'

'I see.' This visit isn't only about professional pride. He needs to know who's being truthful. It's about his principles, honour, doing what's right. I fight the urge to rub my burning eyes. It's not personal. It's not about wanting to see me or missing me or to say he made a mistake in Barcelona when he forced me to leave.

'I didn't mean to upset you, Charley.'

'You haven't.' My laugh is hollow. 'I'm just tired. Which is why I'll tell you everything now – so you can make up your mind and then get on with your life.' The thought causes a slow agony to creep along my nerve endings.

'Good. I– Any chance of a coffee while I listen?'

'Fine.'

Bringing two cups of hot, strong liquid velvet in from the kitchen a few minutes later, I feel better. Making coffee has given me time to push away some of the turmoil. I need to be clear and concise and firm. Because I want him to believe me. God, do I want him to, so much.

Settling across from him, my drink goes cold as I tell him everything. What happened, what I did, how I felt, what it cost me. It's emotional and hard, and at times my voice shakes and I struggle to get the words out. My nose tingles with suppressed tears and I gulp back regret until it's a sharp ache at the back of my throat. Alex sits and listens intently, eyes focused, occasionally sipping his coffee.

'That last conversation with Tony you overheard in the suite,' I say, almost finished, 'was me trying to get him to back off. I was scared and I felt vulnerable. I also couldn't let him walk away thinking he'd won. Again.' Glancing up, I brush my fringe from my eyes. 'But I promise completely and absolutely what I said wasn't true. It wasn't about the claim. The very last thing I expected was to sleep with you and when I did, it wasn't to get anything from you. I was ... caught up in it. Our chemistry took me totally by surprise.'

'Yes,' he admits quietly. 'Me too.'

His comment makes me brave. 'Alex?'

'Yes?'

'You didn't have to come here.' He raises his eyebrows quizzically and I go red. I haven't blushed once since I last saw him, but here I go again. 'I mean, you could have phoned. Was there a specific reason for *seeing* me?' I try not to look hopeful, or like I'm asking for anything.

He frowns, 'I needed to see your face when you told me. To decide if you were sincere or not.'

'Oh,' I croak.

Sharp disappointment pins me to my seat. I can't move, something heavy settling behind my rib cage. It's messy, it's complicated and it'd probably never work out but I wanted to know if our heady time together in Barcelona was a one-off or something real. Not that it matters. I leave the city next weekend and I don't think Alex is the type to have a long-distance relationship. And it's coming through loud and clear that if he liked me in Barcelona, it's not how he feels now. It's too late. I blew it. And he did too, by not stopping to listen.

Springing from the sofa, I swallow to get my voice working. 'Well, now you've done that you can go.' I need him gone. Before I embarrass myself. 'Thanks for popping in.' I fling open the lounge door and point down the hallway. 'You must have loads of important things to do.' Hint, hint get out.

'I haven't finished my coffee yet.'

'I just remembered that I have somewhere to be,' I blather wildly, checking my watch, 'so if you don't mind.' I make a shooing motion.

'I'm not a sheep, stop herding me,' he mutters ruefully, but places his cup on the table and walks down the hall. 'Still, I get the message. I'm going.'

I open the door. 'Sorry about the coffee.'

He stops in the doorway and turns, searching for something in my expression. 'I'll go then.'

'Yes,' I nod, switching my attention to my scarlet toenails.

'I'll call you with my decision after I've spoken with Tony.'

I want him to believe me without talking to bastard-face. I want him to look inside me and see I'm telling the truth. But why should he when, from the very first moment we met, I deceived him? When his last serious relationship taught him people use him for his status and wealth? I'm expecting too much. 'There's no need,' I say brightly, fixing my gaze over his left shoulder. 'Just pop it in the post in writing. Jess can forward it if necessary.' *I don't want to see you or hear your voice again, it would be too much.* 'And if you find in the end you believe me,' I gulp, 'promise to deal with bast– Tony appropriately.'

'I will.' It sounds like a vow.

'Good. Bye then.'

His palm against the door stops it swinging shut.

'Charley, I'd much prefer it if—'

'*Alex.*' I bite, and he freezes. 'I appreciate you tracking me down to hear me out, but please go. Now.'

'Just one thing,' he says, holding the door against my attempts to push it closed.

'What?' I growl, exasperated.

'I just wanted to say that,' he rubs the back of his neck, 'I wish things were different.'

Staring into his lovely blue eyes: 'Me too,' I mutter. 'Goodbye, Alex.' As soon as he drops his hand, I swing the door shut with a resounding thud.

There's a long silence before I hear his footsteps walk away.

Chapter Twenty Five

I slide slowly to the floor against the wall once he's gone, staring at the carpet between the frayed cuffs of my jeans. Tears blur my vision and a ball of hurt unfurls in my chest. My head droops forward like a flower deprived of oxygen and light. The sorrow is raw and fresh, like a scab pulled off a healing wound.

Alex is a good guy at heart, but damn him for coming here. For bringing everything back; what I did and what we might have been to each other if we'd met in another time and place. Big fat tears roll down my face and I wrap my arms round my upraised knees, holding myself together. I want to howl, but am afraid if I start I won't be able to stop. So I sit there, and I realise it can't be infatuation. Not if I'm this devastated. But I can't let another guy wreck me like Tony did, though in polar opposite ways, one with sweetness and the other with darkness.

'No. You're moving on, remember? Get up, Charley. This second.'

Pushing up from the floor, I breathe through my mouth so I don't inhale his scent as I stride into the lounge. Bugger. He's forgotten his coat. Oh well, he's likely got hundreds of the things, he can buy another one easily enough. If not, I can parcel it up and ask Jess to drop it into head office. Folding it, I shove it into the hallway cupboard, out of sight, out of mind. If only I could do that with its owner.

Returning to the lounge, I scoop our mugs up and put them in the sink, trying not to rub my thumb along the rim where Alex's lips touched it, because that would be juvenile. I rush down the hallway to my bedroom to start boxing up more stuff. Keep moving, keep doing and you'll be okay.

Twenty minutes later the doorbell rings again. *Leave me alone,* I groan under my breath. I wait, hoping if I keep quiet they'll go away.

Another ring and then a sharp knock and then, 'Charley, open up,' Alex's impatient voice orders. 'I know you're still in there. I've been outside for almost half an hour and you never left.'

God, will this torture never end?

'So you're stalking me now?' I walk into the hallway and call through the door. 'What do you want? Have you come back for your coat?'

A mutter of disbelief is swiftly followed by an odd laugh. 'No. I didn't even realise I'd left it.'

'What then?' I demand, wrenching open the door.

'I've been sitting outside in the car thinking.'

'And?'

'And I can't leave it like this now I've seen you.' He leans against the door frame as though it's propping him up.

'Leave what like what? You told me what your plan is, we agreed you can write with the outcome. It's fine. Whatever you decide Alex, I'll accept. I told you, I'm getting on with my life.'

'Us. Leave us like this,' he states softly, stepping forward and rubbing his thumb along my forehead. 'Smudge of ink.' He breathes when I raise questioning eyebrows. His eyes go hot and dark.

I stumble back against the opposite wall. 'There is no us. That was obvious when you sent me home so swiftly. And you were pretty clear earlier that you came here for professional reasons, not to see me because you wanted to.'

'Then it was me who lied this time. I was scared. Am scared,' he says boldly. 'It would be a big risk for me to get involved.'

241

What's he saying? That he wants to be involved with me, or can't be? I gulp, stupid hope fluttering in my stomach like a flock of birds launching into flight. 'That's right,' I say softly. 'Because everything I said today could be a lie. I could be exactly like Louise.'

'But I don't think it is, and I don't think you are,' he stuns me by admitting. 'We shared something that weekend and you were honest and open, warm and unguarded with your opinions. You were concerned about me, you wanted to help. I don't think you can fake that, even if there were things you weren't telling me. More than that,' his mouth spreads into the crooked smile I love so much, 'I think you liked me, just for me.'

'Wow.'

'I know.' Stepping over my threshold and closing the door with a quiet click: 'Did you? Do you?'

I tug the bottom of my top down, twist nervous fingers in it. He's asking me to make the first move, roll the dice and see where it lands, but I'm not sure I can. 'Even with your cynicism and your mistrust of female staff and your need to keep any relationship private because of Louise playing games and that I might be a liar … you still want to know the answer to that question?'

'Yes,' he answers, looking very serious and intense and far too sexy.

'Even though you haven't spoken to Tony yet and heard his version of events?'

'Yes!' Sliding closer, he crowds me up against the wall and grabs hold of my face in both hands so I have to look at him. 'Just try, Charley. Try. I've had weeks to think about that weekend, about you. Wondering if my instincts in Barcelona were off, debating whether I should follow logic or gut feeling.' His touch changes, fingers pushing through my hair. 'I'm ashamed to say I hoped you'd complain to the agency so I could write you off completely. But you didn't and I couldn't let it go, couldn't forget you, so I went down to the casino and…'

'What is it, Alex?' I whisper, super-aware of his touch, but more

242

concerned with his words.

Taking a deep breath, he tilts my face upwards. 'I think we might be a risk worth taking. So answer my question will you, put a guy out of his misery. Do you like me just for me, or not?'

'What were your instincts about me? And what about the clause and bad press because you're going against it?'

Groaning in mock frustration: 'Instincts? That you make me feel better. About everything. You understand me and don't see the CEO thing as either a bonus or a barrier. That I should trust you because you're different from other women. Good different. Clause? You're not an employee, and even if you were, I've decided I really don't care.'

'Oh,' I squeak, relief and joy thundering through me. 'In that case—' I shove him backwards and our bodies crash into the other wall as I push in and kiss him, hot and deep, throwing all of my craving for his glorious body and sexy sweetness into the connection between our mouths.

I want him so much. I've missed this, missed him. It feels so good, so right when he lifts me in his arms, big, warm, demanding hands on my hips, kissing me like he'll never stop. My pulse goes crazy, my breathing shallow as I cling onto him.

He sets me on my feet but keeps holding me tight and our clothes fall in heaps and puddles along the hallway as we strip each other, needing to get closer, needing naked skin. Alex runs sweltering kisses down my throat, bends his head to my breasts to nip and lick his way down to suck my nipples and I can hardly breathe. Hurried hands grasp and massage and grab.

'Bedroom?' he pants against my mouth.

Throwing my arm out to the side in a half-hearted gesture, I take his lovely, kissable lips again, begging for more. Yet, as Alex walks me backward into the bedroom, I can feel a change. He slows down, lightens the touch of his hands round my waist, lifts his mouth a fraction, and when he stands back to look at me and brushes my fringe out of my eyes, it reminds me of our last time together in Barcelona, before our argument. The tension, the silence, the sense it meant something more than simply glorious sex. The feeling we had an amazing connection.

I look him up and down. We're in our underwear, and though he looks a little leaner, he's as ripped as ever, shoulders broad and well developed, thighs muscular and hairy, and his erection straining against his jockey shorts. I'm panting too, heaving, sweat gathering along my nape, knickers damp with need. I'm enough of a modern girl to know that I don't need a man to survive, but having a relationship for the sake of it and wanting a particular guy to be happy are two different things. And I want Alex. He's my guy, I realise. It's not just *like*. I don't just want to keep having spectacular sex with him.

I fell for him in Barcelona.

I'm in love with him.

As crazy as it is, it's the truth. Kind of love at first sight, but strung out over one life-changing weekend.

So I do the hardest thing. I put my hand against the twin wings of his graceful collarbones and push him lightly away, my fingertips skimming along his smooth, tanned skin.

'I can't.' I shake my head, gulping. 'I'm sorry, but I just can't.'

'*You can't*? You're not playing games with me, are you Charley?' His eyes gleam as he waits for me to explain myself.

'No! No way. But, I'm sorry. I can't do this,' I flick a hand between our bodies, 'again, until everything is resolved. If it goes wrong … well.' I can hardly tell him it'll hurt too much because I love him, not when he's only talked about *like* and *being involved*. I mean, what does he even want? Friends with benefits? Dating? A more serious relationship? Is he even free to have a relationship, with his ex's scrutiny of him? Would he do the commuting thing, given I'm soon back home?

He's said some nice stuff about a risk worth taking, but how does he actually feel about me? I don't know, and I'm not ready to ask. What I do know is I've already given too many pieces of myself to him and can't give any more. 'There can't be any more lies or misunderstandings or uncertainty,' I offer at last, crossing my arms over my boobs. 'So I guess you'll be going now.' *That sex is off the table*, I finish silently.

But, instead, the gleam in his gaze increases to approval and he gives me another world-shaking, crooked smile.

'It kills me to say it,' he looks down at his bulging shorts and shakes his head wryly, 'but I understand. And I agree. I need to resolve what happened between you and Tony. And I'm on the cusp of finally signing the divorce papers. We should wait, if only for a few days. Then we can talk properly about everything. And I'm going, but only because I can't promise to keep my hands off you if I don't.' He pauses. 'Come here.' Bringing me in for a quick, hard hug, he drops a kiss on my mouth, squeezes my bum, then leads me down the corridor so we can gather our clothes and get dressed, sharing smiles. It is so unbelievably sweet he's willing to wait, and wants to, that I almost drag him back to my room and tell him I've changed my mind.

'I'll be in touch,' he says five minutes later, as he backs out of the front door, making me giggle when he pops back round it and steals a last hot, sloppy kiss. 'I promise.' He taps me on the nose, 'Stay out of trouble.'

After he's left, I sink back against the door, taking in long, deep breaths. He is so adorable and I'm head over heels. I laugh at his last comment. Never mind what he said – I'm already in trouble.

Chapter Twenty Six

It gets worse the next day.

Instead of the phone call I dread from Alex, saying he's spoken to Tony and never wants to see me again, a harried-looking delivery driver arrives at my door carrying a fantastical, gobsmacking, massive bunch of flowers. Red, yellow, green, bright pink, they remind me of the sound and colours of the market in Barcelona the morning we played hooky.

Jess strolls out of the kitchen carrying a plate of sandwiches as I place my signature on the electronic gizmo for the delivery man. 'Woah!' she says, coming to a standstill. 'Look at those. Are they for me?'

I frown as I close the door behind the man, my stomach dropping. Maybe I've assumed wrong, they could be from Jake, though I'm not sure he's the flowers type from what she's told me.

Plucking a card out of the foliage, my stomach lifts again.

Charley

'Nope, sorry. Me,' I grin.

'Come on then, give up the goods,' she smiles. 'I've got to get back to school in time for afternoon registration.'

Tearing the tiny envelope open with indecent haste, I cut my finger, sticking it in my mouth to suck up the blood. Jess rolls her eyes. *Will this girl ever grow out of her clumsiness?* I can practically

246

read the words in large scroll above her head. Dropping my hand, I stick my tongue out at her and read Alex's card aloud.

Flowers from my new favourite place, for my new favourite girl.
See you soon.
A x

His new favourite girl. 'Oh, no,' I moan. 'Is he trying to kill me? I thought I was in trouble but ... now what am I supposed to do?'

'Don't worry, it won't last for long,' she says. 'They all get bored with the fancy stuff after a while,' she frowns. 'Saying that, they're very nice and erm, bright, but I kind of expected something a bit more posh and expensive from a billionaire.'

'They're perfect,' I scowl, walking into the kitchen to start rooting around in the cupboards for something to put them in. 'They're to remind me of the great time we had together in Barcelona.'

'Oops, my mistake!' she smiles, producing a vase from under the sink and filling it with water for me as I find the scissors and start cutting open the cellophane to get to the flowers. 'I stand corrected. Just promise me you'll be careful,' her tone changes, 'I don't want to see you hurt again.' She passes me the vase. 'I've got to get back to work. I'll see you this evening.'

After I've arranged the flowers and put them in the middle of the lounge coffee table with a satisfied smile, I go back to my chaotic room to box up books and CDs. Jess's words keep spinning through my mind. I don't want to get hurt either, but every time I think about Alex's flowers I feel warm. It's thoughtful, it's romantic and it's a positive thing to focus on against the discomfort of packing up my things to leave the home I love.

Over the course of the afternoon I keep realising I'm staring into space with a soppy grin on my face. Boy, I really am a goner.

Once Jess gets home from work we start fixing dinner together whilst she chatters about what happened at work and the funny thing a year-nine pupil told her. She trails off, glancing into the lounge. 'They are nice flowers,' she says grudgingly.

'Thanks very much,' I tease, putting a pan on the hob to boil water for rice.

'Charley.' Her voice is serious.

'Yeah?'

'About you moving home—'

'There's no other choice. We've talked this to death. We can't afford it and I won't let you lose this place.'

'But I've been thinking. We could sell up and rent another place together or we could rent this place out and—'

'Stop it,' I say briskly, adding salt to the water. I can't look at her or I'll cave, and that wouldn't be fair to her. 'I appreciate it, you know I do, but we'd still need money, which I haven't got, and there isn't time for what you're talking about. You're a great friend, but this is my problem not yours. You've got your job, and I know you love the rat-bags you teach, and,' I inject breeziness into my voice, 'you've got Jake. For as long as you want him.' Going over to the corner unit, I hunt for the chilli sauce. 'And living together could never have been forever. At some point we're going to find guys we want to settle down with, so—'

Making an exasperated sound, she pushes past me and pulls the jar from the unit. 'You've changed your tune.' Setting out an onion, minced beef, plump red peppers and a bottle of Worcestershire sauce: 'Before Barcelona it was all, *I'm a career girl, I've got other things to focus on at the moment, the last thing I need is a man mucking things up.*'

'Yeah, well...' I traipse over to stand next to her, watching as she deftly peels the onion under cold running water.

'I know what you're doing, Charley.' She lifts one eyebrow and slides a sideways look at me through her shiny blonde hair, 'and I understand. I just wish—' She sighs.

'I know.' I squeeze her shoulder.

The doorbell rings. Glancing at Jess's onion-juice-covered

248

hands, I wipe my hands on a tea towel. 'I'll get it.'

'Okay. More flowers?'

'I doubt it!'

Shrugging, I pad along the hallway carpet. 'Hello—' My intended greeting dies on my lips when I swing the door open to find Alex's driver on my doorstep.

'Good evening, Miss Caswell.'

'Hi Evan. Is everything all right? I'm not supposed to be somewhere am I? Is Alex okay?' I say anxiously, peering over his shoulder into the communal corridor.

'Everything is fine. Mr Demetrio sent this over for you.' Bending over, he picks up a wrapped package leaning against the wall and holds it towards me.

'Oh. Thank you.' What now? Is he going to keep showering me with presents? And is it guilt or apology, or something else? 'Do you want to come in? For tea or something? We're just making dinner but—'

'I'm fine, Miss. My wife is expecting me home.' He smiles, 'But thank you for the offer.'

'It's Charley, remember?' I smile back. 'I'll let you go then.'

'Goodnight, Charley.'

'Thanks. Night.'

Shutting the door, I kneel down on the carpet and peel open the layers of classy, embossed white and navy wrapping paper, biting the inside of my cheeks. He doesn't need to keep spending money on me, I hope he knows that. Still, I can't deny I'm enjoying it. Though it's not the price tag I'm interested in, it's the fact he's thinking about me.

'Are you coming to finish making dinner or what?' Jess charges into the hallway. 'Oh. Alex again?'

'Yes.' I lift the lid. 'Oh, wow!' I breathe reverently.

'What—' Jess comes over and looks down into the box. 'Nice,' she says, appreciatively.

'Gorgeous,' I sigh. 'Heavenly.' Pulling out the blue, purple and white swirly mega-high heels I admired so much in Barcelona and letting them dangle from my fingers. 'He remembered.' He bought me shoes.

A scrawled note attached to the inside of the box lid catches my eye.

Wear them, enjoy them. A x

'Well I'm guessing they're going to be painful rather than enjoyable at first,' I comment. 'But they really are beautiful.'

'Okay. I'm not a shoe kind of girl.' Jess is more into biker boots than stilettos. 'And I know I was a bit underwhelmed by the flowers to start with.' Jess leans over me to study Alex's note. 'But I've got to say I'm starting to think you're really lucky. This guy knows what you like. It's sort of sweet. He's courting you.'

'He is not!' I laugh. 'And if he was, it'd be totally arse about face because we've already spent a whole weekend together and—'

'Had amazing sex?' she finishes, grey eyes shining. 'Uh-huh. Still. Just saying. Sweet. Now come on Cee, I'm starving, let's go sort out dinner.' She tuts when I stand up and gaze longingly at the shoes. 'Ok–ay,' she sighs good-naturedly, 'You can go and try them on.'

'Thanks!' Without giving her a chance to change her mind, I go into my room and pull on the shoes, admiring them in the full-length mirror. They're stunning and sexy and Jess has to call me three times for dinner before I take them off and join her.

Two days later Alex calls. We've talked in the meantime, when I called to thank him for the gifts, managing with a big effort to speak like a grown up and not squeal like a little girl, but when he asks me to go and see him at his flat my stomach does a mini-flip.

'Okay,' I murmur. 'What's your address?'

'I'll send Evan for you.'

'No, I'll tube it, thanks.' I'd rather leave on my terms if it all goes wrong.

Thankfully the underground station is only five minutes away from his place because I'm wearing the shoes he bought me and they are *really* high. I'm stupidly nervous as I meander towards his posh apartment block by the flowing Thames, getting slower and slower the closer I get. As I hover by the building entrance, trying to figure out the security panel, a heavily muscled guy comes pounding down the stairs in tight blue and white running gear. After giving me the once-over, he flashes me a cheeky smile and holds the door open. A detached part of me realises he's pretty fit, but there's only one guy who matters.

'Thanks,' I murmur, pushing my way in, nerves flaring and sending tremors through me. I dimly notice black, sparkly tiled floors and white walls and gold trimmings before I walk straight into a lift that seems like it was waiting just for me. Pressing **P** for the penthouse, I stare at my reflection in the mirrored walls. Pride has made me put battle gear on; the new shoes and a black woollen dress that shows off every curve of my body and clashes beautifully with my hair, or so Jess told me in slightly less wholesome words. The aim of the outfit is either that Alex will appreciate it so much he'll want to pull it off, or it will be forever etched in his memory as I walk out of his life. I bite my lip. Has he got his divorce? Has Tony admitted everything? Does Alex want to be friends with benefits or to really *be* with me? Is this where we properly begin?

The plushness of the lift, including the underlying scent of lemon and classical music being piped in from somewhere, yells out that the place belongs to the mega-wealthy. It's expected, given what Alex told me about his lifestyle. What's unexpected, and rocks me back on my heels, is the woman who slams Alex's front door as I step into the wide, carpeted receiving area.

'I wouldn't bother,' she spits, lunging for the lift doors before they slide shut. Clipping into the lift, she turns and hits a button with a long, immaculate nail, giving my tight dress a disdainful look whilst pulling her own unmistakable designer togs straight.

'Whoever you are,' she hisses, 'he's in a foul mood. As always. Bastard.'

I stand open-mouthed as the doors swish the stranger away. Whoever *I* am? Who the heck is she? A friend? An acquaintance? It can't be Louise, can it? Whatever the relationship, she's everything I'm not, a classic petite green-eyed blonde beauty in designer gear. Much more Alex's world than mine. She can't be a girlfriend, Alex wouldn't have lied, would he?

I don't think we have any more secrets. I hope not. We've had enough to feature in an episode of *EastEnders*.

Then I wonder what he did to aggravate her so much. The Alex I know isn't a bastard, though he was leaning that way a bit the day we met, with his stern glances and arrogance and orders. But that's not who he is really.

Whirling around as I hear his door open, I come face to face with Alex ... holding a little girl with remarkable blue eyes.

'Charley!'

What the – he has a *daughter*?

He has a daughter and never told me.

I slump back against the wall, sick, shocked, hit by a surge of anger and sharp disappointment.

Looking at me and flushing, he puts her down and crouches to her level. 'Layla, can you go inside please? I need to speak to this lady quickly.' He runs a gentle hand over her dark-blonde hair and something inside me tugs hard. 'I'll just be a minute. You go and watch some Dora.'

The little girl nods obediently. 'Yes, Daddy. Then Layla can have a dwink?' Fingering the edge of his t-shirt sleeve, her plump fingers splay against his muscular bicep. She's so tiny and he's so big. I melt inside a little but harden myself to it. He lied to me. After the way he reacted to my dishonesty, he didn't see fit to tell me the massive secret he was keeping.

'Then can I have a drink please?' he corrects. 'And yes, I'll get you one soon, okay?'

She thinks about it for a few seconds very seriously and then nods. 'Yes, Daddy, okay.'

As she trots away, Alex whips back to me and I'm ready for him. 'You've got a child?' I explode.

Waiting until his daughter's out of earshot, 'I was going to tell you,' he says defensively.

'Really?' I chuckle, but there's nothing funny about it. 'I'm not the only one good at keeping secrets, am I, Alex?' Shaking my head, 'I can't believe it. All those conversations on the phone that weekend, the way you were so stressed out. It wasn't about Louise, was it? It was about Layla. You're such a hypocrite! You were so judgemental about me lying to you, but you had a child and didn't tell me!'

'We kept our marriage and child private and I wanted it to stay that way,' he whispers furiously, 'I wanted to protect Layla from the scrutiny of the press.' He rubs a hand over his dark hair, blue gaze tormented. 'Charley, I've been fighting Louise for regular access rights since we split, and in Barcelona she was making completely unreasonable demands. And she's always been so impossible about me seeing anyone I couldn't chance upsetting her when I was so close to getting a divorce and joint custody. I couldn't risk telling you about my daughter that weekend,' his voice rises, 'you were a stranger.'

'Who you kissed and then slept with! You told me about Louise, Alex. You could have told me about Layla.'

'Don't throw accusations at me!' he shoots back, eyes cooling, 'I wasn't even close to telling you. When I found out you lied to me and were after something, it didn't help, did it? You, more than anyone, should understand why I've kept this quiet. I was doing my best for my daughter, trying to achieve something good for both of us, something fair. Similar to what you wanted in Barcelona from me.' A bang sounds from the living room and he gives me a wild-eyed look. 'Charley—'

'You need to go, I get it, but…' I run sweaty palms down the front of my tight dress. 'Fine. You didn't tell me in Barcelona for the reasons you've just explained, but were you going to tell me any time soon, Alex?'

He pauses a fraction too long and I have my answer. 'That's a no then,' I say tightly.

'I would have—'

'When?' I demand hotly. 'When she started school, or turned sixteen?'

'I was thinking a few months.' The coolness in his eyes heats with anger. 'But didn't know if you'd be around for long enough.'

That stings. My eyes go blurry. 'Thanks,' I gasp. 'I guess I know where I stand now.' A pretty clear indicator a long-term relationship wasn't on the cards.

'I'm sorry. I didn't mean it like that. Argh.' He tugs on his hair so it does that sexy standy-uppy thing. 'A lot's happened today and I'm still trying to deal with all the ramifications, and God knows you've had a shock—' Another bang and his jaw clenches. 'I'm sorry, but whatever else I feel, my daughter has to come first.'

'But—' *I understand that.*

He cuts me off. 'Please. Give me some space, Charley. Just leave me to it.' All I hear is *leave me alone.* 'I'll call you.'

Of course his child comes first. It's what any halfway-decent parent should do, but God does it hurt that he can set me aside so easily. He's stressed and under pressure, but he's not inviting me in to be a part of it, to help him figure this out. I'm on the outside looking in. He doesn't have faith in me, in us, to protect his daughter. Which tells me everything I need to know.

'Don't bother,' I choke, 'There's no trust, Alex. And without trust?' I rake my eyes over him one last time, my chest aching. '*There's nothing.*' Lurching to the lift, embarrassingly the heel of my shoe catches on the carpet and I stumble, falling heavily against the wall, forehead striking the plaster. Ouch. Bloody typical.

Alex springs out of the doorway and grabs me, eyes anxious. 'Are you all right?'

I rub my head, feeling the bump already swelling. His last sight of me is this irritating, DNA-imprinted clumsiness that's a hundred times worse when I'm around him? Fantastic. 'Yes,' I bite, cheeks flaming, 'I'm just great.' Being held by him is bittersweet, his body through the t-shirt and jeans as warm as ever, muscles in his shoulders flexing. I quiver, knickers pinging. No. Hot sex and a gorgeous face and laughter do not equal lasting love. Commitment and honesty are more important.

I look into his face as his arms squeeze me close. Tears clog my throat, thickening my voice. 'I can't do this. Let me go or don't. Let me in or send me away. Pick one.' A beat. I wait for his decision. There's a cry from the apartment behind him. He drops his arms and my eyes fill up. 'Bye Alex,' I whisper.

Turning my back, I punch the call button. I can't speak. This is unholy agony. Alex doesn't offer any comment, I simply hear a huge sigh and the door shuts with a click. When the lift arrives, I stumble into it, pressing the **GF** button and staring at my feet. I frown as I see the blue, white and purple swirls. I can't stand it. Just before the lift doors slide shut, I kick them off and throw them onto the carpet by his door, where they lie lonely and discarded.

I can't have any reminders of him. It would hurt too much.

As the lift goes down, I realise I didn't ask what he decided about Tony. And I'm not sure I even care any more.

Chapter Twenty Seven

Sighing, I settle into the corner sofa of my local village pub after a windy and uncomfortable walk. The weather has chilled in the past few weeks, snow hitting the ground for the last three days in a row. Usually I love snow, but this year it's plain irritating. It's March; it should be starting to feel like Spring.

'Wine?' My friend Lisa asks, long black hair glossy under the lights.

'Vodka, straight,' I reply grimly, 'the bigger the better.'

'Okay honey,' she says with a sympathetic glance I ignore, 'back in a minute.'

Leaving me with Marc and Maggie, other old school friends, she walks gracefully to the bar, attracting attention from all sides. Lithe and pale, she's pretty in a way that reminds me of fairies and magic.

Tapping my fingers on the pockmarked wooden table, I catch a look passing between my friends, who've been a couple since we were all fifteen. 'Stop it.'

'Charley—' Maggie sits forward, dark hair falling over her round, eager face. Marc sweeps it back, tucking it behind her ear before she has the chance to.

PDA alert. I think of Alex. Regret sharpens my voice. 'Don't. Let's have a nice evening. You know, get blind drunk and try to forget about love.' I sigh as Marc gives Maggie a soppy smile. 'Or not.'

'Sorry,' Marc grabs his girlfriend's hand, his spiky bleached blond hair reminding me of a porcupine. 'We can't help it.'

'Can't help being madly in love?' I arch my eyebrow. 'I know. And I won't ruin it for you, don't worry.' I stare into space. 'I wouldn't want to turn into one of those bitter old women who makes everyone around them miserable and ends up being eaten by her own cats.' I pause. 'Though, at the moment, I haven't got a home or cats.'

'Stop being so dramatic.' Maggie smiles, 'But if we think you're heading that way we'll let you know, don't worry.'

'And if you ever need comforting, I'm sure we can find a local lad more than happy to let you sit in his lap for a hug,' Marc offers, grinning.

The comment reminds me of Alex again and I smile sadly. No. Move on. Forget him. He's forgotten you. Over three weeks and no contact, direct or via Jess. 'Thanks guys,' I reply, tone light, 'but I know I look like crap at the moment.'

'You don't,' Mags answers automatically, turning to Marc, 'does she?'

'Er.' He hesitates for too long and there's a muffled bang from beneath the table. 'Ow!' He flinches. 'Of course not,' he yelps.

'Wow. Convincing.' They're trying too hard. It's forced. I stand up, shrugging out of my coat. 'Okay you two, feel free to talk amongst yourselves, I'm going to help Lisa.'

Sloping across the room, I yank up my grey jeans. I've lost weight and they're hanging off my hip bones. Joining my friend, who's deep in giggling conversation with a random customer, I slouch against the bar. Catching sight of myself in the mirror behind the optics – face pale, shadows under my eyes prominent against my black long-sleeved top – I fix my attention on my surroundings instead.

The pub is bigger than it looks from the outside, like the Tardis in *Dr Who*. It's done out in 80s style; cream walls, red

Axminster carpet, and with an intriguing variety of razor-sharp farming implements hanging from the rafters and walls. So far it's escaped turning into one of those soulless gastro pubs. A hint of yeasty bitter mixes with the scent of cider and though there's no cigarette smoke because of the ban, there's a cloudy fug hanging in the air, puffing out from the open fireplace in the corner. Despite the countrified look, there's a small stage at the front of the L-shaped room, with a microphone and screen set up. Next to it is the battered piano I occasionally play on. My guess is Lisa will try and persuade me to bash out a few tunes tonight, though I'm really not in the mood.

Moving home hasn't been so bad. Although it's hard living with my parents again, I'm in the four-room guest house at the bottom of the garden, rent-free, and have as much freedom as I want. But I'm under constant observation. Mum and Dad have repeatedly asked if I'm okay and apologised for not having the money to lend me. I keep telling them it's all right, they've helped me enough, but avoiding their concerned looks and coddling is wearing. Tom's home setting up his company and he's doing his big-brother act, interrogating me about Alex, offering more than once to track him down and do painful things to him. I'm pretty sure he's not kidding and I know from what little he's said previously he's probably got mad torture skills from his time in the army. But I don't want to hurt Alex, I just want to pretend I never met him. Hard when Tom keeps asking me questions and muttering under his breath.

And the rest of the village ... it's just like old times. Everyone keeps rushing up and hugging me and wanting to know what happened and saying they always knew I'd be back some day. I hate it. And I'm sick of pasting a polite smile on my face. I long to run away and hide, but I've nowhere else to go.

On the upside, all my old friends have welcomed me like I've never been away, and it's been nice to catch up with them. I've been occupying myself searching for jobs and considering my options, and the pressure is off, financially, now that Jess has found a lodger to help cover the mortgage.

But.

But I miss my old life. I miss Jess, our flat, the good old City of London. I don't belong here, any more than I did once upon a time, before I went on my big adventure. I wonder how many days or weeks or months until the longing for what I left behind dwindles, is a forgotten, smudged memory. How long before I will get over finding and then losing Alex.

Because I miss Alex too.

One thing's for sure. The last few months have taught me a lesson. Some risks aren't worth taking, some gambles are unevenly loaded from the beginning and you will never win, however hard you play.

Urgh. I'm getting maudlin. *Snap out of it, Charley. Life goes on, it'll get better.*

Lisa helps by thrusting two pints of beer at me for Maggie and Marc. 'Come on. Let's sit down with a nice glass of wine.'

I follow on her heels. 'But I wanted vodka!'

Setting the drinks on the table, where Maggie and Marc are kissing like it's an Olympic sport, she raises both eyebrows at me and hands me a glass of white. 'Vodka makes you tearful and sloppy,' she says, 'and no one wants that.'

'Fine,' I grumble as I sit down, 'but if it takes me longer to get drunk then you're paying.'

She slides in next to me. 'I'll take the chance.'

Poking my tongue out, I take a gulp of my drink and let the alcohol flow through my veins. As they chatter around me, I drink more, feeling the wine begin to work, mellowing me like an enchanted potion. I relax back against the patterned cushions, dipping into the conversation to offer my opinions on the latest sitcom imported from the States. 'Heap of rubbish,' I challenge, 'home-grown comedies are much better.'

As I raise my glass and drain it, head tipped back, a pair of clear blue eyes catch mine. And all mellowness flees.

Alex. Here. Now. What–?

Coughing and spluttering, I slam the empty glass down and stand. My thighs hit the edge of the table, one of the drinks spilling and splashing all over Marc.

'Charley!' he leaps up, starts mopping himself down.

'Sorry,' I say absently.

'What is it?' Maggie frowns.

'Alex.' I narrow my eyes at him. What the hell does he want and how did he find me? 'He's here.'

Immediately, all three of my friends turn round to stare at him.

And everyone in the pub stops talking. A silence falls over the room and curious glances take in the stranger, along with my reaction. His appearance is bound to create exactly the small-village gossip I dislike. Still, it's a minor worry compared to the pain that tears through me. But I will not fall at his feet, I won't be pathetic and needy. He'll be here to tell me what happened with Tony. That's all.

He nods and lopes across the room, uncaring of the attention he's getting. Lisa grabs hold of my hand in a gesture of solidarity as Alex halts right in front of me, tall and broad and still unbeliev-ably gorgeous in a fitted dark-grey suit and blue shirt that makes his eyes seem brighter than ever. His dark hair is longer and curls slightly at the back of his neck, damp spots on his shoulders. It must be snowing again.

Clenching my teeth, I try to ignore the burning sensation at the back of my eyes at the memory of what happened at his flat.

'Alex,' I say evenly, striving to be cool and breezy. 'How did you find me?'

'Your brother.'

'Tom?' He wouldn't. 'I don't believe you.'

He shrugs, squaring his shoulders. 'Believe what you like, but he pointed me in your direction after we had a little chat.'

'Oh, really?' I cross my arms.

He looks me head on, gaze open. 'I told him I may have treated you in a way he didn't like and that I regretted but, with respect, he needed to tell me where you were. That we're not in some flaky rom-com.' He smiles briefly, before becoming very serious, eyes like homing devices on my face, searching for a signal. 'This is real life, and I need to see you. Finished with the fact that I'm not messing around.'

My mouth drops open. I click it shut. From the corner of my eye, I see Lisa recovering from a similar reaction. 'Are you crazy?' I ask, high-pitched. 'Do you know what he could do to you?'

Giving me the crooked grin I like so much, he nods. I hear Maggie sigh. Marc gives her a disgusted look, and I try not to laugh.

'I think so.' Alex nods, 'And crazy? Yes, maybe.'

Behind him, normal life resumes, people turning back to their own conversations when there's no immediate drama to entertain them. If only they knew the murderous thoughts running through me. I'd like to strangle Alex and Tom, the pair of them. How dare Alex turn up and put me on the spot? And how could Tom give me no warning that Alex was on his way?

Alex edges nearer the table. 'I'm sure you'll give him hell for it later but it doesn't matter right now. We need to talk, Charley.'

I can't pretend I'm not intrigued by what he's come all this way to say, but I don't want to give him the chance to hurt me again. I've had weeks to think about that last conversation. He lied to me in Barcelona, after calling me on my lies. He was in a tight spot that day at his flat, and maybe he does like me, but not enough. Not enough to trust me. Not enough to take a chance. Not enough to see if incredible sex and laughter and understanding could turn into love. 'Sorry, no.' I look away from him, shaking my head.

'You're being stubborn and contrary,' he declares.

'Maybe,' I say softly, sitting down. 'Go home, Alex.'

'No.' He grabs a chair from a nearby table and joins us without invitation.

I gape. 'What are you doing?'

He shrugs casually. 'Waiting.'

'What for?'

'You. To give me five minutes.'

I harrumph and try to ignore him. I'm kind of curious how long he'll sit there, unwanted. Turning to talk to Lisa doesn't help because she keeps looking at him over my shoulder, wide dark eyes drinking him in.

'Stop it,' I hiss at her.

She pouts, 'Sorry.'

'What will you do if I won't give you five minutes?' I turn to Alex.

'Stay here until closing time or until you leave. Come back tomorrow. I know where you live now,' he says, sounding altogether too cocky.

'Stalking is a criminal offence,' I bite, but I can see he means it. Might as well get it done. I sigh. 'Fine, five minutes.'

I notice he's not wearing a coat over his suit. I guess he wasn't bothered about the weather when he was only walking from his car to the pub. Which gives me a way to keep this mercifully brief. Maybe it's a bit cruel, but he'll survive.

'Let's go outside,' I suggest with a small smile, pulling my coat on and buttoning it up.

He glances out the window and winces, 'Okay.'

'I'll be back in five minutes, guys,' I tell my friends, 'and if I'm not, someone *please* come and get me.' Charging over to the exit, I open the door.

Once in the cold, crisp air, I pull him away from the warmth and bustle of the pub, away from the windows and inquisitive eyes, and wrap my arms around my middle, trying not to shiver. Planting my feet in the half foot of snow, glad of my fur-trimmed boots, I stare at him. 'Okay, the clock's ticking.'

'Right.' I can see the vapour in front of him as he breathes out. He must be freezing. 'Yes.'

'Come on then. What do you want to say?'

'Charley.' Moving closer, slipping slightly in the ice, he grabs my hands. I try to tug my fingers away but he holds tight. 'You have to promise to listen to me properly.'

I take a deep breath. He's warm and familiar and I want to scooch closer to him, rest my head on his wide shoulder. But I can't.

'Charley?'

Another shaky breath. He gave me an opportunity to explain once, it's only fair I do the same for him. 'I will.'

He smiles, relieved. 'Good.' Pausing, he peers down into my eyes and I can't move. 'I'm so sorry for what happened.'

'For that night at your flat? For not telling me about Layla?'

'That you had such a rough time with that bastard Tony. I'd seen him the day you came round, but I wasn't in a position to talk about it with Layla there.'

Oh. This isn't about us then, it's about his responsibility to handle the professional situation. And he's kept me waiting for weeks, knowing I was anxious to learn the outcome. Because he owes me nothing? Because he doesn't care after all? Yet he's here now. I'm so confused.

'Right.' I gulp down the basketball-sized lump in my throat, 'And? What happened when you saw him?'

'I knew,' he says simply. 'He bluffed and blustered but I knew he was lying.'

'How?' I frown.

'He couldn't look me in the eye. You said it in the note you left me, remember? I looked him straight in the eye and was certain he was being dishonest.' He shifts, dropping my hands to grab my upper arms. 'You always looked me in the eye, Charley, and I knew you were being truthful, as much as you could be, given the situation you were in, the situation he put you in.' He bares his even white teeth. 'So I called him on it and he lost his temper. Got angry and lost control. Ended up admitting it all. It got nasty after that. He said things about you that made me very angry.' His jaw is rigid, but it could be the temperature getting to him rather than anything else.

'What did you do?' I ask breathlessly, wanting him to say he punched Tony in the mouth, defending my honour. But he's too controlled for that and there's still the reputation of the company and family to uphold.

His smile gleams with a hundred per cent satisfaction. 'I had him thrown out, removed by security. He won't be working for me again. It's over.'

Nodding, I extract myself from his arms and his shadow, where he's blocking the light from the building behind him. 'You corroborated my version of events,' I conclude, 'and you feel responsible for his conduct because he was one of your employees.' I kick my foot in the powdery snow. 'You've done your bit. Well … Thank you.'

Stepping in, lifting my chin with a chilly finger, he speaks clearly and with care. 'Now I know without a doubt you were telling the truth, that what I felt was true. And although I don't agree with what you set out to do that weekend, I can understand why you were so desperate. It wasn't until I heard him say it all that it became real to me. What you'd lost, how you were treated, how awful it was for you.'

I slide my chin from his touch. 'Thanks, I appreciate you saying that,' I mutter half-heartedly. I should be happy Tony's paying the price for his behaviour, glad I now have closure and have been vindicated. But I feel nothing. It's all bitter grey ashes in my mouth. I've already lost everything. It's too late. 'It was good of you to come,' I say flatly. 'You can go now.' Stepping around him, I point out Lisa, who's appeared in the pub doorway, 'Your time's up anyway.' I wave at her to let her know I'm coming in and she tips her chin in acknowledgement, retreating inside.

'Hang on!' Just as I think I'm safe Alex grabs my sleeve and swings me round, pulling us together until we're chest to chest, face to face. He's shaking and I start to feel a little sorry for him. That's why I don't pull away. It is. Running gentle fingers down my face, he smooths a thumb over my cheekbone. 'I'm not done.'

'Alex—' I sigh, 'Please don't.'

'I know it's taken too long for me to tell you, and I'm sorry. But there are reasons. Layla...'

'What about her?' I ask, teeth starting to chatter.

'I was going to tell you about her, I promise. I thought I had more time.' He pulls me closer and I can't pull away. 'That day, I saw Tony in the morning and was supposed to finally sign the divorce papers. We'd agreed joint custody, with a court order in place alongside it. I planned to tell you about Tony that evening and about Layla in due course, once ... I wanted to celebrate my divorce – and freedom – with you. Go on proper dates, explore what was happening between us. I needed to know if you would even be interested in me any more, coming as part of a package deal.' I open my mouth to answer but he shushes me. I let him, because after feeling so bleak for so long, some of the colour is starting to seep back into my world. 'You're so focused on rebuilding your career, and I know you want to go travelling at some point, so I wasn't sure. But I would have found a time to tell you properly. You need to believe that.' His blue eyes gaze into mine and I can read the conviction in them.

I nod, wrapping my hands around his wrists. They're still hot despite the freezing temperature. 'So tell me what happened.'

He expels a breath, another vaporous cloud. 'Louise wouldn't sign. Got really angry. Wouldn't accept there was no settlement and claimed the maintenance I was going to pay her for Layla wasn't enough. I called her bluff and she walked out.' He shakes his head, scowling. 'I was frantic, was thinking, this is *never* going to end, I'm not going to see my daughter grow up and I will never be free of Louise. I went home and got changed and was expecting you and was in a complete sodding mess because of my bloody ex and then she turned up and left Layla with me. *If you want our brat that badly you can have her.*'

'What? Just like that? Turnaround of the century!'

'She wasn't going to get the money she wanted and she told me Layla just got in her way anyway.'

265

'That's vile.'

'You've got it,' he nods, expression outraged. 'I didn't have time to think, the flat wasn't childproofed at all, I thought I had a few weeks to sort that out, and then you—'

'Turned up to talk.'

'I panicked,' he admits, shivering. 'I didn't know what to deal with first, or what I was going to do about work. I was completely unprepared. All I knew was, after years of fighting and conflict, I had my daughter, however temporarily. But I'm really sorry you got the raw end of the situation.'

I nod. It makes sense. I squeeze his wrists. 'You love her, she's your kid. You had to put her first and you didn't know how to do that without putting me last. I get that.'

'So you can also accept I'd do anything to protect her and make her happy?'

This is where he gives me the brush-off. Backing out of his reach. 'Of course I do.'

'Especially now she's going to be living with me permanently.' His voice holds a mixture of trepidation and joy as he pulls me back to him.

'You've got full custody?'

'Yes. It's done. Louise has signed, I've signed, it's been filed.'

'Did she decide Layla's better off with you?'

He laughs. 'Not exactly.'

'What then?'

He shudders, yanks me closer for warmth. 'God, it's cold. Layla was cramping her style. She's on the hunt for a new man.'

'But won't she just ask for her back when she's landed hubby number two?'

'No.' Alex shakes his head.

I frown. 'How can you be so sure?'

'I paid her off.'

'Huh?' I'm shocked. I thought Alex would be the last person to give in to emotional blackmail.

He quirks an eyebrow, reading my thoughts. 'I know. Everything in me said not to. But I sat down and thought about it. Really thought. I didn't want to pay her off because she deceived me, hurt my pride, hurt me. But at the end of the day, I have the money. And it's not that I'm buying my daughter, I'm simply paying to protect her. Layla's well-being is more important than my pride.'

'Good for you. I'm so pleased. So, will Louise get access rights?'

'No.' His lips look a little blue and a shard of guilt scratches at me. 'She doesn't want any.'

'What? How can she bear to be away from her own child? Layla's still practically a baby.'

'Louise is fond of her but I don't think the bond's there. She's too selfish to be a good mum. In a way, this is her putting Layla first. With me, our daughter will have stability. And Layla needs that now, especially after being carted around all these years. Which is why I thought long and hard about what a certain beautiful red-head once told me about only having one chance at this world and changing my situation if I could. So I talked to my parents.' He tips his head forward, heated blue eyes running over my face. 'I'm going to be relinquishing some of my duties – most of them, in fact – so I can cut down on travelling.'

'You are? You talked to them about it. You did it. And do you feel guilty?'

'No, strangely not as much as I thought. It's funny what you can do when you have the right motivation.'

'And Layla is yours.'

'Yes. But I also told them how I felt. How relentless it is. How unhappy I've been.'

I smile in disbelief. 'And did your dad keel over from a heart attack?'

Alex smiles back, rubbing my cheekbone again. I go gooey. I've missed him, against all of my better intentions. 'No. My father is alive and well. He understood, battled with the same feelings himself. I never knew because he always hid it so well.'

'And your mum?'

He laughs wryly, shaking his head. 'It was amazing. She just smiled at me as though I'd done something to make her really proud. My brother Kristian is going to be given a senior role and do most of the travelling. He's more than pleased about it.'

'He is?' He's never told me much about him, but I got the impression from the gossip mags he was one of those European playboys. The kind of guy I mistook Alex for when I first met him. I was so wrong.

'Yes,' he sighs, frustrated. 'I never knew. I didn't realise how jealous he's been of me. I thought he liked his freedom, but he's been bored for a long time. It's interesting what you find out when you stop and talk to people. Really talk.'

'People can surprise you if you let them,' I agree, easing away from him. 'So what are you going to do?'

'I'm going to head up community projects, including an apprenticeship programme. In the UK. That's why I didn't track you down sooner. I've been sorting everything out for handover and I wanted to see you once it was all done.'

'You'll be brilliant.' I avoid his last comment. It sounds like he has it all figured out. Something I'm further away from than I have ever been. What am I still doing out here with him? He hasn't offered me anything. He hasn't told me he wants to be with me. He's talked about protecting Layla. Now I need to protect myself. 'Well, I should go. Thanks for apologising. I understand Layla's your priority. I hope it all works out for you.' Dejected, I move away and crunch through the snow towards the door.

'Wait! I want you to meet Layla,' he blurts.

I whip around, slipping in the snow, arms windmilling. I try to get my balance, but Alex is already there, arms wrapped around my waist to steady me.

'You do?' I squeak. Something in his eyes makes me jerk. I lose my footing again, lurch sideways and we scramble for purchase together. He plants his feet wide, braces me.

268

'Yes. She's the most important person in my life.'

'I totally respect that.' I lean back in his arms carefully. 'So why do you want me to meet her?'

'I'd like there to be two important people. And to be clear, you're the other one.'

'I am?' Wonder holds me still and I feel something tiny and cold land on my cheek. I don't brush it away, too fixed on Alex's face. He is so close, long eyelashes damp, jaw starting to stubble over.

'I know that me having Layla isn't what you signed up for. I didn't feel I could tell you sooner … I know I've sprung her on you. And that's not fair—'

'Layla's not a deal-breaker, Alex.'

'So will you come with me and meet her?'

'I'm not sure.' He's told me lots in the last ten minutes but not the most important thing of all. How does he feel about me? 'When?'

'Now.'

'Now?' I make a show of looking around for her in the churned-up snow. 'Well she's not tiny enough to fit in your pocket, so where is she? In the car?'

'No, she's too young for that. She's with your parents.'

Leaning back further in his muscular arms, I risk our balance. 'You're joking!'

'No.'

'But you're so protective of her. You don't even know them and neither does she.'

'I didn't plan to be gone long and they have my mobile if there are any problems.' He pauses, jeopardises our safety by unwrapping one arm from my middle to brush my fringe out of my eyes. 'And I trust them because they raised a wonderful daughter.'

'Oh.' It's cheesy but something catches in my throat.

'I needed to see you, but I couldn't bring her here in case this went wrong.'

He isn't sure of me. 'Sounds like you have this parenting thing sorted,' I say lightly.

'Maybe, but it would be nice to have some help. I'm not asking you to be her parent.' So, what is he asking? 'At least, not straight away,' he tags on quickly. 'But I am asking you to be with us, if you can forgive me for the clumsy way I handled everything that night at the flat.'

'Be with you? Why exactly?' There is so much hope and fear inside me I feel like my heart is too big for my chest, tears glazing my eyes as I ask the ultimate question.

He laughs and kisses me. 'Because I love you, clumsy.' He kisses me again, hot and hard, then pulls back to gaze into my eyes, 'You have my absolute trust and respect. I will always support you in doing whatever makes you happy. As long as you do it with me.' Those are the perfect words, the very ones I needed to hear. 'I've made some mistakes, I don't think either of us is covered in glory, but—'

With a yell of delight, I push off the ground, knocking us both over into the snow, falling on top of him. Kneeling up, I undo my coat, open it to share my warmth with the guy I love, lying down full length along him. 'Shut up, Alex,' I order, happier than I have been in an aeon, covering his gorgeous face in kisses, planting a sloppy one on his mouth, 'just stop talking! Yes, we've both made mistakes.' If he can say it, I can be brave enough to as well, 'But I love you too.' I stare deep into his eyes, starting to work my hands inside his suit jacket to run them over his sexy, strong, freezing body. He must really love me to have stood outside in this weather for so long. Poor man. 'I love you,' I whisper 'and I'd rather be with you than without.'

Wrapping my arms around his neck, I grab handfuls of his thick, dark hair and drop my mouth to his for a long, hot, involved kiss. I think I hear someone arrive at one point and the front door of the pub swing open with a creak and I'm pretty sure I hear giggling, but then Alex's kiss drags me back down to my own private idea of bliss.

When we surface at last, panting and burning despite the snow,

Alex tightens his fingers around my hips, as if afraid to let go, 'I'll be seeing to it you get compensation for unfair dismissal as well as notice pay.'

I push myself up, climb off him and hold out my hand, avoiding the statement. 'Come on, you're soaked through.'

Grasping my hand, he hauls himself up and for once I'm not clumsy, I stand firm. 'Charley? Did you hear what I said?'

'I'm not sure how I feel about it,' I reply, mixed emotions running through me, 'what will people think of me getting a pay-off when they find out we're together?'

'It's what you're entitled to,' he points out with calm logic. 'Both panels got it wrong. We'll do it all properly through HR and Legal, with a proper agreement, meaning it'll all be confidential.'

Biting the inside of my cheek, I mull it over. 'And you're not worried that this is all part of my plan?'

'No!' He kisses me softly, pulling back to gaze into my eyes. 'It's the right thing for the company to do. But… um…' he rubs the back of his neck, 'I should probably tell you that even with the confidentiality clause, there's still a risk it'll all come out.'

'Why?'

'Because when I threw Tony out, I kind of assaulted him,' He admits sheepishly. 'So he threatened to go to the police and the press.'

'Hang on. What do you mean, assaulted him? That's not like you. Didn't security throw him out?'

'Yes, but once we got outside I sort of lost control of my better instincts. The things he said about you … I, well—'

'What did you do, Alex?' I'm worried now. How badly did he hurt him? And what impact is it going to have on Alex and his family? Their reputation?

His mouth quirks and he mumbles something under his breath. 'Pardon?' I move closer.

'I said I kicked him up the arse and he fell over.'

I snort, 'Sorry, you what?'

'It sounds ridiculous, doesn't it? A bit like that scene in *Bridget Jones* where the two guys have that girlie fight.'

'You've seen Bridget Jones?'

'I don't mind rom-coms,' he defends, and I think he actually blushes.

'Oh my,' I shake my head, 'I have so much to learn about you. But,' I walk my fingers up his damp shirt, 'I think you may be the ideal guy.' Strong but vulnerable, sweet but sexy. I get serious, 'Aren't you worried what Tony will do, though?'

'No, I'll deal with it if I have to,' he says, utterly self-assured, 'and I'm glad it happened.'

'How come?'

'Because,' he tucks my hair behind my ear, 'that's when I realised I was in love with you.'

Something soft and gooey uncurls inside me, but I chortle, 'You knew you loved me because you kicked Tony Ferrier up the arse?'

'I knew I loved you when the HR Manager bawled me out, told me what the consequences might be, and I told her I didn't care and realised I meant it. And I also knew I loved you when I decided to get rid of the no-workplace relationship clause from our contracts. You were right. You can't control people's feelings. I know that now.'

'Oh. Wow.'

'Yes. And as a reward for my selfless actions,' he says gravely, 'you're moving in with me straight away.'

'No. I'm not, Alex.' His face falls. But I won't give into temptation. I need to do this myself. And after doing everything topsy-turvy with Alex so far, I'm in no rush to get it wrong again. 'I don't need rescuing.' Grabbing his lapels, I make a quick decision. 'But I'll talk to HR,' I agree softly, 'I'll accept the money, because you're right, I'm owed it. And I'll move back in with Jess and get my career back on track now my name will no longer be dirt. I'm guessing I'll get a satisfactory reference.' It all falls out of my mouth in a garble, but I know instinctively I'm right. Everything is going to be okay.

'Yes. Fair enough,' Alex responds, but there is still a shadow in his eyes.

I wrap my arms round his neck and stand up on tiptoes. 'I do love you,' I assure him, kissing the corner of his luscious mouth, feeling him relax. 'I do want to be with you,' I kiss an angelic cheekbone, 'and I might even be persuaded to change my mind about moving in with you if you ask me again in a few months' time.' I tell him with my eyes how much I adore him. 'I just want to get this right.'

'I do too. Very much. Okay. In the meantime, I want to get away, just the three of us; you, me and Layla, once you've got to know each other. How do you feel about a weekend in a villa in Barcelona?' he teases.

I take a mock swipe at his head, 'Barcelona? Sure. It's my new favourite place!'

Giggling, I take his arm and lead him to the pub door, 'Now you're going to have to go through the pain of meeting all the locals and letting them drill you. Then we'd better go and introduce you to my parents properly and get your daughter.'

'Which are worse, the locals or your parents?'

I scrunch up my face in thought, then grin, 'Do you know, I'm really not sure?'

Shaking his head, he opens the door for me and we walk inside. It feels like everything in my life is finally normal, that the nightmare of the last six months is over.

My friends stare at us as we come in, smiling at our joined hands, and it reminds me I need to phone Jess and tell her what's happened. That I'm coming home.

Alex squeezes my fingers and I look at him, full of relief, full of love, and grateful that over a lost weekend in Barcelona, we found each other.

I was wrong earlier. Some risks are worth taking, even when the odds are not in your favour. Sometimes if you play hard enough and for long enough you might just win. Luck could be on your side.

I started this journey by thinking I should have been smart enough to say no to crazy Plan B. Now I'm glad I was just crazy enough to say yes.

Newbridge

9 780007 591763